GEARS OF THE CITY

Also by Felix Gilman

THUNDERER

GEARS OF THE CITY

Felix Gilman

BANTAM SPECTRA

GEARS OF THE CITY
A Bantam Spectra Book / January 2009

Published by Bantam Dell
A Division of Random House, Inc.
New York, New York

Book design by Glen Edelstein

Library of Congress Cataloging-in-Publication Data
Gilman, Felix.
Gears of the City / Felix Gilman.
p.   cm.
ISBN 978-0-553-80677-9
I. Title.
PS3607.I452G43   2009
813'.6—dc22
2008035649

Printed in the United States of America
Published simultaneously in Canada

www.bantamdell.com

BVG 10 9 8 7 6 5 4 3 2 1

To my parents

Acknowledgments

Thanks again to Howard Morhaim, Juliet Ulman, and Sarah for their help and advice, and thanks to all at Bantam.

GEARS OF THE CITY

PROLOGUE:

Rumors

For six months, give or take, he lived with the people of the Bright Towers, and he was happy enough there. He drifted from tower to tower, as the music led him. He slept out under brilliant stars on bridges of glass. He learned how to coax melody out of shimmering crystal spar. He picked up bits and pieces of the local language, a clear chiming echoing noise. He joined in the worship of strange temples—he was never happier than when he was at worship. For days at a time he forgot to eat. The city was young and full of potential. He felt his God was near.

The locals gave him a name—a carillon sound, three minor tones, descending. He was quite surprised when he learned what it meant. *The dark man.*

"Dark?"

They shrugged, and told him that he seemed unhappy.

In the time of the Bright Towers, the city's spires were crystalline, vibrant, thin and delicate as blades of grass, and impossibly, pointlessly tall. It was impossible to imagine that they were *built.* They seemed to grow wild. The sun nourished them.

The towers' people shone, too. Their skin was like gold. With his black robes, his brown eyes, the dark man stood out among them like a crack in a mirror.

Those towers—he shuddered just looking at them. They were too beautiful to last. A hard wind or a cruel word might shatter them, raining down green-golden glass on the streets. The towers were a thousand years old, and coal-black cracks were appearing. The dark man had walked in the times that came after, he came to the towers *backward* through the secret ways—insofar as backward and forward meant anything in the city's secret ways—and he knew that hard days were coming.

The sunlight was different, too, brighter, *primal,* like the first hot stars, and mirrored and refracted through a million panes and flutes of gemlike glass. Beautiful and in fact almost intolerable—blindness was common among the people of the towers. The blind wore bright silk scarves around their eyes, and navigated by the creak and chime of the glass, the fluting of the wind, subtle distinctions in the warmth of the mirrored light on their faces. The dark man wrapped his head in black rags, torn from his robes.

The people of the Bright Towers had a different relationship to light and weight and distance from the people he was used to. They had a different relationship to violence. When they saw the whip scars on his back, the bruises he carried, they were simply unable to imagine the slave markets, the pirates, the inquisitors, the ghouls, the cannibals, the policemen—the violence that he'd done and that had been done to him. The concept was unfamiliar—though sometimes one of the people climbed too high into their towers, aiming for the peaks where they believed that their Gods dwelt, and they bloodied themselves on the wild-growing glass of the uppermost untended levels.

Was *he* a holy man, too, they asked? In a manner of speaking, he said. He was harder now than when he'd come to the city, and colder, but he remained devout. Devotion was the one constant in his shifting world, the one solid thing he had to cling to. He told them of his God, and its distant temple, and its music, and they listened politely, but not quite comprehending. They had a different relationship to Gods, and to music.

They fed on light—there was *engineering* in their bloodline, or a miracle, because they fed on light, and their golden skin was traced with jade. Their world was translucent, complexly refracted. They lived in the towers, owned nothing, built nothing, made nothing but music, by which they were surrounded—the wind in the towers, the glassy echo of their voices. They were the gentlest people the city had ever known, or would ever know again. In later times those people would be myths.

* * *

St. Loup came to visit him. Well—St. Loup *called* it a visit. It was in fact a polite form of interrogation. St. Loup was a madman and also a murderer a dozen times over, but his manners were excellent.

"You've found a nice place here," St. Loup said. "A vacation?"

"Where did you come from, St. Loup?"

"Through the same doors as you, I expect. We've missed you at the Hotel."

"Have you? I haven't missed the Hotel at all."

"Oh, you always say that. The place wouldn't be the same without you. Father Turnbull is scheming behind your back, I should warn you."

"And you're here scheming to my face. I don't know anything useful to you, St. Loup."

St. Loup smiled. His eyes were hidden by expensive sunglasses. "So what is it this time, then? What brings you out here?"

"Nothing useful to you."

They stood on a glass bridge. St. Loup had accosted him there, on his way between towers. Now St. Loup gestured out across the Bright Towers, across fields of crystal and crowds greeting the dawn with song. He wore a red silk shirt, with ebony cuff links. Long golden curls spilled over his collar. He said, "Who are these awful people? Why won't they shut up?"

"Go home, St. Loup."

"What can these people possibly know about the Mountain?"

"There's nothing for you here. No secrets, no information."

"Is it your God again? Is that it? You think it's here?"

"I don't know. Maybe."

"Well, best of luck," St. Loup said, insincerely. "So, anyway, the big news is that Potocki is planning another assault on the Mountain. You'll want to come back for that, once you get bored here."

"I'm not coming back, St. Loup."

"You always say that. Look me up when you check in again. I have plans."

St. Loup stepped sideways through shafts of refracted rainbow light and was gone.

* * *

The Bright Towers had no doors. Their people lived in seamless extrusions of crystal and glass, immaculate, near shadowless. It had been hard for the dark man to find a way through. He prowled through Time around them like a thief. He was there when the first crystalline tower-seeds were formed, dense and frozen, no larger than a house. He was there in the ruins, after. He read about them in the history books, he watched the movies. They had a music that no later scholar or documentarian would ever be able to reconstruct. That was irresistible to him. But they had no doors; how, then, was he supposed to open a path to them?

In the end, he came through the cracks.

In their last days the towers began to crack under their own weight. Their first tiny crystalline imperfections had never been resolved, only deferred, as the towers elaborated themselves, stretched into the sun . . . The fissures appeared first as delicate marks, like dust, fingerprints, fine hair, shadows of the sun that disappeared when one blinked. They quickly grew jagged and dark, like bruises, like old age, metastasizing. There was one in every chamber and valve. The warm smooth floor underfoot began to splinter. The fluting and chiming of the wind in the towers became ugly, arrhythmic. The people of the towers saw that their end was coming, and began to put their affairs in order. They saw their culture as a musical one, a hymnal one, and they began to attempt a coda for it—a fitting resolution of their theme and essence.

He came through into a high chamber where some two hundred of them were gathered, cross-legged on the floor, humming and murmuring, brushing and sweeping. A geodesic temple, pillars and shafts of crystal, glass organs and pipes. He came through the darkness and mysterious angles of the cracks in the wall, and the glass shattered behind him. He fell to the floor bleeding.

They never asked his name. The people of the towers had no names.

Briefly they entertained the idea that he was there to save them from the decay of their towers—but only briefly. He preferred not to lie to them. He told them with signs, and later with a little of their language—he was good with languages—that he was only passing through. He had come to hear their music. There would never be anything else like it again. He couldn't bear for it to be lost. Too much was lost and forgotten, swallowed in the rolling ten-thousand-year din of the city. He promised to remember them. They seemed to find the offer more pleasing than not.

He sat silently, blindfolded against the glare, and he listened to their slow and careful harmonies.

The song of their ending: it might take them a hundred years. He wasn't sure how long they lived, whether they were immortal or not. He was not.

St. Loup had guessed correctly. He *had* come here in pursuit of his God. He was a kind of priest, a kind of pilgrim. A devotee of a vanished God, the God of his childhood, a God that had abandoned him. He had chased it across the world, and deeper and deeper into the city, through its temples and sacred spaces. For his God's sake he had spent more years than he liked to remember among the madmen of the Hotel, trading secrets and rumors of magic.

His vanished God was a God of music. The Age of the Bright Towers was an Age of forgotten and beautiful music, and he'd hoped . . . But it wasn't there.

For six months he was happy enough. Each tower housed a dozen temples or more, and each temple had a different music, and he drifted from temple to temple. He joined the music-making, clumsily at first, soon with greater skill. He joined their ceremonies. After ten years in the City Beyond he was used to strange and unfamiliar rituals.

He felt the presence of Gods. But they weren't *his* God.

It was the wrong music. It was the wrong place, and the wrong time. For one thing the vanished God of his childhood had been a perfect and peaceful and timeless music, while the music of the towers was slowly disintegrating. The towers cracked. Discord crept in.

He had come too late. If his God had ever passed this way, it was gone now.

He went up into the highest chambers and cut himself on the wild glass, and burned his skin in the brilliant light, thinking that in the high winds up there who knows what memories or Gods or music might blow, be caught, pinned against the sky: nothing. Only the winds.

He went down again. The cracks darkened the glass like storm clouds.

He tried to explain what he was looking for to a green-eyed girl of the tower-people. He *thought* it was a girl, he found their sexes hard to distinguish. There was a language barrier, and a deeper barrier to comprehension. They were fatalists; they strove for nothing. Gone is gone, she said. Things end, they blow away. She illustrated her point with a figure of speech he failed to understand, to do with light.

He offered to save as many of her people as he could—to evacuate them into a safer time. There were *paths,* he said. He always told himself he wouldn't do that, he wouldn't meddle, that past times were gone and should be left that way; but he was soft-hearted.

She said no. People generally did, he'd found.

She took him to see a wise man, in a chamber full of mirrors, scattered with cracks like the wrinkles on his eerie face, who said: *let it go.* He couldn't. The wise man sent him to a woman who lived in the high chambers, up flights of pearlescent stairs curved like twining ivy, through forests of wild glass. A little old woman who *knew* Gods, a woman who pointed out across the tops of the towers, flashing green and gold in the sun, and north to the distant shadow that was always there on the horizon, in every Age of the city, in every place—the Mountain.

There. I have thought long and hard about the nature of light. If you have lost something, look in the shadows.

The dark man winced, shook his head. He said, *yes, but* . . . He sighed, scratched his beard.

It wasn't the first time he'd been told that. In fact he'd heard it so often he was sick of hearing it. Wherever he went in the city the final answer was always—in a hundred different languages, for a hundred different reasons—the Mountain.

In the Temples of the Prime Mover they said it was the body of a dead God, the first, petrified, and all lesser and subsequent Gods burrowed in its tunnels like maggots. In Croix they said the Builders, whoever or whatever they were, had made the Mountain to lock away the last of the city's secrets. In the Hotel every conversation turned to the Mountain.

He wasn't ready for the Mountain. That terrible cold absence in the city—that wound, that flaw, that inexplicable mystery in even the most enlightened Ages of the city. There was no safe path to the

Mountain. All those mad enough or daring enough to attempt it came back ruined, mad—or not at all. He wasn't ready.

The Mountain? Are you sure?

The Mountain. Yes.

How do I go there?

No answer. There was never any answer. So he went back down the crumbling tower and sat out in the sun and listened to the music.

St. Loup was spying on him. He saw St. Loup hiding among the golden crowds—or looking for shadows to lurk in, scattering his cigarette butts on pristine surfaces—or, as he was now, watching through telescopes from high places.

He waved St. Loup over and the man came smiling.

"If you plan to attack me, St. Loup, would you get it over with?"

"Perish the thought! Perhaps I'm concerned about you."

St. Loup was an acquaintance, a contact, not a friend. Nevertheless they knew each other horribly well. Among the hidden and irregular communities of madmen, paranoids, sorcerers, those who had Broken Through to the city behind and above the city of their births, there was a certain community or anticommunity, there was a guarded and untrustworthy exchange of information. They were the wanderers of the City Beyond, the Via Obscura, the Thousand-Fold Path, the Metacontext, die Träumenstadt, the Gears, the Slew, Time Itself, whatever you wanted to call it. (From time to time he'd suggested the Song, or the Chorus—neither caught on.) They bartered maps and keys and rumors of the Mountain.

Every one of them had his own private obsessions, and each one pointed, in the end, to the Mountain; the impossible, unattainable Mountain. For the dark man it was his God. For St. Loup, if St. Loup could be believed, it was a woman.

"Go home, St. Loup. Leave these people alone. They don't know anything. They don't know the way."

"Everyone has secrets."

"I don't know anything either, St. Loup."

"Then why are you here?"

They watched each other all the time—St. Loup, Arjun, Father

Turnbull, all the rest of them. Who would be first to move? Who would be first to take the Mountain? What did they *know*?

"No reason. It doesn't matter anymore."

"Come back to the Hotel. Potocki's moving and I need allies. I'll make it worth your while. When I hold the Mountain I'll give you as many Gods as you like, and a million choirs to praise them, you odd little man."

"Not yet. I still have other places to look."

"There's only one. You know that."

"Not necessarily. It's a big city."

"It's smaller than it seems. Well, you know where to find me."

St. Loup vanished one way through the Metacontext, and, sighing, the dark man went another way, and he left the Bright Towers behind for streets of grey cobblestones and brick.

He imagined the towers, after he'd gone, cracking all at once with a sound like a spring rain shower, that whole Age of the city, and its people, too, turned instantly weightless, shards and seeds of light, blowing away on the breeze.

But in Winding Hall, and in Perrabia, and Slew, and Volstat, and on the cloud-high deck of the cityship *Annihilator,* and on the wires of the City-Signal, and in the haunted crypts under Red Barrow, and in the Houses of the Red Moon, and in the laboratories of the Zubiri Corporation, and everywhere else he went, forward or back, the answer was always the same. The Mountain. In Slew they said the Mountain was like a cage, and it held the failed Gods prisoner. In the Zubiri laboratories they said the Mountain was like a black hole, and it drew all light and music and spirit and positively charged energies into its maw—they had charts and data to prove it. In a dusty little shop in the rafters of Winding Hall he purchased a *Children's Miscellany of Fairy-Stories* because it had a mountain on the cover. It had a story of a wicked mean old man who came down into the city from a clockwork mountain every night to steal away children's dreams in his grey sack. The pictures were haunting. The dreams looked like angels. He kept the book.

A fairy story, a myth, a machine, a weapon, a dark palace, the Mountain! There was no hiding from it. And at last his need overwhelmed his fear, and he began to plan the impossible ascent.

✳ ✳ ✳

And he *failed*.

And so later, much later—*afterward*—he came fleeing headlong down the Mountain. Its servants pursued him. He tore his shirt—it caught on a dead tree in the park and a white wing of cloth ripped away, fluttering on the bare branch. He ran and his *mind* tore away, too. He saw and heard too much and his self and his soul swelled, strained, tore at the seams.

He fled through Time. They were always there, close on his heels. In the café by the reservoir they waited anxiously behind the railings. He threw himself through a door in the kitchen and the name of the city was torn away. At the station they came walking silently down the tracks. He ran through the coal shed and left the names of his lovers in the dust. There were always two of them, his hollow hunters, faces faded like old photographs, always awkwardly about to speak . . . By the river he crawled under wire, through the muck, and the name of his hunters was left in the mud. He had no father or mother; that fact, too, was torn from him as he tumbled through brass elevator doors and onto rain-slick cobbles. He lost the fairy stories when he lost his jacket, swimming across the freezing and night-dark river—he lost all his stories. That was how it worked: an expansion of possibilities to the limits of the self, and beyond, followed by an inexorable contraction. Shay had not warned him that the Mountain was *defended*. He was burning himself too fast in his headlong flight. He left Shay's name on the bloody floor of the butcher's market. The memory of the Mountain was stolen as he pushed through the parade, through the dancing and music and sequins and flesh. The Mountain's hollow servants still pursued him, slow and deliberate. How could they keep pace with him? It was impossible. But when he hid in the dark of the theater they crossed the stage toward him, tall shadows in the limelight, and when he tumbled fleeing through the trapdoor his own name was torn away from him. He ran panting and crying up a silver staircase in the moonlight, and their shiny patent-leather shoes *clack-clack-clack*ed up the steps behind him. He hurled himself through an arch of bloody stones and the name of his God tore away and its Song went dumb within him, like a stone in his gut. He fell into darkness and silence.

BOOK ONE
After the First Expedition

ONE
Darkness–Naming–Wounding–Flight

The stillness of the air told him he was indoors—perhaps underground. He sat with a brick wall at his back, cool and damp. There was an animal smell.

He wasn't alone in the darkness. Rustling; breathing. Scraping—scraping of scales? Rattling of bars. Some large caged creature, heavy tail sweeping the straw.

As far as he could tell, he was not sharing the creature's cage—a small relief.

Time passed.

The rattling of bars, the rough sweeping of the scales, had a kind of off-kilter rhythm. It was peaceful to listen—to contemplate the complexity of it.

Lizard stink, rotting meat, and rust—the thing in the cage was immense. Beneath that there was the smell of gas, of burning gone cold. Stale tobacco? The stones he sat on were littered with the scraps of old hand-rolled cigarettes. Gas—this part of the city was *gaslit*.

Beneath the creature's noises were the quiet sounds of distant traffic, hooves, and rattling iron-shod wheels. Distant echoes of market-traders shouting. No song . . . A man shouting rhythmic commands; a counterpoint of grumbling and groans. A single motorcar roared in the distance—an unequal place, then. Clanging metal and venting pipes. The hiss and groan of steam engines; the creak and sway of cranes and pylons and bridges. A distant panicked moan and bellow; beasts at market? From all over there was suddenly the shrill of whistles and the low mournful complaint of horns.

This is how a city is built. Bit by bit it all locks tight together. When the light comes back the visual world will force itself on him; in the dark he can build the city himself, from these familiar fragments. He closes his eyes tight.

Listen: this is how a city is built from music.

There is something missing in it.

There was a new noise in the room with him. He pressed back against the wall, opening his eyes in the darkness.

A hoarse voice rumbled and hissed, in syllables he didn't recognize. It spoke in short staccato monosyllables, then in grinding gutturals and long languid cadences. It was working through languages. Each one had a kind of lulling rhythm, until finally there was a language he understood. Then meaning drove out music— but all the voice said was: "It would be courteous if you were to introduce yourself."

He asked, "Is it morning or evening here?"

"I do not know," it said. "I hoped you might."

"I'll say good evening then, because it's dark. I apologize if I have intruded."

"I accept your apology."

The voice was like glass and stones scraping together. A deeper bass and sharper sibilants than any human voice. "The local dialect," it said, and it sighed like a rattling buzz saw. "Ugly. I'd hoped . . ." It fell silent for a while.

He was not sure what to say.

It spoke again: "May I ask how you came here?"

"I don't recall. Where is the door?"

"You did not come through the door. You appear to have come down the chimney."

He reached his arm out behind him and felt along the wall. A few feet to his left was a narrow hole, but . . . "It's barred," he said.

"I *know*," the creature rumbled. "Hence my curiosity."

"I don't know how I came through."

"I hoped you might know of a way out."

"I don't think so."

"Ah." The creature sighed.

"I think I was being chased," he said. "Hunted."

It *hissed*. "It is *bad* to be chased and hunted."

"Yes."

Growling: "It is worse to be trapped."

"I expect so."

"Who hunts you?"

"I don't recall," he said. "Two men. They chased me all across the city. There was no hiding from them."

"Are you a criminal?"

He thought carefully. "I don't think so."

"You do not smell like a monster."

"I hope not."

The beast in the cage shifted and the bars rattled.

He asked, "May I ask your name?"

The beast exhaled deeply; its breath smelled of metals, weeds, the sea. "I have no name. My maker gave me none. He kept all the names for himself. May I ask yours?"

"I forget."

"You are a young man of average size and adequate health; there are many strange smells on you. I will call you *Man*."

"If you like," he said. "What may I call you?"

"I am in a cage. You may as well call me *Beast*."

"Ah. What do you look like?"

The Beast took in a ragged snort of air. "I smell sulfide and phosphor. You have matches on your person."

He patted his clothes. He wore no jacket and his shirt was torn. He wore a silk tie loose around his neck. There were a number of things in his pockets, one of which was a crumpled and nearly empty book of matches. He struck one. (Quickly and deftly in the darkness—he had strong, dexterous musician's fingers.)

He started and jerked back. A yellow eye the size of a man's fist reflected the match's yellow light. It was only a few feet away. The slit of black down the eye's center clenched tight in the light like the narrow bars of the cage. The creature shifted its head, coyly presenting itself: a long snake-skull, crudely formed, green scales and dull ridges. Loose lizard jowls on its thick neck. Its body was long and ridge-backed. It scales were cracked and discolored, its hide was lumpy—scarred and stitched? A fat tail swept the cage and rattled the bars. It was the size of a bull, maybe? It opened its jaw to show yellow teeth. The match burned out.

Rack your brain. What else did you see? Think. But the visual world was never his strength. *The light did not reach to the back of the room, but I think the ceiling was low. I think: no windows. A wooden door to my right. The cage had wheels on its base. The matchbook was red and from the WaneLight Hotel—that pretentious capital L curving, priapic, subtly obscene. What else?*

"You are a remarkably educated lizard," he told it.

"Thank you. I do not frighten you?"

"I've seen stranger things than you. Or I think I have; I don't know. You speak very plainly, for a monster."

"You understand me very plainly, for a man. No one else left in these bitter days understands me. I shall have to be more obscure if I wish to awe you. I am the strangest thing on any street of the city for many miles."

"I meant no offense. I'm sure you are. I'm well traveled but I have heard of nothing like you. Where in the city are we?"

Was he well traveled? He thought so. He felt tired; he carried scars. He remembered nothing.

"We are in the Fosdyke Museum of History and Natural Wonders. In its cellars, to be precise. I was an exhibit once, and now I am a prisoner, and soon perhaps they will kill me. There is nothing else like me left in these last days of the city. And I am in a cage, and you are not."

"Where is this museum?"

"In Fosdyke, on Holcroft Square. The Museum has stood here for far longer than this Age of the city. Like me it has survived out of its time. We are far from any river or lake and near the lower slopes of the Mountain."

At the word *Mountain* a fistful of images flashed in his mind, grey-toned flickers like the phantoms of the cinema. Two vague men in hats and shined shoes approaching implacably. A clock tower, the white face darkened by a complex and spiderish excess of hands. Eyes, half-light, pale faces, men stacked like cordwood in a cellar under a spitting bulb. A garden of grey roses. A silent square of ugly statues. Clouds inert in the sky, as if painted; the birds also still, perfect intricate little china models. (Wires? No.) A tram swaying into a rain-soaked station, shaking as if frightened to stop for him. Gears turning. Time as a trap. A dark basement, a thousand Hollow Men standing in the shadows under a dead bulb. A tarnished silver tray bearing sharp and twisted implements. An old, old man looking down from a high window and snarling *thief* and twitching grey curtains spitefully closed.

"I have never left the city," the creature said. "And perhaps I never will. But I have heard that there are places where madness is associated with the moon—that pointless white rock. There is a word: *lunatic*. Here in Ararat madmen dream of the Mountain. Are you mad?"

"No. I don't know. How would I know? Where—*when* are we?"

"These are the last days of the city," the creature said. "This is where things stagnate. This is where things come to fail and end. Man, are you a failure?"

"Very possibly. At what?"

The lizard shifted on its huge haunches and made a mechanical barking noise that might have been laughter. "I am not satisfied with calling you simply Man. It may offend. Will you permit me to name you?"

Apparently taking his silence for assent, the Beast began.

"There is a story they used to tell in these parts, long ago, before all such stories were forgotten. It was popular among the worshippers of a certain God, a certain harmless but ineffectual spirit referred to only as the Ineffable. It manifested rarely even back when I was young and Gods were many. Its cult was one of those that claimed *exclusivity;* that held out its God as the city's sole creator. As such cults go it was inoffensive; it attracted mostly the elderly and they spent their days writing peevish letters to the editors of local newspapers. There were many worse in this city.

"They said—the Knowers of the Ineffable—that this city once was open fields and hills, babbling brooks and limpid blue pools and shady copses and the like. Yes? A vale as vast as all of Ararat, flowers to every horizon. They say the Ineffable came down from the Mountain to rest among the flowers, to sit cross-legged and ponder the Mysteries. And that He brought with Him His manservant to watch over Him as He sat in contemplation."

The Beast pronounced *Him* with a bitter hacking *H*.

"But they say that while the Ineffable sat in silence, head in the clouds, the manservant grew bored, grew resentful, lonely; that he wandered off. Always he came back, regretting his dereliction of duty; and always he would quickly grow restless again and strike out in some new direction, over gently rolling hills, farther and farther out, until one day he found a beautiful pool in a valley and sat down by it to talk to his reflection. He was lonely, you see."

The Beast gave an exaggerated steam-engine sigh.

"And from the deep blue waters a face arose, within the servant's own, then taking its place: the yellow-eyed face of a serpent—its long body coiling away beneath in the depths. And it spoke. It asked him, *why are you here? Who have you run away from, Man?*

I dunno, he said. *I got bored. Nothing to do.*

Will you go back to Him? the serpent asked.

I dunno.

You don't have to, the serpent told him. And it told him, there are trees over the hill; break off the branches. There are flat stones by the riverbanks. Build four walls; build a home. There you can hide from your master and you need never go back.

"And so," the Beast continued, "he did."

The Beast paused for so long it seemed it might have died. Then it said, in a clattering rush: "Well, even the Ineffable can only ponder the mysteries of the cosmos for so long. He woke and was hungry and needed to bathe and found no food waiting for Him and no water or towels. Beetles had crawled on His skin; birds had pecked at His beard. And He came looking for his manservant. He looked in on him, through the holes in the hut's crude thatching. He saw him lying on a bed of reeds, asleep. Did He wake him? He did not. Did He punish him? Maybe. He gave him what he wanted. Outside the hut's reed-woven door, He laid a dirt track. While the manservant slept, He raised up huts and shacks all along that track. At the end of the track He set a crossroads and three stone roads; at the end of each of those roads, another crossroads and another. He built houses and offices and warehouses and prisons and theaters and tenements and palaces all along those roads. He built a maze around His sleeping manservant, in that one night. *Hide from me, will you?* Imagine Him laughing as He works. In the morning the manservant woke to find himself caged and lost at the heart of something new and mad: the city. Ararat. And he walked out into the crowds.

"There was a dispute among the Knowers of the Ineffable. The story at this point *diverged*. Some said the manservant rose to be a prince of the city; others that he wandered like a lost ghost in the mob and his pocket was picked and his throat slit and his body left in an alley. Or perhaps he got a job. Got married, had children? Or grew old and died of one of the many diseases less well-made creatures like yourself die of. At this point in the story—I have thought a lot about stories—the servant ceases to be interesting. Now the story belongs to the city. The servant, lost on those crowded endless streets, is lost to memory. Lost to himself. Anyway, if I remember rightly, his name was Arjun. Some say the serpent named him Arjun; others that it was always his name. May I name you Arjun?"

"If you like. It sounds familiar. Maybe it was my name before."

"Maybe, Arjun. I am *very* wise."

Beast?"

"Yes?"

"There is only one door in this room. In order to reach it, I must come very close to the bars of your cage, in the dark. Are you dangerous?"

"That door is locked, Arjun; don't bother."

"Ah."

"I am both a prisoner and a treasure."

"I'm sorry."

"Thank you for your pity."

"Then we may be here together for some time, Beast."

"That may be, Arjun—unless you have remembered how you came in here."

"I have not. I think it had to do with music."

"Sometimes I hum to myself to pass the time and I may have been doing that when you appeared. Do you like music? There is little of it in these days. Perhaps I was singing some of the old music."

"I think it had something to do with music. That means nothing to you, Beast?"

"Nothing that would be of use to you."

"It means nothing to me."

"Then we are stuck." The Beast rumbled. "You raised my hopes! I wanted to show myself to the world again."

It seemed impolite—so Arjun was a polite man, then!—not to ask: "Will you tell me what you are, Beast?"

"Why not? It will pass the hours."

The Beast's story began in darkness, in forgetting. In muck and filthy water. In the *sewers*. It had been a simpler creature once. It had been a sewer-thing.

In certain parts of the city, the Beast explained, the sewer-tunnels were very deep and wide. It described great arches of moss-wet stone, dark foul water. Drains and grates and sluices like waterfalls. Galleries of mildew and algae. Humans lived down there—they lived everywhere, they burrowed into every place, hacked out homes in every crack in every wall in the infinite city—and so did stranger things, such as the Beast, for one. It coiled its long body through the dark water. It fed on rats and the occasional unlucky rat-catcher. It listened to the drip and echo of the tunnels. It never had a thought in its head until the spiked noose snapped shut around its neck, sharp spears stabbed its sides, it was hauled unceremoniously from the water, its legs were lashed to its belly with rope, and it was heaved and dragged by dray horses into the light.

"My first thought," the Beast said, "was that I hated the light. Nothing since has changed my mind."

"I'm sorry to hear that."

"For a while I was kept in a cage, on a high wooden platform draped with bunting in vulgar colors, by the front gates of the mansion of the local potentate, a man who styled himself Minister. People came and threw rocks. Or just *gawped*. This went on for some years. The looks on their faces! They'd always known there were monsters beneath the city, but they'd never dreamed they'd see one dragged up into the light. My poor scales went dull in the sun; my eyes went milky in the glare. I was a sorry sight. And yet people came from all over the city; from districts and cantons many, many days away by coach. A cacophony of accents muttering about me. I learned their languages quickly. I have a remarkable brain, I discovered."

"You have no memory of what you were before?"

"I was nothing; I knew nothing. I was an animal. Then I was dragged into the light; now I am a thing in a cage. But there is much more between then and now. You are impatient. I'll be quick. In the hottest summer of the century, when the air was black with flies and thick green weeds choked the rivers, the Minister finally died. I was of no interest by then; I was no *surprise*. They sold me to a circus and I traveled in distant precincts. I was moved from cage to cage sometimes, at spearpoint. The circus changed hands, passed from father to son to grandson to the grandson's hermaphrodite acrobat lover and poisoner, who went mad and was succeeded by a team of sober investors from a bank. They found me . . . discomforting. They kept me in the darkness of the tent and allowed the children who saw me to think I was merely a clever machine. They did not like to think about me. When they died, some faceless cog at the bank decided to sell me along with the rest of the circus animals to a stockyard to be rendered into glue."

"Clearly you escaped."

"Clearly! I had learned a trick or two at the circus. When my mere person was no longer enough to fascinate my public, I learned *tricks*. I learned from an elderly rheum-eyed charlatan to tell fortunes, to read minds. I could not read palms; who would trust me enough to come so close? But I read names and eyes."

"Were you good at it?"

"I was remarkable, Arjun. And when they finally delivered me trussed to the stockyards to be rendered, those simple men who worked there—well, when I told those simple men secrets and prophecies—oh, then they would have done anything for me. Then they would no more render me than they would their own mothers."

"You lied to them," Arjun said. "You must be cunning."

"Ah, but my friend, you misunderstand. I was not a charlatan. I was and am a true prophet. I was surprised, too! I was what they thought I was. It is in the nature of monsters to be . . . malleable."

"You have gifts of prophecy?"

"You are skeptical?"

"I am neither skeptical nor trusting." Arjun shrugged. "I do not remember whether such gifts are normal or not."

"In certain districts in certain times they have been quite everyday. In Saddler's Drum, I have heard, every man had the gift; they'd have considered you blind and deaf. Every child is born bawling, they say, having seen in utero the moment of its death; in Saddler's

Drum dice are considered a baffling joke. But here I am a *monster*. Here and now, in the last days, there is nothing as wonderful as me. And soon they decided I was a God."

"You do not strike me as a God. I can smell you, for one thing. In my experience, Gods are less *substantial*."

"And what is your experience, Arjun?"

"I don't know. But I do not believe you to be a God."

"A reasonable doubt! But then, you have not heard me prophesy."

"I have not."

"Would you like to?"

Arjun—he was quickly growing used to the name; it had a comfortable familiar fit—considered the creature's offer. He felt no great sense of urgency. If he was a prisoner in this small dark world, it was best that he spaced out the few amusements it had to offer. And the Beast seemed to feel no particular urgency either. Judging from the sounds, it was lowering its head and coiling itself, as much as it could in the cramped cage, to sleep.

"Beast? If you can see the future, how did you come to be a prisoner? Could you not have avoided it somehow?"

"You want to hear the end of my story? It is increasingly sad." The creature shifted; its voice came closer again as it lifted its head up, close to the bars. "Well then. As a beast of prophecy I had another burst of fashion, and I was displayed again in the finest salons. But they did not release me; I was *precious*. And in the end fashion swept me away, Arjun. The one great inevitability. The plague of the city—the old city, when it was still vital and young. A madness of youth. I miss it now, but at the time it was deadly. You would not think fashion would touch me, would you, Arjun? As if I were a hemline, or a popular melody, or a school of painting—when I am in fact a monster, a freak, and arguably a God. Should I not be either beneath or above fashion? Or to one side? But no."

The creature's scraping hissing voice was not pleasant to listen to. It was too loud. Arjun wondered whether to ask it to speak more quietly—was that impolite?

"For decades—centuries, quite nearly—I had the ear of Mayors and Princes and Plenipotentiaries and High Priests. Magnates who,

I might add, owed their positions largely to my counsel. To my warnings; to my insights into the nature of opportunity. Archbishop Pnoff of the Immaculate Self used to lead me around the cloisters of his abbey on a golden lead, so that all could see my splendor, and know that it was futile to oppose him. Oh, and he fed me . . . he fed me well."

"How old are you, Beast?"

"*Old*. Fashion, Arjun! The Mayor Fosdyke would not get out of bed without asking me what the day would bring. And wisely so. But his son had traveled in distant districts and picked up progressive ideas from men who regarded themselves as scholars. He found me an embarrassment. I am *ridiculous,* Arjun; that was what he decided, and soon all his constituents agreed. I *am* ridiculous. And I have certain repellent appetites. And I offered young Fosdyke the Second my gifts of fortune-telling, and I told the fortunes of anyone who would visit me even for an hour or a minute, but they only laughed politely, and then not politely; and the future happened to them anyway, in the same old way, so who is to say they weren't right? In the end they kindly packed me away in a marble-pillared wide-windowed room here in this very building; upstairs; in the Mayoral Wing of the Fosdyke Museum of History and Natural Wonders. And there I moldered among antiquities from distant lands, from the deep cities beneath the city, from strange cantons hidden in the city's cracks and folds. For a time I was visited by occasional scholars, who found me interesting. Then they found me ridiculous; they found me shameful; they denied my existence; they stopped coming. A hundred years passed and another hundred. The occasional janitor came to dust my stand. In every generation a curator came into the old wings to catalogue the rubbish there—the vulgar displays of their ignorant forefathers. Twenty years ago children still came, infrequently, on rainy days, exploring the dusty cellars into which I had slithered. Pale bearded Museum-men roped off my corridors but some curious children still came. Too few, too few. Their admiration was sincere but too small to keep me whole. From time to time I forgot what I was, I think; sometimes I thought I was only a *thing*. A statue. An empty shell. Sometimes I was an animal in a cage. Sometimes perhaps I was not there. In silence I became unreal. I returned to clay, as the pious folk of the old city would say; but *I* would say, *this is how my maker made me*. A provisional creature. An *ambiguous* creature. Real enough only to serve his purposes. Cruel father! His surgeries are not merely physical. His laboratories are indescribable. Oh, but you asked how I came here. Arjun, even as an animal I was too terrible for the frightened little men of the present Age. New men came and brought me down here into this little prison and locked me away. Utterly away! I expect in the end they will destroy me, but it has been many years. Even as a mute thing they feared me. These are sad exhausted times, Arjun, and I know things that should not be known, I remember things that everyone has forgotten. I was made to know and to tell."

A hysterical tone had entered the creature's voice; the high whine of a struggling motor. "Of course I saw it coming. How could I not? But what could I do? Here among the relics and the dust, what could I do but wait for onrushing obsolescence?" It crashed to the floor and went silent, save for its heavy breathing.

"I'm sorry."

It snarled.

Arjun asked, "What maker?"

It exhaled.

"You said you woke in the sewers. What laboratories, what surgeries?"

"A figure of speech. I was speaking metaphysically. My makers, the Gods. Are you a religious man?"

"Yes." He didn't know what else to say. "Who locked you away?"

"The Know-Nothings." It made a horrible hacking noise, as if trying to spit. "A species of policeman. This is their city now. They put me down here. You will meet them soon, unless you remember the door by which you came here, and do it quickly."

The Beast couldn't be drawn further. Arjun let it be.

Arjun. Had that been his name before? He rather thought it had, in which case he had recovered one part of what had been lost to him—though he remembered nothing of his parents, or of his childhood, or of anyone—other than the ridiculous lizard in the cage—ever calling him by that name, or any other. What else did he know? He was a man. He was reasonably sure that he was a musician of some sort.

He knew principally that he was looking for something very important. And as soon as he acknowledged that fact, in the silence and darkness of his own head, a rush of desperation hit him: his head suddenly pounded with the urge to escape that little cell and break out into the streets and resume his search for . . . what, exactly?

He couldn't recall.

"Beast?"

"Yes?" It sounded tired, deflated.

"Do you see pasts as well as futures?"

"It's all much the same stuff. Do you"—it seemed to perk up; it shifted heavily—"Do you want me to read you?"

Arjun stood. "I would like that very much, Beast."

"Come closer; you must touch me."

"You did not need me to touch you to tell me my name."

"Names are easy. Names are whores; they're anybody's. I can tell you better things than that. Where you are from and where you must go. What the emptiness inside you is called. Come closer and touch me." Arjun heard its head bumping up against the bars.

He struck a second match. He was startled again by the creature's size, its rough lizard skin, the crudity of its form and the yellowness of its eye. It seemed impossible that it was speaking in those civilized tones. He wondered briefly if it was only a puppet—if some dwarf hidden inside the thick hide worked its levers and voice.

Its huge nostrils flared. Its breath stank. It pressed its heavy head against the bars so that the match's light lit snout and eyes and the rest was in shadow.

Pity and revulsion and fear. It was so lonely, so ugly, so strange. What if it was telling the truth? Arjun did not know where he was, what sort of place he was in; was it possible? With his free hand Arjun reached out, fingers outstretched to touch the scaly snout. And, as his fingers passed between the iron bars, the Beast lunged—bit—taught him an ugly fact about the world.

✭ ✭ ✭

Arjun was aware of nothing but pain for—how long? Pain and the snapping tearing sound of the thing's bite, which played over and over in his head, beneath the blazing pain, like a broken phonograph he had heard once playing over and over in an empty towerblock. He howled and ground his teeth. When the pain went cold and numbness set in and he could think again almost clearly he found that he had, in his agony, torn off his shirt and wrapped it tight around his left hand, which was the pain's throbbing engine. He lay curled on the floor in pain and shock, hot sticky blood soaking the shirt.

The match had burnt out.

Over the sound of his pain Arjun was vaguely aware of the monster talking, in conversational tones. ". . . seem to see you in a room full of stars, full of star-machines, on a dark hill; don't talk to him for too long, Arjun. Unless you already have, of course? Ah, yes . . . this moment tastes *old*. My apologies."

A fresh pulse of pain hit him. It ebbed away slowly.

". . . helter-skelter down the Mountain; clutching the map in your hands; the map being the first thing to fall away from you, bit by bit. All those who dare the Mountain are destroyed. All but one. How many have I sent to their doom? Enough! Down the Mountain; you were warned, of course, in his sly way he tried to warn you, but the young one's no match for the old one's cunning . . ."

The Mountain! A rush of images in his mind again; Arjun couldn't make them out, crowded as they were with the fear and the pain. He knew with a sudden sick certainty that whatever it was he was missing was on the Mountain, lost in that airless distant darkness. His wounds both physical and spiritual throbbed with the certainty of it. The Beast was still talking, low and mumbling, a jumble of phrases and names and places; through his pain Arjun caught *this time he's so old, so cold.* He caught *the Hollow Servants, the Failed Men,* and he caught *the shadows return.* A clattering rush of street names and numbers—Bone Alley, 111th, R Street, Carnyx Street. He heard *fat Mr. Brace-Bel and his beautiful blasphemies;* the Beast rolled the phrase repeatedly on its tongue. Arjun blacked out for a moment thinking of the creature's bloody tongue and severing teeth . . .

". . . Arjun! Arjun!"

There was a new urgency in the creature's voice. "Arjun! Are you listening?"

"What did you do? *Why?*" His voice was hoarse.

"Arjun! Can you not hear them coming?"

He turned in the darkness to stare in darkness at the chimney grate through which he had apparently come.

"No, no, Arjun! Down the stairs! Through the corridors! Our captors are coming! The Know-Nothings in their hobnailed boots! They will destroy you if they find you, Arjun! Run, Arjun, when they open the door!"

The creature was thrashing in its cage; the bars clanged and rattled like a building collapsing.

Arjun stood, in the darkness, on shaking legs, clutching his wet wounded hand to his chest. His forearm was quite numb. Now he, too, could hear footsteps in the world outside, and echoes of some stupid cheerful banter. Now he heard keys rattling in the lock.

Arjun closed his eyes tight. The sudden flaring light as the door opened still stunned him.

The Beast roared and hissed like a dumb frightened animal. A harsh voice yelled at it to *shut the fuck up.*

Arjun opened his eyes again and ran stumbling for the door. Three men blocked it; big men in black leather jackets, carrying blazing lanterns and heavy barbed spears. He crashed into them and they fell back in shock. The Beast roared and slammed against the bars. One of the men had the presence of mind to grab Arjun's arm; Arjun spun round and slammed his forehead into the man's nose. There was a sparking cymbal-clash shock of percussion. Arjun did not know where he had learned to do that.

Outside the door was a narrow red-brick corridor, and a staircase. Arjun ran; after a moment the men behind him picked up their dropped spears and followed him, shouting at him to *stop, you bastard, stop.*

At the top of the stairs was a door. Beyond that was a huge echoing room, cathedral ceilinged. High wide windows let in shafts of moonlight. The room was full of looming shapes, under white funeral cloths. In front of him as he ran Arjun saw a marble arm gesturing out from under one of the cloths, holding a wreath. There on his left was the exposed hind end of a horse, sculpted in brass. The men behind him shouted and stamped and echoed in the emptiness.

Arjun could hear the Beast's roaring, too, echoing all through the empty Museum.

At the far end of the room were huge double doors of brass and dark wood. They were open just a crack. Over the door's arch was a marble frieze. Horses and men and women and coiling snakes and men with the hindquarters of goats and bulls fought—mated?—on the frieze, all in white marble. Someone had methodically chipped away each and every head. A golden plaque caught Arjun's eye and a fragment of its text stuck in his mind: *raised up from Anterior Pumping Station Seven of the Holcroft Municipal Trust sewer system beneath Fosdyke in the Year* . . . but he read no further; he slipped through the crack in the door and out onto the wide stone steps of the Fosdyke Museum. He half fell, half ran down them.

It was late evening and there was some kind of shabby market in the square outside the Museum. It was clearly winding down; stalls were being dismantled or shuttered, their cheap goods placed on wooden carts or the bent backs of old women. Rank grasses throve in the concrete's cracks. Sullen-looking teenagers loped idly among the stalls and sized Arjun up for possible violence. Men in grey flannels and grey caps—every one of them in grey, slumping home or standing in little clumps smoking silently—glanced at Arjun as he staggered past and then ignored him, hunching their shoulders, hands in pockets. A pale woman with a single thick black eyebrow who was packing away a stall with three big metal tureens of reeking fish soup stared at him with nervous distaste: he was shirtless and bloody and strange.

After all the Beast's hysterical talk, he had expected something apocalyptic, awful, the wasteland, the end of days! Not *this*—though with the monster's voice still echoing in his ears, even that ordinary market scene had something sinister about it, something furtive, unhappy, hungry, frightened . . . And then he stumbled and looked up, and saw that behind the pale woman—behind her soup stall, and behind the buildings behind that, an ugly industrial sprawl of tenement windows and fire escapes and water towers—and behind the fat-throated factory chimneys venting smoke and sooty flames—and behind the shallow looming domes of gasometers—and for a vertiginous moment it seemed even behind the dull yellow eye of the moon—behind everything was the vast darkness of the Mountain. Streetlights and firelight crawled its lower slopes, like a bright spill of jewels and treasures, like signs, like bright insistent advertisements for something incomprehensible; but the peak, the peak was so dark. The Mountain was so *close,* here. Elsewhere, everywhere, it was a remote troubling shadow on the horizon; here it *loomed.* How did these people not go mad?

Arjun ducked through the stalls, under their canvases, and into an alley, and another alley, and another. The Beast's litany of street names rang in his head, floated up at him off street signs, until he wasn't sure of the difference between the inside and outside of his mind. He ran where his feet took him, until he could no longer hear the men from the Museum stamping after him and shouting after him, and at that point he collapsed against a damp concrete wall and with relief he blacked out again.

TWO

Which Door?–Three Sisters–Maps, Music–Ghosts–The Bosses' Men

A dog woke him. The mangy thing—naked spine and fly-thin legs, long whining muzzle—was sniffing and licking at the bloody rags on his hand. Arjun kicked it away. It retreated to the end of the alley, where its eyes shone in darkness.

Darkness. It was night, still; he had not slept long.

What light there was in the alley came mostly from that yellow moon—*sulphur* yellow. So this was a part of the city with smog-pumping industries—that was a thing to know. A little light spilled from the windows of some kind of upper-story meeting hall, where someone shouted angrily and some massed unanimous others stamped their feet.

A large, ugly bird settled with a clang on the fire escape above Arjun's head. It darted its yellow eyes, shifted its claws on the rails, and emitted a loud noise like breaking wind. There was something shiny in its claws.

"Fak yoff," it sang. "Faaaaak off. Fakoff."

It took off into the night on heavy thumping wings.

Arjun recalled vaguely that he was not unfamiliar with fever and madness and hallucination. That was something worth knowing about himself.

The alley stank of animals, coal dust, piss, rot.

His whole arm was numb.

He needed help.

He stood, shakily. There were five, six, *seven* unmarked doors in the alley's brick walls. Some of them were painted in peeling red, others in peeling green; all were rusty underneath. Rubbish and slops and ordure were heaped beside each one. He staggered to the closest door and hammered on it with his unwounded hand.

There was no answer and finally Arjun gave up and moved onto the next. When he rested his head against it he heard faint music, as if from a great distance. When he banged on it the music came to an abrupt halt.

The reeking alley wind caught the echo of the shouting in the meeting hall. Something about work and clean living; about enemies and spies; about the Mountain.

A muffled voice from behind the door shouted *go away, leave*—a woman's voice?—*leave us alone*. He kept hammering.

When the door suddenly opened Arjun nearly fell forward into the muzzle of the shotgun the woman inside was holding. He sort of slumped sideways in the doorway.

She had very green and troubled eyes.

Tucking the shotgun under her other arm, she helped Arjun stand, and led him through the door and into the room beyond. Arjun hit his head on a low shelf and she murmured an automatic apology; he stumbled over a pile of leather-bound books on the floor and she did it again. She directed him with some firmness to a musty armchair in the corner. She sat across from him with the shotgun ready to hand.

The room was half lit with candles and hazy with dust. Every inch of space was lined with books and scrolls. His first thought was that it was a scholar's library; his second—having taken account of the little signs and tags on every shelf, and the big brass cash register on the table beside him—was that it was a bookshop.

A pair of yellow feline eyes regarded him distrustfully from under a low shelf.

The woman was quite young, and quite small, which made Arjun realize that he himself was quite small, and slight.

The gun in her lap was absurdly too large for her. She balanced it on her knees. Her dark hair was in ringlets that struck Arjun—he had no idea why—as old-fashioned.

She asked him what he wanted, and he laughed, because the

answer was so obvious, or so impossible, depending on how one approached the question. He held up his gory hand to show her his most immediate and practical concern.

She leaned a little closer to see. She gasped *oh dear*. Her hand rose to her mouth—she wore a number of plain silver rings—and the gun slipped off her lap and hit the floor with a significant thud. It did not go off. The woman scrabbled on the floor for it, and hefted it again into her lap. Arjun had not moved; could not have moved had he wanted to. She flushed a little and put the gun aside.

"I'm sorry," she said. "I thought you might be . . . Never mind. You know. What machine, then?"

"I'm sorry?"

"What machine was it? I suppose it doesn't matter."

"Please," he said. "I don't know what you mean."

"I mean your accident. Where did you work?"

"Oh. I don't know. No machine. It was a bite."

"A *bite*?"

"Yes," he said. "An animal. Please, do you have bandages or ointments? Its bite may be venomous. Or infected. I will try to pay you for them."

"An animal? A dog?"

"No. I don't know." Arjun held his bad hand stiff and throbbing against his chest, and rummaged in his pockets with his good hand. He removed a fold of green and blue notes, clipped together with a gold pin, and some coins of various sizes and shapes with a mess of heads and weapons and birds and animals and flags and numbers stamped on them. He held them out to her. Her green eyes flicked to them for only a second, and she shrugged.

"I don't know what all that is. Is it money? It's not money from around here. It'll only get you into trouble. The pin's nice. If you have a pin like that you don't work in the factories. Unless you stole it, I suppose."

"I do not think I am a thief. Please. My name is Arjun. I do not know where I am. If I have no money that's good here I can work."

"Don't worry," she said. "I know what you are. I know where you came from. This close to the Mountain? You're not the first ghost to come wandering." She came over and held his wrist. He closed his eyes in agony as she pulled at his makeshift bandages. "Poor thing," she said. "Poor lonely thing." It felt as though she was crushing his hand in a vise; he assumed she was only tightening the cloth. He did not cry out. He recalled that he had a gift for *silence*.

She carefully lowered the injured limb and rested it in his lap. He couldn't bear to look at it. Instead Arjun watched her walk across the room and tug with both her hands at a long thin rope that hung down the wall from a hole in the ceiling. Outside in the street a quiet bell sounded. The woman went and waited by the street-front door. She bit at her thumbnail and looked out through bottle-glass windows into the night.

Arjun's eyes were closed when the door opened, and cold air blew in—he'd not realized how warm the shop was until the cold air woke him. He'd been dreaming of a dark river, of being pursued . . .

He tried to sit up and a woman gently pushed him down again. She leaned close over him and looked into his eyes as if inspecting them for hidden fractures.

Arjun studied her, too. It was—was it?—a different woman. The same green eyes, the same olive skin, the same dark hair—but this woman wore her hair longer and tied back, and was thicker set. Where the woman he'd first met had been thin, slight, nervous, this woman was fleshy, and solid, and her two heavy breasts rose in front of his face as she stood; and then Arjun saw that the woman he'd first met was hovering a few feet away, chewing again on her thumbnail. The first woman wore a simple black skirt and shirt, and jewelry; the newcomer wore brown, and her hands were plain. Were they sisters?

It was very important to not become confused among persons and reflections and echoes, Arjun recalled.

The newcomer said, "I'm Marta. Marta Low."

The first woman chimed in, "I'm Ruth. Ruth Low. I should have said. Sorry. This is my shop."

"All right, Ruth," Marta said. "I'm here now. I'll take care of him. Go on, put the kettle on. Take this and crush it up. It's all right, Ruth." Marta squatted in front of Arjun again. "So who are you, then?"

"My name is Arjun, Marta."

"You're not from around here."

"No. Please."

"You were attacked."

"I think so," he said. "It seems unlikely now."

"Anyone chasing you? Don't get strange. I mean the police. I mean the Know-Nothings. I mean bosses' men. *Real* things, real *people*. Anyone like that?"

"There *were* some men. I was asleep in the alley outside for a long time and if they did not find me then, then I think they are not chasing me anymore."

"Did you give them cause?"

"I don't know."

"Did you say anything to them? Anything strange, anything mad? Any of that I-Am-Come-Down-from-the-Mountain-to-Tell-You stuff?"

"I said nothing. I found myself in a dark room and I ran away."

"Are you from the War?"

"What War?"

"I don't know. A lot of you say that. I don't know what War you mean. Where are you from?"

"I do not know."

"What was it like?"

"I do not recall."

"Did you find what you were looking for?"

"I do not recall."

"Poor ghost. Thanks, Ruth, there's a love."

Marta took a clay mug from Ruth's hands. The black liquid in it smelled of aniseed, swirled thickly with broken leaves, gave off heavy fumes—she lifted it to Arjun's mouth, and he let her, passively, thinking *sometimes I am passive, then*—fumes that numbed his head and darkened his vision.

Arjun woke in the darkness of an attic full of moonlit clutter, under sagging rafters. He sat up simply to determine that he was not bound down. The experiment was a success; he lay back again, somewhat relieved.

The Lows were apparently kind to stray cats, some of which had made their toilet in the attic's musty corners.

His numb left hand was bound in bandages that were grey and worn, but smelled freshly of soap and lye. It was extraordinary good fortune to have stumbled across any doctoring of any sort whatsoever; on the other hand it was poor luck to have been maimed by a talking lizard, unless this was a *very* strange part of the city. Arjun was not sure yet whether he was a lucky or an unlucky man.

Ruth had thought he might be a thief. He was, Arjun thought, slight, and wiry, and silent; he might have been a *good* thief. He had a number of scars; perhaps he'd been a soldier—a bandit? Arjun thought not. No, he thought that he was an ordinary man, and those possibilities seemed too strange, too fabulous, too picaresque. They made him smile.

I Am Come Down from the Mountain to Tell You. Perhaps he was a holy man. Perhaps he was a priest. That might explain the sense he had, floating at the edge of his memories, of some profound but indescribable *need*. That might explain why he looked at the city around him and thought: this world is not real.

He was quite sure he'd been a musician. He held up his right hand—his *good* hand—and flexed his fingers. They made silent memory-notes.

Arjun held up his left hand. Under the bandages, he still had his index, his middle, his thumb. A good enough tool for most employment, but worthless for a musician—*mute*. Numbness spread down his aching arm and gripped his heart. He knew that he had lost something, something irreplaceable; he could not be sure how much.

He heard the two women coming up the stairs.

They called you a ghost.

They were sisters. There was a third, they said—at least Ruth began to say it, and Marta shushed her. This was on the third day of Arjun's recovery, and he was clear in his head, and the pain in his phantom fingers was manageable; but he was tired, and weak, and did not press the matter.

The silence was broken by an ugly bird that settled on the sill outside the attic's half-open window, and pressed its lumpy head through the crack. Its feathers were like dirty grey rags and its yellow eyes were strangely human. Its misshapen claws—there were bright rags torn from someone's red dress stuck in them—appeared to be fumbling with dim intelligence to reach round the pane and unbolt the latch. "Faaakyu," it sang. "Oi."

Marta banged the glass against its head with an old book and it dropped away dazed into the alley.

"Horrible thing," Marta said.

"What was it?"

"Just a bird. Don't they have birds where you're from?"

"Yes. Of course. It just reminded me of something."

"Thunners, they call them. Nasty breed. Or Thunders. Or Thunderers."

"Because of the noise they make," Ruth said.

"Because they won't stop fucking shouting," Marta agreed.

"Oh."

Marta bolted the window and turned back to Arjun. "You're looking better, anyway. You can start thinking how to pay us, yeah?" And she squeezed her sister's shoulder and briskly left the room.

Another bird landed on the sill, and peered through the window with a resentful yellow eye. Arjun decided to ignore it.

The attic was stuffed to the rafters with furniture and boxes and books; unsold stock. Arjun lay on an ancient sofa. Ruth sat beside him. The cushions were grey and hard. There was, however, a blanket, which was relatively clean. There'd been food—potatoes, cabbage, and carrots—no meat. The house was cold. These sisters were not poor—not by the standards of some places in the city—but they were far from rich by the standards of all but the most desperate quarters. Names of places and times and parliaments and dukes and churches slipped through the shadows of Arjun's mind, too many and too fast for him quite to grasp them.

"Ruth, you called me a ghost."

"Sometimes people come wandering down the Mountain. We're so close to it here. They're like you. They don't know who they are or where they're from. They come and go. They don't really belong here and they go, soon enough. We try to be kind to them when they're here. There are more than enough people who'll try to be cruel."

"Tell me again, Ruth, where we are. I am still forgetful. Do you have a map?"

"Boxes and *boxes* of 'em," she laughed. "Are you buying?"

"Ruth, where are we?"

She went downstairs; she returned with her arms full. "All right. Here's a few of Fosdyke and environs. There's not much call for them.

Who needs maps to see where they already are? We're stuck here in real life and that's bad enough."

"Thank you, Ruth."

There was nothing there that Arjun recognized. This was a place where the streets were straight and square: a grid, a cage. For the most part they had numbers, not names, though a few were named for the factory complexes they bordered, or the Combines that owned them. Zones of authority were marked out—Holcroft Municipal Trust, Patagan Sewer & Piping, Woeck Oil, Carlyle Syndicated, Standard Auto. Where other ages of the city might have had parks, they had *Undeveloped Area (Ownership Disputed)* or *Reclamation Zones*— empty space penned in by the cage of streets. In a handful of spots the maps *knotted,* the ugly gridlike regularity was interrupted, the streets tangled like still-living things. Ruth's finger picked out Carnyx Street—"That's us. That's where we are"—in the coils of one such area. But those places were so few, and everything around them was so coldly ordered; it made Arjun think that this part of the city had to be very, very old, and very tired. *Condemned Area—Poisons. Condemned Area—Unknown.* This Age of the city was *very* old; poisons and worse things accumulated.

The glass on the window was yellow-grey and streaked with soot. The sky looked sick. A shadow intruded on the lower-left quarter of the skyline, half obscured and half abstracted by distance and by greasy shameful clouds—a shadow that might have been the Mountain. It seemed too large to be contained by the window's pathetic frame. It seemed to press past its bounds. Arjun lay back so that he couldn't see it anymore.

Ruth sat again. "Tell me what you remember, Arjun. About where you're from, I mean; about other places."

He shrugged. "I don't know." He gave up trying to recall and in the same instant a name came to him. "I remember a place called the Iron Rose."

"It sounds beautiful."

"I think it was a prison."

"I've never heard of it, Arjun. Where was it? If I bring you up the maps we can look for it together."

"Let me come down. I feel much better. I want to move and work."

* * *

Ruth found Arjun some old clothes, to replace his bloody rags. Grey flannel trousers of a straight stove-pipe cut; a plain shirt, with patches; inelegant contraptions called *suspenders,* which Ruth had to help him fasten. Everything sagged on him like an empty sack, like an old man's face; the original owner had been shorter than Arjun, but fatter.

Ruth put a hand to her mouth and laughed. "The Dad was a fat man, there's no denying it. You look like a boy in his dad's suit."

"Oh. Am I young?"

Ruth lowered her hand. She seemed unsure what to say. She shrugged and waved her hand to say *yes and no.*

"Do you have a mirror?"

The Low sisters had two shops on Carnyx Street: Nos. 27 and 29. The establishments were connected by a bell rope. Arjun said it was a charming arrangement; Ruth shrugged.

Ruth kept shop in No. 27, where they sold a few books, but not many; Fosdyke's factory workers were mostly illiterate. The bosses did not read. Their wives and daughters sometimes did, but they sent south for their reading matter and would not be seen on Carnyx Street, which was disreputable. Ruth sold a few picture books, most of which, to be honest, were illustrated smut. She also sold music; in dusty sleeves along the walls were black discs, deeply grooved, which Ruth said could by their spinning, by codes engraved in them, cause music to be played, on certain rare machines that weren't manufactured anymore. If you were an enthusiast—and those, too, weren't being made much these days—you had to assemble them for yourself out of junk parts and stolen wire and love. *Machines,* Ruth said, had been Ivy's business, before . . . well, she said she'd talk about that later, maybe.

But mostly Ruth sold maps. It had been one of the Dad's numerous little businesses; and it had been *his* father's before him, and somewhere way back in the family line had been travelers, explorers, peripatetic wanderers of the city, lodgers in odd boardinghouses, consummate fakers of dialects, connoisseurs of exotic omnibus passes and indecipherable street signs. Now there was nowhere to go; everywhere in the city was the same. Same machines, same streets, same houses, same factories, same owners. Now people bought the maps because they were little glimpses of other, better worlds; the Know-Nothings forbade their sale, but there was a steady, albeit small and cultish, demand.

Ruth sighed a lot as she spoke. She flitted from shelf to shelf looking for maps, dusty maps, brittle yellow maps, maps printed on hard cracked leather or carved into dark wood or woven into moth-eaten embroideries, muttering, "Iron Rose, Iron Rose. There's a Rose Theater, here. There's any number of Rose Streets. And here, this mark shows the Temple of the Seven Hundred Rose Petals. Isn't that lovely? Were there temples where you're from? They're all gone, now. Ah, look here, where it says *Territories of the Ivory Rose*. I don't know who that was. Do you?"

"I don't."

"Ivory Rose. Doesn't that sound beautiful? I wonder if it was a woman. None of those people exist anymore. All of those places are gone, except on these old maps."

"Do the people around here buy a lot of maps?"

"Some," Ruth said.

"Not enough," Marta said, appearing at the top of the stairs as if she were a sorcerer. (There was a connecting door on the second floor, between the stacks, that Arjun had not at first noticed.) "But we get by," she said, hefting a small sack of vegetables for dinner. "We feed ourselves. The building is ours. We've always lived here. We answer to no one. We don't have to toady to the bosses and we don't have to wear ourselves out in any factory."

"I'm very glad," Arjun said.

They sat for dinner. There was a small circular table, on which elbows touched in accidental intimacy. Three chairs, three settings; Arjun wondered whose place he had taken. *Ivy's?* There was a vague sense of absence, of incompleteness, which the sisters filled with talk.

Marta worked out of No. 29, she explained. She sold herbs, remedies, poultices, treatments. As she described her work, Arjun had a vague recollection of various wise women and cunning men he'd dealt with in the past, in other parts of the city. He recalled a sinister man in a room full of gimcrack stars; he recalled an old alchemist in a gold-and-black skullcap, in a high airy room full of brass birdcages. Ashmole? He recalled holding that old man's velvet-sleeved wrist and demanding, *I need something to make me hear. Something to open my*

senses. Even if you must blind me in recompense. He did not recall the alchemist's answer.

And anyway, there was nothing of those uncanny folk in Marta,
who ladled out cabbage soup into three clay bowls and sat down to
eat, vigorously, methodically.

Every morning, Marta said, she went out at dawn and gathered
weeds from the waste grounds, moss from the canal sides, mold from
the timbers of old sidings and sheds; whatever grew in the soot and
smog of the factories, like the Dad taught her; mixtures for women in
family trouble, salves for the raw wounds left by the loose rusty teeth
of the factory machines. Cures for accidents of one kind or another.
"Like yours, poor old ghost."

"It was no machine that wounded me."

"So you said. Lots of the ghosts that come down from the
Mountain are missing something. Fingers aren't so bad. You can still
do most work. Do you remember who did it?"

"No. That is, yes; I remember. No, it was not on the Mountain.
It was here, in Fosdyke. It was not quite a who, but a *what*. I was in
the Museum—I *think* it was a Museum."

Arjun paused to eat. He fumbled—his hand made him clumsy.
It embarrassed him. He flushed and spoke too quickly. "Not so far
from here. I ran for a while but not so far or for so long. Is there a
museum here? I came to myself in the cellars, underground, in a
storeroom or a prison room. There was a creature in there with me,
in a cage; a kind of lizard, a kind of reptile, maybe, scaly and yellow-
eyed, much, much larger than a man. Heavy and ancient and I
thought slow until"—he raised his hand bitterly. "It spoke to me. It
told me what my name was. It told me that this part of the city was
called Fosdyke, and you agree, which is how I know that it was not
a dream, unless you sisters are also a dream. It said that it could tell
the future. It said that it was a kind of God. I think it wanted me to
worship it, or at least to marvel at it, but I've seen more wonderful
things, though I may not recall them just now. It smelled bad; it
lived idly in its own waste. Its scales were dull. It looked stuffed until it moved. It was an ugly thing. Maybe it was wonderful once,
long ago. It promised to tell the future if only I would touch it; to
tell me what I was looking for, who I am, what's missing from me;
what sent me up onto the Mountain, if that's really where I fell
from, as you seem to think. I needed it so badly. I felt sorry for the

creature. I touched it. It did *this* to me. I think it started to speak, then, but men came—the men who were holding it, perhaps—and I ran. It told me to run. I paid a price for my prophecy and I was cheated. Does this sound mad? I don't know this part of the city. Low sisters, what should I do?"

Ruth's eyes glittered as Arjun spoke. She'd risen from her chair and put music on the contraption in the corner, and wound it up without taking her eyes off him; now the sound of a dusty and distant piano crept into the room. She sat again with her hands folded under her chin.

"I remember that museum," Ruth said. "The Dad took us there. Years ago. Before the Know-Nothings locked it all away. When we were very little, and the city was so different. There were wonderful things there, from all over the city. From all kinds of places that don't exist anymore. Marta, do you remember, there was a great blue silk flying-machine up on the roof, under glass? There was that painting of the woman weaving her hair into a golden map . . . I haven't thought about the Museum for years."

Marta shrugged. She'd produced a little leather pouch from somewhere under her dress, taken three loose pinches of something sticky and black out of it, and was rolling a cigarette. "There was no bloody talking lizard in it."

Ruth said, "No, Marta, wait; there *were* lizards down there. I mean, *stuffed*. Big cats *and* lizards. Oliphaunts. Chimerae. Monopods—those great hairy things like mushrooms. Down in the basement, remember? All musty and mangy. From some old prince's menagerie, or something."

"I remember. You got lost down there and I had to come and find you." Marta inhaled deeply and passed the cigarette to Ruth. It smelled sweet and thick.

"It was so dark down there. They hardly bothered to light it. No one went down there, even then. I remember feeling so sorry for all of them. Poor dead things. So far from home. Things out of time. No one ever cared for them. No one ever dusted them or pol- ished their plaques or cleaned the glass, if they were in glass. I mean maybe someone came at night, but you never *saw* them do it. I could never imagine who brought those things there in the first place. Who'd sat down and decided where they should go, who'd carried them in, those huge great monsters? Who'd dare? It was like they'd settled there themselves, to go to sleep, when they'd gotten tired of the world."

Ruth held the cigarette delicately; she took short breaths on it and stared into the table's candles.

Marta shook her head. "It was all roped off, Ruth. All those corridors. They were *supposed* to be forgotten. You shouldn't have been down there. I had to come and find you. The Dad had wandered off somewhere, too, to look at old clocks or telescopes or meteorites or something. He always was impatient, even then. His mind always wandered. I found you all curled up under some great hairy monster on its hind legs they called a *bear*. You were hard to wake."

"I don't remember that. I don't remember sleeping down there." Ruth passed the cigarette across the table to Arjun. He took it and breathed the smoke in, thinking only as it was too late that he should have asked what was in it.

"You slept all the time back then," Marta said. "The Dad thought you were sick. I said you were just dreamy."

There was a sudden buzzing in Arjun's head and he coughed, once, quietly; then the coughing echoed back and repeated and he was soon doubled over hacking. He dropped the cigarette in his bowl. The sisters politely ignored him. He heard Ruth say, "Maybe it was a dream, then, but I remember I went down there because I heard a whisper. It was like there was something down there talking to me." He heard Marta say, "No you didn't. You only think you remember it because of what he just said. You know what you're like, Ruth." And he heard Ruth say, "It was saying something about Ivy, about ghosts, I remember it," and he heard Marta snort. After that the argument became too fast and too obscure and too personal for him to follow—it was all *no wonder the Dad . . .* and *no wonder Ivy . . .*

The cigarette had left Arjun slow and hazy. Had the sisters been talking about the Beast? It seemed they'd been talking about some statue, some dead and stuffed and stitched-together thing—not the breathing and all-too-real monster that had maimed him. He looked back and forth from face to blurry face in the candlelight and said nothing, afraid of making a fool of himself, until finally Marta stood up to go to bed, when he attempted to say *good night,* but to judge from her raised eyebrow perhaps said something else entirely. Shortly afterward Ruth retired, too.

Arjun did not know what to do with the dishes. He decided to ignore them.

"It *was* there," he said to the candles. "It *did* speak. The Beast owes me answers."

Arjun took the candle over to a bare table out in the shop front, and began studying his maps. The unfamiliar drug was still in his head and at first his vision blurred and redoubled, and the map-lines seemed to multiply and stand clear of the page, to cast intricate shadows, to vibrate with a pent-up urge to collapse into a single coiling scrawl at the center of the page; but he found that if he covered his left eye with his bound-up left hand, the effect diminished greatly, and after a while disappeared.

He identified the Fosdyke Museum. A little more than a mile from Carnyx Street, on the south side of a space marked as Holcroft Square. That must have been the market he'd stumbled through. Its neighbors on Holcroft Square were a university and a Hall of Trade. He remembered staggering in the darkness past several huge, boarded-up, unlit buildings.

Arjun tried to commit the route to memory.

He raided the shelves. He spent some time staring at a map of exotic and confusing design, lacking legend or label, a black disc depicting the city's streets orbiting in precise concentric grooves around a central hole, an *absence*; it was only when he checked the scrawl on the sleeve again—The Pullman & Jones String & Brass Band, Op. 101—that he realized his error; it was *music . . .*

One after the other, Arjun spread out the maps. One of Ruth's refugee cats at once came stalking across them, trampling the city like a monster of the apocalypse. It was soft-pawed and its fur was a grey so rich it was almost violet by candlelight. Arjun lifted it one-handed from the table and it went off to ambush things in the shadows.

He returned his attention to the maps, in which he observed a troubling inconsistency. At the top of some pages the rigorous street grid decayed into a dense incoherent scrawl of slums. In others the regular streets continued north to the map's edge, losing detail, losing place names, but still running rail-straight. Several of the maps ended in arrows pointing north, captioned TO THE MOUNTAIN. One was cleverly designed so that the street lines departed from their courses at the map's edge and converged to form foothills, slopes, a witch's-hat peak. Another simply stopped dead at an irregular border marked LIMITS OF HOLCROFT MUNICIPAL TRUST CATCHMENT & AUTHORITY; north of that was white space, filled with locally interesting demographic and commercial statistics.

One map—hand-scrawled, with shaking lines, as if it showed some secret and forbidden knowledge—marked the lines of trains, stitched back and forth over the city, tagged with the products they carried: COAL? and MEAT? and ROSES? and GOLD. The map appeared homemade; whose work was it? Hypothetical stations were marked with question marks. The lines arced, switched back, converged toward the north, became vague guesses, abstractions, mere arrows pointing north, *up,* to the Mountain.

But no map Arjun could find reached more than a few miles north of Carnyx Street. He knew without looking that there would be no maps of the Mountain itself. There never were, anywhere.

In all the shelves of maps, and books, and music, Arjun saw nothing that wasn't yellow with age. Was that deliberate? Perhaps Ruth chose to surround herself with old things; she seemed sentimental. Marta was the practical one. That was not quite true, he thought, but true enough that he felt a certain satisfaction in the cleanness and efficiency of the distinction. He was learning to understand the world again!

But perhaps all those things were old because there was simply nothing new being made in the city. The Beast had said these were the last days, and in the glimpse Arjun had had of the city it had struck him as an uncultured place . . . A *tired* place. His mood soured again.

Shortly before Arjun fell asleep, head on the table, it occurred to him that he could *read.* Many people in many districts couldn't. That was a thing worth knowing, too.

The candle burned down. In the morning Ruth winced and bit her lip at the waste of it but said nothing.

It rained all day, alternating between a thin cold spittle and savage sheets of water that forced their way into the shop and leaked from the cracks and spread dark stains across the ceiling plaster.

Arjun helped move the furniture and cover the books and empty the most exposed shelving. It was difficult work, one-handed; he dropped things; he was afraid he was getting underfoot. Ruth and Marta moved deftly around him as if he wasn't there.

Ghost, they'd called him. He stopped Ruth and asked her, "How can I pay you? Why are you helping me?"

She shrugged. "I told you; we get a lot of ghosts down from the Mountain. None of you last long. It's all right."

Marta said, "Mrs. Rawley, who runs the Tearoom, had a man last month. She called him Woodhead after the beer, because he said he remembered drinking it wherever he came from, and didn't remember much else. He kept talking about the War that's coming. It scared her. She sent him over to us because she knows we don't mind."

"Can I speak to him?"

"Vanished somewhere between here and there. Between No. 96 and No. 27. Ruth sat up waiting for him but he never came. He was a strong one, too, Mrs. Rawley says, a soldier, could have been useful."

"So it's all right," Ruth said. "I like having you around. Even if you can never tell me what you saw."

"Bandages off, in a day or two," Marta said. "Then we'll talk about *payment.*"

In the afternoon the Know-Nothings came. The rumor was passed all down Carnyx Street. Ruth observed that Mr. Zeigler had put the red vase in his upper window, which meant that he'd learned, probably from Mrs. Rawley, in whose boozy Tearoom the Know-Nothings sometimes drank, that they were on their way down-street. Ruth banged on the walls to make sure Marta knew; then she hid the maps, and the forbidden books, and told Arjun to hide upstairs. "The bosses' men," she spat, as if that explained the matter. "The fucking filth. *Hide.*"

He waited at the top of the stairs, listening. For a moment he remembered bad years in a cold school far away, hiding from angry Masters; he had an image of cold iron staircases, and high rooms made all of glass. He fished for a memory of *family* and came up empty-handed.

There was shouting from across the street, harsh ugly booming voices. Ruth stood behind the counter downstairs, waiting, a blank expression fixed on her face. But they passed Ruth's shop by and swaggered on down the street.

Ruth untensed and lit a cigarette. "Poor ghost," she said, exhaling. "Poor ghost. We won't let them catch you."

"Why would they want to catch me?"

"Because they're stupid, frightened little men. They say there's a War coming."

"What?"

"Look, I don't want to talk about it, all right? It gives me a headache. I don't want to talk."

For lack of anything better to do, Arjun started sweeping.

The others—his more terrible pursuers—came after sunset.

There were bars on Carnyx Street, and laughter and shouting and music echoed all evening from a half-dozen directions. Shortly after sunset, in one sudden moment, all sound hushed at once, as if the whole street was struck with a surprising shame. The drunk in the street faltered, midsong, and shuffled off in silence; a screaming fight in the garden of No. 15 subsided into grumbling and curses. The little bells over the shop door chimed, and then there was a precise *clack-clack-clack* of footsteps.

"Stay here," Ruth told Arjun, and she left him at the table and stepped out into the front.

She'd been applying the ointment and changing Arjun's bandages. She'd been tracing the lines on his palms with her silver-ringed fingers. She'd told him she was a fortune-teller, and laughed at his expression and said *No, not really*. There were a number of scars; the Beast was not the first thing in the city to have wounded him. There were calluses on his remaining digits, some of which were scribes' calluses, some of which he thought were from musical instruments. He lied to her; he pretended he could tell which instrument had produced each one, and rattled off a list of instruments she'd never heard of: dulcian, cittern, setar, clavichord, theorb . . . The carnyx was a kind of harsh and doom-laden war-horn. Perhaps the street was named for it because they shared the same curve. He lied; he told her he remembered blowing it. The dissimulation gave him confidence and he'd begun to enjoy himself.

Ruth stepped out into the shop front and Arjun heard her say . . . nothing.

The bells were attached by cords to the shop door, so that they sounded when anyone passed through; it suddenly occurred to him that though the bells had begun quietly to chime, and indeed were somehow still chiming, in quiet dull persistent tones, he had not heard the door open or close.

Arjun heard their footsteps, again—*clack-clack*ing around the shop. He knew the shine of their shoes. The *clack-clack* of their boots echoed dully, as if the noise fell into a great blank hole in the world. *The Hollows,* he thought, *the Hollow Servants*. There were two of them, always; he remembered that. They would be busy for a while there. Maps and paintings and photographs confused and upset them; he remembered that, too. *The Failed Men . . .*

There were two cats in the room. One fled beneath a chair and hunched there hissing in flat-eared terror. The other squirmed on its back in an ecstasy of submission.

Two men. Arjun remembered fleeing them, tumbling headlong down the Mountain, through strange and hidden doors, and for a moment he thought he could recall the key to those doors, but there was no time, no time; he tightened and tied the bandage with his good hand and his teeth, and he darted from the table and up the stairs.

On his way out he stole a loaf of hard black bread and some cheese; a few coins; a half-sharp knife from the kitchen. He did it almost without thinking. So that was another fact about himself; he was selfish, and treacherous, in pursuit of whatever it was that he wanted, that he was so desperate to have.

He climbed out of the attic window. The roof was still slippery from the morning's rain, and he slid and scrambled down to the edge, where he was able to lower himself down onto next-door's roof, and from there down onto a jutting window balcony where he stepped carefully among Marta's plant pots, and from there it was not such a dangerous drop into the alley, considering the alternatives.

As he climbed the back fence and fled down the alleys he heard Carnyx Street's conversation resume, as if whatever unpleasant thought had distracted it had passed and been forgotten.

THREE

In or Out?—An Ugly Joke—Among the Paranoids—A Memory of Flight—A Kiss— The Third Sister

Dead end. Arjun threw himself at the fence, scrabbled panting up it, the rusty wire cutting the palm of his good hand, tearing into the bandages on the other. The mesh sagged loose like the hide of a starving beast. It shook with a harsh percussive sound. Atonal—very modern, he thought. His foot slipped on the fence's hollow frame and he fell, landing on his back. Grey dust rose around him—the backyard was heaped with acrid soot, black dunes, waste products of some incomprehensible industrial process. The windows overhead were dark. He stood slowly and looked back through the fence. The alley was empty. No sound of footsteps— only his own heart, its strained gears rattling. The long shadows that had seemed to follow him were only the shadows of chimneys, pipes, laundry. The sun was rising, flushed and sweating. The Hollow Men were gone.

His chest burned, and his legs were weak. He'd fled for hours, imagining the Hollows behind him, not daring to look back. When had he lost them? Had they even chased him at all?

He rested his head on the cold metal of the fence and twined his bruised fingers in it, and he dredged in the darkness for memories. His flight down the Mountain, and how the Hollows had chased him—he caught scattered images, but their sense slipped his grasp. All those streets and corridors, alleys and rooftops; sliding down a silver staircase, his feet slippery with strange muck; and the Hollows always following behind him. They were slow and patient.

Time and distance meant nothing to them. They were inevitable. He belonged among them. They were what happened to those who failed on the Mountain . . .

A horn sounded overhead, booming over the rooftops. Dawn shift. A single motorcar roared down the street and into the distance. Chains rattled and heavy doors unbolted. Horses approached, dragging iron wheels along the cobbles. Arjun clutched the fence, sighed, smiled. He should not be caught trespassing. He had enough problems as it was.

Morning, he thought. The Low sisters would be waking . . .

For the first time since he'd fled the house he thought of the sisters. The sick panic the Hollows radiated had left him, and his thoughts were clear again: he'd left Ruth and Marta alone with those horrors. Perhaps the Hollows were still there in the house—perhaps that was why they hadn't chased him. He imagined them questioning Marta, tormenting Ruth, standing in the darkened doorways with their arms folded. Their presence would stop the clocks and put out the candles.

Arjun flushed with shame. He had to go back. Hooking a foot into the loose wire he launched himself at the fence again. Hunger and exhaustion plucked at his heels. He gasped as he threw himself over.

Down the alley, around and out into the street—he walked quickly, keeping his head down. By the factory's front gate stood a pale giant of a man, banging a rod arrhythmically on the cobbles, marking the last trickle of grey workers into the yard.

"In or out? Hey, you—come on, in or out?"

Arjun pointed, questioningly, at himself, and the huge foreman repeated: "In or out?"

Arjun demurred, backed away. "No, I . . ." The foreman locked the gate in his face.

Machines began booming. Someone was shouting as Arjun walked away, briskly, soon breaking into a run.

But running wasn't a good idea—not in this Age. Men stood smoking on every corner, and any of them might have been policemen. Suspicious faces watched from the windows. An omnibus clattered by, pulled slowly by four looming bony horses, a rusting

cage packed with pale men. Workers? Prisoners? It didn't matter. Their grey eyes tracked him enviously as he ran. Running
screamed: *I am an alien here. A ghost. I am lost.* Arjun forced himself
to slow down, walked with his hands in his pockets.

He *was* lost. He didn't understand the street signs. Numbers,
letters, code repeated. He walked for a while down 1121 Street,
past empty concrete sheds, past the thrusting black towers of the
Patagan Sewer & Piping Plant Seventeen, past crumbling tenements, past a patch of yellow grassland that smelled of sewage. The
numbers of the cross streets climbed and fell. Which way was he
headed? The plan of the city seemed willfully confused, maliciously
hidden from him. Where was Carnyx Street?

It was an unmusical city, or an unmusical *time* in the city. The
clang and crash of the factories set its rhythm. The shift whistles
and bells were its only music. Arjun passed no theaters, no music-
halls, no churches, no choirs. He found this deeply upsetting,
deeply disorienting, as if he was blind or deaf; as if he was missing
a sense that he had no name for, and had forgotten how to use.

The streets emptied and filled again. Grey mobs of men stood
silently by factory gates. Little groups of women scuttled through
the shadows, and their harsh laughter echoed off high fences. Shrill
children played in an empty lot, among the rusting wheel-less
skeletons of junked omnibuses.

Was it safe to ask directions?

Probably not. It wasn't safe to be an alien here.

Three young men in smart black coats strutted down the street,
sharing some hilarious joke, which the tallest was embellishing
with closed-fist gestures of violence. Arjun slipped into an alley and
pressed himself against the wall. He stared at his feet and listened
to them go by.

His shoes were caked with yellow sulphurous mud. His trousers
were torn and blotched. Both hands were bloodied, and his bandages unspooled into dirty rags. His shirt was a disgrace. He ran his
hand unthinkingly through his hair—it was wild enough, and now
it was bloody, too. An alien? He laughed. Nothing so grand. He
looked like a mad tramp. He looked like an escaped psychopath.
He couldn't ask for help looking like this.

A poster on the alley wall showed a picture of the Mountain, jet black, limned with lurid red. VIGILANCE, it said underneath, and below that, in smaller text, *Join the Civic League*. The art had the bitter, strained quality of war propaganda everywhere.

What War were they waiting for? What enemy were they afraid of? A paranoid time.

One of Arjun's jacket's pockets had torn on a fence somewhere, and he'd lost the bread and cheese he'd stolen. In the other pocket the knife still rested heavily.

Twenty minutes later a young woman passed by the alley, holding her skirts and sprinting, running late. She was the first person Arjun had seen who was by herself.

Well, it wasn't the first shameful thing he'd done.

She shrieked when he grabbed her and struggled as he muffled her mouth with his bandaged hand. He pulled her into the alley and she went silent at the sight of the knife.

"Don't make a sound," he told her. His voice cracked, high-pitched and tired and nervous. "Just do what I tell you." Then he was so ashamed of the look in her eyes that he said, "I'm sorry, I'm sorry," without quite meaning to.

She struggled again and he held her against the wall. "I just want directions," he said. "I don't want to. I'm just very lost." He dropped the knife in the dirt. "Please?"

North, through a maze of crisscrossing canals. The hollow clatter of the iron bridges echoed off wet stone walls. Engine thump and cold winds shivered the oily water. Ugly grey birds stalked in the low-tide mud. They called after Arjun in nearly human voices, shrill and cracking like children; they flapped heavily up and dropped on the railings beside him, shouting outraged near-obscenities.

One, braver than the rest, got too close, flapping in his face. Its wings were like dishrags, its beak like a broken bottle. *Oiyu. Yu. Yu.* He slapped it out of the air, and it fell on its back wheezing.

Thunders, Marta had called them. Because of the shouting. They offended him somehow, like an ugly and cynical joke. At whose expense? *Yu. Fackoff. Yu.* They hovered just out of his reach. Did they want him gone, did they want his attention? He hurried and flinched through their territory.

He didn't remember the canals from the night before, not at all.

He crossed empty train tracks, plunging through thick weeds. He didn't remember those either. The tracks ran northeast into the fog, and he thought of that homemade map in Ruth's shop, the trains carrying the product of the city's factories endlessly north to the Mountain, and for a moment he turned without thinking to follow the tracks; but the afternoon was wearing on, and the sun was getting low, and he was no nearer to Carnyx Street; so he crossed the tracks and left them behind. He didn't expect to see them again.

As the sun set a red light burned across high windows, sparked on steel bridges, limned the grey swell of gasometers, and—in the distance—lit something he recognized: the ancient dome of the Museum, softly brushing the sky, rising over the rooftops. It was the one curved and elegant thing among the jut and glower of the factories. There was a statue of something winged and angelic at its apex, red in the light of the setting sun. It was north by northwest, past a few last miles of tenement blocks.

For a moment he remembered the Beast, and what it owed him, and he forgot Carnyx Street.

He walked faster, hoping to get to the Museum before the night closed in.

He got there after dark. The angel on the dome was silver in the moonlight.

The Museum itself was guarded. Five men on the steps, all armed; more around the sides.

They were identifiable as Know-Nothings by . . . what? They had no clear uniform. Most but not all of them were white men, and young. They wore workers' clothes, heavy coats. They showed a fondness for boots and flat leather caps that might have been a badge of membership, or the fashion of this part of the city. An irregular group of some sort—hired thugs? A gang, a movement, a party, not an army, not a police force. Arjun regretted not questioning the Low sisters more carefully.

If the men loitering outside the Museum had anything in common it was that they appeared somewhat better fed than their neighbors, and better dressed. Their boots shone. They wore neckties or cuff links. The little luxuries of leather and color and boot polish marked them as a class apart; as men with a source of income into which it was best not to inquire too closely. A certain arrogance; a certain brutishness. They did not particularly look like evil men, but they looked willing to do evil things, and then laugh it off later as *just business*.

Arjun wondered why they didn't just burn the Museum down; if they hated and feared what was in it so much, why not simply erase it, rather than keep it locked away, alive but rotting? For a moment he considered asking them. If he were truly a ghost here, he could say what he liked without consequence; or he could walk past them and down into the cellars and they couldn't touch him.

Suppose that *he* was real, and *they* were only ghosts; suppose this whole ugly city of factories and slums and ruins and brutal men was only a backdrop for some nasty dream. Then he could simply walk up to them and say, *enough now. That's enough. Go home.* He could march in and claim the prophecy he'd purchased from the monster in the cellars. *You bore me, Know-Nothings. Bring on the Beast.*

Arjun watched them from across the street. The market had emptied out and all the stalls had been packed and wheeled away. The plaza was empty, and they could hardly not have noticed him standing there. Soon enough they'd be bored enough to come over and ask him *what are you looking at, eh?* He slipped quietly away, keeping his head down.

Where was Carnyx Street? South of the Museum, southwest . . . Arjun couldn't quite remember.

A high moon—yellow clouds slunk like cats across it. How long could the Low sisters survive the attentions of the Hollows?

An empty concrete lot, fenced with chains, was strewn with broken boxes, stamped: HOLCROFT COMBINE ENGINE MFG. He built them into a tottering heap, from which he could reach a low-hanging fire escape. He climbed quickly past occupied windows, leaking dim light, the sounds of whining and dull arguments.

On the roof an iron chimney, brown and hooded, bent like a monk, vented clouds of white fog like stale incense. Arjun held his sleeve to his mouth and looked out over the darkening city. Where was Carnyx Street?

He oriented himself by the Mountain—there it was, looming on the skyline, marking the north pole of the city. The high dome of the Museum, off to his right, was tiny by comparison.

The Mountain! Unshakable, unchanging. There was so much he was so close to remembering.

There were old tricks; ways of triangulating between two landmarks—one, the Mountain, permanent, perfect, the same from Age to Age; the others purely local, ephemeral. Rivers came and went, flags and signposts couldn't be trusted, golden pillars and copper roofs got stolen, even marble crumbled; but the explorers of the City Beyond had their tricks. There were no maps, but a smart traveler was never lost.

Arjun remembered Shay snarling: *that way, north, you idiot, can't you see it? Never forget it. Never turn your back on it.* That was a thousand years ago.

In a flash, he remembered another time, another place: golden-haired St. Loup, shimmering in sunglasses, scarlet snakeskin jacket, silk shirt, and shined shoes, checking his watch and smiling, saying: *here comes the storm, chaps.* St. Loup had been a rich man back in real life, something in business or banking or aristocracy. Over his razor-sharp collar spilled golden curls so perfect they seemed to conduct light. *See—it starts on the peaks.* Gesturing north with a wave of a manicured hand. *Lightning, fire. Set your watch by it. Only here, only now, only in this dreary little district.*

Arjun couldn't remember the district, he couldn't remember the place. They'd been on a rooftop? Half a dozen of them, watching the skies. Blood-red and snake-green flashed over the Mountain. *A crack in the armor,* St. Loup had suggested, *the gears grinding, the fires of creation, fireworks and jubilation among the lords and ladies of the Mountain? One hell of a show. What do you think? Useful intelligence? Gentlemen, what do you propose?*

Abra-Melin, shaking, with his gnarled staff and black skullcap and dirty beard, had boomed: *the Gods are angry, you fool.* His huge frame was sagging with age like a condemned building. *The angels make war.* His robes were like a heap of old laundry.

Turnbull had shaken his head: *God is dead.* A plain suit, glasses, an egg-shaped head, the manner of a middling academic or an unbelieving priest. A pedantic little shrug. *God is dead. The Mountain is empty. Sometimes a storm is only a storm.*

Where had this happened? When? Who were these people? Arjun couldn't remember. He couldn't place them. Maybe they *had* no place, no context. Half a dozen madmen on a roof in a storm, talking nonsense. Most or maybe all of them were murderers. Drawn from a half-dozen different Ages, wanderers in the City Beyond, united only by their shared obsession. A clownish variety of clothes from a half-dozen cultures and Ages—all hid knives, guns, poison needles. Uneasy in each other's company, contemptuous of real people and real life. Paranoia was simply common sense among these men—they'd all glimpsed the City Beyond the City, the huge and hostile structure in which other people's ordinary lives were suspended. These were the men who chased the Mountain.

Someone had said: *Why did you bring us here, St. Loup? What do you want for this information? Is this a trap?* Arjun couldn't remember who'd said that. Maybe it was him.

The dust venting from the chimney was thick, drowsy. It smelled of age, exhaustion, old fires, stale food. Arjun swayed with hunger. A sudden explosion of birds from behind the chimney made him duck. Two dozen black beating shapes, tiny machines, rose past his head, through the fog, and out north across the sky, their pattern loosening and tightening again, their forms quickly becoming invisible against the darkness of the Mountain. It made him remember . . .

Another time. Later, earlier? *Elsewhere.* Another rooftop—on top of Potocki's vast factory, south of the Mountain, above streets clogged with cars and noisy intershuttling trams. The madmen of the City Beyond returned again and again to high places.

Arjun remembered: a wide rooftop, a broad concrete plain under a bronze sky, gorgeous with strange pollution. Complex steel machines littered the rooftop, humming and grinding their wheels; delicate wire-mesh mouths sifted oils and grit from the air, to be processed below into food and materiel. The waiting aircraft flexed white plastic wings. Electricity crackled from pylon to pylon. Potocki the Engineer lived in a nest of machines. And there he was, dressed in oily rags, scraggle-bearded, hunched and swollen like a gigantic mole, dragging his lame left leg around the rooftop in circles, conducting his servants, bellowing: *Now! Now! Now!*

Arjun had arrived at Potocki's rooftop too late. He'd taken a taxi to get there, down strange and shifting roads, skidding and swerving forward through history, from the honking jostling ranks out the front of the WaneLight Hotel.

Luxurious, immense—the memory of the Hotel pressed itself into Arjun's mind, too huge to grasp. Bright yellow-black taxis leaving the Hotel like a swarm of greedy wasps, homing in on a rumor: *Potocki's got another prototype. He launches today* . . . The horde descended, armed with cameras, bribes, knives. *Me too, take me with you* . . .

Everything began at the Hotel in those . days—everyone's schemes were hatched there. If the vastness of the city had a center, it was the Mountain—but if its impossible geometry allowed for a *second* center, that would be the Hotel. Power and influence and fame gathered there, connections were made, secrets were bartered. The secrets of power; the secrets of the Gods and the city; the secrets of the Mountain. Years of Arjun's life spent penetrating the mysteries, ingratiating himself with the right people, watching his back, listening for rumors. Gossip at the bar. A note pushed under the bedroom door. A phone call, untraceable, at dead of night, spilling secrets. A whisper overheard in the casinos. Surveillance and countersurveillance systems constantly breaking down, hissing and crackling, leaking information, leaking plans.

The conspirators—the explorers—the secret-hunters—had met in the Bar Caucasus. It was on the south face of the Hotel's forty-fourth floor—a forest of potted palms, a shrine of vulgar brass. There was the scent of a rumor in the stale air. Turnbull was there, and St. Loup, Longfellow, and Monmouth. St. Loup was stylish as ever, golden-haired, in trousers of sapphire-blue leather and a white shirt with a red snake logo. He leaned on the bar and toyed tensely with his drink, which he held like a weapon. Longfellow looked hot and itching in his long black coat. Probably he was wearing his hair shirt again—the pious Longfellow believed the Mountain was the house of God, and hoped to find forgiveness there for unspecified but presumably dreadful sins. Arjun himself was recently returned from one of his futile trips to primitive districts in search of his own God, and still wore pilgrim's robes. The mage Abra-Melin looked out of place in a corner, clutching his ornate staff, glowering at cocktail waitresses. The collector Lord Losond showed off three sleek amber wildcats, sprawled on the bar, chewing their silver leashes. Someone measured out drugs in the back of the room—there was a new *xaw* dealer at the Bar Caucasus, and the air in those days was greasy with the stuff. Wreathed in furtive purple clouds, there was Cantor, there was Karatas, there was Muykrit . . .

All the usual crowd. They said:

Is it true?

Potocki? He's cracked it?

Shut up—shut up. Who's heard what?

Where? Where?

They had raced each other downstairs, squeezing into elevators, sliding down fire escapes, taking secret routes through the staff quarters. They stumbled and slid over each other in the lobby. Muykrit stuck out a muscled leg and tripped Cantor. Losond tripped on his cats' tangled leashes and they savaged his cape and his balding scalp. Abra-Melin stood in the glass doorway making occult gestures that did nothing—then suddenly swinging his staff he cracked Longfellow on his bald head, taking the penitent efficiently out of the running. The mob bowled Abra-Melin over, and surged out into the street. Tourists and scarlet-jacketed porters looked on curiously.

Taxi! Taxi!

Arjun had shared the backseat of a yellow taxi with St. Loup, who sat reading a glossy magazine, pretending to be calm while his hands shook with eagerness and fear. At the time Arjun and St. Loup had had a sort of alliance—something less than friendship, more than mere détente—which usually resulted in Arjun carrying St. Loup's bags, running to keep up, waiting for scraps of information. *Faster, driver,* St. Loup drawled, *if you don't mind.* The roads were strange—it was day, and then night, and then day again, along the route St. Loup picked—and the driver was nervous. The scenery shifted, fashions changed, the skyline rippled. Green raindrops and fat foreign insects blatted against the windscreen. Traffic lights strobed through the night—so, too, did Gods. They were driving down newly made paths through the city, and Gods strutted and blazed beside them, taller than towers, brighter than stars, many-limbed, radioactive;

reshaping the city as they passed . . . St. Loup lunged forward and leaned on the horn. *Out of the fucking way!* The driver started to cry. Neon advertisements in alien languages reflected on the windshield. The skyline was made menacing by ziggurats and fires. *Fucking go faster!* St. Loup shrieked, with his gun against the back of the driver's neck. *We're going to be too late!*

Potocki, the mad Engineer—born in a ditch full of pigs somewhere, or a tunnel, or the inside of a diesel engine. A genius, a mutant, a monster, made out of mad beard and black grease and bony elbows. He'd raised himself up out of the dirt by his own ingenuity, his gift for invention, and he now controlled a dozen factories, all over the city. He owned a hundred hangars full of slumbering tarpaulined prototypes; full of weapons of civic destruction, hidden from the inspectors in unmarked crates. People said he did business with Shay himself, that even the great and hidden Shay himself purchased Potocki's machines. Potocki visited the WaneLight Hotel for rumors and business, never relaxation; he never relaxed. He had only ever exchanged one word with Arjun: *primitive.*

Potocki's great obsession was the Mountain. For their various reasons, they were all obsessed with it; that was what brought them together. What did Potocki want with it? Probably he thought of it as some huge machine, probably he wanted to reverse-engineer it. Arjun wasn't sure. But again and again Potocki constructed machines to breach the Mountain, and again and again he failed.

The first thing everyone learned about the Mountain, when they were first dragged out of their little local neighborhood and into the City Beyond, was that you couldn't just walk there; the streets turned against you, you circled your steps, if you were lucky you only got lost . . . No matter how far north you walked, the Mountain remained remote, away over the rooftops. Did the Mountain retreat? Did new streets pour in to fill the gap as it receded? No one was sure. Perhaps it was a kind of hallucination. No telescope could pierce the darkness of the Mountain. The maze was never the same twice. The way was guarded. Time became a trap that could freeze or end you. If there were secret paths through it, out of the city, and up the Mountain—and the Hotel was full of rumors of secret paths—then no one who'd found one had ever returned.

In a thousand years of scheming, no explorer—as far as anyone could tell—had ever found the secret way to the Mountain. They all tried in the end. Sooner or later their patience gave out, and they went walking . . .

Potocki once built a bulldozing engine, the size of a house, and sent it bludgeoning its way north. It sank in a deep pond. He once built an enormous corkscrew engine to tunnel under the maze of streets. It drilled through a snarl of subterranean gas pipes and exploded. Now he built flying machines. Every few years he had a new prototype—from huge heavy things like winged whales to remote-operated helicopters the size of hummingbirds. None of them ever reached the Mountain: lightning and fog struck them down. They fished up smashed in gutters a thousand years in the future, or as rusting hulks in primitive rivers, mistaken by barbarians for the bones of Gods.

"Sneaky bastard's been quiet this time," St. Loup said. "Well done. Lying low. Well done. Didn't see this coming. When we get there, you know the plan, right?"

"No," Arjun said.

"Nor do I. We'll think of something. You and me together!"

Arjun didn't smile. St. Loup would sell Arjun to Potocki as a slave in the blink of a glittering eye if he thought it would buy passage on Potocki's new machines. They both knew it. Arjun was never very good at pretending not to care . . .

The taxi lurched sideways. A hideous scrape of metal and a burst of sparks. As they barreled north down a great lonely suspension bridge—strung like a silver harp, over a formless midnight river—another car slammed *again* into them. They hit the railings hard and the windows shattered. The other car broke away, swerving right across the empty road, trailing wing mirrors and broken metal, and came sharking back toward them again. Murderous intent was written in its low-slung lines, the one-eyed glare of its headlamps. Its hood, rawly crumpled, pulled back in a snarl. The face at the window, hunched over the wheel, was Muykrit, teeth bared, eyes wide, as he bore down again.

"He's gone mad," St. Loup said. "No patience!"

Muykrit—huge, fat, and pale, filed teeth, clammy skin purpled with savage tattoos. A placid manner, except when enraged, which was frequent. He was from some pre-pre-industrial district—wattle and daub huts, down by a marshy untrafficked river. A barbarian priest-king in the place of his birth, he sacrificed his enemies to crocodiles, or so rumor had it. Ten years ago Shay himself had brought Muykrit through into the City Beyond, which Muykrit conceived of as Hell. He'd been Shay's muscle. Abandoned by Shay, Muykrit hired himself out. He navigated through the secret ways of the City Beyond by blind instinct, and dreamed of plundering the treasure vaults of the Mountain, and raping its women. He wasn't sophisticated. He feared electric light the way he still feared lightning. He had no business being behind the wheel of a car. Was he howling? Impossible to tell over the roar of engines, the squeal of abused tires.

St. Loup leaned across Arjun's lap. His sleek needle-gun was in his hand. An elegant weapon—you wouldn't know it was there, even under St. Loup's tight-fitted jacket. He smelled more of after-shave than of fear. His gun emitted a sad melismatic whine. A wound opened in the flank of Muykrit's car, a thin smile of torn metal. Muykrit's tires burst. His car skidded, spun, pinballed from side to side of the bridge's railings, and finally slammed up against a concrete pillar.

As they passed, and as Arjun looked back through the cracked window, Muykrit's car sat and smoked. No movement. Midnight, and the bridge was silent.

Soon the bridge was far behind them, and the river was gone, and it was day again.

Soon after that they were forcing their way down the crowded roads of Potocki's part of the city. Grey-smocked cyclists scattered. No doubt they broke local traffic laws. Their driver was at that point utterly numb with terror and disorientation, and responded to St. Loup's commands like a puppet.

They crashed through a barrier—already smashed, they weren't the first to arrive—and onto the concrete grounds of Potocki's factory. They rushed up the stairs. Potocki's resentful and underpaid laborers didn't bother to stop them. This wasn't the first time a mob of Potocki's demented rivals had descended on the factory, and the laborers knew it was safest to leave them be. Besides, it was too late for anyone to stop . . .

The launch! Bursting out onto the rooftop, St. Loup first, Arjun following, they found that Abra-Melin was already there: he stood on top of a stack of air-conditioning machines, shaking his staff over his head, threatening to call down the lightning, denouncing Potocki's blasphemy in a harsh and booming voice. No one paid him any attention. Cantor was on his knees, offering up jewels and cash, begging Potocki to take him along for the ride. Lord Losond held out a dossier of photographs and mimeographs: he seemed to be trying blackmail. Some of the others had apparently tried to sabotage or steal Potocki's aircraft, and were being held down and beaten with wrenches by Potocki's hand-picked personal security staff. And the Engineer himself stood at the edge of the roof, as the sun set through the polluted bronze of the sky; and he raised his long apelike arms, and dropped them, and the aircraft rose.

There were two dozen of them. They unfolded themselves out of the junk heaped on the rooftop; hatches irised open to let them emerge; teams of grey laborers heaved open the doors of hangars down on the ground below, from which the mechanical swarm fluttered forth. The air buzzed and crackled. They were made of wire, plastic, and ivory, and each was the size of an elephant. Four wings flapped—two above, two below—and complex vanes spun. They were designed to ride strange winds. Cloth-of-gold mesh billowed out behind them to catch and disperse the lightning. They appeared to be unmanned—scout craft, sent to map the route, if there was one. They rose together into the bronze sky. They were an unlikely flock, mutant jellyfish-birds of the distant future, wheeling east and then north, driving toward the Mountain.

St. Loup shifted anxiously from foot to foot. Arjun held his breath. He felt that there should have been music, a crescendo, cymbals and brass. But there was only the silence of expectation, the distant hum of engines and snap of wings, as the craft became silhouettes, then specks, then . . .

Potocki sat slumped on the edge of the roof, not looking at the sky. He looked exhausted. He seemed to have given up hope at the instant of the launch, not wanting to wait for the bad news. But it came anyway. Distant lightning flashed, once, twice, three times. The black specks of his craft ceased to exist. There was no sound. Then St. Loup sighed, and Abra-Melin howled with laughter, and Cantor sobbed quietly into his handkerchief.

Potocki didn't get up. He spoke in a numb monotone: *get rid of these idiots.* His security staff drew their guns and advanced. But

St. Loup was already running, halfway down the stairs, and Arjun was following. St. Loup had stuffed his pockets with stolen scraps of machinery—gears and gyroscopes—who knew what useful intelligence could be gleaned from Potocki's castoffs? Arjun took with him the memory of those alien craft, rising black against the Mountain, and a moment of utter silence.

The taxi was where they'd left it. The driver sat in the backseat, covering his face, too scared to move. He moaned in terror as St. Loup opened the door. "I'll drive," St. Loup announced. "Arjun, shut him up, would you?"

"It's all right," Arjun had lied, a hand on the driver's shoulder. "Think of it as a bad dream."

"Soft-hearted," St. Loup said. He turned, a huge smile on his face, one hand on the wheel. "So much for Potocki's new prototype. Same time next year, I suppose." St. Loup's other hand lovingly held his needle-gun. "Let's go see if there's anything interesting left of good old Muykrit."

High over Fosdyke's night, Arjun reeled on the edge of the rooftop. His head was full of smoke and memories. For a moment he nearly fell and it seemed the peaked roofs below lurched up to meet him. He sat down with a thump. Memories . . .

St. Loup had . . .

At the Hotel that night, they had . . .

The memories were gone again—vanished like a fever dream. All he had were fragments, without sense; lurid colors; the grinning faces of madmen.

He sat and breathed in cold night air. It was starting to rain.

What was the Hotel? Who was St. Loup, who was Potocki, who were those other men?

What *God*? Was that what he was looking for?

Was that his life?

It was like a nightmare, or a half-remembered and unpleasant film. (For a moment he recalled the private screening rooms at the Hotel, where banned films and classified footage from a thousand and one districts were shown to discerning audiences . . . An aftershock of memory. It faded.) It scared him to think that his head contained those madmen. Was he one of them?

* * *

The fog shifted a little, and Arjun could see clear over Fosdyke. A harsh grid. The formless blocks of factories, tenements, a rubble of low houses in the cracks. Black smoke and flashes of fire, from engines that ran all night, churning out—what? Everything else was the same cold grey.

Fragile specks of light, here and there—and there, over to the east, a single street glowed in the darkness. A necklace of lights scattered in a heap of coal. Carnyx Street—he recognized the curve of it. The moment he grasped its shape he set off at a run, clambering down from the roof, leaving all thoughts of the past behind him. The City Beyond was meaningless, probably a hallucination. The Low sisters might already be . . .

He wove through back alleys. He ran across a black field where monstrous drayhorses dreamed upright in their chains. He stumbled through an alley where men without papers, or too wounded to work, slept in rags; he dodged outstretched hands and kept running. He nearly got lost again; the sound of music drew him in. The bars were open on Carnyx Street, defying the Know-Nothings, and music spilled out.

He heard a piano playing in an upstairs room. It was a cheap and badly tuned instrument, clacking and thumping in a small room. It was a simple tune; the piano started and halted again and again. He followed the sound without quite meaning to, without quite realizing what he was doing. He circled it, through dirt alleys, over back fences and darting—for fear of dogs—across weed-cracked yards. He turned a corner under that window and found himself stepping out onto Carnyx Street, through a crowded garden. Scrubby but green grass; torches burning along the fence; a lush shadow-growth of hedges. Drinkers at the benches looked up at him as he passed—men and women, mostly old, some young, curious but not hostile. A murmur of conversation.

Arjun crossed the garden and left by the gate. He emerged onto Carnyx Street between a shop that sold secondhand clothes—violet and blue lace and green bows and red ribbons pressed up against bottle-glass windows—and the rich black stink of a tobacco shop. Now the piano was gone, but Arjun could hear the scratchy sound of Ruth's music-machine—long-dead music, *ghost* music gently welcomed back into the air.

Carnyx Street curved; it described a sinuous serpentine *S*, and there was a serpentine shimmer to the colors in the shop windows and the lights in the windows above. Arjun surprised himself; though he'd never seen the street front of Ruth's shop he recognized it at once. He walked faster. It was late and Ruth's door was locked. Arjun climbed up the shallow stone steps and knocked on the glass—the thick and bleary and whorled window glass, green-tinted, through which the shop's dark interior was visible only as shadows and void. A single candle, unattended on a shelf, was a blazing mote in the darkness. No answer. The music-machine had gone silent.

Arjun knocked again. He didn't dare call out.

Any of those shifting glassy shadows might be the Hollows, still patiently waiting, silent in the dark. They had nothing better to do. They were the Failed Men . . .

Arjun fought back mad memories.

He remembered Marta coming into Ruth's shop at the balcony, at the door over the stairhead. The two houses were connected— joined at the hip—and maybe they'd retreated to Marta's, hidden there. He ran down the street.

Marta's door was locked, too, but there were sounds of movement from the backyard: low voices and coughing. There was a glow of gaslight.

He climbed the fence. On the other side he dropped down into mud.

There were grey figures moving in the moonlit yard. They were hunched and despairing. Lame legs shuffled across the concrete. Their heads were bowed, and they muttered and whispered.

By the back door, in the dim light of a half-shuttered lantern, stood Marta. She wore plain black. One of the grey men stood before her, reaching out his pale arms . . .

Arjun shouted something. He wasn't sure what. He charged forward.

To his astonishment, the grey men scattered. Shocked faces turned to him—filthy, tangle-bearded—and swore in panic. Two men, with remarkable speed considering their hunched frames, heaved themselves over the back fence and away.

"It's the fucking Know-Nothings!"

Three more men, fleeing, fell at the fence. One was missing a leg, one an arm.

"Run!"

Another, a woman, fell to her knees. Three men stood sheepishly by the back fence, lined up like schoolboys waiting to be flogged. One white-haired old man yelled in terror, began to cough, and was sick in a corner.

"What the bloody hell are you doing?" Marta's deep voice cut through the panic. "Arjun? What do you think you're doing?"

The back door opened and Ruth emerged from the house. She carried a heavy wooden water-bucket, and a heap of grey rags. "Arjun?"

"Yes." For a moment, he wasn't sure where he was. The men and women in the courtyard were just that: men and women. Scarred and hungry-looking. "Yes? I'm sorry. I . . ."

"I thought you were gone," Ruth said. "You came back."

"Get him out of here," Marta said. "He's more trouble than he's worth."

"Come inside," Ruth said. "Come away."

She left the rags and the bucket on the steps, and retreated into the light of the house. Her beauty as she turned her face away made him dizzy. When Arjun had first stumbled into Carnyx Street the beauty of the Low sisters had somehow not struck him. He'd been lost and confused; he'd been blind.

She led him back over the stairs and into her house. The dusty room was lit by a single candle. She started up the music-machine's delicate engine.

"You scared Marta's patients away," she said. They were paperless men, she explained; criminals, homeless, dissidents, and undesirables. They were prone to fevers. They came at night, once a fortnight, to be treated under cover of darkness and away from the eyes of the Know-Nothings.

"You scared them," she said.

"Ah. I thought they were . . ." He let the sentence hang. She looked at him curiously, as if something about him fascinated her.

"You're filthy," she said.

"I was lost," he explained.

She touched his dirty hand; the stumps of his fingers. There were the beginnings of tears in her eyes.

"Poor ghost," she said.

"I should not have left you."

"I never thought you'd come back."

"I shouldn't have left you with those . . . those men. Did they hurt you? I shouldn't have brought those men down on you."

"What men?"

"From the Mountain, Ruth. My pursuers. The Hollow Men. The unhappy men. Do you not remember?"

"Oh, poor ghost."

"Do you not remember?"

"Maybe you imagined them. You had a fever." She was still holding his hand; she squeezed it gently.

"I did. That's true." He couldn't bring himself to argue; her kindness overwhelmed him. He could not understand her kindness to him.

The disc on the music-machine skipped and snarled and wound down. Ruth went to replace the disc, and rewound the handle. Long-dead strings sang in the dusty room. When she came back she brought hot tea, and she held one of her pungent cigarettes in her hand. She passed them from her lips to his; he did not refuse either.

"You came back. I never imagined you'd come back. Ghosts never stay. I thought you'd just . . . drifted away. I thought you'd maybe found your way back where you came from. I hoped you'd found whatever you were looking for."

"I found nothing. I lost myself. I should not have left."

"You won't be able to help yourself. You'll remember one day soon and then you'll walk out of here. Will you tell me when you go? Will you tell me what you've seen?"

"Ruth, we vanish because something *catches* us."

"I don't believe that."

"We don't belong here."

"No. You belong somewhere *better*."

She was holding his hand again, warm and tight. There were still tears on her cheeks. He brushed them away with his thumb. First one cheek, then when she did not recoil from his dirty and worn and thin hands, but simply smiled at him, the other. Then, laughing—it was like a starved and ragged sob—he kissed her.

✳   ✳   ✳

. . . so he was not as tired as he'd thought he was; he surprised
himself with his own strength and capacity for pleasure; he'd not
have thought he was able even to climb the stairs to the bedroom,
which in fact they almost tumbled up, weightlessly, together, the
old boards and timbers creaking both urgently and musically under
their feet.

He was self-conscious at first, and ashamed; the dirt, the scars,
he was unwashed, rake-thin. The clothes she pulled from him were
stained and ragged and filthy, the hands he touched her with were
cut and blistered, he was no better than one of the wretches in the
garden—she didn't seem to care. She saw something in him. She sat
astride him; she bit him. She held him like she was trying to save
him from falling. She continued both crying and smiling throughout the act. His greasy hands tangled in her thick hair; her drug-
scented fingers ran softly across his raw stubble. The city's dirt did
not dismay her. She reclaimed it and made it beautiful. She saw past
his outward deficiencies into . . . what? What did she hope to reach
through this congress with ghosts? But she seemed suddenly *very*
beautiful, and he didn't let the question trouble him unduly.

The bed sagged, and creaked, and sprung loose wires, and was too
small for two, but even so he fell deeply asleep.

When Arjun woke, Ruth was sitting on the side of the bed, still
pulling her stockings on, and Marta stood in the open door, her
arms folded, watching them sadly. It was early morning, cold and
bright.

"Another sister lost to another ghost?"

Ruth shook her head fiercely. "You won't lose me, Marta."

"Maybe," Marta said. "Who knows?"

"*I* know."

"No one knows."

Arjun sat up. "Low sisters, please. I don't want to bring you any
harm. You saved my life, and I stole from you, and ran from you. I
want to make amends."

Ruth said, "You don't owe us anything."

"How are you going to repay us?" Marta asked.

"I lost myself out there. I have forgotten my name, my purpose,
why I came to this city. The Mountain is barred to me. The Beast is

locked away and I cannot reach it. There are terrible memories gathering behind me; I can't make sense of my own life. I need a purpose. I've learned something about myself: I cannot live without a purpose. Let me work for you."

Ruth had crossed to the dresser. She was clothed again and affixing her earrings. Her back was to him and she watched in the mirror as Marta stepped into the room.

"We have work for ghosts," Marta said. "If you're stuck here you can make yourself useful."

"Anything."

"Then bring back our sister."

Arjun, surprised, looked to Ruth's face in the mirror. Her dark eyes watched him from the glass, pleading and urgent and hopeful.

FOUR

An Unconventional Understanding of Time–A Prophecy Confirmed?– "Come Back One More Time"– Some Inauspicious Predecessors– Secret Societies

Arjun would not presume to criticize the Low sisters. All that he would say was that their understanding of time was . . . *unconventional*.

They believed, unshakably, that everything in Ararat first started to go sour when Ivy left them. Before that was light, and warmth, and the shops on Carnyx Street were filled with wonders; back when Ivy had sat in her shop at No. 43 and tended her old records and her music-machines. And not *just* music-machines, Ruth said. Ivy's place was full of old devices of all kinds, scavenged from dumps, from attics, from the rubble of demolished buildings; half broken, rusting, often of obscure purpose, so that it was hard to tell what was a device in its own right and what was only a long-lost part of some larger apparatus. Ivy used to sit cross-legged on the floor among her machines, her hands full of screws and wires, grease streaking her fingers and her furrowed brow. She got it from the Dad—that fascination with machines, with the secrets in them.

After the Dad left things had been hard for a time, but Ivy was the last straw.

She'd been the most beautiful of the Low sisters by far, Ruth said, there was no question, and when she'd emerged from the world of things and machines she could make men do anything for her, as if they were just more wind-up toys, but she rarely bothered. In her own way she was a very innocent creature. Without Ruth and Marta she might have forgotten to eat for days on end. Scattered all around her shop were devices that spun and clattered and counted off numbers, and things that cast light, and things that cast shadows, and things that walked on tiny tottering metal legs. She was the most brilliant of the sisters. After she and the Dad came back from . . .

"Yes," Marta said. "That's enough, Ruth." And Ruth went to busy her restless hands making tea.

"The machines are gone," Marta said. When Ivy went away, she left the music and music-makers behind, having never cared for music, having never in fact quite forgiven the Dad for leaving the music shop to her and burdening her life with noise; having always suspected that the man was trying to make some sort of joke at her expense, which Marta allowed was very possible. So Ivy left the music, but she had all those other rusting machines packed up in boxes and sent on. Ruth took on Ivy's remaining stock. Three sisters became two. And Ararat went *bad*.

The factories encroached on Carnyx Street. Ezra Street and Capra Street and Ball-and-Chain Lane and Lewis Circle, all of which had been beautiful once, and free, now belonged to Holcroft Municipal Trust, Holcroft Municipal Trust, Patagan Sewer & Piping, and Holcroft again, respectively. The Know-Nothings settled into those places and shut them down. They closed the Museum, and the theaters, and the meeting halls. They closed the last few long-empty temples and dynamited and steam-shoveled them away. Fewer and fewer customers came to Carnyx Street, to what was left of Carnyx Street; the factories worked them too hard, paid them too little, kept them in company stores, running up company debt, buying company stock . . .

Of course, Arjun observed, the Low sisters were still young, and Ivy couldn't have been gone for more than a year or two, while the city Arjun had gone wandering in had been sliding into exhaustion and drudgery for decades; those towering factory complexes were not built in a day. By any sensible reckoning the process of city-death was very far advanced when Ivy left Carnyx Street. Nevertheless the sisters remained adamant; the rot began with Ivy's departure, with the breaking of their circle.

If it were Ruth alone, Arjun might have argued, but Marta was practically minded and did not seem overimaginative or oversensitive, and if both agreed—well, who was he to say how the city appeared to them?

He asked, "Why did she go?"

"She was taken," Marta said.

"Who took her?"

"A ghost," Ruth said.

"One of you lot," Marta said. "We can't touch him. Maybe you can, who knows? Set a ghost to catch a ghost."

His name was Mr. Brace-Bel, and he was a very unusual ghost. He'd arrived on Carnyx Street without a penny in his pockets, but in splendid and aristocratic clothing of a bygone age; wig and ruff, velvet and buckle, silk and brocade—somewhat torn and scorched, but still fine. He appeared neither haunted nor hunted; he was not lost and nervous and forgetful like other ghosts. He pronounced himself to be unutterably bored with the ugliness and squalor of the times, and winced with theatrical disgust at the debased men who inhabited them. His voice was loud and hooting. He made enemies in the pubs, in Rawley's Tearoom; he seemed to relish making enemies. He dared the drinkers to gamble, he put up his golden watch as stake, and he cleared out every man in the room. He declared that he was bored with his good fortune. When hotheaded young Thayer laid hands on him Brace-Bel produced a tiny silver pistol from his pocket, and waved it like a conductor.

He was a strikingly ugly little man, Marta said; wet-lipped and droop-eyed and fat-jowled, a rash of pockmarks on his cheeks, a feverish energy in his beady eyes. In repose his body appeared soft and fat and idle, almost boneless; when he walked, rapidly, urgently, gesturing with his plump hands to illustrate some obscenity or philosophical point, or to call attention to something that particularly disgusted him, or delighted him, or both—then he moved with the jerky confidence of some exotic bird.

"Brace-Bel," Arjun said. "I know that name."

Marta nodded as if her suspicions were confirmed.

"But I remember nothing about him," Arjun said. "He was from another time, another place?"

"He said so," Marta said. "And he spoke like he was."

"He kept bragging about the old city," Ruth said. "*His* city. About princes and kings and brilliant scholars and playwrights and wits. Gods and miracles. Monsters. He said he was a great man back then. He had . . . *things*. He had a silver stick, with a pommel, like a crystal of mercury, and it gave off a kind of light, like no light I've ever seen, except sometimes when there's lightning over the Mountain. Like it was crawling, *whispering,* like there was something inside it. Something wonderful. It's hard to describe."

"Ivy fell for him," Marta said. "She was so innocent. She couldn't see how bad he was. She only saw that he was so strange, and so different, and he'd seen such wonderful things. Even if half of it was lies. I tried to tell her he was dangerous and she just screamed at me. Or laughed at me. And then one day she just went away with him."

"We got a letter," Ruth said.

"Yes," Marta said. "A letter, three months later, telling us to send on her things. Her machines. None of her clothes; just the machines. She gave us an address. Nothing else. Not a word asking after us, or the Street. Ivy could be thoughtless—she was so brilliant sometimes she forgot her manners—but no sister of ours could be that *cold.*"

"You think she did not send the letter herself? Was it in her hand?"

"Yes," Marta said. "But maybe that man made her write it. Maybe he copied it. Who knows? We wrote back. We said we'd not send on a thing until she came to see us."

"If she *had* to go," Ruth said, "we wouldn't have stopped her. How could we? We'd have wished her well."

"Of course," Marta said. "Of course. But not like that. Not *stolen* from us."

"Of course," Arjun agreed.

"Men came," Ruth said. "He hired thugs to come take her things. What could we do? They came with guns."

"We followed them back," Marta said. "*That's* what we could do. He has an estate on Barking Hill. Fuck only knows how he got it."

"Gambled for it," Ruth said. "Or stole it."

"We camped at his gate," Marta said. "For two days. We shouted across the lawn. We *begged* him to let her go."

"He had a *lot* of women there," Ruth said. "We could see them through the windows, we could hear their voices. All in strange clothes. He had lights and music and women."

"He never answered," Marta said. "He just ignored us. So we went away, and we gathered up our friends, and about a week later we sent some men up there to sort it out. There were a lot of men on the Street who loved Ivy. And people on the Street stick together, anyway."

"Smith, and Miller, and Sol, Basso, Thayer. Ah, most of those men are gone now," Ruth said. "Moved away."

"Sol died in the fire at the Fielding Foundry," Marta said. "Miller got murdered by the Know-Nothings for talking out of turn."

"I *do* know Brace-Bel's name," Arjun said. "The Beast in the Museum named him. In return for my blood the Beast spoke prophecy: *Brace-Bel, and his beautiful blasphemies.*"

There was a confused pause in the conversation.

"What happened?" he asked. "At the estate, I mean."

"Brace-Bel had prepared his defenses," Marta said. "His devices."

"His magic," Ruth said.

"If you like," Marta said. "Brace-Bel's a ghost and he knew ghost tricks. Things he'd brought from his city, or *your* city, or the Mountain. Sol and Smith came back and they wouldn't talk about it. Miller came back and he said he didn't remember anything. Thayer babbled about lights and voices, and kept crying, and he's never been right in the head since. Basso never came back at all."

"Brace-Bel's a *monster*," Ruth said. "How could we have known? Poor Thayer."

"We *should* have known," Marta said.

"Every month I write to her," Ruth said. "I tell her how the Street is."

"You know he doesn't let her read those letters," Marta said. "It's a waste of ink."

"I like it. It matters to me."

"How can I pass his defenses?" Arjun asked. "What if I end up like Thayer, or Basso?"

"You won't," said Ruth. "I believe in you. You're a ghost, same as him. You can match his magic."

"I have magic of my own? I don't remember any."

"You *will*," Ruth said. "You're electric with it."

"Are you afraid?" Marta asked.

He looked from face to face—Marta scrutinizing him carefully, practically, calculating his weight and worth; Ruth's face nervous, half elated. He lied, *no.*

. . . *Brace-Bel.* Arjun lay awake that night. The Beast had said that name; surely that was confirmation of the Beast's prophetic powers. By chasing down Brace-Bel he could set himself back on his proper path . . . to whatever the *absence* in him was, whatever he'd gone seeking in the first place.

There was an obsession in him, confused and unfocused. The grinning and menacing faces of the madmen at the mysterious Hotel; the darkness of the Mountain. What had he been looking for there?

"You're different," Ruth had said. "You remembered something."

He'd shaken his head. "Nothing important."

Ruth was half awake, dreaming or thinking about something. He didn't know what. He stroked her dark hair as she lay there, and wondered if Ivy still lived, and how Ruth would take it if she were dead; how best to break the news, if it came to it . . .

The next day it rained, a yellow and acrid downpour that rattled off the roofs and made the streets hazy and dark.

"One more day won't make any difference," Marta said. "Gather your strength. No sense catching a fever."

She busied herself preparing food for him to carry. She avoided looking him in the eye.

She asked, "Do you want a weapon?"

"Would it help, do you think?"

"It might."

"I feel I have never been lucky with weapons."

"Well, you can't just *talk* to him."

"Perhaps I can! I'll appeal to his fellow-feeling. It's hard to be a man out of his time."

"It's not funny," she said. "Now let me take a look at your hand."

When you've found Ivy, come back to us," Ruth said. "Come back one more time, before you disappear."

"Ruth . . ."

"No. Not now. When you bring Ivy back things will be better. Then we'll talk. When you come back. If you come back."

"I . . ."

"Good. Go on, then. Please. It's stopped raining."

Arjun set out east along Carnyx Street in the afternoon. The paving-stones were wet and the sky full of black clouds through which a straw-yellow sun cast a cold clean light.

Brace-Bel's mansion was more than a day's travel south and east. Arjun carried a bag slung over his shoulder, containing food and a blanket.

Ruth had cut his hair short, and he'd shaved with the Dad's old straight razor. He wore a suit borrowed from the Dad's old wardrobe. It was pinstriped and it fit badly. The Dad had been short and fat. It smelled of mothballs and there were ancient scribbled notes-to-self in the pockets: *buy eggs* and *rent due on No. 43* and *Ask Stevens about the* MONEY and *Poss. 7-minute anomaly b/w Ezra Street fountain & Capra Street Theater?* and *See Smith about the key; see Kaplan about Smith* and *Thunders roost b/w Odradek & 121A; nets? Poison?* and RE-MEMBER *Ivy's Birthday(?)*.

Also in the pockets: a wallet thinly lined with what money the Low sisters had been able to spare, and a folded map on which Ruth had sketched the omnibus routes for at least the first third of the journey, after which Arjun would have to improvise, or walk. And also everything he'd had in his pockets when he'd first come tumbling through Ruth's door, a sad little pile of miscellany that she'd kept safe for his return while he went wandering: the red matchbook from the WaneLight Hotel, a worn and crumpled theater ticket for something called *The Marriage Blessing,* a citation to appear in Lord Chymerstry's Court for false preaching, on the back of which someone—Arjun himself?—had scribbled a ten-digit number. Some lengths of wire, a pencil stub, some coins.

He had no work papers, no residency papers; according to Marta, there used to be a forger on Carnyx Street, but the Know-Nothings had beaten him and hauled him off one night last year. Arjun would have to get by paperless.

Arjun stopped, on a whim, at the end of the street, outside a public house that called itself the White Horse.

He made his way down damp stone steps into the bar. It was half subterranean, sawdust-floored and filled with rough wooden benches. Someone had painted the walls with horses in primitive style, vast and powerful and surging; others had defaced them with curses and obscenities.

Two men played chess in the corner. A third slumped drunkenly under the dartboard. The landlord sat smoking at the bar. He did not respond to Arjun's greeting, and appeared not to listen to Arjun's question; but he answered, "Mr. Brace-Bel? Yeah, I remember him." He spat.

The landlord squinted suspiciously. "Not a friend," Arjun assured him. "He owes me money," he improvised.

"Big fucking surprise."

"May I ask you another question?"

"I won't bite."

"Do you know where I can find a Mr. Thayer?"

Thayer still lived on Carnyx Street, back west, in a flat over the tobacco shop, in the care of his elderly mother. Old Mother Thayer, half blind, half deaf, not quite right in the head herself, seemed to take Arjun for a doctor of some sort; he did not disabuse her.

Thayer slumped in an armchair in the half-dark and silence. He was a large man, with a boxer's hands folded in his lap, but gone soft and fat and pale. He looked Arjun up and down without getting up; only his head moved. He was blind in one eye. He asked, "Where are you from?"

"I don't know," Arjun said.

"Not from around here. I can smell it on you."

"I think that's right. You seem quite astute, Mr. Thayer. I was told you were sick."

Thayer's mother, hovering in the doorway, said, "He can't go outside, sir."

Without moving from his chair Thayer craned his neck around and screamed at her with sudden unhinged rage to *fuck off*. She started to sob; Arjun led her gently from the room, sat her on her bed, and returned.

"I don't *want* to go outside," Thayer said. "Nor would you, friend, if you saw what I saw."

"At Brace-Bel's mansion? What are his defenses?"

Thayer snapped, "Who *are* you?"

"I'm a friend of the Low sisters, same as you."

"Good luck to you, then, friend."

"What are his defenses?"

Thayer closed his eyes and breathed deeply for nearly a minute. He appeared to reach a decision; he opened his eyes suddenly and said, "He's got man-traps in the grass. Fuck that, though, Basso used to do a lot of second-story work, you know? He knew his way round a man-trap. But there were trip wires and alarms that Basso didn't understand."

"What else?"

"There were . . . things in the trees. Like shadows. They touched you and you froze. There were lights that made you go blind." Thayer raised a fat finger to his dead white eye. "If you were lucky. Sol and Miller never made it to the mansion. We left Sol crying by the fishpond; he said it was a fucking *mirror*. I don't know what he saw in it. I was *shitting* myself, you know, and I didn't want to listen. We left Miller laughing and wanking himself in the rose garden. Who fucking knows, right?"

Arjun said, "Did you make it to the house?"

"It was night. We broke open a window. It took fucking ages. I don't think we were right in the head by then, it was like we were drunk. I mean we'd had a few before we went, loosen the nerves, that's good business, but it was like we were . . . The house was all dark on the ground floor, and all lights upstairs. There was music."

"Is Ivy alive?"

"There were girls, friend. Lots of 'em. Dancing. They wore masks. Maybe one of 'em was Ivy. What's Ivy to you?"

"Her sisters saved my life, Mr. Thayer. They have shown me great kindness."

"They're kind with the rent, I'll tell you that; not like their Dad. So what have you got that's going to beat Brace-Bel, friend?"

Arjun shook his head. "I don't know."

"All that dancing and masks . . . not *just* dancing, know what I mean? Dirty stuff—he made us watch. He made us join in. He's a fucking monster. He's in touch with . . . *things*. The old Gods. What have you got, ghost?"

"I don't know. Someone or something has tampered with my memory, Mr. Thayer. Like you I have been wounded in my mind. In my self. I remember things bit by bit but . . ."

"You mean you won't tell me."

"I mean I don't know. What was he in touch with?"

Thayer moved. One of his thick pale arms lurched into sideways grasping motion; clammy fingers hard as roots closed round Arjun's wrist. Thayer growled, "Tell me, ghost. What have *you* got? What's backing *you*?"

"Nothing, Mr. Thayer." Arjun tried to pull away—his hand flaring with pain—and Thayer's grip tightened.

"What's backing you? What's your plan?" Thayer's whole massive body surged up from the chair and drove Arjun back against the wall. "Why are you here?" Thayer's broad pale face forced itself so close that his spittle sprayed Arjun with every word: "Fucking *ghosts*." Thayer's hand closed around Arjun's throat. "What are you and him planning?"

Instinct took over Arjun's limbs—some rapid twisting motion of shoulders and elbows. A hold-breaking move; a wrestler's trick. Where had he learned it? When? He hardly knew what he'd done. Unfortunately Thayer, too, knew how to grapple. He had a bouncer's confident grip, and was twice Arjun's size; the effect of Arjun's resistance was to topple them both to the floor, Thayer's heavy body on top, pinning and crushing and snorting stale breath . . . They struggled. Thayer regained his grip on Arjun's throat and lost it again. Arjun drove a knee into Thayer's flab but the angle was bad and there was no force to it. Thayer regained his grip again. Thayer's cheeks quivered and flushed red. There was a murderous light in his eye.

"Who'll . . ." Arjun forced out a painful breath past Thayer's squeezing fists. "Who'll tell Ruth I failed?"

Thayer relaxed his grip but did not let go.

"Can you tell the Low sisters I failed, Mr. Thayer? Can you face them? Will you send a letter?"

Thayer did not get up. He seemed to be confused. Arjun scrutinized his heavy body for vulnerabilities. He had just decided that gouging Thayer's one good eye was a suitable opening gambit when Thayer's mother appeared overhead, ineffectually flogging Thayer's back with a mildewed dish towel, shrieking, "Stop that stop that *stop that*."

Thayer recoiled, rolled over.

Arjun scrambled to his feet. Thayer remained sprawled. Thayer's mother dropped the towel and started to sob.

"I'm sorry, madam." Arjun held both of her thin hands in his. "I'm so very sorry."

Thayer started to get up again, so Arjun picked up his bag and ran downstairs and outside.

With the rains over it turned into a warm and sunny afternoon. The Mountain was at Arjun's back as he walked and he did not have to look at it. His brush with death put him in high spirits. He felt invulnerable; better, he felt *fortunate*. He let the omnibus go by and decided to walk. The factory towers, their complex rigging of scaffold and strut and girder and pipe, glittered in the light.

Since Arjun was walking down empty streets, between wire fences and vast bare lots, he felt safe talking to himself to test his bruised voice. It croaked. As he passed a Patagan Waste Mgmt. scrap yard Arjun decided to hum, and then to sing. His voice, he discovered, was quite good; limited in range and power, but still acceptable. And he knew so many songs! The words were lost; he had only a few tantalizing scraps of lyric and he filled in the melody with *la-la-la*. But the music alone was a remarkable recovery! Hymnal and protest song, drinking song and chant, playground song, wedding song, mourning song . . . He walked steadily west and south. With every street he recovered another fragment of self; he polished and set them.

. . . what was Ruth doing? How was she waiting for him? Was she alone or with her sister? Eager to share those precious fragments with her, he picked up his pace.

He caught the omnibus when it started to get dark, when the streets began to feel unsafe. He squeezed onto a crowded bench and rode in silence through the evening.

⁂

At midnight the omnibus left Arjun at its terminus. The guards shooed the last passengers out through the gates and they staggered away. Those with no homes to go to, and those too drunk to find them, and Arjun, climbed the railings and slept in the graveyard behind the depot.

He woke to shouting. It took him a moment to identify the source of the noise; it was coming from the trees, from the rooftops, from little ugly forms perched along the spikes of the railings. The birds. *Thunders*. Dozens of evil bright eyes caught the dawn's red light. They honked and hooted, barking and boasting in their nearly human voices.

Four of them flapped their way down among the homeless men. Their flight was ungainly, but their movements were rapid. They closed in on an old man who wore grey rags and a bright red scarf. Three of them tugged at the scarf with beaks and claws, while the fourth—a leader?—hovered close to the man's face, howling its arrogant greed.

The other sleepers, woken, scuttled away, clutching their possessions. One man had carried a bottle; its green glass was bright enough to attract the birds, and they pecked at his heels and shoulders.

Arjun swung his bag at the birds and knocked the ringleader to the dirt, where the scarf's owner quickly stamped it dead. The other birds hopped back a pace and hung their grey heads nervously.

Four more landed. With their numbers swollen the birds regained their courage, puffed out their chests, shouted a challenge, hopped in closer.

"I *remember* you." Arjun crouched in front of them.

The old man grabbed his scarf and ran for it.

The creatures paused, twitching their heads.

They were not quite birds, not quite natural. They were both more and less than birds.

"You used to be something else."

They shouted nonsense-word curses and flapped their wings.

"In a different place you were different things. I don't think I ever liked you greatly but you were *better* things."

They took tiny fluttering steps forward, and tiny steps back. They seemed nervous to approach.

"Do you remember any other speech? Do you have names?"

They'd fallen silent and grave, solemn the way children could sometimes be, like a little grey choir.

Arjun came slowly closer.

"Everything's changed. Do you remember?"

They came fluttering suddenly at his head, shrieking and screaming in their booming flat voices. He flailed them away. They vanished into the night sky behind him.

Arjun spent the next morning lost in monotonous identical streets, residential blocks, red-brick, grey-brick, blank windows, roofs high enough to darken the narrow street below but low enough to seem humble and cramped. He asked for directions and received conflicting answers. It was past noon before he found an open lot from which he could see the distant rise of Barking Hill, beautiful and stately—that soft haze on its skyline was not smoke, it was *trees*. It was midafternoon when he reached its foot, where the streets narrowed and climbed sharply.

There was a checkpoint in the street.

Four men stood, hands in pockets of long brown coats, around a small wooden table in the middle of the street. A fifth man sat at the table, leaning back in his chair, drumming his fingers idly.

They looked up at Arjun as they saw him come close. He nodded and turned briskly away down a side street.

He followed around the Hill's sprawling perimeter. Every street that turned inward—and there were few of them, as the Hill was ringed around protectively with fenced lots and solid flat-blocks—had a similar checkpoint. Sometimes more men, sometimes fewer.

On a street numbered *eleven* he saw three men in worker's overalls pass; the men at the checkpoint sprung to attention and questioned them thoroughly.

On a street numbered *thirty-three* he saw a black motorcar, sleek and expensive, precious and rare, pull through with a wave and a nod.

Police? Know-Nothings? Some other gang, local to this part of the city? Hired security for the mansions on the Hill? Arjun didn't dare get close enough to the checkpoints to find out. They slouched and smoked and were unmilitary in their bearing, but they seemed alert, suspicious.

Arjun had had some *trick,* he knew, some *art;* he could almost remember it. Once he'd known how to pass all barricades, all walls, all doors. The knowledge itched at the back of his mind. Scattered and buried fragments. He turned over the dust of his memories with an archeologist's patient care.

A name, a shard of meaning. *Shay!* The back of Shay's grizzled, white-haired head retreating through a closing door, and Arjun following, desperate not to lose him in the unraveling maze of the city . . .

Who *was* Shay?

The narrow street numbered *thirty-three* surrounded Arjun with steep ranks of doors, marching up the hill.

On a whim he darted to the nearest door and tugged at its handle. It remained obstinately locked.

It was a trick of the *will* . . . A matter of *seeing.* Hearing?

"Oi! What do you think you're doing?"

. . . and they were advancing down the street, two men closing aggressively in while the rest waited around the table where their captain sat. There was a tone of almost comical outrage in their voices, as if they simply could not *believe* Arjun's effrontery.

Arjun took a step back and they sped up, started running, boots pounding down the hill. He considered fleeing, but they had guns, and the street was long and straight and offered no hiding places. He raised his hands.

They dragged him back to the checkpoint.

The man lounging at the table looked him up and down with disgust. He was short, and fat, and dark-skinned, and past middle age. His hair was grey-white and grizzled.

His colleagues, who surrounded Arjun, some glaring, some smirking, were all taller and younger, and most were shaven-headed. They were smart; two of them wore their collars turned up, one wore his short hair oiled and slick, and all of them had shiny, shiny boots.

The man at the desk seemed to have passed beyond such things; he wore his rumpled black suit with an air of elegant, exhausted impatience. His tie was loose. He tapped his pen on the desk and drawled, "Where do you work?"

"Where I can, sir. I have no regular employment."

A pile of papers on the desk was weighted down with a gun. The man toyed with it as he spoke.

"Where are you from?"

"Northeast of here, sir. Carnyx Street, in Fosdyke."

"Carnyx? Never heard of it. Fosdyke's a shit-hole. Let's see your papers."

"I have no papers," Arjun admitted.

"Big surprise. What's your business here?"

"I have a message for a man on the Hill. May I pass?"

"No, you may not."

"You're policemen?"

"Never you mind what we are."

"Know-Nothings?"

"That's the Civic League to you. It has a proper name. Only malcontents call us what you just said. Who's been talking to you about Know-Nothings?"

"My apologies. The Civic League, of course."

"What man who lives on the Hill?"

"I would rather not say."

"Who cares what you want? What man on the Hill?"

"A Mr. Brace-Bel."

The man at the table smirked. The men around him nodded grimly; they seemed oddly nervous.

The man at the table said, "You're one of *his*."

"I am not one of his anything, sir. I have a message. I take work where I can find it and I was well paid to carry this message." Arjun opened his wallet. "See, sir, there's money to spare on this job." He left it hanging suggestively open.

The man at the table rolled his eyes. "Put that away."

Arjun flushed. "Of course."

"Let's hear the message."

"I can't, sir. I'm sworn to secrecy."

"That fucking pervert. Brace-Bel. We're very interested in him." The men around the table nodded again, closing in. "What's he up to, then?"

"I don't know, sir."

"He doesn't belong here. He's not natural." The man tilted his chair back. "You say *Know-Nothings*. People mean it like a curse, but it's not. Do you know what the League means? It's not about this job, son. It's not about guarding rich men's houses, or factories, or breaking strikes, or kicking in heads. Do you think we like that? Of course not; it's just a job. Everyone has to make compromises. The real work we do—it's about things men aren't supposed to know. Things we're supposed to forget. The bad old days when the city was haunted. The evil things they do up on the Mountain. All those ghosts like you who come down and say there's a War coming, and it's going to be bad. *We Know Nothing Of It.* See?"

Entirely confused, Arjun said, "Certainly, sir."

"*Maury,* son. Call me Inspector. I know what you are."

"I'm a messenger, Inspector."

"Somehow that ghost Brace-Bel comes wandering into town. Normally when ghosts come down off the Mountain, or they slip in through the cracks in the city, we pick 'em up off the street and we *dispose* 'em. Like stray cats. Lost things. And the bosses, the councilmen, they tell us, *good job.* Ghosts upset people; you're bad for business. But this one's different. This one's got money, and he's made powerful friends. How'd he do that, eh? Fucked if I know. He's a clever one. He's got tricks and devices, uncanny stuff. He's doing all kinds of black magic up there. But we're not allowed to touch him. We're not even allowed to get close to him. What are we going to do about that?"

"I don't know, Inspector."

"I'll tell you what we're *not* going to do. We're not going to let you see him. Last thing we need is you ghosts forming conspiracies against us."

"I am from Fosdyke, Inspector, born and raised . . ."

"Don't waste my time."

". . . very well."

"What should we do with you?"

"I have no love for Brace-Bel. Let me pass, let me see him, and I'll come back to you; I'll tell you what I saw."

"Aren't you a slippery one? You wait here. Colfax!" One of the men nodded at the sound of his name. "Go let the Lodge know what we've got here."

Colfax set off at a lumbering jog.

Maury continued staring Arjun up and down.

Arjun shrugged. His legs were nervous and aching so he sat down in the street.

A brief flurry of rain came and went.

A little later a convoy of three horse-drawn delivery carts came, loaded with barrels of beer and vegetables. The drivers studiously avoided eye contact with Arjun while Maury checked their papers. Then they went on up the Hill, the horses straining at the steep incline and the barrels shaking and sloshing with every slow step.

Maury's manner was not unfriendly, now that he'd decided to his full satisfaction who and what Arjun was. He even offered Arjun a cigarette, and shrugged and smiled when it was refused: "Don't they do this where you're from, ghost?"

"I don't really recall."

"Huh. Of course you don't."

They chatted. Though it seemed Maury intended murder, there wasn't much apparent malice in it; but then, in Maury's eyes, if Arjun understood the drift of the man's conversation, Arjun was not so much a person as a thing; or not even a thing, but an illusion or reflection of a thing; an infection of unreality in the solid world.

Colfax came back and whispered in Maury's ear. Maury nodded. No action was taken.

Arjun said, "There are better places in the city than this, Inspector. There are places where no one need work, where everyone lives a life of leisure and ease. Machines serve them. There are places where men have mastered flight." Was that true? Arjun wasn't sure; he hoped only to pique Maury's interest. "There are places where music plays from every streetlamp and paving stone. There are places where Gods descend among the crowds. If it's sex or money that interests you there are places where . . ."

There was an ugly rash on the side of Maury's bulbous nose. All Maury's attention went to scratching it.

Maury didn't listen, but he was quite happy to talk. "Who are the Know-Nothings?" Arjun asked. "I mean the Civic League. I admit it. This is not my city. Who are you?" Maury lit up another cigarette and answered, at length, cheerily, with a long and incomprehensible history and geography of Chapters and Lodges and

Orders; a story of beatings and backroom deals; a slow erratic rise from gang to secret society to mob to hired thugs to party to unofficial to semiofficial police force. Maury claimed to be a person of some importance in the movement, more importance than Arjun thought likely, given his current posting. Perhaps it hardly mattered what lies Maury told to someone who was not real. And as Maury talked and kept talking, never looking at Arjun, drumming his fingers on the table—the day-to-day work of Lodge 32A, which was Maury's Lodge, the declining quality of new recruits, *et cetera*— Arjun thought: *no, there is hostility in it.* Maury talked as if he thought that by affirming the minutiae and the tedium of his city, his *real* city, he could drive the alien and impossible out of it; he could render Arjun silent and invisible.

Arjun had to repeat his question twice before Maury heard it: "Do you serve the Mountain?"

"What?"

"Or fight it? Who runs this city?"

"None of your business."

"If war comes, what side are the Know-Nothings on?"

"Who's been talking to you about war?"

"No one important."

"Then keep your mouth shut."

Maury chatted to Colfax about some colleague's failing marriage; they agreed that it was no big surprise.

"In the Fosdyke Museum you keep a Beast," Arjun said. "An uncanny creature, from another Age of the city. It should have died long ago. What is it? Why do you keep it?"

Maury stopped smiling. "What *beast*?"

"A lizard, a gigantic lizard. I don't know what it is. It talks. Why do you keep it?"

"We kill things like that, ghost. We don't keep 'em."

"I saw it. It spoke to me."

Maury looked long and hard at him.

"Well, we'll see about this."

"What do you mean?"

"None of your business."

Arjun panicked. "Don't harm it. Please, I need to speak to it again."

"Mind your business." As Arjun started to stand, Maury's men closed in around him; he sat back down. Maury took out a pen—shook it violently to make the ink move—and scribbled something down on the papers at his table.

"Going to be a cold night, eh? Shift changes in an hour. Then you can come along back to the Chapterhouse with us."

Just as the sun set behind the Hill there was an explosion.

"Fuck!"

A series of aftershocks echoed down the Hill as Maury jumped up from his chair. Black smoke jotted an exclamation over the top of the hill.

Maury's men gathered around him, shielding their eyes and staring up the road.

"The Odradek estate?"

"Harrington, more like."

"There was a riot at Odradek's textile works."

"Fuck. Black Mask have been putting bricks in the windows of Harrington's offices for months. *Fuck*."

"We caught Maskers trying to blow up Odradek's wife's motor-car last fucking week."

"Shit."

"I knew there was something in those barrels . . ."

"Oh no, it did *not* fucking come past *us,* shut your fucking mouth, Colfax . . ."

"Shut up, all of you," Maury yelled. "Colfax, Burke, with me. Let's see what's left. Ah, shit, Harrington had his kids there . . . Lewis, Waley, stay here. No one passes. *You.*" He rounded on Arjun, "Did your lot fucking do this?"

"I can hardly be a ghost *and* a revolutionary, Inspector. Where would I find the time?"

"Aren't you fucking clever?"

There was another, quieter explosion—or perhaps the sound of walls crumbling—and a cloud of dust.

"Fuck, fuck, fuck . . ." Maury started running, stiff-legged and wheezing. Colfax and Burke followed. Maury called over his shoulder, "Lewis, get rid of *that* shit."

✵ ✵ ✵

Lewis handed his half-smoked cigarette to Waley—the job wouldn't take long, that gesture said—and drew his gun.

"Let me go," Arjun said. "I'll disappear. I don't belong here; this was a mistake."

"Shut up. Turn around."

"I can show you wonders."

"Turn around."

"Not on the street," Waley said. "There's children live here, they shouldn't have to see it. Down the alley."

"Let me go and it'll be like I was never here."

"Turn around."

Arjun turned around. He fumbled in his pockets. He had no weapon; not so much as a penknife.

His fingers brushed the glossy paper of the matchbook from the WaneLight Hotel. A small miracle; a matchbook from a hotel that existed only in another world.

He withdrew the matchbook, readied a match to strike, and turned back again.

"What's that supposed to be?"

"It's a matchbook, Mr. Lewis."

"Last cigarette?" Lewis asked. "Don't see why not."

"If it seems unfamiliar in design," Arjun said, "it is because it comes from another city. A better and more beautiful city. Do you want to hear about the luxuries of the WaneLight Hotel? Every prince and potentate in that Age of the city stays in the WaneLight Hotel."

"Shut it, ghost."

"Then do you want to hear what these matches can do?"

Lewis lowered his gun, an uncertain look on his face.

"If I *strike* this match, what will happen to you?"

"Nothing."

"The WaneLight Hotel protects its guests, Mr. Lewis. This is a ghost trick, Mr. Lewis, this is an uncanny device. If I strike this match you burn."

Lewis lifted the gun again and Arjun raised the matchbook, tensed his elbow as if to strike.

"Ghost tricks, Mr. Lewis. You're right to fear us."

For all Arjun knew it was true. What was the Hotel? Where was it? He had no idea. He remembered only enough to know that it was uncanny, and unpleasant. Maybe its artifacts *were* deadly, maybe its name *was* a curse. Who knew?

Lewis neither raised the gun nor put it away. Waley screwed up his face and advised Lewis that Arjun's story was bollocks, but made no move to draw his own weapon. Arjun's tensed arm began to ache.

There was a noise of crashing and running feet from the crest of the Hill. Over Lewis's clenched shoulders Arjun watched four men come running down the road. They yelled as they ran and waved their arms, in which they held pistols and knives. What appeared at first to be evening shadows on their faces turned out to be black masks, oil-black rags covering their mouths and noses, leaving only wild eyes and dirty hair visible.

They'd sent barrels rolling downhill before them; that was the crashing clanking sound. The barrels spun and sparked. Metal rims struck cobbles with a deep church-bell peal and the barrels bounced and leapt downhill. Some of them were in flames.

Lewis and Waley turned, swore, and fired wildly at the approaching spectacle, and the black-masked men behind it.

As Lewis swore, fumbled in his pockets, cracked open his weapon, and began to reload, Arjun jumped on his back and grappled for his arm. Lewis dropped the gun.

The barrels went bouncing again, and Lewis was kneeling on the ground, reaching back for Arjun's eyes, as Arjun held his elbow tight around Lewis's neck . . .

The barrels struck a crack in the cobbles and bounced *again*—one of them burst, spilling flaming timber and hot ringing metal down the street—and Waley was pointing his gun at Arjun and shouting . . .

Then the barrels came thundering down on them, and they all tumbled out of the way as best they could.

When Arjun looked up from the gutter he'd thrown himself into, the black-masked men were there.

One of them kicked Lewis back down into the gutter.

Another shot Lewis, and then Waley, in the back of their heads, spattering gore on the cobbles. He bent to pick up Lewis's and Waley's guns, and wiped them clean on the back of Lewis's coat.

A third approached Arjun, and Arjun tensed himself again for flight, but the man put his gun away and pulled off his mask. Underneath was a handsome young face, sweat-soaked and soot-streaked, beaming a smile full of crooked teeth. The man extended a hand to Arjun and said, "Thanks."

The hand was missing an index finger. He seemed to be offering it not to shake, but to be *seen*. Arjun raised his own maimed hand in response and the man's smile widened.

"You're welcome," Arjun said.

"Are you coming, then?"

"I have business on the Hill."

"Business is done, mate."

"Not mine."

"Good luck, then. Your funeral. Look out for more of these filth."

The handsome young man pulled his mask back on and ran off after his fellows, who were already vanishing into the evening fog that filled the low places of the city.

For now, the crest of the Hill was bare of enemies. Arjun went up it at a run.

Black smoke rose over the Hill. There was a noise of men shouting, bells ringing. There was a clatter of buckets and ladders, ropes and axes, perhaps hoses. It was all far away on the other side of the Hill, and Arjun kept his distance. He wandered among tree-lined high-walled streets, in and out of pools of gaslight and shadow. Dogs barked and howled their outrage at the invasion of their peace, but even they eventually settled again. The trees and the fences muffled the noise and soon Arjun was out of earshot of it all.

He counted off numbers and addresses. The estates on Barking Hill sprawled. Through the iron gateposts he saw rolling lawns, orchards, a painstaking and manicured facsimile of nature; and another, and another, until it came to seem quite monotonous. Another lawn, another stand of oaks, and behind them, those white marble mansions, lights in the windows, faceless and repetitive in their mathematical perfection.

In the silence Arjun's thoughts turned inward, and he wondered at his own calm. He'd been within moments of death; he'd seen two men murdered at his feet; he remained unclear as to who exactly the Know-Nothings and the Black Masks were, and what the point of the violence might have been. Any of the people behind those fences, in those beautiful mansions, would have been reduced to shaking and sobbing by the day he'd had; how could he be so unconcerned? Something in his past had numbed him to horror; something valuable and human in him, he thought, had been lost. Maybe he *was* a ghost.

Brace-Bel's gate had no number, but a plaque bore his name. By the grace of Thayer's elderly mother and the black-masked terrorists Arjun was there, alive and intact.

Ruth would have eaten dinner, and the house would be dark; would she be able to sleep tonight?

The fence around Brace-Bel's garden was high, but the trees that grew outside it and stretched over it were so comically easy to climb that the fence couldn't seriously be meant to keep people out. At most it was a warning; it might almost have been an invitation.

FIVE

Xaw–Market–Ancient Monsters–Wizardry–Ghosts of the Coming War

Ruth

Through the window of the shop at No. 37, Ruth watched Arjun walk away down the Street. In the thick whorled glass of the windows his body blurred, twisted, was soon a black angular refraction indistinguishable from the trees or the lampposts. The curve of the Street took him out of sight entirely. Seized by a sudden excitement Ruth ran upstairs to the window of the third-floor bathroom, which looked over No. 39's roof, and allowed a view of a tiny vulnerable figure that might have been Arjun passing south off the Street across the little patch of waste-ground behind No. 92, and under a yellow sky bruised by grey clouds.

The bathroom was, she noticed, appallingly dusty. "Not been up here in *ages*." Her voice echoed. The Dad had been an overambitious builder; the house was too large, too full of empty spaces, too full of drafts and dust.

Ruth considered cleaning—she was too restless.

Instead she wound up one of the music-machines to play a shimmering soulful number by the Pullman & Jones Band, and smoked one and then another of the pungent *xaw* cigarettes. The music built from minor to major, to a crescendo of trumpets. Her senses sharpened by the *xaw*, it seemed the air filled with sudden brightness. She adjusted the needle and played it again. The afternoon sky darkened.

The room was full of ghosts.

For instance the music-machine, which operated
forgotten principles, and could no longer be manu
been rescued by Ivy and their father from a rubbish-ti

Ruth had rescued the music herself; the record had
a lot to be destroyed by the Know-Nothings, but she had been
friends with one of the guards at school and had been able to persuade him to let her salvage as much as she could fit under her coat.
No one remembered who the Pullman & Jones Band was. The
record's sepia-toned sleeve showed a group of smiling young people, mostly black, men in pinstripe suits and women in dark
dresses, in a lush park, in front of an unrecognizable city of domed
and glittering buildings. She was achingly proud of having saved
them from the fire.

The intoxicating synesthetic *xaw* was taken from a virulent
purple weed that grew only on certain rusty surfaces. The Dad
claimed to have discovered it in his explorations of the city's waste-
grounds. It bore all the marks of having been *engineered,* he'd said after long study, though for what purpose he wasn't sure—most
likely something religious. The name *xaw* came from an old book
Ruth had read, where *xaw* was the drug the young wizard used to
call on the powers that defeated the King of Shadows . . . It was
probably the wrong name for whatever the weed really was.
Certainly smoking it gave Ruth no magical powers. It heightened
memory and the senses, it calmed the nerves. Now Ruth and Marta
cultivated it in the backyard, on chicken wire and the insides of old
machines, and as far as they knew were the only people who remembered it at all.

Everything in the room was a ghost of a different and better
time. None of it was more than a temporary escape. The room was
a stalled project, a plan of a jailbreak that had gone nowhere.

They needed Ivy back. Ivy was the clever one. Without Ivy they
were stuck.

No customers came. Evening fell. The market was open.

W rapped in a grey shawl—not so much to protect against the cold
as to mask her face—Ruth visited the market.

The market's legal status was unclear—that was the way things
usually were, the Know-Nothings preferring to leave people unsure

what they would or would not tolerate, or for how long, or under what conditions. The market wasn't exactly *hidden,* but it moved from night to night, and you had to know someone who knew someone if you wanted to find it. Tonight it was in an empty barn on the end of Anchor Street. It sold non-Company goods, and *stolen* Company goods, and sometimes illegal goods. Some of the young men behind the seedy stalls selling incongruously bright and new tools were, Ruth knew, Black Masks. Others were just thieves. Most of them knew her, and smiled, nodded, had enough sense not to say her name out loud, because you never knew who might be listening . . .

"Miss *Low*!"

She sighed. "Good evening, Mr. Zeigler."

Out of breath, running to catch up with her; drainpipe-tall and thin, grey-haired; cheerful, smiling, bowing, kissing her hand with awkward avuncular courtliness. Mr. Charles Zeigler, resident of No. 87 Carnyx Street, Flat 2C, unmarried, a sort of friend of her father's from the old days—or at least, they'd shared similar interests. He was now a part-time, lowest-grade accountant for a subsidiary of Holcroft Municipal; he wore his frizzy hair long and wild and kept in a basement down-street a junked and jury-rigged printing press with which he put out *Sightings,* a cheap newsletter on the uncanny and anomalous, that would surely one day get him in serious trouble unless he learned more caution than he seemed capable of.

"Find anything interesting tonight, Miss Low?"

An old picture book. An odd mirror of antique design. Groceries, while she was there—vegetables, wine, a scrawny rabbit. "Not much," she said. "Yourself?"

Zeigler was a tenant. A bachelor rent-scraper in a little room. Flat 2C had once belonged to Ruth's father, like a number of the houses on Carnyx Street, and now it belonged to the Low sisters. Those debts and obligations were about all the Dad had left behind, when he left. Zeigler was probably behind on the rent—he usually was. Ruth couldn't remember. She'd have to ask Marta.

"Not much. Not much! But I hear you have a guest."

She slowly withdrew her hand from the man's grasp. "Shh, Mr. Zeigler. Please." She felt a sudden panic; she thought of how tiny and vulnerable Arjun had appeared through the windows, receding . . . "Mr. Zeigler, some things are private. Some things aren't safe to talk about. He's only a lodger, he's only a friend. You won't give anyone the wrong idea, will you?"

"Of *course* not." Zeigler looked sincerely hurt. "Of course not, my dear." He took her hand again, patted it. Then he whispered, "I hear he went walking away south this afternoon. Just between you and me, may we prepare for the return of your much-missed sister?"

He let go of her hand. His fingers twitched at the jacket pocket that contained his notepad. His bushy eyebrows twitched. Ruth sighed. "Good *night,* Mr. Zeigler."

As she came onto Carnyx Street from the unnamed alley behind the Morgans' house someone grabbed her arm, and she nearly dropped her groceries; but it was only old Mrs. Morgan, confused, in a panic, asking after Marta.

"What is it? Maybe I can help?"

"I was looking for Marta, dear . . . it's Mrs. Thayer, she's in tears, poor thing, says that poor boy's gone again. You know how he gets."

"Don't worry, Mrs. Morgan. I'll talk to him."

Thayer always went to the same place when he went outside; up to the roof of the Foundry, among the water towers, where he sat grey and fat as a pigeon and threatened to jump. Ruth had to drop her groceries to clamber up the fire escape to reach him. It was Marta's turn really, but there was no sense wasting time waiting for her. You never knew; maybe today would be the day that Thayer finally *did* jump. She found him heaving and groaning on the edge of the roof. It was better not to say sorry, however badly you felt it, because it only upset him; better just to sit with him. She touched his arm. Despite the cold he was damp with sweat. From time to time he bellowed, "I'll do it!" A small sympathetic crowd gathered in the street below. By the time Thayer was ready to come down—shoulders slumped and sighing, same as always—Ruth was hungry and thirsty and desperate for bed.

But Marta was waiting at home, sitting at the kitchen table with a glass of wine in her hand and a concerned look on her face.

"I know," Ruth said.

"We need to talk."

"Do we have to?"

"You know you shouldn't. Why do you always do it? Is it because of *him?*"

Ruth sighed, sat down. "Go on, then."

"It never ends happily with ghosts. Why do you put yourself through it?"

Marta was right; it had never ended happily.

They came and went—the ghosts who tumbled down the Mountain, lost and confused, half in the world and half out of it, heroic and pathetic and beautiful . . . Last winter there'd been the pilot. Sandy-haired, handsome, smelling of smoke and engines. He'd gone up on the Mountain on some wonderful winged machine, something like—to judge from the wreckage—a balsa-wood bicycle with wings of silk, and a heavy iron steam engine. He'd had no name that he could remember, so Ruth called him Altair, because that was stitched on his parachute—*Altair Aerodynamics Manufacturing*. He'd broken his legs in the fall down the Mountain and into the world. He didn't remember where he was from, or why he'd gone up on the Mountain. He thought he was a kind of explorer; he remembered flying his machine into dark clouds over the Mountain, and the flash and ozone of lightning, and nothing else. Zeigler found him half dead in the empty lot south of Capra Street, and the Lows and Zeigler brought him raving back through the streets and installed him in the bed in the attic. He'd been angry and confused at first, then . . . Ruth shouldn't have fallen for him, but she did. In the spring, when he was walking again, albeit on crutches, and not far from the house, he vanished. Did he find the way back to his city, his own time? Did something take him? She'd never know.

Before that there was the astronomer, who came wandering lost down the street on a summer night, frantically asking anyone who'd stop for him: *why are the stars so different here?* A little ugly man, kind and clever. The stars, he'd explained, were different on the other side of the Mountain. He stayed all summer. He'd forgotten his own name, he'd forgotten the city he came from, but he was full to bursting with stories, myths, and science about the stars, the sky, the clouds. He'd used the stars to mark his path up the Mountain; having been thrown back down in a different place, he was lost. He said he was lucky to have landed lost among such kind friends. When he vanished one night Ruth told herself he'd found his way back to his own stars, and she cried for a day.

Before that there were others. The thief, the soldier, the pilgrim, the sculptress . . .

"Every time," Marta said. "Every ghost that blows through. You always let yourself get hurt. They never stay. That's not how the city works."

They didn't have to stay, Ruth thought. That wasn't the point. And anyway—"This one's different." The words were out of her mouth before she thought about them, and when Marta snorted and said, *"how?"* she couldn't answer.

That night she dreamed, among other things, about Arjun—who carried some mystery silently with him, walking with her through a labyrinth under the city, the walls etched in gold and onyx, where every gate was guarded by a thin slithering dragon that asked riddles, the answers to which were all about alien times and places in the city, mostly about Gods. And somehow she knew all the answers, and Arjun followed through the gates after her, and for some reason both of them wore red robes, shimmering and rustling. And as they progressed through the maze the walls pressed in closer and closer so that they were walking arm in arm and almost leaning on each other, breathing together—and that dream shifted as dreams do into a dream about the Beast beneath the Museum. She walked in the dusty velvet-roped corridors, among the hulks of ancient stuffed monsters, glass eyes and stretched skin and bristling lifeless fur, dull scales, molting wings stretched out on iron frames, yellow cracked tusks, broken fangs, and heavy legs on the grey hide of which generations of naughty children had scratched their names. She *remembered*. It had been shortly after her mother had died, when the Dad still brought the girls with him everywhere he went, and shortly before the Know-Nothings locked the Museum away. While the Dad and Ivy were upstairs among the machines, Ruth, who didn't share their fascination with machines, slipped away, downstairs, past the ropes, and found herself lost among the ancient animals. Sloth, minotaur. All long dead. Auk, mammoth, chimera. The plaques were so covered with dust she had to ruin the sleeve of her dress wiping the things legible. Amphisbaena, dragon. Then, like dust shifting and falling, there had been a soft *voice*. It had called her *Middle Child*.

She would have given any adult a kick in the shins for that, but from that long-dead thing looming still and shadowy over her it seemed acceptable.

Middle Child, you remind me of someone.

She had climbed up onto its platform and settled cross-legged beneath its shadow, curious to hear what it would say next. For a long time it was silent, and then it spoke prophecy:

You will never marry.

. . . which was a great relief, at the time, and exactly the best way to make friends with her, and make up for the *Middle Child* business.

You must always keep a close watch on your sister.

. . . which she'd always tried to do.

You must stay close to your father.

. . . which at the time had seemed to go without saying.

There was something else on the edge of her memory, some terribly important warning; but then she was torn out of sleep by the shriek of two of Marta's horrible stray cats fighting in the room below.

Twenty minutes later she found herself outside the Museum. In the cold of the night she was no longer sure the Beast had been real; nor was she able to tell herself it was only a dream. It nagged at her. As if she didn't have enough strange memories to haunt her! But this one, at least, could be resolved quite easily if only she could get into the Museum, if she could *somehow* . . .

She shivered, wrapped her hands in her scarf, approached slowly, coughing to announce her presence, so that the night guards wouldn't take her for a threat.

There were two of them, standing by the great double doors, at the top of the marble steps. They were backlit by smoky torches and so heavily dressed in layers of wool and leather and fur hats that they loomed like bears.

"Hello, Henry," she said. "Hello, Siddon. Cold night."

She knew them both. They weren't bad lads. Henry—the elder, the less bright of the two—had mooned after Ivy for a summer three years ago. Siddon, the younger, had broken his leg and lost most of the skin on his left arm when he slipped and fell among the grinders in the Glassworks, and if not for Marta's herbs the infection would have been a lot worse—so it was no surprise when he gave Ruth a friendly smile and waved her up the steps, and said, "Cold fucking night, Miss Low. Boring, too. Come stand by the torches a moment."

She did. Siddon affected to bow to her, welcoming her to the Museum; he gave her a sly suggestive smile.

Henry furrowed his brow. "You're out late, Miss Low."

"Couldn't sleep," she said. "Bad dreams, you know?"

Henry nodded solemnly.

In a conspiratorial whisper, Siddon said, "He thinks the Mountain sends bad dreams, you know, Miss Low."

Henry scowled. "I only said sometimes it *seems* . . ."

Siddon laughed. "Long nights, Miss Low. We all say all sorts of strange things. Do you mind if I call you Ruth? I shouldn't when I'm on duty, so to speak, but no one's here who minds . . ."

"Of course you can, Siddon."

There was a long silence: Siddon, quite obviously trying to think of something charming to say, only a few minutes away from gathering his nerve to ask Henry to mind the Museum while maybe he and Ruth went for a *walk*; Henry narrowing his dull eyes as if something about the scene bothered and upset him; and Ruth realizing that there was no possible way of broaching the subject of the Museum's contents and the mysteries it might contain with these two, that there was no hope of tricking them, that if she asked to be allowed in, they would simply say *no,* and maybe if she was lucky, for old time's sake, they would forget she'd asked, but that was the best she could expect . . .

"I don't come out this way, much," she said. "Do they have you out here every night?"

Siddon tapped the side of his nose. "Important stuff in here. Secrets. Count yourself lucky you never have to see this stuff." He looked ready to say more; then Henry coughed, and Siddon's face closed into a stiff blank smile.

They made small talk about Marta, and Siddon's sister, and Siddon's sister's baby; and Ruth shifted restlessly from foot to foot. She felt almost able to sense the presence of the impossible creature beneath the Museum, its weight, its warmth, its strange smell; she felt almost able to hear its whispering dusty voice beneath Siddon's laughter and Henry's grumbling. Birds gathered in the eaves above, in the cracks of the Museum's marble facade, settling like memories. Siddon made a daring joke at the expense of Holcroft Municipal's bosses, apparently to show he wasn't *just* your ordinary loyal Know-Nothing . . .

"I should be getting going," Ruth said. "If you're here some other night I should bring you something to drink, maybe."

"Someone's always here, Ruth. A little thank-you's always appreciated."

The next day she was in an unaccountably good mood. It was a good day for business; the bell rang and customers crept in, opened their wallets, walked out with forbidden books stuffed in their coat pockets. She had a sense that things were moving again, unfreezing, stirring from the dust: Ivy would return, Arjun would bring her back, the mistakes of the past would be wiped away . . .

The picture book she'd picked up at last night's market turned out to be charming. It dealt with a young wizard—who dressed very oddly, in what she could only think of as a dress and a kind of sparkly tea towel wrapped around his head—who set out to rescue a princess from the headquarters of a wicked Combine, who had the remarkable power to open quite ordinary doors and manholes and pass through them into far-off parts of the city, or draw through them monsters, genies, storms, flying horses, golems, dancing-girls. The bright pages were brittle with age, and she turned them slowly, carefully, admiring the details, the colors, the vibrant exotic vines that curled around every structure in that long-forgotten city.

It struck Ruth as a good omen. It made her laugh. But she hid it every time the doorbell rang, because it was most certainly forbidden, and if the wrong person saw it . . .

The book made her think of Ivy. *Doors.* Before she left, Ivy had been obsessed with *doors*. With gates, gratings, bridges, and tunnels—with distances and measurements and the spaces between things. They'd had a game when they were girls, and Ivy had taken it too seriously—*doors*. Same as the Dad, before what happened to *him*. Ivy would have laughed at the little picture book, called it a childish fantasy, whereas *her* investigations were scientific, were not about escape, but understanding, and control. Ruth vividly remembered the screaming row the sisters had had, shortly before

Ivy—frantic and depressed as her experiments and explorations one by one failed, her mathematics refused to work out, and she was trapped and unable to break free from the city—was desperate enough and unwise enough to go off with that unpleasant Brace-Bel creature. Ruth remembered—all three of them standing in that same cluttered shop front, picking up and throwing fragile books and records, sneering and crying and snarling, arguing over whether Ivy needed her sisters, whether they were holding her back, or whether Ivy was, as Marta said, a bitch, heartless, worse than their father . . . The room still seemed to echo with it. Ruth refused (it was a sunny day; warmth slanted in through the thick windows) to be upset at the memory. Ivy would be free soon, home again, happy to see her sisters; they could apologize and begin again, together, through dreams, cunning, patience, science, to un-lock the puzzle of the city and pass beyond it into better and brighter times. Up the Mountain, into the clouds, down into the warmth of memories; it didn't matter.

In the evening—as Arjun, miles to the south and east, climbed over Brace-Bel's low fence—Ruth went walking, hands in her pockets, down the street, meaning to check on Thayer and his poor mother, and noticing how the clouds behind the roofs and the chimney-pots were like blood and grey feathers. Like when Marta's cats got hold of a pigeon. She was never sure whether to take clouds as *significant* or not. The Dad had briefly had a period of fascination with clouds, which he theorized were a kind of abstract and roiling map of the city below, color-flattened, like one of his "pho-tographs," and which might, if you studied them in the right way, offer *directions,* expose secret paths not visible in the solid world be-low—but Ivy had said all that was nonsense, evidence of early senil-ity; clouds were only clouds. Ruth had no idea who was right.

She was shocked out of her thoughts by the sound of shouting and running feet. Instinctively she ducked into a doorway and tried to look inconspicuous.

A man came running down the darkening street, darting in and out of the slants of window light, so that his motion seemed stiff, jerky, hectic, helpless. The first thing Ruth noticed about him was his eyes; they had the frightened and lost look that said that he didn't know where he was, that he'd come tumbling down the Mountain with his memory ruined and found himself in some alien city. The second thing she noticed was that he carried a rifle, clutching it in his arms like a baby, and wore a grey-black military-looking uniform, torn as if by sharp wire, and that he seemed vaguely familiar, as if she'd met him before under better circumstances. He was shrieking something incoherent. Behind him people were shouting, "Stop, you idiot!" and, "Just wait a moment!" and, "Keep that fucking noise down, or the Know-Nothings'll be here!"

Ruth stepped out into the street in front of the running man, her arms spread wide to show she wasn't an enemy, trying to say something to calm him; but he simply crashed into her, knocked her aside, and kept running.

As he staggered away he was calling out something about a war, about his lost men, about the airships.

One of *those,* Ruth thought. One of the ones from the War. (What War? Against the Mountain, presumably. When? Why? No one knew, yet. Lost soldiers like him came through every so often, and upset everyone with their ranting.)

The man turned into an alley and his shouting—*this is all ruins, where am I, who are you people*—echoed dully and faded.

Zeigler helped Ruth to her feet. Her hip was bruised where she'd fallen in the gutter. "I'm all right," she told him. "I'm fine."

He offered her a handkerchief; there was dirt on her face. "Poor man," he said. "One of *those.*"

Her hip hurt abominably. "Most of them manage not to break my bloody leg."

"Oh dear, is it really . . . ?"

"I'm only showing off, Mr. Zeigler. I'm fine."

Zeigler cupped a hand to his ear and craned his head, but the soldier was gone from earshot. He shook his head. "Ghosts, I've always said, are like the omnibus; you wait and you wait and two come at once."

Ruth sighed, smiled. "That's true, Mr. Zeigler. That's quite good."

They went looking down the alley for the soldier, but he was gone, vanished into the night as if cleaned away by patient, silent street sweepers.

SIX

A Garden for Paranoids—
"Are You New?"—The Dancers—
The Whip—An Inelegant Combat

Arjun

In the violet light of the evening sky the plants in the garden
seemed both exotic and artificial, lush and yet flat. The effect was
heightened by the presence among the trees and the bushes and the
vines of what were, on closer inspection, only *paintings* of flowers
and vines, on the side of the grottos and nooks and marble chambers with which the garden was generously, extravagantly ap-
pointed. Those paintings were executed so skillfully that in the
uncomfortable and ambiguous light it was easy to take them for
real things, until one ran one's hands over their cold stone surfaces.
And after wandering awhile Arjun realized that all of the strangest
and wildest plants—the swollen, obscene, and organic things, in
lurid shades; the predatory thorns and strangling sinewy tentacles;
the funeral-cloth flowers; the asymmetries and improbabilities—
were in the paintings, not in life. Only so much could be done to
pervert flowers and trees.

There was an obscene hedge maze. Arjun avoided it.

The marble structures had their own varieties and eccentricities.
Grim sepulchers rubbed shoulders with rose-draped lovers' nooks;
or with hissing fountains; with tall carved needles of stone; with
what seemed to be shrines, in which statues of exotically dressed
individuals adopted strange and significant poses; or with . . . but

Arjun steered clear of all Brace-Bel's buildings and statues. They were, he thought, quite likely to be booby-trapped.

Though they came in a mad cacophony of styles, stolen from a hundred Ages of the city, each of them was quite clearly new construction; fresh stone, clean-lined, and unworn. None of them could be more than a few years old.

There was distant music, coming from the mansion that overlooked the house. Once there was a sound that might have been a shriek, or might have been laughter. No birds; no rustle of vermin; a cold and lifeless un-city. Only a faint buzz and click and cold electric whine.

Arjun took a winding route through the garden—the wide graveled path also seemed likely to be rigged, or watched. He trampled the flower beds and shoved through thorny bushes, one eye on the warm light of the mansion's windows, one on the ground at his feet, in which he detected a number of dangers—everything in Brace-Bel's garden was ersatz except the dangers.

Some of them were crude and obvious. The flower beds sprouted iron mantraps. Even in the half-light they were impossible to miss—their function was possibly ornamental. Here and there Brace-Bel had strung razor wire at neck height between trees. No intruder with the sense to not run blindly could have been caught by it; perhaps Brace-Bel only wanted to ensure that his guests took the time to appreciate his garden.

There were wires at ankle height attached to shotguns, or bells. Those took more care to avoid. Arjun found that he had a great capacity for patience and caution.

There were traps that could not reasonably exist—not here, not yet. In the branches, in the shadows of the marble shrines, glittered the hard unblinking eyes of *cameras*; devices for which Thayer and Basso and Miller and the rest would have had no name, which they would not, being local folk, have known to avoid. Arjun ducked and crept and hid from their gaze. He remembered, vaguely, a place in the city where every street corner carried one of those little devices like a hidden knife; he remembered he'd gone there to plead with a bank manager for release of a sealed safe-deposit box containing a certain valuable key, and he remembered quite clearly the manager's insincere smile of refusal and the dull brass of the box, but couldn't remember what the key opened, or why he . . .

One thing at a time. Whatever door it opened you must have passed through, because here you are; it's behind you now. Brace-Bel is the step before you.

On the elegant arch of a little white bridge across an artificial stream Arjun noted two black boxes, one on either side of the walkway, just above ankle height. He knelt close but did not touch them. Their smooth cool material was not quite metal. A wire ran away from them into the grass and up to the house. Between the two boxes was an invisible etheric force—Arjun remembered that without knowing how or why or where he'd seen those devices before—a force that if interrupted would trigger an alarm. Even the empty air in Brace-Bel's garden was watchful for intruders.

And there were traps that could not reasonably exist *anywhere*; fragments of ancient superstitions, dragged up and nailed up on the trees; things that Thayer and Basso and the rest would not have known to take seriously, even if they'd noticed them, having never traveled in parts of the city where such things were not jokes, or quaint curiosities, but real and deadly weapons in the bitter night-time wars of gutter-witches and fortune-tellers and madmen and paranoids. Arjun surprised and dismayed himself with his own knowledge of those nasty little tricks. The horseshoes didn't worry him too much; they were set to catch ghosts and devils, and he was, whatever people said, flesh and blood. Some of the spiderweb constructions of twig and wire and feather and bird-skull hung in the branches were set to catch nightmares, and those didn't concern him. Others were set to release those nightmares on those who brushed past them. Poor mad Thayer, perhaps, had blundered into something like that—or perhaps there was hallucinating gas, or a needle, if one tripped the wrong wire. Some of the devices glowed, like marsh gas; others blinked a steady electric light, red, green, *tiny*, like distant stars. Brace-Bel's garden was a contest of light and shadow; shadow was winning.

Arjun ducked his head and watched his step.

A line of salt; a splash of blood; a knot of hair; a severed hand dangling spiderlike from rusty wires; a withered bird—corpse nailed upside down to a tree trunk; all those were snares or wards of one kind or another. Out of the corner of his eye Arjun saw a word of power chalked on the side of a stand pipe—SODOM—a curse of judgment and fire, a wicked word to utter or invoke in *any* city, let

alone one of Ararat's fragile substance—and he spoke the counter-
word at once, by instinct, and then couldn't remember what it was.

Perhaps it was all hocus-pocus and superstition; perhaps not. Arjun
took no chances. He made it to the house apparently unscathed. If
some curse had been placed on his soul, he thought, it wouldn't be the
first and it would have to fight for its prize. If a camera had caught
sight of him and triggered a silent alarm, he'd find out soon.

The lower floors of the house were dark. From the upper windows there was light and music; a fast waltz.

Arjun climbed a drainpipe round the back, by what appeared to
be the servants' quarters. There was a heap of stinking refuse there,
days or weeks old; Brace-Bel's household was wasteful and ill-kept.
He entered through an open second-story window.

He found himself in a cold room containing two mirrors, two claus-
trophobically small claw-footed bathtubs, and a scatter of clothing
on the damp, moldy floorboards.

The room confirmed his guess: these were servants' quarters. For
one thing, Brace-Bel surely bathed in more style; for another, the
man who'd made that garden would not leave his windows unlocked. So Brace-Bel's servants were unreliable, then. That might be
worth knowing.

Outside was a corridor, uncarpeted, unadorned, lit by a single
candle on a side table. On the white walls was a thin spatter of something that might have been blood.

The corridor ran in two directions, into and away from the heart
of the house. Arjun headed toward the music.

The servants' quarters had their own staircase, an iron spiral leading down into shadow and up into light. As Arjun came close he
heard it clatter under the weight of running feet; by the time he
turned the corner there was no one there.

The corridor at the top of the stairs was empty, too.

The music was louder now, sounding through the door at the
end of the hall. At this distance it was clear that it was not well
played. An amateurish quartet sawed away in and out of pitch.
Someone hit a drum at seemingly random intervals—possibly the

same individual who clashed the cymbals as and when the mood took him.

Arjun pushed open the door and blinked in the light. Something blue in feathers rushed past him, shoes clacking. His eyes landed on a dark and wide-eyed face that he realized was his own, in a mirror. There was a smell of cigarettes and makeup, paint and sweat. A young woman sat on a low stool polishing her boots; she looked up and asked him, "Are you new?"

I said, are you new?"

"Maybe he's mute."

"Or deaf. The boss doesn't have anyone deaf yet."

"You're supposed to call him Master."

"Yeah? You're supposed to be the most beautiful woman in the world. I don't point out *your* shortcomings."

"Fuck you. So, *are* you new?"

"What are you, stupid? He *broke* in. Like old Basso."

The room appeared to be a dressing room; an antechamber, full of mirrors and costumes, to the room beyond in which the music played.

Four women looked Arjun up and down. Two sat on stools. A third leaned against the window, smoking. A fourth stood in front of a mirror, attaching gaudy rings to her ears and nose; "He *broke* in," she repeated.

They were wary but not frightened, Arjun thought. They seemed curious to see what he'd do.

"I told you I heard an explosion earlier."

"Is he an anarchist? He doesn't have a mask."

"Ask him yourself."

On further inspection they were not all women. Two of them were young men dressed and made up as women, and one of the actual women wore a fake red beard, which she pulled aside in order to smoke. All of them, in fact, were in quite improbable costumes. In addition to the ridiculous beard, the smoking woman wore what appeared to be a parody of armor: clanking parts of metal and chain, spiked and dented, that left most of her flesh exposed and anyway were made thinly out of tin and would crumple at the first touch. One of the young men wore a long dress stylized with flames and coruscating golden thread, and his eyes were somehow tinted red. The other wore black furs and his white boots were like bulls' hooves.

The fourth woman, who wore the rings—who was now attaching further baubles to a gold chain that swung between her ears and her lip—appeared to be being devoured by a jewelry-shop locust swarm. Emeralds contested passionately with rubies over the prize of her flesh. Most of her back was bare, though little studs and bars and glittering things pierced her, marking rail-track lines down her spine. She was bruised by purple cane-strokes, by sore burn-marks, by the marks of needles . . .

"Are you Brace-Bel's prisoners?" Arjun asked. "I came here to free Ivy Low, but . . ."

"Hah!" The woman's jewels clanked as she laughed. She moved to the far door; she opened it a crack and the clumsy music tumbled into the room. "*Just* like Basso. Why's it always Ivy? What's that bitch got that I haven't?"

"I found a path through the garden," Arjun said. "Help me find Ivy and we can all escape."

"That's sweet."

The armored woman finished her cigarette and attached her fake beard. Her arm rattled as she opened the door.

Behind it was a ballroom. The floor was a dark polished wood; the walls were invisible in the darkness. There was a suggestion of heavy curtains. The room was huge and only darkly lit, by sparks of electric light and reflected glitter from the jewels and sequins and masks of the dancers who swept and circled that troubling space.

"Our cue," said the armored woman. "The boss'll go crazy if we miss it, mister whoever-you-are. Ladies and gents; after you." And the jeweled woman and the flaming man and the bull filed out into the ballroom and joined the dance. The door closed behind them, leaving Arjun in the dressing room, not quite alone; his reflection, dark and puzzled, watched him from a half-dozen mirrors.

Arjun and his reflections shrugged and opened the door.

A woman in a costume that appeared to be made largely out of leaves drifted toward him, performing elaborate waving gestures with her bare arms. She was counting under her breath and appeared to be having trouble remembering her steps. She looked bored and tired. When she found Arjun blocking her path she stopped dead and swore.

"Shit. Am I out of line or are you? Wait, who *are* you?"

Arjun put a finger to his lips, and stepped around her. A young and surprisingly fat man came past, circling counterclockwise, dressed in something that appeared to be a kind of clock, as if open wounds had exposed his organs and they'd turned out, to his murderer's surprise, to be glittering clockwork. The fat man ignored Arjun, his attention fixed on his feet, and on a structure of gears and wires and brass that was coming unstitched from his shirt, and had to be held in place with his free left hand (the right hand brandished a kind of tuning fork). And behind him, in the center of the room, Arjun saw Ivy.

There was no question about it. She had both Ruth's and Marta's features; Ruth's beauty and strangeness, and Marta's solidity and seriousness. She was taller than either of her sisters. She seemed both younger and older than them. There was something cold about her face, and something haughty; but then, she could hardly not appear haughty, while she was at the center of that elaborate dance, orbited subserviently by some ten or twenty dancers.

She stepped sideways out of the heart of the dance and her place was taken by a young woman in filthy rags.

It was only as an afterthought that Arjun noticed what Ivy was wearing. White feathers clung tightly to her and white wings hung weightlessly from her arms, stark and brilliant against her dark hair and eyes.

Arjun approached her and was about to speak when a door in the room's far wall opened, and a new figure pushed through the room's red curtains.

It was a man, perhaps in his forties, and fat—pendulously so—and sweaty, and acne covered, and naked. His hair was wild, as if recently removed from the constraints of a wig. His pale flesh was bruised, like the jeweled woman's had been. A short and stiff penis bobbed like the bill of a heron. In his hand he held a long three-tailed whip.

The newcomer came running through the room, hooting and

scattering the dancers. His eyes were wide and black and mad; they nearly *revolved*. He snorted. He blundered into the heart of the dance and flailed at the young woman in rags with his whip.

The other dancers withdrew silently into the room's shadowy corners.

The ragged woman shrieked under his blows. She was hardly more than a child. He crowed and struck again.

Arjun caught the man's whip-hand on the backswing, by the fleshy wrist. He yanked it backward, seizing the whip and throwing it aside, sending the man sprawling in his ugly nakedness on the polished floor.

The girl pulled her torn rags closer around herself and sniffed, but stayed in her place.

The naked man drew himself up to his full height, which was not impressive, and fixed Arjun with a glittering mad eye, which somehow was. He seemed entirely unembarrassed at his own nudity. "Did I not give the most express instructions," he barked. "Did I not make plain my one inviolable command in this place where nothing is inviolable save this one, this *one* Goddammit command: do not under any circumstances interrupt me at the moment of . . . Now wait, sir; you are not one of mine, are you?"

"Mr. Brace-Bel, I assume? Keep your distance, please."

Brace-Bel stepped eagerly toward Arjun, and Arjun stepped back, cursing himself as he did so for what it cost him in control of the situation; but Brace-Bel was wildly intoxicated and there was no hope of intimidating him.

"Has our summoning succeeded? What part of the city are you from? What doors did you open? What message have you brought me? What have we unlocked, spirit? Who or what have we finally *finally* angered? Speak, ghost!"

"I'm here for Ivy Low, Mr. Brace-Bel."

"What?"

"Will you release her?"

"Certainly not! She's *mine*."

"What on earth are you doing here, Mr. Brace-Bel?"

"Oh shut up." Brace-Bel sagged. His wheeling eyes went dim and tired. "You're only another thief. Or worse, some Know-Nothing or policeman or busybody. Gods damn you as they surely have me. No matter how far I go there are always busybodies. Why won't you leave me alone?"

"Is this some kind of ritual? It seems familiar, somehow."

"Mind your business. Mr. Basso, please!"

Arjun had not fully noticed, among the dancers—but not dancing, only watching and waiting—a large man in a grey wool suit and flat cap, who now appeared holding a silvered and crystal-handled stick.

Arjun picked up the whip again, and held it ready.

"No, Mr. Basso," Brace-Bel said. "I'll thrash this dog myself. If you please!"

Basso threw the stick to Brace-Bel, who caught it neatly. There was a new intensity in his eyes as he advanced on Arjun. He held the stick by its foot, thrusting the shining crystal forward; then, laughing, "This is only a man! I'll need no trickery tonight!" he reversed his grip and lunged with the silver-shod foot of his weapon.

Arjun knocked the stick aside with the whip's long handle, and stepped back. Brace-Bel lunged again.

Some of the dancers, released from their duties, lit cigarettes as they watched this new show.

Brace-Bel advanced on surprisingly nimble legs, full of febrile energy. He lunged the cane's silver foot at Arjun's face; he swung it sideways at Arjun's legs. Arjun parried and fell back.

It was an inelegant and unpredictable combat. Brace-Bel was clearly well trained with his weapon, and for all his fat he was quick and surefooted; but whatever drugs he'd ingested before the ritual were taking their toll on him. He executed skilled maneuvers at a point somewhere well to Arjun's left. He giggled and nearly tripped. After a flurry of deadly lunges and feints he sighed, stepped back, and began trying to wipe his cane clean with his sweaty hands, having apparently forgotten Arjun's presence, until a blow to the head with the whip's handle reminded him that the job was still unfinished, and he charged again. Another effect of the drug was an indifference to pain; or perhaps, to judge from the bruises and welts on his naked body, he'd long since made a friend of pain.

And Arjun found his own capabilities . . . erratic. It seemed that at some point in the past, in his forgotten wanderings, he'd learned how to fence—and the whip's long handle was a passable weapon—

but the memories were inaccessible to his thinking mind. So some-times, by *instinct,* he'd parry and deftly riposte, striking Brace-Bel's soft belly and winding him, or rattling the teeth in his globular head, and at those moments it seemed Arjun was rather the better fighter; but the next second he had no idea what he was doing, and could only retreat clumsily. Not knowing his own abilities, he couldn't plan; he could only defend from moment to moment. He feinted without thinking; then, having thought, he couldn't re-member how to follow the motion through and left himself open. Brace-Bel, scratching his balls thoughtfully, said, "Aha!" and lunged only a moment too late. Later Arjun dropped his weapon, and was only saved by the fact that Brace-Bel's attention was focused on the glitter of reflected electric light in the crystal on the end of his cane . . .

Basso stepped in and punched Arjun smartly in the nose. Sparks exploded in his brain and his nose started to bleed. The dancers sighed or shouted or clapped. Arjun fell back. Basso withdrew dis-creetly and let Brace-Bel take his place; the naked fat man pressed himself up against Arjun, holding him against the wall with the cane at his throat. Arjun looked around, trapped, panicked, and his eyes met Ivy's, where she sat on the edge of the bandstand recently vacated by Brace-Bel's musicians. Her look of cold unsympathetic curiosity—*out of that face so much like Ruth's*—chilled him. The fight went out of him.

Brace-Bel pressed his face up against Arjun's and glared into his eyes. His breath was rank and greasy.

"Tell your masters, Know-Nothing, I won't be trifled with! By the Gods I'll send you back to them in such a state! Pain is the great teacher, Know-Nothing, and I'll *teach.* By the Gods! . . . wait a mo-ment; don't I know you?"

Arjun wheezed: "Not . . . not a Know- . . . Noth . . ."

Brace-Bel relaxed the cane. "I *do* know you!"

"You are . . . ah . . . very familiar, Mr. Brace-Bel. But . . . I have had . . . *trouble* with my memory."

"Aren't you that little dark fellow who worked for old Holbach?"

"That sounds familiar."

"One of Olympia's?"

"One of Olympia's what?"

"One of what do you *think*?"

"Please, sir, your cane."

"Are you or aren't you?"

"You would know better than me, Mr. Brace-Bel. I remember nothing. If you know me, if you know anything of my past, I beg you to . . ."

"Ah! Now I see. You went up on the *Mountain*."

"So I understand."

"More fool you. You people and your *explorations*. Was your expedition a success? Did you chart it?"

"I don't think so. Please, Mr. Brace-Bel, if you would take one step back . . ."

"Your exploration was always outward, you see, and physical; mine was inward and more subtle."

"Mr. Brace-Bel, if you can tell me anything . . ."

"See?" Brace-Bel—*finally!*—stepped away from Arjun, and gestured with his cane at the dancers, who mostly stood in a row against the far wall. There were about fifteen, twenty of them, each more ridiculously dressed than the last—men and women, thin and fat, young and old. Seeing themselves observed by their master they straightened up and hid their cigarettes behind their backs and pulled their masks back on, if they had them. "See?" Brace-Bel repeated, as if the point was too obvious to be worth explaining.

SEVEN

Brace-Bel Explains Himself—
Under the Rose—A Man Out of Time—
A Little Song about the Dawn

Brace-Bel

My name is Brace-Bel, and a byword for evil. Here, now, in
these last days, my reputation is still young; a poisoned seed
yet to grow. My time, like yours, was many centuries ago, and far
away, and I am forgotten. Like you I am a man out of time. Once I
was before my times; now I am behind them. But if all time in the
city is one time—as I believe that it is—and down some strange
turn of hidden streets we may wander into years thought lost to us
and find the long-dead still living and breathing and fucking into
existence generations paradoxically unborn in one place and gone
to dust in another—well *then* there still exist places where mothers
warn their children to behave or Brace-Bel will take them; where
preachers bellow against Brace-Bellism; where gutter-witches invoke those potent syllables *Brace* and *Bell* against their enemies, to
make maidens sterile and young men mad. A byword for evil. And
why? Brace-Bel; it's a pretty sound. My father was a nobleman and
noted merchant of wines, and well thought of in the councils of
princes. My mother—well, in truth she was a serpent, a foulness, a
barren womb; had my father's seed been planted in more hospitable
soil it might have grown straight and true, and not into the ugly fat
creature you see before you. For science teaches us that it is the father's seed from which the child grows, and the mother provides

only a temporary housing, which may fall short of adequacy, but can not exceed it, so the mother may contribute to the child's defects, but not to its excellencies; and this is why all men of learning and sensitivity revile their mothers. A serpent! Yet she was publicly reckoned a great woman of the city, and notable for her work with orphans and charity and sponsorship of the arts and other things that make me sick to think of. No, the black stain on the Brace-Bel name is my work alone, mine alone, and . . .

. . . yes, yes. I'll be getting to you—Arjun? Odd name. Where was I? I am suddenly very tired. I make use of certain drugs in preparation for the ritual. They give me vigor but confuse my thoughts. Where shall I begin?

I was only an indifferent student of divinity. I'll not bore you with the details of the scandal which resulted in my first expulsion, my first return in disgrace to my father's house, and in the *hanging* of my tutor and partner in depravity, who was of less noble family . . . Now, were it sane to punish crimes of love or passion, then punishment would fall in some scientific and regular fashion, and there is no question that I was more deeply at fault than him; that arbitrary scattering of punishments taught me all I ever needed to know of the law.

It is well known that a man will spend his seed in the moment of hanging. I watched him struggle and jerk on the rope. A public hanging, in Tiber's Square. Afterward they cast the body into the Gods' imperious fire. What dry and dark pleasure did it give the priests and the judge to procure that joyless spending? I realized that I had been outdone in depravity. It was not Law. There *is* no Law. Much sinned against, I am. I promised I would meet the city's challenge; I would exceed it in depravity.

When I returned home my father struck me, and I struck him back, and soon I was on my own in the city and . . .

No, sir! Damn you, sir, no! I will not clothe myself! My nakedness offends you? Here I bare my soul to you, and you balk at a little flesh?

Mr. Basso, take my arm please. I need to sit.

Dancers, away!

Where is Ivy? Basso, bring Ivy to me. Well, *find* her then. Am I not the master here?

Come, sit closer, Arjun. My voice is tired.

* * *

I had a little flat in Foyle's Ward. There I was attended by guests, so long as my father's money lasted. I was never physically well favored, even when younger, and that money was much of my charm. Those were happy days, though I had not yet found my purpose. The quality of whores has declined precipitously in this city.

Godsdamn it, where is Ivy? She calms me when I am sick. The drug tires me and the ritual tires me. Nightly I bang my head against the walls of reality like a moth against a flame; is it any wonder I am tired?

. . . *happy* days. I made the mistake of embarking on an affair of sorts with a young relative of the Countess Ilona. A little too vigorous a hand with the whip left marks on him that were *unpresentable* in company. And that time *he* received only a dressing down, while I, the less noble man, spent a season in the Iron Rose . . .

Yes, Arjun, it's a prison! Gods, do you remember *nothing*? What monstrous defenses the Mountain must have. It puts my garden to shame. I was wise to flee from it.

The Iron Rose was a prison, then: far to the south, and far lost in time; five great ancient towers broken and slumping, bound together with iron. A maze. A thousand cells, a thousand thousand; the Rose's million bloody petals exceeded all record keeping. Traitors and poisoners and witches and blasphemers and seditionists—criminals by the reckonings of one or other of the city's thousand lords and laws—laws so various and perverse and contradictory that there was never a man in all of Ararat who was not a criminal by *someone's* reckoning some*where,* and so it was pure chance who did or not end up in the Rose.

In these last days the whole *city* is a prison. I have never cared for democracy or leveling.

During my incarceration I wrote, and my letters were smuggled out. Wonderful slashing letters to my old clucking tutors in the School of Divinity, expounding upon my theories. So blasphemous were those letters that those old men might have been struck blind reading them. What more could they do to me? I was already in the Rose.

And through those letters I came to the attention of Nicolas Maine and his Atlas-makers.

No? Nothing, Arjun? No memory? Not a glimmer? Yes, I

think I see a glimmer in those pretty dark eyes of yours . . . I most certainly *did* see you among them, in the last days. No? Still nothing?

Maine, then, brought together all the most brilliant minds of the city, among whom I was most certainly to be counted, even in those days when the city was full of wit and brilliance—now, in this stagnant backwater of time, I am entirely without peer—and he set them to the work of mapping the city; of recording not only every last street but every last fact about those streets and the men and Gods who walked them; every last idea in the city; the last great work of knowledge. A blasphemous business, said the priests and censors, because it was not for men to reduce to understanding the perfect complexity of the city—and so my blasphemous path traveled alongside Maine's, for a time. I contributed the Atlas-entries on the *Prison-State,* and the *Orgasm,* and the twin Gods of the Iron Rose, and on *Menstruation,* and on *Suicide,* and on *Prostitution,* and on a great many other topics. I essayed a number of contributions on the *Womb* and on *The Maternal Impulse,* which were repeatedly rejected, I'm sorry to say.

You? You came in the last days, long after Maine was exiled, in the days when he'd briefly come back, only to die . . . You had inquiries of a theological nature. You wanted to find a God or possibly get rid of one. I think you were one of Olympia Autun's lovers. Awful arrogant woman. Because she played a few flummery lawyer's tricks in court to spring me from prison once or twice she considered it her place to lecture me on my proclivities. She took exception to my fondness for the whip. Once she struck me! And you were one of Holbach's creatures. You were a translator for him, weren't you?

Well?

Akomof fen lindur olmik, agalom dolmik!

Hah! Don't look so offended. My Tuvar is weak and I only remember their curses. Well, then, you were his translator; there's no doubt in my mind.

You were there for the end.

Hold me up! Hold me! I do not remember the stairs being so treacherous. Look how they slip and slide beneath my feet.

Carry me swiftly to my toilet or I cannot be accountable for what will happen to your shoes, sir.

Oh, Basso, who is this oaf who handles me so roughly?

Oh yes. Yes. I remember.

Ahhh.

Don't be shy. You may sit on the bathtub, there.

The end? The end of what? Oh yes. How tiresome. Let me tell you of my theories, instead, my marvelous theories.

By fucking we are brought into this world and by fucking we shall pass beyond it.

That's the essence of it. All else is footnotes.

Help me downstairs, will you?

See? My dancers, my girls and boys and men and women, my creatures. In old Ararat I had my pick of the finest dancers and beauties of the city's most splendid brothels; I had my pick of the wildest freaks of its circuses and sideshows. All those brilliant impoverished artists, eager for my patronage! Here I make do with more ordinary persons. There are no dancers, no freaks, and no artists left in the last days. Yes, yes, wave to them as we pass.

Ivy alone is not ordinary. You shall not take her from me.

Each one incarnates symbolically a God of the ancient city. I have only seventeen dancers here, because money is not inexhaustible; but the Gods were infinite in number, as many as the moods of the city, its cobbles and leaves and windows and iron bars. Thus we have frequent changes of costume, and some must do multiplicitous service.

See this one? I dress her in armor; she stands for the God Addartta, bloody in battle, resplendent in victory; God of the triumphal march and the conqueror's golden statues and the bringing back of spoils in chariots down cheering stamping streets. But she is also Querl, the mailed fist of the lawman. And she is also Vulmea, God of freebooters and bandits and drunks. The whore beneath those clothes has a gifted tongue but she also has the clap; be warned.

This one in the jewels is Orillia, spirit of the lights, spirit of the illuminations, of torchlight and gaslight and bright glass and open fires blazing over the dark hills of the city, the bright flash of its arcades—in these grey days it is hard to imagine the city was bright, once, but it was. She also does service as Keba, the whore. And so on and so on. This one here who rings with chimes is all the spirits of music the city had, which were *many*. This one in rags is the Beggar, and also the Typhon, murderous stinking river-spirit, greedy for sacrifices. This young man in his mirror-masks is Lavilokan, God, of course, of the mirrors. This is the Spider. Ivy, wherever she's gone, stands for the Bird, most beautiful white-winged bird of *freedom,* on which I meditated long and hard during my time in the Iron Rose. Ivy is my favorite and you shall not have her. This young lady here is . . .

Are you listening?

It began as a perversion. It began as a sick thought, of an imprisoned libertine and lecher, thinking, how might I most terribly outrage against decency? Arrest me, will they, for debauchery? They'll see what debauchery means!

I dressed up whores as the Gods and I fucked them.

You do not appear shocked. Have you forgotten the Gods, too? What a funny blank little man you are.

It rather discomforts me, not to be shocking. Are you not perhaps a *little* . . . ?

Yes, well, it quickly became clear that this delightful practice was more than a mere perversion—I should not say that, for it has always been my case that a pure and beautiful perversion's a finer thing than any dull utilitarian *purpose*. But anyway. In this forbidden union with the divine—in this ecstatic union—I found myself becoming closer and closer to the divinities of the city. Elevated, in the moment of ecstasy, to what lay above the ordinary matter of the city; descending, in submission and degradation, to what lay below it. Piercing the curtain of the real with a thrust. A thrust!

Pardon me.

A dance of submission to the divine, and dominance over it. More—of *unity* with the divine. As your dull old Professor Holbach sought to understand the Gods of the city with his mind and his mathematics and his grey brain—so I mastered them with my prick.

I confess that the ritual has grown baroque, has grown elaborate, over the years; once it was me and a whore and a bird-mask and perhaps a whip or candle; now the cast's swollen and the props become . . . operatic.

I once wrote a piece for the opera, in fact.

What do you *think* happened? They banned my opera and burned the sheet music and put me back in the Iron Rose.

I am suddenly very tired. Have I mentioned the drug? It takes its toll. Let us retire. You look quite exhausted, too. Mr. Basso! Show our guest to a room. No, I insist. My Creatures! I sleep alone tonight for the drug leaves me flaccid—but any pretty thing that wishes to curry favor may attend me in the morning. I include you, Mr. Whatever-your-name-is-*Arjun*-is-it, in my offer. No? Shame.

Go, sleep. Do not let me catch you talking to Ivy. Remember there are always a thousand watchful eyes in Brace-Bel's house. I have been too long in prison and I have become a kind of warden myself.

Are you awake?

Yes?

Splendid!

I cannot sleep. Is the bed acceptable?

No, no, don't worry; you need fear no assault from me. I take no one against their will. An unfree choice is useless for my purposes. Mine is a liberatory philosophy, a liberatory art, a science of escape!

Shush, shush. If you would be more comfortable I will sit on the chair, and leave the bed to you.

It is the small hours of the night. I keep no clocks in the house because my devices interfere with their workings, but you can tell time by that horrid yellow moon. The moon in these last days is like the stub of a cigarette, the skull of a rat, the pus in a blinded eye.

Now my story becomes strange; better told at night. I will tell you how I came to this place and this time.

So, then—in and out of gaol. I grew pale. In Mensonge's custody I grew fat, like a eunuch, for what other pleasures but gluttony did I have? I scribbled by candlelight and discussed my ideas with rats. Though the Rose was my most frequent residence, I saw a great many other gaols. I recall when Mass How held me in the clay cells beneath their Parliament. They sent pious back-benchers to slobber for precious drops of repentance, which I denied them. I observed that ours was a city of a thousand Gods, and great antiquity: there were places where my practices were sanctified, and those of my interrogators were thought foul and unnatural. I told them of the followers of the Wasting Queen, who dwelled in the east in their narrow towers, and considered increase of persons to be blasphemy, a theft of souls from the storehouses of the Gods, and a practice that crowded the city and invited disease; those excellent people favored only barren pleasures; why should not I? So the Parliament concluded that I was in league with foreign powers; this did not hasten my release, or gentle my confinement. You saw the stripes on my back, did you not? Over the years some were administered with love, but others, so many, were administered in spite, or fear, or the wicked self-denied lusts of torturers and priests, and . . .

In and out of gaol. Your lover Olympia did much work on my behalf, begrudgingly but . . .

Do you remember her? You do? You do not? What a cold man you are!

It must have been shortly after your arrival that I was confined again in the Iron Rose. Its vast and dark twisting capillaries were like home to me by then. Arrested for blasphemy under Seal of the Duke of Baltic Street, no thanks to Olympia, no thanks to her—she was, perhaps, too busy with you, and neglecting her duties. Eh? Eh?

They deprived me of human contact.

They had a most ingenious method of driving me mad. They allowed me writing implements, and paper, and so every day—I had no window, but one knew when it was day and when it was night; one sensed it; a fresh sadness sank over the prison every morning, and fresh horror broke every night—every day I wrote. Letters; a novel; a treatise.

Every evening they took my work away. When they returned it in the morning it was subtly changed. My ideas were subtly disordered. Affirmations were made negations; sharp contradictions twisted into spineless agreement; paradoxes unknotted. Characters who had taken part in my fictional debaucheries with openhearted glee now only *pretended* pleasure; one could tell that underneath they suffered. Can you imagine any torment more terrible?

How was it possible? How did my gaolers find the time? I wrote all day, every day, from the first moment the torches were lit to the moment they were snuffed. How was there time in the day's remainder for even the most skillful forger to produce such subtle parodies? There was not. I concluded that there must be a doppelganger in the cell next to mine, writing as I wrote, hour for hour, a constant evil mirror of my own scribbling hand—a creature that was almost but not quite my double. Perhaps, I thought, they gave him *my* work every morning, and he underwent the same torments as I; never knowing which were his thoughts and which were mine, which mine and which his. At last they silenced me. Me! At last I was unable to write, not trusting my own thoughts. My thoughts were taken from me. They were all I ever had. It was never truly about the flesh, never truly, no one understood that . . .

I sat in silence for I know not how long. I became less than a worm, turning under the earth; a fat pale grub.

One day there was a terrible sound of riot and alarm. No, first there was the distant smell of fire and smoke. The clatter of knives. Distant screams. There were often screams in the Rose, but they were the screams of prisoners, they had a tone of resignation to them, they spoke their lines of agony like practiced players; now I heard the screams of *gaolers,* full of outrage and surprise and offense. There had been an escape, somewhere in the endless corridors above me. The screams of my gaolers were the sweetest sound I had ever heard. In the inviolate privacy of my cell I began to masturbate.

I expected the noise to quieten, to last no longer than my own pleasure in it, to be put down. Instead it grew, and grew. They came closer—those children.

They came down the corridors of my cell like a fresh wild wind. They were laughing and shouting. A flash of bright silk . . . Then they were gone. They moved faster than any natural human person; I believe they were touched by some God. In those days the city was full of talk of those children, the Thunderers, and Silk their leader, and their gaol-breaking enterprises; but for all my long experience in gaols that was the only time I saw them. For all my long study of the Gods and for all my many rituals I never broke the barrier between man and God, but those ragged children had been touched by some miraculous effortless grace.

They were gone before I could call out. They were not there for me.

My cell door hung open.

I quickly found that all the doors on my floor were open; Silk and his cohorts must have tripped a switch somewhere, or broken a chain. All the prisoners of the Duke of Baltic Street milled around in their nightshirts or nakedness, in the unguarded hallways. My doppelganger was not among them. I attempted to assert order, to offer leadership or at least advice, but some thuggish criminal— some vulgar burglar or murderer—recognized me as the blasphemer Brace-Bel, and it seemed that the first order of business for these newly free men would be to punish the deviant in their midst, and so, cursing mankind, I fled.

I fled down dark corridors, in the wake of the miraculous Silk. Everywhere was in disarray. I passed free men struggling toward the light, carrying the lame and the sick on their backs; and I passed creatures that could think of no better use for their freedom than to rob and plunder each other in the darkness.

I should have fled upward to freedom but my curiosity drove me down, and down, in Silk's path. Soon I was lost.

How much do you remember of the workings of this city, Arjun?

I see. To have forgotten so much! It must be agony.

Suffice it to say that the Rose is an unusual place—a place of unusual density—of suffering, of history, of hope and fear and *power*—and in this city, certain things follow from that. Just as the moon may perturb the tides, so the weight of the Rose and places like it perturbs the city's cartography, distorts its time and its space.

In these last days, when there are no Gods, people have forgotten that the city is a living thing.

Pressing further into the Rose I found myself lost in alien places. There were signs on the walls in alien languages, and I am a learned man and yet there were soon languages and letters I did not recognize, some of which frankly made me uneasy. I lost myself among people who spoke strange languages; people who had strange eyes; people who seemed unaware that they were in prison at all, who made pale and ragged societies for themselves in the hallways, with their savage kings marked out by the keys hung around their necks; people who had strange anatomies, as if someone yet more daringly perverse than I ever was had fathered by-blows on cats, or dogs, or birds, or snakes, or animals I could not name, or even flowers; people who were scarcely people. I developed a familiarity with *electric light*; at first it made me wonder if I had a fever. There were places where the corridors contracted, smaller and smaller, to house prisoners scarcely larger than dolls. There were places where the ceiling was so high it was lost in darkness, and vast imprisoned men shambled in the torchlight—and I thought *I* had grown fat on prison food and no exercise! This took many days, yes? Many weeks. Some days I drank water from cracks in the ceiling, and fed on moss and mushrooms; some days I starved. I traveled many miles beyond the walls of the Iron Rose as it stood in my city, our city.

I wish I could see your eyes. Do you remember the Rose? Damn this feeble moon! In the old days the moon was bone-white and cast a wild light. Poets worshipped it. The moon in these years is only fit for pity.

Sometimes, during my, my *rituals,* in the moment of ecstasy, I saw what I saw when I lost myself under the Rose. I saw the world falling away. I saw the *real* breaking like a mirror. I could never hold on to it; a few brief shimmering gasps and there I was, back in the world again.

Let's go for a walk in the garden. The traps will not touch us. I am master here. I need to be in the open air.

Only you can understand me. We are lonely ghosts, out of our time. It is a great pleasure to talk. The flesh is a fine thing but words are my greatest pleasure.

Lost under the Rose, I wondered if I had gone mad. I had often been *called* mad. Once the priests of Tiber tried to exorcise mad spirits from me, a process that involved fire, for Tiber—do you recall it? — was a God of avenging fire. These burns, here and here, remember it for me. The pain did not make me *less* mad. The electrical therapy was the latest thing, in those days; one of our colleagues on the Atlas, Dr. Hermann, invented it. May he be damned for it.

Never mind. I was *not* mad.

You're curious about my devices, my traps? That one, in the branch above your head, places a sickness in the lungs. Hold your torch a little closer: you'll see the coal in its heart. Go on, it will not harm you while I am here.

What? Shay gave it to me.

You start as if you know the name. I am not surprised.

Shay, then. Bear with me a little longer.

I was thoroughly lost, and despairing. I'd seen enough of miracles. I desired nothing more than to return to my little flat in Foyle. To dally with my favorite girls and boys. To dispute philosophical abstractions with my friends of the Atlas, about whom I had grown sentimental. Even to return to my comfortable little cell, and my writing paper, and the company of my doppelganger. Perhaps he, I thought, my doppelganger, had been released in my place—Olympia would surely have procured my release by then, I thought, at Sessions or Assizes or Common Pleas or Oyer and Terminer; the rattling rusty wheels of Law would have turned. And my doppelganger would have gone out into the city in my skin, to enjoy the simple pleasures of my life, while I had taken his place among the unreal creatures of the uncanny prison that spawned him.

Yet where was the way back? Where was the way forward? I pressed on, hopelessly lost.

I was fleeing when Shay found me. There was a place where white-coated men and women moved slowly, silently, *dutifully* through the corridors, making notes, communicating in curt nods that all was to their satisfaction. Slope-browed and red-eyed! So long as you passed among them slowly, head down, in silence, and gave no cause for alarm, they seemed not to notice you as an intruder. If your nerve or your patience broke and you stepped too quickly, they turned on you in sudden savagery; beneath their white coats they carried sharp instruments of surgery. Do not disturb the silence of those doctors!

I was not patient, or quiet. I have always lacked self-government.

They pursued me silently through white-walled halls. I have never been a strong man. I wheezed and sweated. I was close to despair, close to lying down and letting them work their corrections upon my flesh, which I could hardly deny was imperfect—when Shay appeared before me.

He was short, and thin, and strutted. That laughing young man—his hair long, and white, and bound in a vain tail, thick and greasy. Sheep's wool snagged on a wire fence. His thin smile—his dreadful pride.

He came stalking past me, past where I knelt gasping. At first I took him for one of my pursuers, and I thought they had flanked me, and I hung my head and submitted to the stab of his instruments; but his long coat was black, not white, and bulged with his various devices.

I closed my eyes, and I heard him converse with my pursuers. The sound was like insects' wings; like mathematics; like the scrape of knives on bone.

I did not hear them go. But one moment the corridor echoed and buzzed with their conversation, and the next all was silent. I lifted my head to see that strange young man close and button his coat; in its lining I saw the sharp glitter of certain *instruments*.

"A fellow explorer," he said, and helped me to my feet. He was short, a little plump—older than at first I had thought, but vigorous. The strong sure hands of a burglar or grave robber. "The Doctors of Marfelon are dangerous but they don't mind doing business. Fresh knives! I once learned some very useful techniques from them. I bought you, too, but don't feel obligated to me."

I disliked his sneer; I mistrusted him.

A golden-black monkey ran around his feet. A singed and scarred little thing. Extraordinary claws clattered on the tiled floor. It had uncommonly intelligent red eyes and it seemed to *whisper*. He picked it up as he had me, as if it were weightless, as if it were a toy; and all together we went down the hall.

See? This, here, in the grass, is another of his toys; a little piece of devilish circuitry. Hah—*that's* a word I was not born to know! If you step on it it will burn off your foot. You, too, are a very determined explorer to have come through my garden unharmed.

We walked together, just as you and I are walking.

Shay was a vigorous man; a man of animal spirits. The monkey curled round his shoulder and burdened him not at all. I scurried to keep pace with him.

He led me on a path through doors I'd hardly noticed, each of which opened to his touch, up ladders and down stairs and through tunnels in between walls, and he led me out into the fresh night air.

No delight in this life has ever compared to those first breaths of cold air.

"That," Shay told me, "is the last free thing I will do for you."

He pointed out over the city. From where we stood—atop the Rose's topmost tower—I could see the Mountain, in the far north, squatting over the horizon like a beast over its felled prey. That was where he pointed.

"Come work for me," he said. "I've been watching you," he said. "I like your style, but you're going nowhere the way you're going."

A barbaric and insolent manner of speech!

"You're nowhere near strong enough," he said, "for what's under the Rose. Not alone."

He gave me to understand that he would show me the secret ways under and behind the city, if I would be his servant, his admiring servant. "It's a lonely business I'm in," he said. "There's a lot of lonely years ahead of me. I like the way you keep house, Brace-Bel. Come work for me."

He wanted me, in other words, for his majordomo, his butler; his pander; as they say here, his *pimp*. He maintained a number of properties, here and there, about the city, and they were in disrepair; and perhaps he was lonely. I would serve him, and in return he would show me how to master those properties of the city that had so nearly devoured me. He would show me the Mountain. Of course, he said nothing in so many words. He made *implications,* and smiled his teasing smile. I told him to go to Hell! Brace-Bel is no man's servant, except in play. I would find my way to the other side by my own methods or not at all. It would be *my* triumph; I would not haggle for it. I said other proud foolish things.

He simply shrugged. "If you change your mind," he said, "you know my name." He lit a cigarette, and he stepped behind a chimney.

I followed, of course. The smoke lingered; he had vanished.

Don't ask how I got down from the tower. Don't ask. I had no fear of heights before that night; now I shudder to climb the stairs.

I returned to my home. At the time I lived in Faugere; you could see the lights of the Arcades from my library windows, a constant temptation away from reading and toward drink and laughter, just as I liked it. I kept few servants. Respectable servants would not work for the notorious Brace-Bel. My butler was a man I met in gaol, who once strangled his wife. Enormous *hands*; like a brace of squid. He welcomed me home; my servants were used to my long absences and sudden returns. I slept in silk sheets. I sent Hands to market to buy coffee and tobacco.

In the morning I went to visit my colleagues of the Atlas. I'd seen wondrous things; I wished to discuss them. I feared, I think, that I might forget what I'd seen if I did not share it. It might vanish like a dream. *Holbach,* I thought: if a thing's shared with him it *cannot* be imaginary; it must be very much a part of the workaday world. He will publish the wonder in the learned journals and pin it like a butterfly to the stuff of the real. Good old dull Holbach. But I found his house deserted.

I made inquiries.

Does none of this refresh your recollection?

Holbach had been arrested, I learned, and held in the Iron Rose. There were rumors that he had escaped and fled north. The rest of our colleagues had been arrested, also, on the orders of the Countess Ilona, or forced into hiding. Liancourt the playwright they had *beheaded.* That silly musical play had got him into trouble. The Atlas was constantly in trouble, of course, with censors or priests or angry mobs, because this city has always feared free thought; still, this had the air of finality. Maine had returned from exile and was dead, perhaps poisoned. There were riots. There were rumors that the whole ugly business was the scheme of some rival of the Countess—Red Barrow, perhaps, or the Parliament, or Mensonge, or Cimenti. I don't know. I hoped you might . . . ? No?

That was far from the worst of it.

I questioned further. In those days in the city there were subtle webs of confidence and trust between the highest and the lowest people. Holbach prostituted his science to the Countess, and was—before she turned on him, that dangerous woman—in her highest councils. I corresponded with Holbach on matters theological. My investigations and my pleasures required the services of panders and whores, and I was often seen in vile places. In the company of whores there were men and women who served the Countess as spies and agents—the wheel spun, the heart pumped, and the blood circulated. Now the city is like a dead thing, stiff and silent and cold.

I questioned further, in vile places. It seemed my own escape from the Rose had not been noticed, for there had been a general riot at the Rose and indeed over all of the Countess's districts, and elsewhere. But my association with the Atlas was well known, and I feared the Countess's men might be looking for me. I adopted an assumed name, like a spy in my own city. And I skulked, and I *listened*.

Rumors swirled around the Atlas like carrion-crows. Those men and women of the Atlas who'd not been beheaded, it seemed, were all dead. Maine first, then others. In the city in those weeks there was a plague, plague wrestled with riot to see who should prey on the city's poor flesh. A choking foul blackness of the lungs. It rose from the rivers and from dark places. Rumor had it that the plague had begun with Maine's death, and that it pursued all those who'd had dealings with him, or the Atlas. I snorted. I was skeptical. *I will not pay for these fancies,* I said, and sometimes there was an *altercation,* and then there was one more drinking-establishment in the city where Brace-Bel was not welcome! *Fancies*—for it was *always* the case, when there was sickness, that some preacher or other would blame the makers of plays or the writers of forbidden books, and the mob was always eager to believe them.

Yet on further investigation it appeared that the mob was quite correct.

I counted the dead. Lauterbach, dry dull economist; Vannon, the etymologist; Marlowe, one of our pet radicals, theorist of revolution; Aumont, the architect; Helvensi, armchair general, who wrote on horsemanship and siege-engines and the sniper-rifle; credulous Bayley, who offered us his theories on the werewolf; Lycian, Dumont, Gilfoyle, hardened explorers, carriers of theodolites, astrolabe, and pistol; too many, too many others, all dead of the plague. It was a bad plague but it did not strike the common folk near so bad as it struck those of us of wit and learning.

There was something haunting the streets in those days. A blackness in the fog. A stink in the gutters. Rumor had it that some God had gone mad. *Beware the water,* people said. *Do not go out of doors. The River-God is hungry.*

In my house, now, the River-God is played by a young man named Marley. It frightens me terribly to touch him, but I steel myself to it. The drugs help.

I *felt* it. I felt it pursuing me.

A shiver passes across your face, Arjun. I wonder if you are aware how eloquently your face speaks. Your voice is silent, but your body remembers, and shudders.

You *remember* this.

Once, as I left a whorehouse on Baruch Street, I felt something brush against my face. The next morning I had to ply rotten teeth from that side of my jaw.

When I returned to Baruch Street, the whorehouse had been torched. The plague, they said, had come in the night.

I did not dare attempt to charter passage from Ararat by boat; the docks were always watched by spies, and besides the plague was worst by the water. Instead I fled west. The shadow followed at my heels. I felt it in my dreams. When I woke my sweat stank. Why did it want me? I do not know. Perhaps my daring explorations in blasphemy and perversity had finally angered something more . . . *ultimate* than the censors and priests who had formerly been my tormentors. Terror mingled sweatily with pride. I had been marked for persecution by the Gods themselves!

For a while I hid in the highest bolt-hole I could find—on the roof of a condemned hotel, among pigeon-roosts. One day I returned from scavenging for scraps to find all the pigeons dead.

No place in the city was safe.

What, then, if I went *beyond* the city?

If you change your mind, Shay had said, *you know my name.*

I called out to him—feeling foolish—as if he were a pantomime devil. He did not appear.

I paid for an advertisement to be placed in the paper. I checked the post-office box but he never responded.

I painted his name on the wall of my hiding place. I spelled it out in candles on my roof. Nothing.

I went into the alley with hammer and chisel and carved it on the wall. S—H—A—Y. Acting on some unclear instinct I appended my name, and the date.

That night Shay came to me.

He wore a grey coat. His head was shaved, a knob of ash-white stubble. Was he older, or younger? He was thinner. I could hardly doubt that he was the same man—not with those cold eyes.

"I was out for a walk," he said. "A hundred years tomorrow, when what did I see? Under all that ivy. All that graffiti. My own name, and yours. I keep a close eye on my name. Changed your mind, eh?"

He saw my desperation; my terror amused him.

I remember this because it was strange. "The old fool's gone and let one of his creatures loose," he said. "This part of the city's done for. They should put yellow tape round it and call it condemned."

"So come with me," he said. "But I would have given you cushy duty last time. Now you won't get off that easy. I want you with me when I go for the Mountain. You can carry my bags."

I threw myself on the floor. I kissed his feet. I did not balk when he blindfolded me.

Have you noticed how beautiful my house is at night? How lovely my garden?

Shay did not give me those. I earned them with my own wits and charm, and with the devices Shay left behind. I have for instance a die that comes up one, or six, or what-have-you, just as I will it; hold the dots in your mind's eye and the little thing eagerly jumps to your bidding. A profitable trick. There are others greater than that.

I will always be rich. If I were poor I would kill myself. The city's mirrors are clouded; its scribes are drunk; in our various translations across time and place the fine details of our selves may undergo change and transformation. Nevertheless our essence persists. It is of Brace-Bel's essence that he be a rich man. Just as it is apparently of your essence that you be poor, and lost, and confused. My condolences. But we all have something for which to reproach our creators. I for instance have gout. Moreover I have spent seven of every ten years of my manhood in chains.

Shay brought me here. I mean to this time, this place, not to this house. Shay made his home in this Age some way to the north. In an empty warehouse. Do not go looking for it. I stripped it bare of wonders when I quit his service.

I do not recall the route between our Age and this. I was blindfolded. He led me through alleys, up and down stairs. I heard doors unlock. For a time I thought we were pursued, but he only laughed, and the footsteps receded. If I knew the way I would have followed it back long ago.

We lived in the warehouse. Shay taught me the use of his devices. Amulets. Keys to surprising locks. Cloaks. Charms of concealment and devices of augury. Ah, what *didn't* he have? What *hadn't* he collected on his travels? He made machines to suit his whims out of the birds of the air and the rats and lizards of the sewers. Twisted and unhappy things that had been burdened by surgery with something very much like the power of speech. I am a cruel man and a perverse man, but those poor creatures filled me with pity and loathing. *I have laboratories,* Shay said, as if that explained everything. He laughed and called me a very provincial coward and hypocrite. That clawed monkey which he claimed to have purchased in a market in the Under-City of a far-off time guarded our door and was unable to close its poor red eyes. It was scaled in places, part lizard.

I inspected him closely, as servants do their masters. He was not so young as I had first thought—a man in early middle age, a little tired sometimes when he thought my eyes were not on him—when he forgot that I was a *man,* not a possession. I had mistaken energy and pride for youth.

Many of his devices were terrible weapons. Those Shay took with him when he went. I let his creatures go when he left and I imagine they starved in the concrete hideousness of this city. I am left with the dregs of his collection.

We did not often go outside. Why would we? I looked out from the high windows over the rooftops and it made me shudder. This is an *ugly* time.

I asked him what was on the Mountain, of course, why he meant to assault it. And *how.* In the old days of the Atlas, sometimes our explorers went north to the Mountain. Always it ended in madness—if they came back at all. The Mountain has always been an evil thing. Shay would not answer me. He told me it was not my place to ask.

I cooked for him, and cleaned. The monkey and I developed a jealous mutual dislike, one servant to another.

One day Shay went away and did not come back. That is to say, one morning I woke, and he was not there; and by nightfall he was *still* not there.

I reasoned carefully.

Suppose that those who inhabit the Mountain had spied out Shay's intentions—which is hardly improbable, for any denizen of this dejected and fearful Age will tell you that the Mountain spies on them constantly, and they surely must be at least half right. Suppose that the Mountain's servants had stolen Shay away, or killed him. Yet they had left me unharmed, as if I were beneath their notice. Were that the case then I was free, though I was lost in a strange and hideous time. I certainly had no intention of revenging my erstwhile master; let the Mountain have him!

Or suppose that Shay had gone up the Mountain without me; then it would be wise to flee before he returned.

Suppose that Shay *never* intended to go up the Mountain. He was a brilliant man, the most brilliant I have ever met, and the most remarkably well traveled. He had a number of striking scars. He was a man who'd survived much. Perhaps, rather than face the terrors of the Mountain himself, he brought travelers, adventurers, madmen, obsessives, daring and dangerous men, all would-be visionaries, into his orbit, and into some small part of his confidence; and he hinted to them of the Mountain, and the wonders hidden there—let *them* go! Let *them* face it first! Well, I said, if that's the case, you may fuck yourself, Mr. Shay; I am no one's pawn, no one's monkey. I have seen what the Mountain does to people.

For instance look at you, poor ghost.

I considered other possibilities; I have never learned the truth. Nor do I care to. Is Shay dead? Well, that's a nice question, isn't it. Even if he's dead here there are times in the city when he may be alive, and what's time to Mr. Shay but a flimsy veil? One day he may come for me. Or he may not. I intend to enjoy what time I have, regardless.

I do not like the dawn. Ha! In the play of Mr. Liancourt that brought down the wrath of the Countess and doomed the Atlas there was a very silly hymn to the dawn. A pretty tune but idiotic words. What a thing to die for!

Dawn is so ugly here. Look how the factories poison it. Those rosy fingers are nicotine-stained and filthy. They paw the horizon like they're picking its pocket.

An ugly time. They talk daily here about war; ever since I arrived there have been rumors of war, from some quarter or other; from the Mountain if no mundane enemy is available. I think they cannot bear to live in this time. They long for the end. They know these are the last days.

Dawn brings sobriety. I do not like to be sober.

We have talked all night. My servants will be waking now, and doing the housework.

Once I thought, by my rituals, to pierce the veil of reality; to see the city as the Gods see it, mutable, infinite, miraculous; to break the walls of the city down and force my way into . . .

Never mind. Do you know why I keep up my rituals? This tired charade? Because I cannot bear the thought that I might die in this time. I cannot bear to be stranded here.

Sometimes when I performed my rituals I felt that I was close, so very close . . .

I hope to bring the Gods back. To call them back into being! To open the way. To follow them home. If I *provoke* them, if my little performances outrage them, if they come in *anger,* so be it. I will still have opened the way home.

I long for the comforts of home. The city I grew up in seems unbearably beautiful to me now. Even its priests, even its judges, even its cruel princes. Their robes and finery and arrogant display had a certain . . . richness. Life in the last days is thin and grey. I would happily go back into my little cell, if I could look out of the window over the towers of old Ararat.

I, Brace-Bel, the great libertine, the great debaucher, the great hater and despoiler of the good and the pure! Like a toothless old woman mooning after the days of her childhood. Sentimental in my old age, and I am not yet an old man. Shameful. And yet there it is.

When I first recognized you, I thought: *at last my rituals have succeeded.* I have called up a phantom from the old days. I have opened the door. I have fucked into being a miracle. I have scribed the spell with my whip! Oh, how wonderful! No wonder I could not sleep. Ah, but you recall nothing, do you? I have watched your face closely for hours and you recall nothing.

It is pure accident that brings you here. You came for Ivy, and not for me. You told me that but I did not believe you at first.

Leave me alone, will you? Let me watch the dawn. Go to bed, go to bed.

Liancourt's little song about the dawn. I was never musical, but sometimes music awakens the memory, it transports us home. How did it go?

Now I remember you, Arjun. You worked with Liancourt on that silly play. He did the words and you did the music. I remember you beavering away in the conservatory. Stay a moment. How did it go? Tumpty-tumpty-tum-tum-tum-tum. No, not quite. La-la-la-la-la . . .

What? You look quite stricken! Your eyes . . . Steady, steady; what's come over you?

EIGHT

Music and Memory–Housework–
"Ivy's Clever"–The WaneLight
Hotel–Doors

Arjun

Brace-Bel slept late. Even in sleep the words kept pouring out of him. He muttered; sometimes he shrieked. It echoed down the stairs. The household was apparently used to it.

Arjun didn't sleep at all. The "bed" Brace-Bel's servants had made for him was a velvet-covered loveseat. To sleep on it one had to curl like a bent note. Arjun ached where Brace-Bel had struck him, and his wounded hand throbbed again, and his head thronged with memories. Memories returned one by one like birds coming to roost.

That *song*—the few notes Brace-Bel had sung in his tuneless grating voice. That was the heart of it; the heart of *him*. Everything else wove in and around the bright thread of that song. Gad, his home in the far southern mountains, the Choristers, his God, and the absence of his God, which struck him all over again now as a fresh wound, a loss that left him gasping; the long trek north, by horse, by cart, on foot, by train, by slow barge, across deserts, plains, hills, the sea, into the city, Ararat, the impossible, legendary, infinite city, in search of his absconded God; the day—the music, his memories, looped back again, he snatched a moment of his childhood from the stream—when he first sang in the Choir, the gypsy girl, a faded scent-memory of his mother, before the Choristry took him from his first home; then an *accelerando* of vio-

lent and terrifying and wonderful city-memories, assaultive, confusing, like the first moment he stepped off the boat and into the
surging crowds of the docks. The Atlas; Olympia; the boy Silk; the
monster of the canals; *Shay* . . .

The song was the key to himself. It was unfortunate, then, that
Arjun knew it only from Brace-Bel's half-hearted and unmusical
rendition. As he lay awake struggling to order his memories, part
of his mind was trying to weave the music back together—to remember the next notes. There were laws and principles of composi-
tion floating in his head according to which it should have been
possible to reconstruct, to develop, to reanimate the scrap of music
Brace-Bel had half remembered; he couldn't do it. It far surpassed
his talents. It hovered on the edge of awareness like an angel. It was
not merely music; it was *Music*. But naming it brought it no closer,
in fact perhaps only drove it away. He twisted and turned on his
side; the arm of the loveseat poked his spine.

. . . and after *Shay,* how he'd traveled *beyond* the city, and into its
hidden places, and past and future times, and seen things he could
hardly, now, make sense of. He remembered how Shay had taught
him to open the city's secret doors, and then . . . Memories flickered
across Arjun's mind like unspooling film. The moving pictures, the
cinema; that was something he suddenly remembered. Gods, how
long had he wandered? There had been traces of his God everywhere, like a trail marked for him through the city, but he'd never
found it. The Martyrs of the Bloody Scalp. Gradek's Academy. The
slave market on Caspar Street. The river-pirates of the Flood Years.
(The faded lash-scars on Arjun's back began to itch like a bulb's filament burning at the flick of a switch.) The Unlicensed Operators
who gave up their bodies to inhabit the city's wires and mathematics and flickering screens, and guided him on through a dark time.
(He wanted to share the news with the Low sisters. *This is a bad time
but there have been worse; this is* not *the end of things*. Was it good or bad
news?) The incident of the duel on Hawker's Common. (He remembered learning to fence, and a number of occasions on which
that skill had saved his life; he suddenly, childishly, itched for a re-
match with Brace-Bel.) The monomaniacal Replacement Men of
Ako, who took the place of their sleeping masters, and lived un-
comprehendingly half-existences. The Glorious Revolution—one
of many. The Bank Theater and the spies among Lord Wolfe's

Players. The WaneLight Hotel! He searched in his pockets and drew out the matchbook and turned it over and over in his hands. He remembered his years at the Hotel, digging into its secrets, hunting for clues, bartering for rumors . . .

He remembered searching for the way to the Mountain. For *years*. He remembered his childhood in the far south, beyond the walls of the city, in the Choristry, that cold and serene monastery. It had been made of stone and glass. They had kept goats, libraries, quiet young men, and severe pious young women. His God had lived there, in the high spires. Then it had vanished and his world had fallen apart.

He remembered the trek north to the city—to Ararat, City of Gods and heart of the world. It had taken him a year, summer to summer, across plains and deserts and rivers and seas. He remembered how the crowds at the docks had swallowed him, the haze of sweat and salt and spice that enveloped the harbor.

He remembered the moment he decided that his God, which had fled for the city, had now left the city for the Mountain, and that he, too, had no choice but to go deeper into the heart of things. He'd been reading a newspaper, sitting in a railway carriage, when he'd caught a glimpse from the greasy window of the shadow of the Mountain and thought, as if out of nowhere: *of course. They're right, of course. They've been right all this time. The Mountain.*

He remembered his years in the WaneLight Hotel.

He could not remember going up. He could not remember falling down.

There were still holes in his memory, still shadows.

They'd come in time. He decided not to force the matter. The music slipstreamed, a chromatic glide, an awakening theme, and he remembered Olympia again, the flat in Foyle Square, the theaters . . .

Years. And he'd never found his God. Rumors of the Mountain at every step. Years . . .

. . . *Shay.* Arjun remembered his apprenticeship to that unnerving man. He remembered a thin elderly man with straggling dirty white hair and a worn suit, a sneer, a peevish snarl; not the strong laughing young man Brace-Bel spoke of. And he remembered that sometimes Shay had called himself Lemuel, and sometimes he'd heard rumors of a man who must have been Shay who called himself Cuttle, or, or . . .

Brace-Bel's story was disturbing, and strange. Shay, it seemed, had wanted Brace-Bel for something, had armed him and pointed him at the Mountain. It made Arjun wonder what purpose Shay might have had in teaching *him,* in bringing him out of the city and into the secret paths behind the city. Among the uncommunity of the travelers in the City Beyond—and now Arjun began truly to remember smiling St. Loup, sour old Father Turnbull the defrocked, the mad Engineer Potocki, Longfellow the penitent, Abra-Melin of the shaking staff, so many dozens of others—Shay was *special.* Ubiquitous, apocryphal. Uniquely deadly, because he was *first,* and his plans were laid before yours and around yours. Always absent— wherever you were, you always *just missed him.* Rumors of sightings of him sold for gold, blood, kingdoms. St. Loup had once confessed (lied?) that it was Shay who first brought him through. Turnbull admitted it casually: "Actually at first I rather thought, ha-ha, that he might be the *devil.* But we were all young once, and naïve. I followed him anyway, of course."

It began to worry him; Arjun couldn't grasp the shape and scale of that great machine . . . and he found that he'd nearly forgotten the precious fragment of music. His back ached. He felt restless, full of energy, fresh strength. A flash of sun through the curtains stung his eyes and he realized that it was nearly noon. Perhaps he *had* slept a little, after all. He could hardly be blamed if he had trouble distinguishing dreams from reality. It was nearly noon, and Ruth would be wondering what had happened to him, whether he had failed, like all the others. He had a sudden powerful urge to move, to act, to begin again.

He had his memory again. The last few gaps would fill themselves soon enough. Maybe in time he would remember what happened on the Mountain! In a peculiar way, the Beast had led him to Brace-Bel, to where he needed to be.

He looked at his maimed hand, still strange to him, still sometimes sore. He didn't consider the debt paid. There was more that the Beast could tell him—it had begun to tell him what happened on the Mountain. It had begun to tell him the way back up.

Somehow, he had to free it from its captors.

He twitched the curtains and looked out over the green and sunlit and deadly garden. Perhaps Brace-Bel's weapons might prove useful.

First things first. He had made a promise to the Low sisters, who had saved his life. He got up, bones creaking, and went in search of Ivy.

The Bird stood in the hallway outside, perched prettily on a stepladder, wiping the windows with a wet rag.

On closer inspection it turned out to be a thin young woman in feathers. It was not Ivy. Though she'd worn the Bird costume the night before, it had apparently been passed on to another member of the household—a pale girl on whom it hung loosely and ridiculously. In the daylight the costume was more grey than white, and the patches of tape and string that held it together were painfully obvious. It barely covered the bruised bony thighs of the girl on the ladder.

"Morning," she said.

"Good morning. My name is Arjun."

"I know. That was a strange business last night. We weren't expecting it. Was it rehearsed?"

"No. Brace-Bel was not expecting me either. I broke in. Our fight was an impromptu performance."

"Shit." She frowned. "Then I lost money on you."

"I'm sorry."

The girl shrugged. "Never mind."

"Last night Ivy Low wore your costume."

"She wears it at *night*," the girl explained. "The Bird's Mr. Brace-Bel's favorite. So's Ivy."

"You wear it during the day?"

"Looks like it, doesn't it?" She stepped down from the ladder and wrung out her rag into a greasy bucket. She met Arjun's eye. "Don't ask. The boss says, it's *part* of it, same as the whippings and the you-know-what. Bringing the Gods down to do housework." She imitated Brace-Bel's ranting voice—"Breaking down the barriers between the mundane and the miraculous"—and laughed. "Better than most jobs."

"I wasn't going to ask."

"Ivy doesn't have to do it. The housework. She does whatever she likes all day and she never has to work. She's so pretty and clever. No one said the boss had to be fair."

"No one said anyone had to be fair," Arjun agreed.

"My name's Stevie."

"Good morning."

She smiled, showing bad teeth, pauper's teeth, and self-consciously frowned her mouth closed again. She said, "If you're going to stay he'll dress you up, too. Some of the girls say it's no job for a man but I say that's no one's business, and you wouldn't be the only one."

"I don't plan to stay."

"Where are you from?"

"That's hard to explain. A long way away."

"Some people say everyone who's a little bit odd is some kind of ghost, who drifted down from the Mountain. I say some people are just a bit odd. My uncle got hit in the head with a steam shovel and he never remembered my aunt's name after that and he had to write down his own house number, but he wasn't any kind of ghost."

"In the general case, you're probably right to be skeptical," Arjun said. "But I really have come down from the Mountain. And before that from somewhere very different from here. And before that, from outside the city, even."

She gave him a long calculating look, as if waiting for him to try to sell her something dubious. He shrugged.

"So," she said. "What about Brace-Bel? Is he really from somewhere else? Was there ever really a Bird, or God of lights, or . . . ? Or is he just mad? Knocked on the head? Too many drugs?"

"Do you have money on that, too?"

"Yeah." She gave a yellow-brown smile.

"Well, good news, then. Help me find Ivy, and I'll tell you a few stories."

She thought about it for a moment, then threw the rag with a wet ringing slap into the bucket and said, "Fuck it. Brace-Bel doesn't notice if the place is clean or filthy. I don't know where Ivy is. She gets into odd places. Come on, then."

No idea."

In Brace-Bel's shadowy kitchen an old woman chopped pale white tubers with a heavy cleaver and ladled them into the soup. Her costume's arms and legs and bristly protuberances rattled the pans overhead and dragged in the soup and nearly caught fire on the stove. She was either a spider, or a beetle, or a threshing machine, or perhaps a many-wired telegraph switchboard. As she moved the costume's complex elaborations slipped in and out of shadow and steam and Arjun could not quite comprehend them.

"No idea," she repeated.

"Come on," Stevie wheedled. "You haven't seen her all day?"

The face underneath the costume was round and grey, cracked and lined in the stove light. The old woman gave her name as Mrs. Down. She looked at Arjun and Stevie with frank contempt. "Probably still in bed," she said.

Arjun sniffed the air, thick with meat-smells, and nearly salivated. "Mrs. Down, may I . . . ?"

"Out, the both of you. You'll eat when Brace-Bel says you'll eat."

Stevie led Arjun along the cobwebbed balconies of the third floor, from which much of the garden was visible, but they caught no glimpse of Ivy.

"Horrible old cow," she muttered.

"Ivy?"

"Mrs. Down. Used to be a madam, can you believe it, in a brothel up north, before Brace-Bel found her. Sick in the head. Wrapped round his fat little finger, she is."

She leaned over the edge of the balcony, craning her head for a better view of the hedge-maze, scratching her bony hip. "Ivy's a cow, too, mind you."

"I'm here to rescue her."

"That's sweet."

"Her sisters sent me. They miss her."

"Huh. She's never mentioned sisters. Can't picture her with a family. Stuck-up and cold. Is she rich?"

"No."

"Huh." Stevie poked her head around the door of a room with mosaics on the floor, where two thin young men in rags and jewels sat cross-legged, smoking, sewing uniforms together. Ivy? They shrugged; they hadn't seen her.

"I always thought she was rich. Hah. She acts like she's a fucking executive's daughter or something."

"How does Brace-Bel keep her here? I promised her sisters . . ."

"How does he keep her here? He *doesn't* keep her here. Arjun, she just about runs this place." Stevie stepped out onto another un-tended balcony, waved a feathered hand out over the gardens. "All those horrible machines and things? She's the only one who under-stands even half of them. What, you thought Brace-Bel knew how to make them work? He can't even stand up straight half the time, can he? She makes up all the dances and things. Ivy's *clever*."

Stevie grabbed Arjun's wrist. Her grip was surprisingly strong. There was a nervous smile on her face. "Don't tell Brace-Bel I said all this, will you? But it's got to be obvious, right? He'd be helpless without her. She runs this place. I don't know what she wants out of him, or us, or all this, but. He worships the ground she walks on, you know. He's like a kind of child. When she gets bored with him he'll just die, I think. It's sick. She's a bit mad, actually. She still thinks all this stuff, the dances, the other stuff, it's all going to maybe do something, I don't even know what. Like *magic*. This is her show these days. You're going to have to drag her out of here kicking and screaming, I think."

She let go of Arjun's wrist. She was panting a little. "So that's that."

"Ah." Arjun leaned against the balcony. The garden below was pleasant and unthreatening by daylight, and there was a cool breeze. For a moment he felt lost. He shrugged. "Then I'll talk to her. We'll see. I made a promise."

They stood in companionable silence for a while, in the gentle sunlight. The treetops around them rustled. Stevie plucked broken feathers from the arms of her costume and let them flutter down.

"So," she said. "Who *are* you, then? Where *are* you from?"

She had bruised and vulnerable eyes—half trusting, half suspi-cious. Part of her wanted him to tell her that he was a fake, that Brace-Bel was a fake, that Ivy was only mad and the whole thing only a sham; part of her wanted him to tell her something beautiful and strange.

He began trying to tell her about his God. Her mousy eyebrows rose. She lived in a godless Age. She understood the concept only vaguely, first as something the Know-Nothings had taught her to be frightened of, then as something Brace-Bel had—inadvertently—taught her to laugh at. He tried telling her about his monastic childhood in the mountains outside the city, but it was clear that she couldn't quite believe it or imagine it. The silence, the peace, the simplicity, the music; she was a city child.

He realized that he was turning the little red matchbook from the WaneLight Hotel over and over in his fingers. He held it up to her. "Have you ever heard of this place?" She shook her head. "Well then. It was the most famous and important place in the city once, a long time ago, and I don't know how far away . . ."

Far to the south. Back in the old days the WaneLight Hotel stood in a high place, so far south that the Mountain was only a distant grey smudge on the horizon; and even then the Mountain was only visible on the clearest summer days, and only if one went out onto the highest north-facing roofs and teetered on the unsteady tiles.

How long ago? Long enough ago that it had been forgotten by Stevie's time, but long after the time of the Atlas-makers and Olympia and Silk and the rest. Time had meant very little to Arjun in his years of searching up and down the city for his God.

It was a place where people traded and schemed and murdered for, among other things, secrets. He had gone there in search of the secret path to the Mountain.

Far to the south, and high. Far from the haunting presence of the Mountain. On the south side the roof was colonized by elegant little cafés and observatories and glass-canopied hothouses and aviaries. On the north it was unadorned industrial space: vents and chimneys, antennae and pylons. To see the Mountain from the WaneLight Hotel one had to creep through that swamp of iron and wire and out to the edge. The roof curved and angled and swooped at odd angles like something organic, like a complex and chaotic equation, in a way that was soft and seductive when viewed from the ground, far below—and to sophisticated sensibilities it was even erotic—but was merely frightening and nauseous to those who worked on the roof.

To stand safely on the edge one had to clutch at nearby reedy antennae or the mushrooming vent-pipes for comfort. Then one felt the crackling subtle power of the WaneLight Hotel's communications and signaling arrays rush through one's skin, and could almost hear in the stridulant hiss the whisper of powerful secrets of business, politics, crime, religion. If one clutched the vent-pipes instead one's skin sweated with the dreadful demonic heat rising from the Hotel's belly and one felt sick and ashamed. But those were necessary compromises if one wanted to lean out over the edge into blue vertiginous sky—not looking, trying not to look, at the great sweep of flags and parapets below, the windows from which music spilled, and laughter, and shouting, and screams, and weeping, for the perfect and significant number of ninety-nine floors, and below that the motorcars circling the Hotel tiny as toys with touching hectic speed—if one wanted to look out over the edge and see the faintest suggestion in the infinite distance of the Mountain. On cloudy days even that was impossible.

The WaneLight Hotel would countenance no competition; therefore it was placed as far as it was possible to get from the Mountain, while still being nowhere near the city's walls and somehow deep in the city's heart. It was complex and paradoxical but its builders had been very clever indeed.

When Arjun came to the Hotel it was already so old that its builders were long forgotten. Ownership of the Hotel itself had changed hands a hundred times. Occasionally a controlling interest had been acquired by outsiders; more often alliances and consortia formed among the wealthier and more connected of the long-term guests, who found that there were certain advantages of access and communications to being owners of the Hotel's various infrastructures.

When Arjun began working there, management of the Hotel was in the hands of something called Bodley Estate Investments & Properties, and Arjun was interviewed in a windowless white-walled office just off the lobby by a young tie-wearing Bodley. The regular staff called all representatives of Bodley EI&P *Bodleys,* and there was indeed something blandly interchangeable about them. It was common knowledge among the staff that the Bodleys were only a front for a combination of owners led by Mr. Monmouth, whose gambling operation now brazenly spanned the entire East Wing of the twenty-fifth floor. It was also common knowledge among the staff that all common knowledge about the Hotel was wrong.

When Arjun first approached the Hotel he came to it too late. He followed rumors of it back from a later more degraded Age, through twisting alleys of time, relying on harsh music as his guide. When he first found it, it was after a fire had ruined the beautiful south face, and the structure seemed twisted, melted, deflated. The rooms were half empty and the guests were a seedy bunch who sold drugs, or guns, or whores, or slaves, and had no secrets worth paying for. He stayed for one week before realizing his error: no one in those latter days of the Hotel would know the secret path to the Mountain. So he went through the Hotel's nightclubs where a thin repetitive jazz was playing—and through the kitchens where hood-eyed immigrant workers sang something deeply self-pitying as they chopped and slit and garnished poison squid and lurid spiny anemones—and opening a door on the other side of which a suicidal guest warbled feebly in her bloody bath—and through a door on the other side of which he found a way back into the institution's glory days. He emerged into a summer day of wild wet heat and searing blue sky. A profusion of bright flags and crystal and lights and laughter greeted him. The ostentatious extravagance of suits and dresses and black sunglasses all around told him: this is the time, these are the days!

The WaneLight Hotel was not *formally* a seat of government. That came later: when the building was crumbling and real power had long since moved elsewhere an ineffectual Council would headquarter itself there, and take over the Hotel's famous elegant letterhead, and steal what remained of its glamour, until the taxes stopped coming in and they could not afford to stop the roof collapsing.

At the height of the Hotel's influence it was simply known as a place where powerful people came to meet each other, came to do business. Ambassadors from all over the city lived there—the Hotel catered to all tastes and cultures, and there was nothing it could not copy. It cocooned in luxury the presidents and owners of every corporation of significance. It indulged the antics of the stars of whatever entertainments were popular at the time. The city's finest athletes roomed there in their spoiled retirements, reverting one by one into a cosseted muscular second infancy, swollen gigantically by the drugs the Hotel's staff slipped into their food—an illusion of continued virility for which the athletes would drain their bank accounts and prostitute their endorsements for the Hotel's clients, and that would, in the end, turn them violent and ogreish, so that floors thirty-one and thirty-two were not safe for regular guests, and the cleaning staff there went armed with cattle prods.

It housed—so the rumor went—a small, shifting, and secretive community of . . . call them *travelers*. Those who wandered in the City Beyond, in the Metacontext, among the shifting Gears of the city—the visionaries, the madmen, the lost, the unmoored in time. They came to the Hotel to scheme, to deal, to share their various obsessions. (St. Loup claimed to be in pursuit of the most beautiful woman in the world; the magus Abra-Melin sought a sacred Grail; Longfellow dreamed of some God, somewhere, with the authority to forgive him for his apparently monstrous crimes; for Monmouth it was a particular and improbable flavor of ice cream; the thuggish Crebillon only wanted to find his way home to the city of his birth—he had scores to settle.) They haggled over secrets—the paths, the rumors, the keys and the doors; sightings of the mysterious and omnipresent Shay, who for so many of them had been their first sinister introduction to the City Beyond, who had pulled back the walls and given them their first terrifying glimpse of the spin of the Gears.

They told each other stories of the Mountain.

If anyone in the city, anywhere, possessed a map of the safe path to the Mountain, then someone in the Hotel would know about it. It would be available, for a price.

Who were they? The Hotel's crowds teemed. Everyone in the Hotel had something to sell, held secrets close to their chests. Arjun had no contacts. No invitation. Who, among the Hotel's guests, was an alien, who was merely eccentric and affected? Who was a fake and who was the real thing? Hard to tell. Arjun needed time to observe. To spy. To ingratiate. He needed a job.

The Bodleys put Arjun to work on the roof, because he was slight and nimble and unafraid of heights, but unsuitable for working with guests. They gave him overalls, and a pan, and an assortment of tuning-fork brushes, and sent him up there to join the teams who groomed bird shit and dead pigeons from the shivering antennae.

Arjun worked on the roof for more than a year. That was nothing remarkable. There were men who'd been working on the roof for ten years, twenty, all still hoping that one day they'd be noticed or notice something compromising and their long-awaited political careers would begin.

In the winter it rained and stormed and the cleaning teams wore waxy indigo cloaks. The guests were guarded and suspicious; angry sullen static crawled along the wires and the chimneys groaned. In summer the guests were happy and greedy and every minute in some room somewhere a deal was made and the Hotel's silvery antennae quivered and purred.

Arjun applied for a transfer to the engineering teams who tuned the antennae and tended their frequencies. He failed the examination. The invigilating Bodley shook his head. "You must be from one of the *backward* districts, right?" And fair enough; Arjun never *had* learned to understand machines. And another six months went by.

All sorts of birds gathered on the roofs. Not just pigeons—swifts, hawks, parakeets, parrots. All kinds of engineered birds and surgical creations—muttering messenger birds, scaled and bladed and strutting war-birds, chiming clock-birds. Something about the Hotel's vibrations attracted them. Parliaments of ravens gathered among the wires and did their own business, up there on the roofs; and in the mornings Arjun's crew had a special spike-and-bag to clear up the bodies of defeated challengers . . .

The wires buzzed and the antennae murmured. Some of Arjun's crew believed they could *hear* the secrets the guests whispered down below. On at least two occasions, during Arjun's time on the roof, a clever cleaner invented a device to snoop on the wires—and both men disappeared shortly after, and blandly smiling Bodleys shrugged and lied, *it's just turnover, you know?*

And Arjun learned how to hear the music in the wires.

At first he thought he was mad. The heights and the winds and the vibrations in the ether drove many of the roof-workers to madness. (And the *waiting,* the endless waiting, in hopes that some guest might notice them, that they might be welcomed below, that they might get to make *deals.*)

He heard it as a kind of code, a kind of itch. He slowly learned to piece it together as music.

It was *terrible.*

The Hotel piped music everywhere—to soothe, to inflame, to

inspire awe, greed, nervousness, misery—whatever was most conducive to business. To Arjun's ears, it was a jangling, manipulative abomination. Since Day One he had *suffered* during his long daily elevator rides between the roof and his quarters in the basement—in the service elevators the Hotel played bright and cheery muzak. He was profoundly upset to find that even the roof was no longer a sanctuary from the noise.

And one morning, around that time, the elevator opened briefly on forty-four and Arjun saw *Shay* in the corridor shaking someone's hand and smiling hugely and handing over a briefcase. Sunglasses, tan, red silk shirt, cropped white hair . . . but the doors closed again before Arjun could say anything, and he never saw Shay there again, though he made inquiries, and he heard *rumors*. And not long after that, one of the guests on sixty-one, a defrocked priest named Turnbull, invited Arjun to *come and talk about this Shay chap, then*. Sometimes he went by *Father* Turnbull, though his faith had long since inverted into an obsessive hatred of the deity. Turnbull, like Arjun, like Brace-Bel, like most of their kind, had been lifted from the city of his birth into the Metacontext by Shay, for Shay's own mysterious reasons, with vague promises that what Turnbull sought—the final proof of God's nonexistence—could be found on the Mountain. And then Turnbull had been left behind. *What do you know about Shay? Where is he? What've you heard? What are they saying about him these days?*

And through Turnbull, Arjun met Dr. Quayle, and through Quayle he met Mr. Mangalore, and through the services he performed for Mangalore he developed an uneasy working relationship with the brutish enforcers Slough and Muykrit, who introduced him to the hairshirted penitent Longfellow, who gave him access to the mad magus Abra-Melin, at one of whose séances he met St. Loup, who persuaded him to go in on a deal with Li-Paz, one of whose girls knew Cantor, who told him the great comical secret about Mr. Monmouth, who, under threat of blackmail, offered Arjun an introduction to Potocki, who . . . A dangerous business, his introduction to the uncommunity of travelers. They were solitary, unsympathetic, untrustworthy by nature. Everyone who Broke Through did so alone. They didn't care about the consequences of their actions.

Their very existence was an act of ontological violence—few of them scrupled over human life. The secret nature of the world was profoundly corrupt, and they all knew it. But what choice did Arjun have? He did what he needed to do. For nearly a year he assisted the serpentine St. Loup with his schemes, and at the end he had nothing to show for it except an introduction to the dissipated Lord Losond, the collector, who introduced Arjun to his wife, who . . .

Arjun had come to the Hotel to find the way to the Mountain. That was a story in itself, how he had first heard rumors of the Hotel (it was all coming back to him now, as he spoke, as he walked with Stevie through the corridors of Brace-Bel's house). He sought the Mountain because his God lived there—so he believed; it must. There was nowhere else left to look. Inward and upward. Since his God left him—alone in that distant crumbling monastery, an abandoned child, in silent halls that had once been full of music—his search had taken him upward and inward and deeper into the city.

He spent ten years in the Hotel. He ran away after rumors of music and Gods, again and again, and again and again he came back disappointed. He schemed. The pursuit of secrets became its own purpose. Sometimes he forgot *why* he was searching for the Mountain, sometimes for months at a time. Sometimes he forgot the difference between himself and St. Loup or Abra-Melin or Turnbull or the other madmen. Sometimes there was no difference.

But that was beside the point. He remembered his God now. He wanted to tell Stevie about the *music*.

Arjun complained to the Bodleys about the leaking music, and they ignored him. He complained to the other cleaners on his crew and they suggested earplugs. He filed a more *formal* complaint, attaching extra pages to the Bodley EI&P Grievance & Suggestion Form so that he could detail, at length, precisely how vile and debased the Hotel's music was. It relieved his feelings a little. Three weeks later a Bodley summoned him to interview.

The Bodley, whose name was Frank, claimed to be sensitive, musically minded—though to Arjun Frank seemed indistinguishable from his fellows. Frank listened to Arjun's complaints and made him an offer—and soon Arjun found himself working under

Frank the Bodley's staff in the darkened and humming and machine-filled nerve center of the Hotel's musical systems.

There were eleven men in the Music Department, seven women, two indeterminate, one Bodley. Quarters were close and hygiene poor. They drank and smoked furiously in their darkened carrels, watching the feed from the cameras that were hidden in every corridor and every room, fiddling with buttons and dials, headphones on their nodding twitching heads—massaging constantly the Hotel's moods and tempo.

Frank assigned Arjun on a probationary basis to the east side of floor sixty-two, where no one very important lived, and where the bars and gymnasia were out of fashion.

"No," Frank said, one week later. "Oh dear no. You're making them uneasy. What *was* that you were playing? You're bad for business. This is about *getting business done,* Arjun. Look at the way Esme does it; do it the way she does it. Otherwise we may have to let you go back to the roof."

And Arjun—who was very eager not to lose access to the cameras, because who knew what secrets he might learn from them?—swallowed his pride and copied Esme.

And the *point* Arjun wanted to make, he told Stevie, was that, as he worked for Frank the Bodley, as he sat in that nerve center listening to all the Hotel's whispering insinuating music hissing and twining together, he remembered the Voice of his God. Because the Hotel's music was its *opposite,* was everything the Voice was *not*; the Hotel's constant song was all lies, was all manipulation, it cheated and twisted, it *stole* from all its listeners. It was there to make gamblers take that one last shot that would ruin them; it was there to make men forget their wives and children and all their promises; it was there to make people squander themselves. And when—after a few weeks of shame, and drinking, and a promotion to the feeds for the seventy-third and twenty-ninth floors—Arjun first learned to hear the Hotel's music as a whole, he heard his God, too: his God was all the notes *not* played. He tore off his headphones and walked out. Frank the Bodley tried to stop him and Arjun took a swing, and the

Bodley's bland face, to no one's particular surprise, turned out to be made of soft inhuman clay and a tangle of emerald circuitry. Fortunately by that time Arjun was moonlighting for Mr. Mangalore, and no longer needed the job. But the Music, Arjun said . . .

But Stevie, as it turned out, didn't much care about the music, and cared even less for Gods. She wanted to know about the clothes, and the food, and the hotel's beds, and the lights, and the women who gambled, the dresses they wore, the wine . . . For a moment Arjun was nonplussed, almost stammered. But he liked the girl; there was something charming about her eagerness, so he rallied and tried to remember. "The women all wore heels so high they walked like storks, Stevie. Black, and red, and . . ."

"Show me."

"What?"

She grabbed his arm again. "Show me. All these things. I believe you, all right? Let me," she started taking the ridiculous wings off, "let me get a few things, and you can take me there, right? Doors, time, streets. You *said.*"

He held her bony hand. "It's been a long time. I've forgotten a lot. I pushed too close to the Mountain and I hurt myself."

"Can you still do it, or not?"

"I don't know." He laughed. "I actually don't know."

"Well fucking *try,* then." She looked close to tears. "Come on, come on. Take me there and I promise I'll . . ."

"Don't. Please, don't promise anything. No deals. No charge. I'll try, Stevie. First I need *music.*"

She narrowed her eyes suspiciously. Then she whistled a cheerful little tune.

". . . not quite like that. Come on."

He turned toward the door, and stopped short. It was occupied; Brace-Bel's enforcer, Basso, leaned against the door frame, smirking. "Aren't you two cozy?"

"Basso," Stevie said, "We were only . . ."

"Don't you have chores? Get lost, Stevie."

She picked up her wings and ran, ducking through the doorway under Basso's outstretched arm, eyes on the ground, not saying a word.

"We were only talking," Arjun said. "She offered to show me around. You didn't have to talk to her like that."

Basso laughed, not unpleasantly. Prominent on his hip, under his loose shirt, was the handle of a knife. "That's sweet," he said. "But you don't tell us how to run things, all right? Now, you and me, let's go for a walk."

NINE

Whispers–Old Experiments–
The Survivor–Arrest

Ruth

Ruth **spent the** morning waiting for the doorbell to ring; every
time she heard footsteps in the streets she thought it would be
Arjun, and Ivy, and her heart leapt into her throat. She was too restless to read or work—instead she moved things aimlessly from shelf
to shelf, rearranging, reorganizing, and restructuring, in what she
slowly came to realize was *exactly* the neurotic, fussy, coldly precise
and perfectionist manner Ivy had sometimes had—as if Ruth were
trying to call her sister home by some magic of impersonation. She
laughed and decided to let the books on the table under the slope of
the stairs *stay* in a mess, then. She sat back down and began to roll a
cigarette.

There was a whispering sound. While she'd been working she'd
hardly been aware of it, but now—it was unmistakably *not* just
birds, or the pipes, or the wind in the eaves. A scratching, a hissing,
a vague and distant chattering.

It was coming from the cellar.

That meant going next door to Marta's place to get the key to
the cellar door. The cellar had been the Dad's territory, and Marta
was still funny about that whole business. Getting the key would
have meant an awkward conversation, had Marta not, fortunately,
been out somewhere, gathering, visiting, maybe just walking, but
in any case leaving the key in the oak jewelry box on the dusty bot-
tom shelf in the back room.

Ruth got one of the lamps from under the stairs.

The cellar door, set down a short flight of cold stone steps in the corner of the backyard, was cobwebbed and clogged with old leaves, and the hinges were rusty, and Ruth had to grunt and strain to open it. How long had it been since anyone had been down there? Not since Ivy, and that bad night when Ivy had gone down and come back nearly screaming with rage . . .

As the door slowly scraped open the sound of whispering—electric, many-throated—escaped, and for a moment the sound made Ruth think of the voice of the Beast, and then she remembered: *radios.*

There was a word, and a noise, she hadn't heard in a few years—not since she was a child.

For about six months, when she was very small, the Dad had had a phase of experiments with old radios. (After the phase with the birds; around the time of the great rusty gear collection; before the phase with the clocks.) No one else in the city remembered the devices—like the music-machines, like all the rest of that stuff, they were forgotten, anomalous, beyond the capacity of the Combines or their factories to reproduce.

But the Dad had discovered a schematic in an old manual, and he'd dug the rusting dented machines out of junk heaps on weekends, and he'd made his own out of parts he traded for with other . . . enthusiasts. He tinkered with and tuned them. All they ever picked up was a hollow hiss and crackle, like night rain falling out over the reservoirs; occasionally the distant ghost or echo of a voice, a scrap of peculiar music, but nothing more, nothing useful or comprehensible. And no wonder—after all, the last of the old broadcasting towers had closed down long before the Dad's time, long before the Dad's Dad's time, even.

When the Dad got drunk he liked to say that maybe if you tuned them right the radios would reach back to past Ages of the city, where those who were dead were not yet entirely forgotten. He once got drunk enough to tell his daughters that maybe, maybe their dead mother was somewhere in some distant part of the city tuning her *own* radio, separated from them only by static; when he sobered up and found that Ivy, the youngest, had taken him literally, he laughed. Afterward he felt guilty—at least after Marta reproved him—and he lost interest in the machines. One by one their irreplaceable power sources ran down. Later Ivy dismantled most of them to see how they worked. Now the few remaining devices sat on a high shelf, in the far corner of the cellar, under a shroud of dust and grime, and they were *whispering*.

She held the lamp up to them, absurdly, as if she could see their lips moving.

The words were distant, crackling, incomprehensible. A tidal *whoosh* swept back and forth, obliterating meaning.

It was cold in the cellar; her skin crawled and her hair bristled with static.

The cellar was huge, and deep, and its corners shadowed. The Dad had built the house over complex foundations, and sledge-hammered through into adjacent buried spaces. The darkness thronged with uncomfortable memories. The light of the lamp made the eyes of the Dad's mangy stuffed birds and vermin glitter.

Ruth had never been down there much. Nor had Marta, for that matter. Only Ivy, who'd always been so clever with the machines, who'd shared their father's fascinations, had really been welcome in the cellar when he was working.

The radios chattered and sighed.

What were the devices picking up? What barriers were falling?

She had no idea how the things operated. She turned the stiff dials and knobs, but it seemed to make no difference.

There was a tone of panic in the whispering that unnerved her and excited her at once.

Still, to be on the safe side, she lowered the machines to the floor, got a thick blanket from upstairs, and covered them up. Grunting and cursing, she dragged breeze blocks in place to hold the blanket down. It wouldn't do to have the wrong person hear those strange voices.

She went walking past the Museum, glancing nervously at the guards, listening intently, opening her ears to any sound as if she were a radio herself.

Nothing. No sound of the creature's voice, no whispering. She flushed with embarrassment. What had she been expecting?

The guards at the door were different. She didn't recognize either of them. Siddon's and Henry's shifts had ended, of course; they'd gone home to bed, or off to other duties, or back to their regular jobs. Like most low-ranking Know-Nothings, Siddon and Henry still worked ordinary jobs at the factories, for the Combines. They spent their nights and their free days working for the Know-Nothings for a little extra cash or for the prospect of advancement; or because the Know-Nothings could get them free shifts away from the noise and dark of the factory floor, or because they just liked hurting people.

The two on the door today looked like real bastards.

She nearly stumbled right into a drift of grey young women on their way between factory shifts and home shifts. She stopped, collected herself, turned home, where she waited, and waited.

The doorbell rang and instantly Zeigler came running in, eyes gleaming, stage-whispering, "I've *found* him."

"Arjun?"

"Who?"

". . . never mind. Forget it. Who?" She put down her book.

"Our," he glanced, with theatrical caution, at the slowly closing door. "Our *soldier*. Our ghost."

"From last night? I thought he vanished."

"So did I! Fair enough, fair enough, they do that, don't they? But I happened to overhear Mrs. Salt talking to Mr. Thatch, she says there's some beggar or paperless skulking around the back of the old barn, the Patagan one, you know, and I thought, hmm, sounds interesting . . ."

"And you went poking around? I know you."

"It was him. Poor man. Huddled in a corner. Reduced to scrubbing up grass to eat. Quite lost, couldn't give his own name, his rank, anything. I offered him something to eat. I asked him a few questions but . . ."

He took out his notebook, and held up the page—blank, save for the words *interview 37* and *War?*

"I scared him," Zeigler said. "Perhaps, if you're not too busy, a woman's touch . . . ?"

But Ruth was already getting her purse, and her coat, and getting ready to lock up the shop behind her.

* * *

The man hadn't moved. He sat at the back of the barn, in the loft, up the iron ladder, and half hidden by shadows and a heap of old machinery. His back was against the rusting wall, his legs stretched out stiffly before him as if broken and stretchered. He stared blankly up into the shafts of dusty light that fell through the ceiling. He seemed to be counting under his breath. When he heard Ruth approach—as she stepped carefully up off the unsteady ladder—he scrabbled for his rifle. She held up her hands.

Zeigler, below, hissed, "Are you all right?"

"It's all right," she said. "Wait a moment."

The man lowered his weapon again.

Ruth came slowly closer. She sat down beside him with a sigh and a, "Cigarette?"

He took one, automatically held it in his lips for her match. That told her something; many of the ghosts from far off parts had no idea what to do with a cigarette. The pilot Altair had smoked ferociously, as if trying to burn himself up; but her astronomer had regarded the practice as charmingly quaint; and the strange intense red-haired, spike-haired sculptress—who'd come wandering down Ezra Street lost, frightened, touching the surfaces of buildings and trees and the cobbles with her strong hands as if everything in the world was fake and poorly made—had said, "Ruth, are you mad? Put that shit out!"

So he smoked; this man was from a part of the city not altogether unlike her own.

He was looking at her a little more calmly now.

His ragged uniform was familiar, in an odd way. It seemed like a translation, an intensification, of something with which she was intimately acquainted—and, she thought, *unpleasantly* acquainted. She disliked the uniform. The man himself, helpless, confused, she couldn't help but pity.

She let him finish the cigarette.

He stubbed it out under the heel of his boot, smiling for the first time, and suddenly he reminded her of *any* of the Know-Nothings, and she was a little afraid of him.

"Are you all right?" Zeigler called. "Hang on. I'm coming up."

"Stay," she said.

She waited for the soldier to ask her something. He stayed

silent. After a while he closed his eyes. He still had a faint smile on his lips.

He was enjoying the peace, she realized. Perhaps he thought she was a dream, the silence and shade of the barn were a dream of a wounded and dying man, and he was afraid that if he said anything the moment would be over, and he would wake on the battlefield, on the Mountain . . .

"My name's Ruth," she said. "If you can't remember yours, don't worry. That happens. You're not the first. This close to the Mountain, we see a lot of ghosts, lost, we can *help*."

He winced at the word *Mountain*.

"Were you a soldier?" She thought he might be able to answer that question.

"I didn't bloody want to be."

"You remember? Where are you from?"

He shook his head. He looked sad. "I don't remember. I've been sitting here all day and I don't remember. All of this," he waved a hand, "it looks like I know it all, but I don't remember, it doesn't make sense."

"The city you're from, before you went on the . . . *before*, it was like this one?"

"I don't know. I don't bloody know. I look at it and I think: *I know all this.* Then I think: *all this is gone.*"

"You were in a war. Sometimes we see . . . people like you, who say they were in a war."

"We went up . . . *there*. I remember we had a song, about how all the rich bastards on the Mountain had castles of gold and rivers of wine and all that, and we weren't going to put up with them anymore, and we were going to sort a few things out. The things they'd done—wicked. Shay, that name comes back to me, I don't know why."

"Who's Shay?"

The soldier shook his head, irritated, eyes still firmly shut—"I don't remember, some man on the Mountain, they tell me to bloody hate and I do it. Rifle, pack, special issue, like in the old days. What old days? I don't fucking know. I never signed on for this. Up the Mountain. And then all I remember is . . . shadows. Wire. A flash, like a flash of dark. Bumping lost in the dark into my men. Then I was running down that street, screaming."

He opened his eyes. "I knocked you down, didn't I? That was you? Sorry, love. I thought it was all a big cruel joke. After the War this is all gone. Rubble. That's all I remember. Now it's all back again." He smiled and closed his eyes again. "If I can remember my name I'll go down the factory, get my old job back. Go down the nearest League Chapterhouse, say, *reporting for duty, sir. Went on a bit of a bender. All all right again.*"

A shiver ran down Ruth's spine. "You were a Know-N . . ."

The rusty barn door screeched open, and there were boots on the concrete floor below. She heard Zeigler's voice, full of false cheer, saying, "Good afternoon, officers, is this company property, sorry, sorry, just poking around a bit, bird-watching, yes, I'll just be . . ."

A young man's voice drawled, "Shut it, you old fool."

She recognized the voice: it was Siddon, the young Know-Nothing who'd stood guard on the Museum the night before. He sounded tired, angry.

She put a hand over the soldier's mouth. He opened his eyes in shock. "Stay quiet," she hissed. "I don't care if you were a Know-Nothing. These boys aren't your friends anymore. Not after what you've seen. Right? Yes? *Quiet.*"

His eyes were full of hurt and confusion and fear.

The men below—it sounded like three, four of them—poked around the junked machinery, the rotting hay bales, the old dry oil drums, and the stagnant water barrels.

She looked all around for an escape from the loft, but there were no windows, no places to hide, and it was only a matter of time before one of the Know-Nothings below came clanging up the ladder—in the end it was Siddon.

He shook his head. He glanced at Ruth for a moment, then away. "I didn't see you," he said.

The soldier reached for his rifle and Siddon came quickly up over the edge of the ladder, lunged forward, and put his black boot firmly down on the weapon's stock. The soldier snatched his bruised fingers back, and looked up with a stupid, trusting expression on his face. His bloodshot and tired eyes took in Siddon's boots, his long black coat, his collars and cuffs, his black cap. "Hey—don't I know you?"

"Leave him alone," Ruth said. "He's just not well, a bit mad, he's no trouble, he's been stealing chickens, that's all, so we came to tell him to . . ."

Siddon ignored her. He looked at the man at his feet and horror and loathing crept palely over his face; he breathed deeply and swore under his breath and his eyes went blank, flat, distant.

Two more Know-Nothings rose up over the edge of the ladder, and—while the soldier tried to say, *wait, I'm one of you, the League, I think I remember, what Chapterhouse are you from,* the two of them lifted him up roughly by the shoulders, and Siddon stepped forward and, not looking at him, stiffly not looking, eyes trained up at the shafts of light that fell through the ceiling, slit his throat.

The other two Know-Nothings let the body go.

"Oh, fucking hell!"

"*Covered* in fucking blood."

"What about her?"

Siddon shook his head. "She didn't see anything, she didn't hear anything, she's not one of *Them*. Local girl. I know her. Nice girls, no harm in them, bit mad. Father was mad. Leave her, all right?"

He turned and smiled at her, wiping off his knife.

She slapped him as hard as she could in the face. He staggered, his lip bled; it wasn't enough.

"You son of a bitch, Siddon. Why did you do that? Why did you *do* that? He wasn't any harm."

He still had a patronizing smile on his face, even as he dabbed at his bloody lip with his sleeve. "It's not for you to decide, Ruth, you know that. This is the way things are. He was a ghost. A monster. He shouldn't have been here. You want to live in *his* world, instead?"

"You bastard, Siddon, you hypocrite. Monster? He was only a man. He was *lost*. Monster? I know what you're guarding in that Museum. I know what kind of monster you've got down there." Siddon flinched. She realized it was stupid to go on, but she couldn't stop herself: "I've seen it, you bastards, you're not even honest, why are you keeping that thing, why . . . ?"

She trailed off. She was shaking. Siddon and his colleagues looked suddenly pale and nervous, as if they'd been caught stealing from petty cash.

"Fuck it then," Siddon said. "Let's take her in. The old man, too."

TEN

Threats–Fire and Smoke– An Awkward Dinner–Weapons– Pursuit

Arjun

Sorry about last night," Basso said. "How's the bruise?"

Basso was a tall man—taller than Arjun—and he stood too close, as they walked together across the lawns of Brace-Bel's estate. He had the ropey build of a man who was made to be thin, but started every morning with chin-ups, and press-ups, and dumbbells. He was pale and hollow-cheeked, scarred and unshaven, and he smiled a lot. He wore a single golden earring. Sometimes he tugged self-consciously at it. Otherwise his manner of dress was entirely ordinary; unlike the others, he wore no costume.

"I've had worse," Arjun said.

"All a bit of a misunderstanding."

"In fairness, I *did* break in, Mr. Basso; I can't complain."

Basso seemed delighted by this. "No harm done, then!"

Basso *leaned* against things. Somehow even while walking he managed always to be leaning, smirking, glancing idly around in odd directions, as if making a note of vulnerabilities and valuables.

Basso asked, "How's the old street?"

"Carnyx Street? I don't really know. I was only there briefly. It was the only place in this city I have liked."

"How's Thayer and that lot?"

"I met only Thayer. He is a ruin of a man. But somehow you seem unscathed by Brace-Bel's traps, Mr. Basso."

"I'm a lucky lad. Shame about Thayer. A good man."

"Is it true that only Ivy understands the devices?"

"I don't know that that's your business."

"What did you do before coming into Brace-Bel's service, Mr. Basso?"

"I *know* that's not your business. No offense."

"No offense taken."

"You and me, we're in the same boat," Basso said. "Ruth and Marta asked you nicely, right? They went all misty-eyed? They told you how much Ivy meant to them, how wonderful she was, how wonderful the city used to be? How when Ivy was back they'd all go somewhere wonderful together and you could come, too? How they'd escape everything ugly, and you could come, too?"

"Not really," Arjun said.

"What *did* they promise you, then?"

"They saved my life. I know no one else in the city. They only had to ask."

Basso—who was leading Arjun across an unweeded and wild tennis lawn—shrugged. "You're not a bad man, Arjun. The Low sisters are good women."

"There was also the matter of a prophecy, in which Brace-Bel was mentioned. For personal reasons it is important for me to be here; I can't explain why."

"Huh." Basso stooped and lifted an ancient mossy yellow tennis ball from the weeds and tossed it in his hand. "Is that so?"

"Why did you come to work for Brace-Bel, Mr. Basso?"

"Ivy had a word with me."

"Ivy seems to be more the mistress here than a prisoner."

"She's a clever one, all right."

"What did she promise you, Mr. Basso?"

"Maybe she only had to ask nicely."

"Is that true?"

"Where are you from, Arjun? Brace-Bel thought you were from his time, his city. Is *that* true?"

"Yes. We met once or twice. We didn't know each other well."

"Small fucking city."

"Few dare the Mountain. Fewer find the way. There is a certain . . . community. Among the obsessives one meets the same people again and again. It's not so strange."

"Do you know the way back?"

"No."

Basso sighed. "That's a shame."

"I went up on the Mountain. They took my memory of the path back. It seems they have defenses."

"What's up there, then? What kind of forces? What've they got in the way of weapons? Everyone says there's going to be a war one day. Our bosses want what they've got or their bosses are just sick of looking down on us. Are they getting ready for war?"

"I don't know."

They walked for a while longer.

Basso said, "If Ivy wants to help you, she'll help you. If Brace-Bel wants to help you, he'll help you. Do you understand? But if you're here to steal from them, it'll be my job to break your neck."

"I understand."

"Don't be here to steal Ivy away, or I'll kill you."

"I understand."

"Here she is, then."

Basso pointed out across the lawn to a stone shrine, where Ivy sat, in a simple white dress, legs folded, apparently waiting impatiently. Her head was tilted up toward a little black device in the shrine's low ceiling, from which a distant muttering voice could be heard.

Ivy Low, my name is . . ."

But she stood, without looking at Arjun, without listening to him, and strode over to Basso.

"Basso," she said. "There are men at the gate."

"Sorry, Ivy. I was looking for this bloke, like you asked me."

"That's all right," she said. "I heard them talking, over the listening-tubes. They're scared to come in."

"Who is it?"

"Know-Nothings. That pest Maury again. They're here about last night's explosions. They have questions."

"I'll go talk to them."

"They want to know, did we see anything? Did we hear anything? Did we see anyone fleeing the scene?"

"Well, Miss Low, did we?"

"We did *not,* Mr. Basso. The whole household was fast asleep at an early hour."

"Understood."

"Don't let them talk to Brace-Bel. You know how he is. Say he's ill."

Basso nodded and walked off down the garden path.

Arjun had been studying Ivy's face. She was eerily similar to Ruth, but a Ruth *narrowed,* somehow, perfected, stiffened—machine-tooled to a fine degree of precision. Perhaps it was the eyes, or the charged elaborate curls of her dark hair; perhaps it was the way she stood.

"Ivy," Arjun said, "your sisters sent me . . ."

"Shut up a moment. Let me take a look at you."

"Ivy . . ."

"A ghost. A visitor. You don't look like much. Do you know the way out, then?"

"I don't know. I don't . . ."

"You don't remember. Yes. I've heard that story before. The Mountain, the fall, its awful defenses. Poor old you. How did you get there?"

"Ivy, your sisters miss you."

"Did I ask about my sisters? How did you get there? How do I get *out?*"

"I don't know."

"Well—*think.*"

It was midafternoon when she let him go. His head reeling from questions and her sharp voice, he walked back across the lawns.

Out of long habit he'd tried to mislead—but he couldn't lie to her. She was a great deal cleverer than he was, and impatient.

He couldn't tell her what she wanted to know either. He didn't have the answers. All he had were handfuls of mad images, some scraps of music.

You're a mess, she said. *Go get something to eat. And* think. *I'm not done with you yet.*

He tried to find Stevie, but she seemed to have hidden herself. He took some bread and cheese from the pantry. Mrs. Down forbade it, but he defied her. He ate in the library, which was silent, and echoing, and in fact largely empty of books; it was not an Age for books. The pride of the poor collection were three copies of Brace-Bel's own works, scavenged presumably from flea markets out in the city somewhere. One of the books was a scholarly edition of *Brace-Bel's Collected Letters,* full of condescending annotations by a Professor Kay S. Pooler, who'd lived and worked at some intermediate time between Brace-Bel's own life and these last days of the city. Her notes tried to explain Brace-Bel's times by analogies to her own now-almost-equally-distant times, and the main effect of the fat hardbound volume was to leave Arjun headachy and disturbed. He reshelved it and went for a walk.

In the late afternoon a thin grey smoke was still visible over the top of the Hill. Arjun watched it from the second-floor windows on the landing of the great staircase.

Something in the wreckage of the night before still burned. The handiwork of the black-masked men lingered awkwardly, outstaying its welcome.

"Who are they?" Arjun asked.

"Huh?" Basso, who'd been at work on the stairs, rested his broom on the banisters and came to the window.

"The men who did this. Four men in black masks came running past and . . ."

"Do I look like I know anything about that?"

"Mr. Basso, you very much look as though you might."

"Maybe I do. Maybe I used to know some people. All right. You see, the Black Masks are for the workers. In the old days we used to march, and we used to down tools if the bosses weren't treating us right, but now when you do that the Know-Nothings come crack your skull; so sometimes someone cracks back. Whoever's estate got blown up, they probably own some factory where something happened. Or somebody did something. Or something. I dunno."

"So the Black Masks blew up their boss's home? Perhaps there were women and children there."

"Perhaps," Basso acknowledged. "There's women and children everywhere. Ask Brace-Bel what he thinks of *families*. Besides if you don't . . ."

"I hear my name invoked." Brace-Bel descended the stairs from the upper floors like a pale cloud. He wore a silk dressing gown and held a wet cloth to his forehead. "Oh. A fire. Shut up, Basso. Do not bore our guest. He like me is from a finer time. The dull ephemera of *politics* is no explanation for the beauty of this act. Arjun, the end of time is the condition of the impoverishment of the imagination. Look out over the city for a thousand miles and all you will see is repetition. The same simple figures played over and over on poor instruments. Whoever set that fire interrupted the monotony for a night. That curling smoke is a question mark over the world. An exclamation! Perhaps I should work in fire, not words."

"Perhaps you should, Mr. Brace-Bel," Arjun said. "I want to talk to you about Ivy. About Shay."

"Later, later." Brace-Bel, taking slow, achy steps, descended toward the main hall.

"I want to talk to you about your devices and weapons."

"Later. My head throbs like an open pox sore."

The household ate dinner together. They sat around a great circular table and fumbled expensive cutlery and ravenously dug into Mrs. Down's beef stew. In the light from the fireplace their costumes cast strange and monstrous shadows on the walls. Stained napkins were folded into the shapes of peacocks and roses. Brace-Bel led his household in a blasphemous toast against all priests and all Gods and all authority and against the nest of vileness that was his mother and mothers in general, who had birthed him into this city and thus cast his pure and refined spirit in that fat uncomely form, a flesh from which there was little escape; and against *fathers,* too, while he was at it . . .

His servants made a vague pretense at listening, at first, in the grudging way of employees in the presence of an eccentric boss; when it became clear that Brace-Bel intended to talk for a while they went back to their eating, and whispered among themselves.

Brace-Bel sat down with a thump and a sigh of relief passed round the table.

His face was very waxy and pale and yellow. He drooped and sagged and repeatedly dropped his spoon into the stew. Ivy sat at his left and largely ignored him. When he pawed at her she slapped his hand away; he looked momentarily hurt, and then appeared to forget the insult.

From time to time Brace-Bel's eyes lighted on Arjun, who sat at the far edge of the table. A look of surprise and shrewd suspicion crossed his face.

Brace-Bel kept his stick, with its strange glittering crystal, close at hand, lying on the table by his wineglass, and fingered it thoughtfully.

Arjun sat between thin pale Stevie, still dressed in grey feathers, and a tattooed young man in a plain business suit. Stevie's eyes were fixed on her plate; he tried to talk to her but she mumbled and turned away. He wondered what Basso had said to her to make her afraid.

He decided that his presence was unnerving her. "Excuse me," he said, and he put down his napkin and stood. He circled round the table. He asked the young shaven-headed man on Ivy's left to swap places, and was told to fuck off. Arjun dug a few coins from his pockets and offered them. It seemed to be an acceptable trade; the young man took them with a grunt and slouched away from the table, carrying his plate and his fork like weapons in tight little fists.

Arjun sat. "Ivy," he said, "I promised your sisters I would bring you home. Will you come?"

"Of course not. Why should I?"

"Will you tell me why not?"

"I believe in what Mr. Brace-Bel is doing here. I *belong* here."

"Yes," Brace-Bel said. "Yes, we are on the verge of a remarkable breakthrough into . . ."

She sighed coldly; he blushed, went silent, amused himself by poking at his stew as if trying to murder it.

Arjun said, "I would go back to your sisters and tell them you are happy here, but they might not believe me. I am not very persuasive, as you can see. Will you come back with me for a day, to tell them you're well? Frankly I think they fear you may be dead. Come back for a day. Mr. Brace-Bel will survive without you for a day or two."

"They don't want me back for a day."

"I'm sure they would."

"They want me back *forever*."

"Yes, perhaps, but . . ."

"Families," Brace-Bel announced drunkenly, "are a *curse*. I am a better father to my creatures than any they were born with. And a better mother, too. I'll birth them all into a better world. I'll sire Gods and Goddesses out of them!" Brace-Bel stood, rang his wineglass with a fork for silence, then lost his thread and sat down again. "Why are you still here?" he demanded, rounding on Arjun, leaning across Ivy—who moved her chair deftly back out of his way—and gesturing with his fork.

"Everyone expects me to disappear. I don't know why."

"I wish *I* could disappear." Brace-Bel frowned. "Why are you still here? Ivy's mine. I need her."

"I promised to bring her home," Arjun said.

"She doesn't want to come. She told you that herself."

The table had gone quiet. Brace-Bel's servants flicked their eyes from Arjun, to Ivy, to their master.

"How I can be sure she means it?" Arjun asked.

Brace-Bel shrugged. "Most women do not know their own heart; not Ivy. Ivy is a woman of unusual genius."

"How did you make your fortune, Mr. Brace-Bel?"

"Money comes easily to me, because I disdain it."

"Why do the police and the Know-Nothings leave you alone here? They hunted me; when they suspected I was an alien here they were ready to shoot me. You flaunt it. They tolerate you. Why?"

"A fair question."

"You told me yourself that you have a great stock of unusual devices. Something in your horrible garden drove poor Mr. Thayer mad. I am very unsure about Basso; his eagerness to serve you after what you did to his colleagues strikes me as suspicious. You play with minds."

"A fair point. I understand your implication."

"You see, then—I cannot be sure that Ivy's will is her own."

"What evidence would suffice to persuade you?"

"I don't know."

"Then you are in a difficult position, Arjun."

"Yes. Here I am."

"Here you are indeed. This house does have other work, you know. I am a busy man. Your presence is a *distraction*."

"I'm sorry—I must compound the offense. I came here both for the Low sisters' sake, and for my own reasons. A creature told me your name. A Beast. A *lizard*. Suddenly the name *dragon* rises in my memory. Others I've told of this have thought me mad, but I think you'll hear me out."

"I suppose I will."

"It told me it spoke prophecy. It did *this* to my hand. It promised in return to tell me who I am, why I came here, where I must go. But we were interrupted. It gave me your name. The Know-Nothings hold it captive in a cellar under a museum. Perhaps it sent me to you because you can save it."

"Me?"

"It owes me prophecy. It may be able to tell me what happened to me on the Mountain, how I can return there. First I have to free it. What weapons do you have, Mr. Brace-Bel? Do you have something to confuse guards? Something to open locks or bend bars? I suspect you might."

"The Know-Nothings hold this creature? I don't pick fights with powers greater than me, my friend. My position here is precarious."

"You told me your story. Of *course* you pick fights."

Brace-Bel smiled. "I only want to go home, my friend."

"Perhaps the creature can help you."

"Now I wonder if you came here to steal my devices."

Arjun thought for a moment. Ivy was watching him closely; it was important to impress her with his honesty. "I have considered it. I would if I thought I could."

Brace-Bel's red eyes narrowed. "A thief," he spat.

"They're not yours. You took them from Shay."

"Shay left me stranded here. I felt myself entitled."

"I met Shay," Arjun said. "If I recall rightly he injured me, too. I need his devices, now."

"You can't have them."

"What if I promised to bring them back?"

Brace-Bel drummed his fat fingers on the tablecloth. "I should have Basso whip you out of here."

"I wonder why you haven't already," Arjun admitted. "It's very gracious of you to feed me."

"Perhaps I'm lonely. Lonely for the company of men who remember the old days. Look at you! You were touched by the miraculous. I can see it in your eyes." Brace-Bel reached out and fondled Ivy's leg. "Not even Ivy, my dear Ivy, can say that. There are things you will understand that no one else can." Ivy rolled her eyes. "I still suspect that my ritual summoned you here for that very purpose. My own ghost. I will not force you to leave. In fact"—Brace-Bel flung his fork across the table, to clatter against the wall behind Basso's head—"I *forbid* you to leave. I wish to observe you. Mr. Basso, please make a note of my wishes."

Arjun shrugged. He had been unclear all day whether he was a guest, or an unwelcome invader, or a prisoner; it was something of a relief to have his situation clarified. "I don't intend to leave. I hope to talk to you again in the morning when you may be more open to persuasion."

"I am rarely awake in the mornings. I have grand plans for tonight's debauchery."

"I'll wait. I can be patient."

"Has it occurred to you that if I've mesmerized Ivy, and Basso, it follows that I could mesmerize *you*? I could make you forget your mission. I could make you serve me. Does that not worry you?"

"Not especially, Mr. Brace-Bel. I believe myself to be quite strong-willed."

Brace-Bel raised an eyebrow. "You think your mind is invulnerable? A question, Arjun: what happened to you on the Mountain?"

While Arjun thought that over, the household rose from dinner. Apparently Basso or Ivy had given some signal. The servants flocked, hissing and gossiping, away from the table and toward the dressing rooms.

Brace-Bel was picking his teeth with a silver pin. "Will you join us, Arjun?"

"I . . . I think I would prefer not to."

"Shame. You can watch if you please. Maybe we'll summon up a more sporting and playful ghost tonight. Maybe you will be the first of many. Stay with us and bring us good luck. Try not to vanish in the night."

* * *

Arjun watched the proceedings for a while, standing on the edge of the ballroom in the shadows.

Now that he knew what he was seeing the whole thing seemed rather pathetic and sordid. Brace-Bel's servants mostly seemed *bored*. Their motions were listless, their costumes absurd, their steps heavy.

When Brace-Bel started laying into Stevie with the whip—he'd been performing some ritual of obeisance to her with a silver goblet and blood-red wine, and when he suddenly cast it aside and stood, eyes wild, Ivy was there to press the whip into his hand, and she stood behind him smiling, hands folded—when Brace-Bel started with the whip Arjun's first instinct was to wrestle the weapon away again and try his luck a second time with Basso; but soon the whip was in *Stevie's* hand and Brace-Bel was on his knees, a white helpless shape like a peeled potato, and Arjun, not knowing what else to do, walked away in silence. As he left Brace-Bel's whole household began in unison to rut, with a great shaking of feathers and clattering of jewels and horns and gears and chain mail. Even the chamber orchestra downed their instruments and descended into the fray. Arjun turned at the door to see Ivy, alone, standing aloof from the scene. She smiled coldly at him. Her eyes shone by candlelight. He closed the door and left them to it.

Distant moans and shrieks and grunts followed Arjun downstairs.

In the morning the household felt cold and bruised, awkward and exhausted. Another night's work and the barriers of reality remained stubbornly unbroken, and the Gods kept their distance.

Arjun took Brace-Bel's *Collected Letters* down into the garden and sat with it in one of the shrines. He read Brace-Bel's long impassioned diatribe against the asylums of Ararat and the priests and judges who wielded the word *madness* as a weapon against free thought and . . .

According to the scholars who'd annotated Brace-Bel's letter his accusations were largely unreasonable. But Arjun had spent time in a madhouse, and he remembered the bars; he remembered being *watched*.

He realized that Ivy was there in the garden watching him; it seemed she'd been watching him for some time.

"How was last night's . . . ah . . . ?" he asked.

She didn't answer.

"I remember Brace-Bel," he said. "In his own time he was considered mad. Much of what he says is true. There *were* Gods, there *were* better times in the city, there *are* doors, there *are* paths. I have walked them myself. But Brace-Bel will never find them, Ivy. He's a fool. You're wasting your time here."

She raised an eyebrow. He felt himself being minutely scrutinized for flaws.

He wondered what kind of desperation would cause a woman of her evident intelligence to follow Brace-Bel, to remain with Brace-Bel, to put her hopes in Brace-Bel after night after night of failure and absurdity.

"And you?" she said. "What about you?"

"What *about* me?"

She stepped closer. "You know what I fucking want."

"I imagine, since you're here with Brace-Bel, since your own time is what it is, that you want to leave the world behind. To escape."

"To *understand*. That's part of it. Can you help me?"

"Yes. Come home. There are better times out there, and I remember the way. Come home to your sisters, and we can all go together."

She leaned in very close. Her eyes were the green of diodes, synthetic chemicals, strange stars. She sneered. "You want to be part of the fucking family, do you? If you had any sense you'd run away now and never come back, and you'd go alone. You don't understand *anything*."

Her sudden anger shocked him. Anger and . . . hurt?

"You told Brace-Bel something about a Beast that talked," she said. She flashed him a brilliant smile, and for a moment she reminded him again of Ruth, and he was charmed; then he saw how cold her eyes were. "Now *that's* interesting. Tell me everything about it."

He told her. She listened in silence, nodding with excitement, as if the story of the Beast reminded her of something important, confirmed something she'd begun to doubt. Without warning she walked off. He tried to follow but she stalked fearlessly across the trapped and deadly garden where he only dared *creep,* and he lost her among the willows and shrines.

After that she avoided Arjun for the rest of the day. So did Stevie.

Brace-Bel saw him reading the *Letters* and pronounced a terrible curse on all scholars and antiquarians, then withdrew to prepare for the evening's performance.

Arjun declined to participate. He fell asleep while the household was still at work.

Alarms woke him; or rather the memory of alarms—there was a terrible mechanical howl and drone that suddenly cut short with a whine and a crackle in the moment before he woke, and Arjun wondered, as he stumbled to his feet, in the dark, head pounding, if he'd dreamed it—but the house was full of shouting and movement and banging doors, and he knew at once that something dreadful was at the door.

He fumbled for the lamp on the shelf. He couldn't light it. No spark, only a dismal fart of inert gas.

They have found you again.

He ran out into the corridor. The shouting was coming from upstairs, from the ballroom. He staggered in the dark into a dressing table and broke a vase and bruised his hip.

He found the ballroom door shut. Behind it he heard Brace-Bel's voice, Basso's voice.

He pushed the door open.

Inside was shifting darkness, windowless, packed with nervous sweaty bodies costumed in inhuman shapes. Only the crystal on Brace-Bel's stick gave a cold light; it reflected in Brace-Bel's eyes, and Basso's eyes, and Ivy's, and off Stevie's jewels, and the boy's mirror-plates, and off white feathers and brass buttons.

Basso was pointing a gun at Arjun. He lowered it with a sigh and said, "Only you. False fuckin' alarm. What were you doing in the garden?"

"No," said Brace-Bel, pulling on his trousers. "There's something else coming." He raised his stick; the crystal was very bright now, in the dark. "See?"

"Something set off the alarms," Ivy said. "And then *silenced* them. Arjun can't know how to do that. Even I don't know how to do that."

"Only a few minutes ago," Brace-Bel said, buttoning up his coat, "each of our musicians suffered the embarrassment of a broken string or a snapped reed. All of our candles guttered. The electric light died. My watch—see?—has gone still. I'll wager good money that the milk in the pantry is spoiled. Arjun is a sad and somber little man and his presence may kill a joyful mood, but can he break clocks? He cannot. Something comes. At last something comes."

"Brace-Bel," Arjun said. "There's something I should have told you. I am being pursued. There are two men who pursued me down the Mountain, and have pursued me since. I am very afraid of them. If I run from here I think they will leave you alone. Ivy, will you come now?"

Basso raised the gun again, and looked from Ivy to Arjun and back again.

Brace-Bel appeared not to have heard; he was staring with eager anticipation at the darkness of the doorway.

There was a hollow and distant sound of footsteps; slow, methodical, regular as the ticking of a clock.

Brace-Bel's servants shuffled nervously in the dark. "You should all run," Arjun said. "Go on, go on!"

"At last," Brace-Bel said. "At *last*. Can you feel them coming? This is magic. *This* is the uncanny. The walls of reality shake. The doors are opening. Together we have called them here. Something comes and the laws of science tremble." He removed his watch and stamped it flat.

"You don't go nowhere," Basso said. "You don't go nowhere, Arjun. You come here and tell me what this is."

"They are *Gods*," Brace-Bel said. "Feel how everything quivers at their coming."

The footsteps grew closer.

"They are not Gods," Arjun said. "They are the Hollows." He felt suddenly ashamed and embarrassed, and mumbled, "That's only a name. I don't know what they are."

Ivy's eyes were wild and excited, her cheeks flushed; she hovered between Brace-Bel and Arjun and seemed unsure whether to be frightened or thrilled or both.

"Close that fucking door," Basso said.

Arjun and Brace-Bel said, *"Doors won't keep them out."*

And in fact it seemed clear that no door *could* have kept the Hollows out, for they appeared in the middle of the ballroom without passing through the doorway, and no one saw them enter. *Two.* They stepped out silently from the crowd of Brace-Bel's servants. The young man in mirrors stepped aside, tinkling, to let one of them pass. Mrs. Down, who wore rags, flinched from the other. They stood side by side in the cold light of Brace-Bel's crystal.

They wore dark suits. They were of average height, and no particular build. Their faces were not quite clear in the shadows and glitter of the ballroom, but appeared doughy, baggy, *scarred,* poorly shaven. One was pale, one dark. Their blank eyes were fixed on Arjun, who was about to speak, who was about to ask, *what did I do to offend you, who is your master,* when Brace-Bel stepped forward.

"Welcome! Welcome. I have *waited* for this moment. Since I was stranded here. No doubt it pains you to come forward to these terrible last days of the city but your presence here is . . ." Brace-Bel lowered himself stiffly to his knees and shuffled forward with his head bowed.

Basso lowered his gun, uncertain, and Arjun stepped back, toward the doors, looking around for Ivy; she'd gone.

The intruders looked blankly at Arjun, and blankly down at Brace-Bel. They appeared confused. There was a coldness in the air around them.

There was a distinct sense of *shame*; they radiated it. Arjun felt very conscious of his own wrongness and awkwardness. Brace-Bel's servants blushed and shifted.

Only Brace-Bel seemed oblivious to shame.

"I don't know your names," Brace-Bel said. "As you can see I am a pious man but I don't know your names. Once I raged against your kind, but I have learned the error of my ways. I have made a particular study of the Gods of the old city; look around you!" He gestured at his servants.

The intruders moved their heads with camera-shutter sudden-ness to regard each of Brace-Bel's servants in turn.

Stevie attempted a curtsy, and stumbled.

When she lifted her head one of the two Hollows was suddenly standing over her, examining her head to toe with scrupulous ex-acting slowness. She raised her eyes to it and something passed be-tween them; it was impossible to be sure what. Arjun watched as Stevie's eyes fixed intently on the thing's unremarkable face. She seemed to be trying to solve a complex nagging puzzle; she seemed to be trying to recall something important. It was easier for Arjun to look at Stevie than at the one of the two that stood over her. She bit her lip as if on the verge of saying: I remember you! She didn't rise from her crouch but her face seemed poised finely between ter-ror and contempt—as if she was unsure whether that one of the two was a boss to be bowed to and pleased and amused, or a beggar to be driven from her door. The thing awoke contradictory emotions, none pleasant.

Stevie had played the Spirit of the Lights in the evening's per-formance. She wore a thin dress of sequins and shimmer that left her bony and bruised back bare. There were fake jewels in her hair and her ears and hung on her neck and woven into her dress. She wore bracelets and bangles. She'd carried a candle in a stained-glass lantern—it had gone cold and dark as the Hollows approached and she'd left it at her feet. She stepped back and stumbled on it, shat-tering it, as the thing reached a hand slowly toward her hair. Its thin fingers shook with—displeasure? Outrage? Fingers brushed and knotted and tangled in her lank yellow hair and she tugged loose with a shriek. And then as she staggered away for the safety of the crowd and found that crowd inching away from her, refusing to look at her, creeping into the shadows—then the glass jewels of her dress began to glitter with a nervous uncertain light.

Arjun stepped forward and called for the intruders to *Stop,* but their interest was momentarily diverted from him.

While the one stood watching Stevie shriek—its hands hang-ing loose at its side, twitching, as though it was not sure what to do with itself—the other held a hank of Mrs. Down's rags in its fist, and those rags now *stank,* and seemed to stretch like snakes and writhe. And it seemed there was a third, and perhaps a fourth, step-ping into the crowd and fixing on the young man in the mirrors, who was now bleeding from a hundred sharp incisions, and on the pierced girl, who also bled, and whose flesh now crawled and bulged as things grew and delved beneath; something sharp like a hooked steel finger erupted from her cheek spraying blood. All this was visible by the light of Stevie's jewels, which burned and blazed now and lit the room with glare and stark shadows. The young man in mirrors began to divide against himself; a sharp dark fault line opened down his screaming face. A fifth Hollow and a sixth moved in the crowd. Arjun called for them to *Stop* again, but they still ignored him. Stevie's hair caught fire; Arjun reached for her hand and withdrew, his fingers blistered. He remembered now those men in their dark suits; he remembered them emerging from the shadows of doorways and windows as he turned up and up onto the streets that led to the Mountain. They were merciless to things that were not in their place. That was what they had been made for. They found Brace-Bel's display unacceptable; they would turn it neatly against itself until it was not there anymore. He could not remember how to stop them. He could not *remember*.

Basso shoved Arjun aside, raised his arm, fired a shot; one of the Hollows dropped silently to the floor. A moment later Basso's body jerked and shuddered as a dozen bullets struck it from all sides, and Basso dropped dead.

Stevie was now impossible to look at. She was a terrible brightness that burned the retinas and filled the room with shadows and after-images: the sun's flashing light caught in the glass of a high window, and behind that window a thin girl, suspended, screaming. Then there was an explosion, and then darkness, full of motion.

"I was warned," Brace-Bel said. He stood at Arjun's shoulder. His voice was madly calm. "Mr. Shay warned me. He wanted me to assault the Mountain, you may recall. Are these the guardians of the Mountain?"

"They're the Hollows," Arjun said.

"Are they the guardians of the Mountain?"

"I expect so. *Yes*."

"Then Shay armed me against them. I wonder—will this work?"

Brace-Bel raised his stick, then rapped it sharply on the floor. As Arjun's eyes adjusted to the shadows he could see the men in dark suits—six? Seven? More?—approaching with some curiosity Brace-Bel's stick, and the glowing crystal on it. They identified it as a thing that should not exist and swarmed in like sharks. Distant undersea shadows rippled across their white faces and the stone's light glittered in a dozen dark eyes.

"Come on, then!" Brace-Bel said. "I have no idea, Arjun," he added, "how this device is intended to operate."

Arjun silently withdrew. He stumbled against a young man half naked in furs who crouched sobbing on the floor; Arjun lifted him by his arm and sent him with a shove on his way through the door.

Brace-Bel lifted the stick higher and let it shine brighter. Dark intent shapes pressed in around it and around him. He shivered; his whole fat body shook. He muttered. The forms around him lengthened as they approached. It was now hard to tell their shapes from their shadows. There was strain and stretching, shiver and scrape. As Arjun closed his eyes there was *shattering*. When he opened them again the Hollows were gone.

The electric lights in the ceiling flickered into life and the bloody room was starkly visible again.

The curtains were singed and the windows shattered; a cold wind blew in.

Brace-Bel stood quaking. Tears ran down his sallow cheeks. The stick—did it still shine? It was hard to say now—fell from his hand. "Tonight was to end in pleasure," he said. "Such cruelty! Such . . . Where is Ivy? Oh Gods, where is Ivy?"

Seven servants had died, including Basso; Ivy wasn't among them. She came back into the room once it was silent and looked around and said: "We have to bury these bodies."

"They were brave men and women," Brace-Bel said. "Each was a great love."

"Yeah," Ivy said. "The police'll be here soon, or the Know-Nothings, after all that bloody noise and light."

There were no shovels in Brace-Bel's house—no useful implements of any kind, in fact—and the bodies could not be buried. Instead the survivors dragged the dead down to the wine cellar. Brace-Bel was too overcome to assist. Arjun dragged Stevie by her blackened withered arms; he wore gloves and a cloth over his face, and managed not to vomit. Ivy locked the cellar door, and disposed of the key.

After that the servants dispersed. They collected their meager belongings from their rooms and vanished into the night. They shucked their fabulous costumes and pulled on plain sweaters and skirts. They crept up to Arjun and whispered: *what were they?*—and he shrugged—and *will more of them come?*—and he couldn't answer. They left one by one, as if scared to be together, as if unable to look at each other. Brace-Bel, sobbing, didn't seem to notice their leaving. Ivy seemed not to care; she'd lost interest in them. By morning only Ivy and Arjun remained to keep Brace-Bel company. They were unable to clean the ballroom floor of blood.

In the morning there was a cold grey fog, and all the windows were broken and the house was cold, and besides the whole building stank of blood and burning, so Arjun and Ivy brought Brace-Bel outside into the garden to sit in one of the shrines. Brace-Bel wore a thick shiny green bathrobe and hugged himself like a miserable caterpillar. He stared glassily and muttered. He yearned doglike after Ivy with his eyes. "I am quite shattered," he said. "Quite shattered. Everything comes to ruin."

Ivy scavenged in the dewy grass of the garden, and found nothing but torn wires, broken glass, fused plastic, torn webs, inert lumps of metal and bone. "Everything's broken," she said. "They broke everything." She shook her head. She stood with her hands on her hips, as if awed at the methodical and precise destruction.

She lifted Brace-Bel's stick from his nerveless and limp hand. She shook it and peered at the crystal. "Does this look flawed to you?"

Arjun shook his head. "I don't know."

"Does it look broken? Does it look used up?"

"Ivy, I don't know. Does it matter? The Hollow Men are all gone."

She looked at him like he was stupid. "There'll be more. There are always more of that sort of thing. Don't you know anything?"

"I'm constantly surprised by how little I know."

"Pathetic. I'll be ready for them if they come again."

She gave Brace-Bel his stick back. Then she went back to searching in the grass. "Come away," Arjun said. She ignored him.

At midmorning the Know-Nothings drew up at the gate.

They came mob-handed. Two flat-backed horse-drawn vehicles like little black omnibuses carried six men apiece. A closed wagon shuttered in black canvas followed. The men disembarked and stood at the gate, scowling and swearing, rubbing their hands and stamping their feet to keep warm. They wore long black coats. There were not enough cigarettes to go round. The horses steamed and shifted. Their leader made a megaphone out of his cupped hands and called out, "Morning, all. All well, Mr. Brace-Bel?" It was Inspector Maury, from the checkpoint, in fine good humor. "Lot of noise last night, Mr. Brace-Bel!"

"Hide him," Ivy told Arjun. He nodded, helped Brace-Bel to his feet, and led him back into the house, by a circuitous route that was not visible from the gate. He sat Brace-Bel on a bench in the library, and watched from the window as Ivy went down to meet Maury.

"Look," Brace-Bel said, pulling books from the shelves. "All blank. All gone." Arjun shushed him.

Ivy was a tiny form in the distance. He saw her open the gate. He saw her shrug and point back at the house. *A fire in the kitchen,* was what she'd be saying. *Nothing to worry about. No Black Masks here, no ghosts, no nothing.*

Arjun had tried to warn her how much Maury, how much the Know-Nothings, hated Brace-Bel, how much they resented his wealth and his impunity; but she'd been so coldly confident of her ability to lie to them, to confuse and charm them, that he was almost surprised to see them grab her by her arms and drag her, seemingly too stunned to resist, into the back of the black wagon.

For a moment it occurred to him that she'd *wanted* to be arrested. She frightened him; he was willing to believe strange things about her.

Then the Know-Nothings entered the garden—slowly, nervously. When no unnatural curse blasted them, when their feet didn't burst into flames, no one was turned into a frog or a pig, no one went blind and no one went mad—then they realized that Brace-Bel's garden, if it had ever had any power or mystery, was stripped of it now, was just grass and weeds and paving-stones, was just a place in the city like any other; and then they picked up their pace. They were laughing with each other as they approached the house and joking about who'd get to have a go on Brace-Bel's whores and who'd have to settle for the rent boys . . .

Arjun dragged Brace-Bel up off the bench, and together they fled out the back of the house by the servants' quarters and the overflowing bins and rubbish heaps, which had *still* not been cleared away, and maybe now never would be. Behind them, as they fled for the estate's rear gate, there was the sound of Know-Nothings shouting, *stop, you fuckers, stop,* and the crash of their boots, and the hateful barking of their dogs. Before them, across the road, as Arjun fumbled with the rusted padlock on the gate and Brace-Bel slumped bonelessly against the wall, there was the faint sound of someone in the garden of the next estate over practicing a simple tune, badly, on an expensive flute, while a nervous-sounding tutor muttered encouragement, *yes, Mrs. Shandy, that's excellent progress, very good,* and as Arjun listened to the stumbling, halting music and in his mind gently *mended* and completed it, the padlock suddenly leapt in his hands chiming like a bell, and when he fell through the gate, pulling Brace-Bel after him, it was warm, and he was lying on soft grass, and the blue sky overhead sang with swallows and larks, and he had no idea where he was or how he'd got there.

ELEVEN

A Warning–Authority–Family
Arguments–Corruption–Resistance

Ruth

The **Know-Nothings** took Ruth and Zeigler back to the Chapter-house. Ruth walked in silence. Silence was best—talking only made them angry, only showed weakness. Zeigler, stunned, outraged, frightened, seemed inclined to argue; she put an arm on his elbow to say, *keep quiet*.

The local Chapterhouse stood in what used to be the Hall of Trade, on Holcroft Square, across from the Museum. The old ornate pillars and friezes of the Hall of Trade were blackened with soot and grime. The grand brass-bound doors to the old lobby were locked, forgotten, jammed with decades of wet windblown rubbish and leaves; the Know-Nothings went in and out by the back door, the old servants' entrance. A small sign by the side of the door read CIVIC LEAGUE LOCAL 141C, beneath which was a list of the League's local corporate sponsors—Holcroft, Patagan, Axis, half a dozen others. Otherwise the building was unmarked. Everyone knew what it housed.

Inside it smelled of beer, cigarettes, oil lamps; sweat and fear. The sound of typing rattled through the corridors. Young men lounged with their feet up on the tables, played cards or darts, stared into space—aimless, stupid, restless time-wasting. Some of them were people Ruth recognized. In the outside world a few of them were almost friends—she didn't much like Know-Nothings on principle, but people did what they had to to get by, and . . .

In here things were different. They looked at her coldly—like a *thing*. A ghost. She shivered, went pale.

"In here," Siddon said.

They put her and Zeigler in separate rooms.

And to her surprise, her slowly growing relief, they didn't beat her, didn't so much as lay a hand on her. Her questioner was an old man, round and grey and shoulderless, with the look of one of those who'd been in the League so long that they'd settled into it as a kind of comfortable retirement. He was almost courtly. He called her *a pretty young thing,* and she didn't tell him to get lost, she batted her eyelashes and spoke softly, thinking: *better to be ashamed of yourself later than shot in the head now.*

"What did that . . . ghost say to you?"

"I don't remember. I don't know." Plead ignorance. That was what they liked to hear.

"What did you mean about a, a monster?"

"Don't know. I'm sorry, I don't know. I had a dream, once. That Museum scares me, sir. Who knows what's in it? I don't know. I was upset, because of the . . ."

I don't know. That was the catechism. Over and over. The interrogator nodded, coughed, smiled, stared at her with weak pale eyes. *I don't know anything about anything.*

It wasn't an interrogation; it was a warning. *Keep your mouth shut.* She bowed her head. She could take a hint. *I never saw anything. I don't know anything.* By the end of the day she almost believed it.

They released her and Zeigler both at the same time. It was evening, and cold. Zeigler's nose was bloody and his scalp bruised, his spectacles broken, the fingers of his left hand swelling and the nails going black. "They took my notes, Ruth, can you believe it?"

The warmth of relief ebbed away, and Ruth began to shake with the fear and anger she'd been holding back all day—but the Know-Nothings were still watching, so all she said was, "Shh, please, Mr. Zeigler."

She helped him home.

Maury

Inspector Maury rode across the city in the back of the black motor-wagon, sat on the hard rattling benches, under the darkness of black canvas, in the constant smell of leaking fuel, in the constant drone of the wagon's engine.

The motor-wagon was a rare and remarkable thing. It was one of the perks of his rank and his special status, his roving and open-ended jurisdiction—as were the security detail who rode behind in the motorcar.

Even by motor-powered vehicles, it was a long trip from Brace-Bel's house on Barking Hill northwest to Fosdyke, and Holcroft Plaza, and the Museum.

The woman—Low comma Ivy—the *prisoner*—sat on the bench across from him, and stared defiantly into his eyes. A contest of wills was taking place, and he wasn't entirely sure he was winning.

She'd answered *none* of his questions about Brace-Bel, or about the Arjun fellow who'd fled with him, or about anything at all, until, on a whim, he'd said, "Arjun, then—don't pretend you never talked to him—he says there's some kind of monster in the old Fosdyke Museum—did he tell you anything about that?" She smiled; her eyes lit up.

"The Beast. The lizard. It has scars, Inspector—I've seen it. I may even know who made it, in what laboratories."

She wouldn't say anything more, so of course he slapped her around a bit. In fact he bloodied her up a little more than felt proper, with a pretty face like that. But she seemed indifferent to pain, contemptuous of it. He had a sense that she was waiting, somewhat bored, for him to reach an obvious conclusion. She made him feel unimaginative and small. He stopped and lit a cigarette to cover the shaking of his hands.

"Fosdyke," he told his bodyguards. "You heard. There's something sick going on in the Fosdyke Chapterhouse." That was the nature of Maury's special rank and status. Internal investigations. He *watched the watchmen*. That was a line from an old book he'd had burned. "We're going to have some fucking questions for the Fosdyke Local. Take this bitch with us. Back of the·wagon, tie her hands."

Now he sat across from her, in the back of the wagon, and tried to meet her gaze.

Maury's wife had died, what, ten years ago? Since then he hadn't had much in the way of dealings with women—what one did with ghosts, of course, not counting. His wife had been a good woman, but plain, and thick as two short planks. He didn't have much experience with beauty. The Low woman made him uncomfortable. He felt his authority slipping in her presence. Once, as they went north through Marriot, he jumped up and slapped her, and she sneered back at him, "Did that help, Inspector?" It didn't much. He didn't do it again. The wagon rattled and strained up and down hills, over iron bridges, into the night.

And so Inspector Maury hit Local 141C at just past midnight like a *storm,* like a wicked gale blown down from the Mountain, that rattles the windows and strips the trees and fills strong men with nightmares—that bloody woman might not have been scared of him, but those lads were all right. Midnight shift in the Chapterhouse, skeleton crew, a few pale unbloodied lads hanging around over the last gaslamp in the mess hall, drinking, smoking, farting, telling each other ghost stories; none of them ready for Maury, who'd been building up a great head of steam in the back of the wagon, and was ready to explode. "You want to see my fucking papers, boy? Do you? Are you challenging my fucking authority?" *No sir, no sir,* too fucking right they weren't. Maury's own personal staff flanked him, cracking their knuckles, ready for the word, ready for just so much as a *nod* from Maury—and he thought about it, he definitely thought about it. Local 141C's night shift looked ready to piss themselves. Can't get the quality anymore. This lot had a particular look to them—furtive, corrupt. "I hear you've been keeping *secrets.*" Oh, they knew—he could smell it. "Keys to the Museum, boys. Let's go digging." They didn't dare say no. Throughout all this the prisoner, the Low woman, Ivy, stood by his side like she was his own personal bodyguard or advisor or something, and it didn't seem quite right, but it didn't seem exactly wrong either.

Through the locked halls, filled with shrouded and dusty relics— between two great bronze knights on horseback, offering up their swords as if in surrender—under a stone arch carved with fat writhing snakes—through a room of cracked beads and brittle yellow fans—the lads from Local 141C making their various excuses all the way. "So glad you're here, sir, to be frank keeping the thing alive never sat right with me, orders are orders, so glad you're here to set things right." *Clever lad, that one. Watch that one.* Down through the corridors, smelling of torches, mildew, cigarette smoke; across a vault of velvet ropes, empty plinths, dark spaces; through a plain unmarked door like any other storage-room door. The smell that escaped through the crack in the door—indescribable. Metals and acids. Formaldehyde? Death and Time. A sense of weight. A *hiss* . . . And suddenly Maury felt a kind of furtive, overpowering fascination. Whatever was in the room, he wasn't willing to share it.

"It's caged? Fucking answer me—it's caged? Right. Wait outside. All of you. And take her away," he said, waving a hand at no one in particular. "The prisoner. What's she doing here? Lock her up. Local cells, go on."

For a moment it looked, absurdly, as though the woman might object—might *refuse*. Then she gave a tiny, ironical bow—as if to say, *all right. This once.* No time to worry about that now—more important things to worry about.

Then he was alone.

He went in alone.

A small room, but dark. The torchlight that slanted through the half-open door only deepened the shadows. No windows. Underground, of course—felt somehow like it was *deep* underground. Buried. The yellow headlamp eye of the thing in the cage . . .

Maury noticed—he'd been an Inspector for longer than he cared to remember, he kept a cool head and he noticed these things—that the floor was littered with cigarette butts; and he pictured with sudden savage clarity all the men of Local 141C coming down here, alone, furtive, mumbling, chain-smoking, night after night, waiting for the creature to . . . speak?

It blinked at him and said nothing.

He got a torch from the corridor outside and held it close. The dark pupils contracted, dwindled into the yellow of its eyes, vanished like tiny black bats retreating into a yellow moon. Intelligence fled, leaving dullness behind. The eyes themselves—misshapen. Uneven. The folds, nearly human, scarred and stitched. The huge shoulders hunched, the tail dragged. "Fuck, you're ugly."

It settled back on its haunches.

"What the fuck *are* you?"

A long tongue the color of spoiled meat flickered across its jaw.

"Speak to *me,* then."

It sat there in dumb animal silence.

He shivered, shook himself, laughed. "Fuck you, then, you horrible thing. Back in the dark for you."

When he left, he locked the door behind him and slipped the key into his pocket.

Time to find a bed somewhere. Time to find a bed, and put the thing out of his mind. Go blank, which was something he was good at doing. Big day tomorrow.

Ruth

Marta was scarcely two years older than Ruth. That never stopped her from going maternal at times like these. At first it was, "What happened to you, you left the shop shut all day, where'd you wander off to this time?" And she scowled and crossed her arms like a fishwife. But then she saw the look on Ruth's face, and Ruth told her the story, and at once Marta was full of a fierce frightened kindness—she alternated all night, and the next morning, too, between concern for Ruth and rage at the fucking Know-Nothings, fucking *Siddon,* that treacherous little shit . . .

"You know you shouldn't," she said over breakfast. "Oh, Ruth, you know you shouldn't do those things."

"That poor man," Ruth said, meaning the murdered soldier. "Someone had to help him," she explained. For some reason it was always easier to talk to Marta about those things when Marta was frightened—when she was calm those conversations turned into shouting matches. "What could I do? Leave him to Zeigler? They'd both be dead."

"You're lucky you're not dead." Marta sighed. "Following those ghosts—*this* is the world we have to live in, Ruth."

"For now, maybe."

Marta shook her head. They finished their breakfast in an exasperated affectionate silence. The arguments were long familiar to both of them—living in the shadow of the Mountain, in the shadow of their father, with their extraordinary sister, the Low sisters argued about the supernatural the way other families who bore more normal burdens might argue about money.

"I have to see Macaulay about his leg," Marta said. "Will you be all right this morning?"

"Of *course* I will, Marta."

"Stay out of trouble, then."

Outside it was not quite dawn yet, and Fosdyke's shifts were beginning, the whistles were sounding. Carnyx Street—home to the eccentric, the dissolute, the irregularly employed, those who lived on their wits—was still half asleep. The list of chores Ruth had been neglecting was long and forbidding. She put things off for another morning. Not being shot in the head and thrown in a ditch—that was enough of an accomplishment for the day. She read; sometimes she started shaking. Eventually she fell asleep, and dreamed of impossible creatures, ghosts of unusual beauty and brilliance, a world in which she, herself, was perfect, inviolate, alien and immaterial, a ghost or a dream.

Martha banged the table. "What *happened?*"

"Huh? What?"

"Is this you and Zeigler—did you do this?"

Ruth blinked; her head was full of muzzy grey clouds; it appeared to be afternoon. She repeated, "What?"

"They didn't say anything, yesterday? No? I'm sorry, Ruth, I just—there's bloody great motor-wagons outside the Museum, and the Chapterhouse."

"Executives. Someone important."

"New men, with guns. Have you been asleep all morning? Everyone's talking. The Square's full of new men with guns, Know-Nothings, and there's something going on. They're up to something. Shouting—Macaulay said he was walking that way and he heard shots. This can't be good. Can't be."

"Marta, what were you doing out by the Museum?"

She stopped, went silent, shrugged. "I don't know, Ruth. You're not the only one who *remembers* things."

Maury

In fact there was no shooting—it came close once or twice, but cooler heads prevailed. There was a scuffle—one of Maury's boys, Pake, got into a bit of a fight with two of the local lads, had to bloody a few noses. Otherwise the men of Local 141C shouted, simmered, sulked. They telegrammed for confirmation—and found that Maury's authority was unchallengeable. In the end they accepted the inevitable. They were in enough trouble already.

"You're all going to be up on fucking charges," Maury said, "every last one of you, if I get my way. What have you been playing at here? What is that thing?"

Maury had the key men questioned in separate rooms—the Chief Officer, the Local Secretary, the Holcroft Rep, the First and Second Investigators. He told his boys, "No violence yet—nothing too nasty. Go easy." He sat across the table from those sweating, nondescript, frightened men, waited a carefully measured time for them to speak.

They all had the same story.

The monster in the basement had been there before their time—and when they'd first joined the League, twenty, thirty years ago, the men who'd recruited them had said it had been there before their time, too.

They said it was just—sort of *down there.* They never talked to it. None of them ever went down there.

Well, that was a lie, for starters; Maury had seen the cigarette butts scattered down there by the monster's cage. He sighed, and told his lads, "Break this lying bastard's finger—one finger! No more. Don't go crazy. Not yet."

Sobbing, they admitted that sometimes—sometimes—they went down there to look at it, to see the horror of it for themselves, but nothing more, nothing more . . .

That would have to do for the moment; more intensive interrogation methods would require additional paperwork.

They said they didn't know why the creature was still alive. They said they'd just never got round to killing it. They said the paperwork wasn't in place, they weren't sure they were allowed. They looked honestly confused.

They all swore that they never fed the creature—not once in

thirty years. They still swore to it even after Maury had more fingers broken.

Maury spent most of the afternoon typing up charges against the local officers. He typed one-fingered, with a great deal of fumbling, swearing, backtracking. His mood was foul; a whole Chapterhouse corrupted!

Maury was loyal to the cause. Too many of the League, especially the young lads, joined up for the bit extra in the pay-packet, the chance for promotion, the social life, the thrill of a bit of violence. They didn't really *fear*. They didn't get out of the Chapterhouse enough. Maury, raised in the shadow of the Mountain, haunted all his long life, scarred by a hundred encounters with unnatural things, knew how to fear. Nearly his earliest memory was of a bloodied and torn and ash-shrouded ghost who'd reached from the darkness of an alley mouth, pulled little Maury from the afternoon's game of stick-and-ball, away from the other little boys and girls and into the shadows, and said, *all you people are gone—the War wipes you away—you're not real,* and had proceeded to . . .

Maury had very definite ideas about what was and what wasn't real. The rattle and ring of the typewriter; the sweaty institutional smell of the Chapterhouse; a stack of neatly typed-up charges and indictments!

Without quite meaning to, or thinking about it, Maury got up, walked across the empty evening Square, through the cold rain, turning the Museum keys over and over in his hand, and went down into the presence of the Beast.

Still in its cage. Its head lay flat on the ground, at a mournful angle. It opened one eye to regard him.

He carried a gun. He could have shot it. But then he wouldn't have evidence for his charges against the local officers. "A few more days," he whispered. "You monster."

It was silent.

"There's new management here now," he said. "That's bad news for you. I'm in charge here now."

It flicked its tongue.

"Look at you. You ugly bastard. Never seen nothing like you. Those bars had better be strong."

He gave a curt laugh. "Big fucking lizard. Look at you." He laughed again, louder; it boomed in the little room. "Never was one for pets, me. The wife had a rabbit but it died. Lizard. Ridiculous thing. If I had kids I'd tell them about you, but they'd never believe me."

He scowled.

"That ghost said you speak. That woman, Ivy, says you speak. Why won't you speak to me?"

It stayed silent. After a while, he laughed again. "Just a dumb animal. Speak; it's your last chance. No? Just a thing. I knew it. I'm sick of looking at you."

He watched it awhile longer.

Ivy—there was another problem.

At first Maury's lads had locked her up in one of the Chapterhouse's cells, but that hadn't worked out; they'd needed all the cells to separately interrogate the local League boys. Acting on their own initiative, they'd moved her across the Square, into the Museum. They'd locked her in one of the storage rooms on the upper floor, among cracked and dusty paintings, shrouded statues, gold and marble relics—horrible stuff, Maury hated it. She seemed quite at home there—like a queen from one of those old stories, in a chamber of treasures.

He visited her in the evening. The room was half dark and felt haunted; she stood by the narrow window in the light from the streetlamps.

She said, "Can I help you, Inspector Maury?"

"If I want your help I'll fucking tell you."

She turned back to the window, ignoring his bluster.

Her beauty confused him. He wasn't even sure she was so beautiful, really; maybe it was only the light.

Young enough to be your bloody daughter, Maury.

Well, so what? He wasn't fucking *courting* her. She was his prisoner. She was a whore for fuck-knows-what sort of alien powers, that dreadful ghost Brace-Bel, she knew things about that monster . . .

He said, "Are you all right in here?"

"Yes, thank you, Inspector."

"It won't talk to me."

"Take me to it," she said. "It'll talk to me."

"Oh no. Oh no. You stay where you are. I'm not having you two *plotting*. Tell me what to say to it."

After a long silence, she said, "Maybe you bore it, Inspector Maury. You can't threaten it. Try making a deal."

That was all she'd say. No point roughing her up—Maury had learned that. As he turned to go, without meaning to, he said, "Thank you," and he felt another little bit of his authority slip.

A whole new storm of shit in the morning!

It turned out that the local Holcroft Rep—the officer whose job it was to liaise between League Local 141C and the Holcroft Municipal Trust that sponsored them—had sent off a telegram of his own, complaining about the Local's ill treatment at Maury's hands. And so now suddenly there were men from Holcroft poking around, smooth men in suits and ties, junior executives, a class of men who always made Maury uncomfortable.

They wanted to know what the *hell* was going on.

Who ran the League? Who was in charge here? It was hard to say. The city was a big place, and the League was notoriously, obsessively secretive about its operations, and the Combines were even worse. Need to know. Asking questions not encouraged, not at all. Paranoia was the order of the day, not only a survival instinct but the organizing principle of the polity. Sometimes it seemed like the League answered to the various Combines and Trusts, who paid all wages, sponsored all operations; and it seemed that the League's men were only there to keep the city's business running smoothly, to maintain a very profitable status quo. Then again, there were times when it seemed the League was a power unto itself, the city was the League's to mold and shape, and the Combines existed only to fund it. There were people who said the League and the Combines both served the Mountain, come to think of it—who knows?—Maury wasn't a philosopher.

The executives from Holcroft wanted to know what Maury thought he was doing—charges against half the Local? Was he mad? Disruptive. Embarrassing. Bad for business.

Who was in charge, when things got complex, was usually a matter of who shouted loudest and who drew first. Maury saw the young executives off. They had the money, but he had the guns, and the *fear*.

And all day, at the back of his mind: the monster. Its eyes. The secrets it withheld from him. In the evening, when the executives were gone, he went back down to its cell. Impossible. Fascinating. Tormenting.

"This is your fucking fault, you know."

It ignored him.

"You stink."

He checked that there was no one at the door. Whispering, self-conscious, he said, "Why won't you talk to me? If you talk to me maybe I'll let you live."

It hissed and scraped its dull head against the bars. It fixed him with a contemptuous yellow eye, as if to say that it knew he was lying, and despised him. Magnificent eyes—something complex and mysterious worked in their depths, like golden gears.

When he went to see Ivy, she laughed at him. "You're so literal-minded, Inspector. Life? Try offering it something it *wants*."

He stopped in the hallway outside for a cigarette. The Museum's halls were full of statues of forgotten Gods—horrible things, too many limbs, *awful* expressions. *This is what it's like to be corrupted,* Maury thought. He'd thought the fall would be harder, somehow.

The junior Holcroft executives brought reinforcements, and over the next couple of weeks the situation got—*complex.*

Mr. Wantyard himself made a personal visit to the Chapter-house. *Wantyard*—Holcroft Municipal Trust's Chief of Operations for the Fosdyke, Fleet Wark, and North Bara Districts. A big man in the Combine. Grizzled, gouty, red-faced, and quick to anger, bullying, expensively tailored in pinstripes and scarlet silk ties. *What's going on? Inspector Maury, what is the meaning of this?*

So Maury took Wantyard down into the bowels of the Museum, into the monster's stinking cell, and let him see for himself.

Wantyard peered into the shadows, caught his breath as if about to retch, and recoiled in horror. "Kill it," he snarled. "Kill it at once."

Maury felt obscurely disappointed—in Wantyard? In himself?

"Wait," Wantyard said. "Leave it for a while. Let's get the bloody hell out of this place, Inspector."

After that Wantyard seemed to settle into the Chapterhouse,

and the Museum. He was around twice daily. He brought his own staff with him. He took on the Chapterhouse and the Museum as a new project, and devoted himself to it with red-faced intensity.

And Maury found himself cut out of the loop. The situation had been wrenched from his control.

Suddenly there were questions about the deaths of his men back at Barking Hill, Lewis and Waley. Suddenly there were questions about Maury's character.

Bureaucratic warfare—it gave him a fucking headache. Vicious as knives in an alley—knives at least were *quick*.

He went and visited the prisoner—Ivy—and she sat by him and listened to his grumbling. (He'd had furniture moved up into her room—he'd found himself worrying about her comfort.) She nodded and said, *yes, I see*. It wasn't exactly sympathy, she wasn't *sympathetic,* but it was at least a kind of cool and scientific curiosity, which was better than nothing. A kind of closeness. Once his strained emotions got the better of him and he smiled and put a questioning hand on her thigh. The look on her face—that cold mocking smile! Never again. He'd never do *that* again. He wanked himself to sleep that night like he was a fucking teenager. He toyed with the possibility of raping her. He didn't quite dare. People would hear. People would talk.

They were already talking. They noticed his nightly visits to the prisoner, and how, whenever he could get a minute away from meetings and hostile telegrams, he slipped across the windblown Square and down into the Museum's bowels to commune with the monster.

"What *are* you?" he asked it.

It stared blankly at him.

"What do you eat? How do you *work*?"

It shifted—its rough scales made a noise like a sigh.

"Are you a God? Like all those statues upstairs? Is that what you are?"

It appeared to fall asleep.

"Why won't you talk to me? If you think I won't understand you you're wrong. I do a stupid job but I'm not a stupid man. Talk to me."

It ignored him.

"Well, fuck you then."

＊　＊　＊

Back and forth across the windblown Square, Maury went, from Chapterhouse to Museum and back again.

There was usually a twice-weekly market at the far end of the Square, but it had been canceled. Who gave that order? Maybe Wantyard. Maybe Maury did it himself; he'd signed enough papers that he might have forgotten.

So who were these people who hung around the corners of the Square, looking dismal, worried, frightened? Who watched him from the shadows, as if they were screwing up their courage to ask him: *What's going on? What are you doing to our Museum?*

One of them was a dead ringer for Ivy. He tried to grab her but she outran him.

Wantyard summoned Maury into his temporary office, in the dusty former curator's office of the Museum.

"I've had my doubts about you, Inspector."

"Mr. Wantyard . . ."

"But you did well to expose this . . . unpleasantness. This place, the Museum, don't know how it lasted so long. Under my nose." He scowled. "Makes me look bad. Should have come to me first, Inspector."

"Mr. Wantyard, the investigation . . ."

"Shut up, Maury. I'm handling this now."

"Yes, sir."

"Have you seen the people outside, Inspector? Watching us? Like they don't have jobs to go to. Makes me sick. They *know,* Inspector." Maury started to speak, but Wantyard cut him off with a wave of his hand. "The people have long memories. They *dream,* Inspector. They sense something unnatural here. It's all gone too far to be resolved quietly. Make a public announcement, Inspector. Let them know. A show of force. Starting tomorrow we destroy this place, bit by bit, those awful statues, those mirrors, the paintings, the machines, all that machinery and witchcraft, Inspector, that *monster.*"

He dabbed at his sweating forehead and jowls with a silk handkerchief. "Bit by bit, Maury. Drag it out into the daylight, into the

Square, and smash it. Burn it. The monster last. We want people to *see*. Go on, get to work."

The posters went up. Eager young Know-Nothings went running through the streets nailing them up on trees and doors: *By Order of Inspector John Maury of the Civic League and Holcroft Municipal Trust, the Building Popularly Known as the "Museum of History and Natural Wonders" Is to Be Purged of Its Contents . . .*

And now the situation slipped further out of Maury's grasp. Someone else was visiting the monster—once, when he crept down at night, unable to sleep, he found a fresh lamp by the edge of the cage, a fresh smell of cigarette smoke. Who was it? "Are you talking to them, monster? Why won't you talk to me?" No answer. Still no answer. "Fuck you, then—tomorrow you get the fire."

He went to visit Ivy, and found Wantyard there—questioning her, so he said, but in fact from the look of it paying court to her like a love-struck schoolboy. "Get away, Maury," Wantyard said. "Get back to work. Are we ready to begin the destruction yet?"

They weren't, yet. First they had to order hammers, kindling, pallets, and crates to move the Museum's contents out into the street. More paperwork, which somehow fell to Maury. And late that evening—as he sat alone in his makeshift office, and looked across the Square at the one lit window in the Museum, where Wantyard was still talking to Ivy, *his* Ivy—Maury made a decision: he misaddressed the requisition forms.

"That buys you a few days," he told the monster. "Maybe I can tell them it was just a mistake. A few days, no more. I won't do it again. If you want to talk, now's your time."

It moved its head from side to side—so *slow*.

"What would happen if I let you loose? Would you run? You look so fucking fat and lazy."

It stayed silent.

"You know, I just realized there's no lock on this cage. There's no door. How did they ever get you in here? Who locked you away?"

Its tongue flickered across its scarred jaw.

"I think you can fucking *move* when you want to. I think you'd charge up those stairs like a bull. I think you'd kill anything in your way. I think you'd make the streets shake. Broken windows. Screaming children. I bet you'd roar. You snuffle like an old man in that cage, but I bet in the open air you'd *roar*. Yellow eyes like the moon. Shattered cobbles and bloody claw-prints there in the morning. Nightmares all over the city. They'd never forget you. They'd never find you. I bet we'd never find you."

It hissed.

"Fuck I'd like to see that."

It bared its irregular teeth. He fought back an urge to place his hand within the bars, to experience the bloody thrill of its teeth . . .

"Fuck, I need more sleep." He felt suddenly almost sick with exhaustion. "I wouldn't let you loose if I could. You'll never go free. I have a job to do. People are starting to talk. Soon we'll burn you."

Ruth

Ruth sat at the kitchen table with her head in her hands. Marta sat across from her, drinking her aniseed tea. The Know-Nothings' poster was stretched out on the table between them. Ruth read it over and over as if hoping to find a loophole. *By order of Inspector John Maury of the Civic League* . . .

The poster spoke of the "contents" of the Museum—contemptuously, as if it was only a warehouse full of old food cans or oil drums or something. There was no mention of the Beast. Was it possible that they hadn't found it?

Of course not. Of course not. They planned to kill it.

There was nothing like it left in the city, and they planned to kill it.

Her eyes watered—she felt so angry, so helpless.

She wished Arjun had come back. Not particularly because she thought he could do anything to stop the Know-Nothings or save the Beast, but only because it was so *depressing*. She'd given up hope of him returning. Another ghost, vanished—the city worked the way it worked, and there was no point hoping otherwise.

She blinked back tears. She said, "Fuck that," out loud, and Marta started. "We have to stop them," she said.

"How?" Marta said. "There's no way. Those kind of men get their way. That's just how the city works."

"We can't just let it die. It's the last . . . It *knows* things."

Marta sighed. She swirled the thick leaves in her tea.

"We have to do *something*," Ruth said.

Marta looked into her tea leaves for a long time, and said nothing.

TWELVE

The Swallows of Quinet Green– Spoliation–The Carnyx Street Action Committee–Faster–Masks and Games

Arjun

Arjun lay on the soft grass and watched the sky. Clouds drifted in the warm blue heavens. The light had the clarity of high places, and it seemed that he could see every precise black or white feather of the swallows that drifted on the breeze. He smelled flowers for which he had no names. Apart from the fluting of the birds there was a huge and echoing silence.

Birds! Flowers! The earth rotated beneath him, its vast weight tumbling through infinity. The Metacontext was open to him again! The City Beyond was all around him!

Brace-Bel lunged, looming, filling the sky with his round sweating face. "You know Shay's secret! Where have you brought us? Bring me home at once!" And he grabbed at Arjun's lapels and bore down on him with all his weight.

Arjun struck Brace-Bel smartly in the throat and he rolled off, gasping. When dealing with Brace-Bel, he'd decided, it was all a question of who was to be master.

Arjun stood.

They appeared to be in a park, on beautifully manicured lawns, at the edge of a steep grassy bank. They'd come through the open door of an unmanned information booth. A handful of brightly colored tourist brochures had spilled through after them—according to which they were in some place called Quinet Green. He'd never heard of it.

On the far horizon there were barely visible kites. Behind them were the hazy phantoms of a city skyline. Otherwise they were alone.

They were far from the Mountain.

He helped Brace-Bel to his feet. The fat man regarded him warily. "I propose a truce, Mr. Brace-B—"

Brace-Bel swung his stick for Arjun's knees, and Arjun, who'd seen the spark of cunning in Brace-Bel's bloodshot eyes, and was ready, stepped in to wrestle the stick away. They fell together and rolled down the grassy bank, to land in the sand trap of an empty golf course.

"A truce!" Brace-Bel said. "Let me stand! A truce!"

Arjun held the stick. He examined the crystal on its tip. "How does it work, Brace-Bel?"

"I paid dearly for that knowledge, Arjun—why should I give it to you for free? Take me home."

"No, Brace-Bel. For one thing, I don't think I remember the way back. It's been so long."

"Then leave me alone. This time is good enough for me. There are flowers; there is beauty."

"You have to come back with me, Brace-Bel."

"To that ugly Age? To that fear, that darkness? Don't be absurd. *You* go face your death on the Mountain, if you must—I shall remain here. This time will do well enough for Brace-Bel."

Arjun tossed the stick back to Brace-Bel. "What else do you carry, Brace-Bel? What other weapons have you got in your pockets? Your rings, that necklace—too vulgar to be jewelry. Did Shay give them to you? Are they *devices*?"

Brace-Bel's hand went involuntarily to his necklace.

"Brace-Bel, I must free the Beast. It's well guarded. Ivy, too, wherever she is. I need your weapons. I think the Beast sent me to you so that we could save it. And you—I thought you loved Ivy. Don't you want to save her?"

"She needs no saving, Arjun."

"Come back with me, and I promise when we're done, before I go up the Mountain, I shall take you home."

Brace-Bel sighed. "Very well." He reached out, shook Arjun's hand, and, grunting with sudden effort, pushed him over; then he ran panting and sliding up the bank.

Arjun got up, gave chase. Ahead, Brace-Bel clambered up over the edge of the bank and was framed for a moment against the blue sky. The swallows of the Green swooped and fluttered by in the warm breeze. There were no birds so beautiful in the city of the Low sisters, in the shadow of the Mountain. They reminded Arjun of something; they gave him an idea. They scattered as he ran after Brace-Bel.

Ruth

The spoliation of the Museum began. It was a few days behind schedule, but once it got under way the Know-Nothings threw themselves into it with savage enthusiasm. They transferred in reinforcements, warm bodies, extra hands and backs. They requisitioned cranes and cables and teams of dray-horses and motorized, smoke-belching hauling-engines, and they began dragging the dusty and forgotten relics of the abandoned Museum out into the light to be destroyed. They lashed heavy cables round statues of ancient Gods, and dragged them down the steps. Sometimes the statues fell and marble arms and heads shattered, and they gave a raucous cheer. They broke the frames of paintings and threw the canvases on the fire—portraits of ancient queens or long-dead whores, street scenes of forgotten parts of the city, magnificent or squalid, dreamlike or nightmarish, fanciful or dourly naturalistic—all burned. Ash blew down the streets, and scraps of butterfly-bright colors.

Glass and electronics could be stamped underfoot, the jeweled shards swept into the corners. In the case of stone statues, sledge-hammers were employed. The gold stuff they melted—the local Holcroft Municipal operation donated engines from the forges to the cause. Harder metals, ceramics, and plastics—that stuff they hauled away to the big fire-pits in the factories. The scrap would serve the War effort, in the event of War. A man from Patagan Sewer & Piping had given a confused and vaguely threatening speech to that effect, and swung the first hammer.

It went on and on. Morning shift, afternoon shift, night shift. Day in, day out. The Museum predated all living memory. Who knew how much *crap* there was in it?

There was a cheerful atmosphere in the Square among the Know-Nothings. Overtime pay for interesting work in the open air! The Holcroft people put out food and beer at long trestle tables. Good times. Everything they saw was something to tell the grandkids about. And the things they dragged out were so preposterous you couldn't help but laugh as they smashed, so awful you couldn't help but shudder and cheer as they burned.

What kind of people had worshipped those squirming steel snake-Goddesses, those ox-headed fat boys?

What kind of madmen painted those unnerving chromatic abstractions, those many-angled women?

Who'd dare the skies in these flimsy machines, who'd pierce their skin with this squirmy insectile jewelry?

You wouldn't want to know. Swing the hammers!

For the first couple of days, a large crowd showed up. The district's Holcroft and Patagan factories ended shifts early to let the locals watch the spoliation. There were scattered cheers and applause. "About time, about time!" The things in the Museum were *horrors*. "Smash it! Fucking *smash* it! Good lads!" But by the third day the brutality of it, the monotony of it, began to wear on the audience. For nearly everyone there was a moment, a sudden moment, when something so beautiful was dragged out into the light that their hearts clenched and they were unable to bear seeing it destroyed—a winged angel in sandstone, a painted sunset catching the actual sun, a dress on a mannequin, a sword, a delicate machine. Slowly the crowd drifted away.

Now, at the edge of the Square, there was a small perpetual protest. Half a dozen to a dozen men and women, standing solemnly, watching the burning. Bearing witness.

Generally Ruth was among them.

Nothing living had been dragged down those steps. She panicked every time she saw some stuffed monster or four-legged statue hauled out—but so far there'd been no sign of the Beast. Perhaps they were saving it for last.

It was an awkward and diffident kind of protest—no one dared go too far. The Know-Nothings could get violent. The protesters stood in silence and radiated disapproval and sorrow. Oddballs, weirdos, dejected idealists, the underemployed, the borderline paperless. On the first day they'd brought a banner—SAVE OUR MUSEUM—but a bunch of drunken Know-Nothings had taken it and thrown it on the fire. Some people brought their children, who picked their noses and sometimes laughed and swore and sometimes started crying when the Know-Nothings yelled at them to *fuck off*.

They were mostly from Carnyx, or neighboring streets. In times of emergency—depression, disease, factory closings—Carnyx Street's householders formed Committees. Marta was a leading organizer. At Ruth's urging, Marta had visited their neighbors, called in favors, and convened a Temporary Action Committee. It met in the back room of Ruth's shop. After long debate the Committee had organized this protest; this pointless, futile protest. It made Ruth want to scream.

I t isn't enough," she said.

Marta shook her head. "What do you expect, Ruth?"

It was late in the evening. Over in the Square the Know-Nothings had knocked off for the night. Around the table in the Low sisters' back room sat Ruth, Marta, and the rest of the Committee. The room was half lit and they spoke in low voices. There were too many people in the room, and they banged elbows and rubbed against each other whenever they sat forward or back; the conspiratorial atmosphere kept collapsing into awkward laughter.

Zeigler was there. Next to Zeigler's skinny body loomed Mr. Frayn—who was one of the foremen at a Holcroft slaughterhouse, and resembled one of his bulls, fat and pale, dressed in a too-tight grey sweater. Next to Ruth sat Mrs. Rawley, widowed proprietor of the Tearoom, one of the local public houses. Across from her sat blinking bespectacled Thorpe from the glassworks, who wrote poetry in which everything in the world was compared to either mirrors or window glass. Durrell, the sign-painter, sat beside him. The thin and feral Schiller, who lived on the south end of Carnyx Street, paced around the room. Schiller worked freelance putting stray dogs to death. He played the violin surprisingly well. He eyed Marta's refugee cats with professional interest.

These were the pillars of the local community.

Ruth had Zeigler's sympathy—he shook with excitement at the thought of the creature hidden in the Museum, he moaned with horror whenever he saw another treasure dragged out and wrecked. Mrs. Rawley was on Ruth's side, too—no one hated the Know-Nothings like Mrs. Rawley. They threw their weight around and made trouble in her pub, and once, long ago, they'd *questioned* her for consorting with ghosts; she blamed them for the death of her husband; she'd disowned the son who'd joined them.

The others were having cold feet.

"We agreed on a dignified protest," Frayn said. "This is a bad business. This is a bad decision by the bosses. Unwise. No one can say I'm any kind of toady to the bosses. You all know me. Ruth, you know me. I'm old enough to be your dad—sorry, sorry. I know. But I remember the place before they locked it away, is what I'm saying. They had these flying machines there, up on the glass dome on the roof. Beautiful things—I used to dream about them. So I hate this as much as anyone. I don't see anything wrong with letting the bosses know we're not happy. But I have a wife and a family and a job, Ruth, and I don't want to do anything mad."

"We've done all we can," Durrell said. "We've made our point. I say we call off the protests before we push the Know-Nothings too far."

"Hear, hear," Schiller said. "How do we know this thing isn't a figment of your imagination, anyway? How do we know the Know-Nothings aren't right, maybe it should be killed. Why should we care?"

The argument dragged on. Nothing Ruth said could sway them. She wasn't even sure what she was hoping for—what did she expect these ordinary frightened people to do? "Facts are facts," Marta said. "There's nothing we can do."

"Then I'll talk to someone who *can*," Ruth said.

Arjun

Arjun made his way back across the city, across Time, through the secret ways. Brace-Bel followed.

They'd reached a kind of understanding. Or at least, the struggle had gone out of Brace-Bel, who now walked in silence, despairing, sometimes sobbing over the names of his dead servants, over the ruin of his dreams and hopes and dignity. He screamed in his sleep.

At first they both flinched from every shadow, avoided crowds and alley mouths, expecting to be attacked at any moment by the terrible creatures that had pursued Arjun and murdered Brace-Bel's household. It didn't happen. It seemed that for the time being Arjun's hunters had lost his trail.

"Do you never learn? They called *me* incorrigible, Arjun—but I defied no power so dreadful as those Hollow Men. If you go up the Mountain again they will destroy you."

They were chased by street gangs through concrete streets, under electric lights and obscene advertising billboards. They were menaced by large purple-eyed cats. At night, in cobbled streets slick with sewage, under the shadow of great granite towers, a Vampire took an interest in them. More than one kind of policeman asked for their papers. But those were only the usual risks of going walking through Time, through the infinite urban Metacontext, without a map. And sometimes they passed through gentle and beautiful places, through *musical* places, and Arjun was tempted to stop where he was. They stood at the top of a hill overlooking azure mists and the spires of temples each lit by their various Gods, and Brace-Bel was moved to spontaneous poetry.

At every turn Arjun went north, toward the Mountain, and forward in Time, toward the end of things. As the Mountain loomed closer the horrible sights became more frequent, and the beautiful ones were left behind.

He found and opened door after door. The art of it came back to him. He *remembered* how it was done—how Shay had shown him how it was done. First one found one's key; for Arjun it was music. The song of birds, the drone of muzak, opera echoing from the theaters, the howling of drunks—whatever the city offered him. Then one had to set aside all distractions, which included Brace-Bel sobbing, or saying, *faster, faster, you fool,* and the shouting of whatever happened to be pursuing them at the time; the roar of vehicles, the fires crackling, dogs barking, factories pounding, flags snapping in the breeze, the noises of markets and engines and football games and cattle and rain and wind . . . *Ignore all that. Now listen to the music; now listen to the way its echoes spread out and make the city; so that this, now, is the center from which things are made. Now take that infi-*

nitely unfolding city of echoes and turn *it. This is the indescribable part, and this is the impossible part, because describing it kills it, and that is the hardest thing not to do . . .*

It came back to him quickly, almost easily. Almost exactly like playing an instrument. And at first it was easy to find the way, to open whatever doors he wanted. But as he came closer and closer to the Mountain, to the Low sisters' city, a kind of gravity overtook him, and the path was harder and harder. He pushed against a strange pressure. Dull and flat notes crept into the splendid music of the city. There were fewer and fewer doors. He began to fear that the Age of the Low sisters was somehow closed to him. He pushed on.

They walked down a grey street, through a haze of diesel fumes, looking for doors—in the clang and drone of the foundries Arjun felt the presence of a door. "How does it work?" Brace-Bel said.

"I don't know." He wasn't inclined to explain anything for free; he still wanted Brace-Bel's help. Besides, he didn't know the answer.

"What kind of place *is* our city?"

"I don't know, Brace-Bel. This is how things are." There were theories out there, among the travelers, among Arjun's peers—but those men were all mad.

"What kind of thing is the Mountain, to be at the heart of all this?"

"I don't know, Brace-Bel."

There were theories—in the laboratories in Zubiri they spoke of the Mountain as a *singularity,* a weight around which the possibilities of the city revolved. In the bloody war shrines of the Red Moon they said that the Mountain was the home of the cruel Gods of the city, the one unconquerable place in the world, the ultimate challenge. In Huiringa, and Slew, and on Crabbe's Lake, they said that the city was built by the Gods, that it blazed and sparked with their energies, and the Mountain was the black cold slag-heap of the wastes the great work left behind—but Crabbe's Lake and Slew and Huiringa were Ages of heavy industry, and that was just how they saw the world. In Pyx they thought the Mountain was the graveyard where Gods went to die.

In the bars where the madmen and seers who'd Broken Through gathered, the rumor was that it was a kind of machine—

the maker and unmaker of the city. The engine of time and possibility. The prison, the fountain of Gods. The most coveted weapon
in the world. St. Loup sometimes said it was a palace, and smiled
his handsome smile over the prospect of its harems and its women.
Abra-Melin and Ashmole believed it was a kind of vast alchemical
crucible. One by one those madmen got greedy, went looking for
the way up, and never came back . . .

Arjun had heard a hundred theories. He didn't know what to
believe. He had no head for science or theory. They didn't seem
worth discussing with Brace-Bel.

"How do you do it?" Brace-Bel said. "How do you know where
you're going?"

"I don't know, exactly. There's an art to it."

"I remember how I followed Shay through these secret paths. To
follow *again,* helpless and lost—it would offend my dignity if I had
any left. You begin to remind me of him, Arjun."

Arjun stopped short in the street. He turned to Brace-Bel, and
nearly hit him. A horrible comparison! There was a smug light in
Brace-Bel's eyes; he had meant to provoke.

Arjun breathed deeply. He calmed himself. "When we're done,
Brace-Bel, I'll take you wherever you want to go. I'll show you
whatever you want."

"But for now you must keep secrets, make demands?"

"For now I need you."

Arjun's nerves were fraying. Events in the Low sisters' city were
proceeding without him. He might arrive only to find that their
Time was done, their history already written. Something was
wrong with their world. Some awful mean-spirited pressure
weighed down on it, stifling all hopeful possibilities. Who ruled
their city?

He went north, and the Mountain loomed closer and closer,
cold and bitter, and his mood darkened.

Maury

Maury went down into the depths of the Museum—again. He
couldn't sleep. His back ached dreadfully—all day he'd been out
there in the Square, come sun, come rain, overseeing the destruction. Jangling his keys. His hand was stiff from swinging that

bloody hammer. Was it night outside? He wasn't sure. He hadn't been sleeping right for days. His head buzzed with grey panic. The Museum was full of empty spaces, the rooms were yawning voids full of spinning dust, the walls bore the ghost-marks of the paintings that had been torn down and burned. Not long now. Not much longer. Soon there would be nothing left, and he wouldn't be able to stall the death of the Beast any longer. It would die, and he would never know what it had been, what secrets it hid. He felt close to panic.

Down into the basements and the red-brick corridor; the swaying glow of his lantern illuminated scenes of devastation, emptiness—when the Know-Nothings dragged things out, they weren't gentle or careful. The flagstones were littered with fragments: broken glass, torn-off doorknobs, stone fingers snapped off statues, stone hands in gestures of benediction. Dials, gears, levers, antennae . . .

There were voices coming from the Beast's room.

Fucking hell. Was *that* the creature's voice? Was that what it sounded like? That hissing, scraping sound—like knives clashing together. Like jammed gears. Like bones breaking. That *echo* . . .

He stopped still in the corridor. He leaned against the wall. His heart beat madly. That voice—nothing human could speak in that voice.

What was it saying? He couldn't make out the words.

There was a second voice—a woman's voice.

He crept closer.

It was Ivy Low. What was she doing there?

He heard the monster's voice saying something about its *cruel father,* about *laboratories,* about the *unstitching,* about *the Hollow Men.*

He heard the woman ask it something about the Mountain.

He heard the word *Shay.* The monster pronounced it like a curse, and the woman laughed. Was it a name or a place?

The creature said: *Will you kill him? Do we have a deal?*

Maury's skin crawled with gooseflesh. All of Maury's long and distinguished career . . . All those years tormenting scared, helpless little ghosts . . . He'd never been so close to anything so uncanny, so dreadful. It was *speaking.* The things it might tell him!

What are you?

How are you possible?

Who runs this city? All these years, who have I been working for?

The door was ajar. He threw it open.

Ivy turned to look at him. She sighed. "Inspector Maury."

She sat on an upturned bucket next to the cage.

The thing in the cage was still and silent. It appeared to be asleep. The light of Maury's lantern picked out its scars and stitches.

Suddenly Maury couldn't think what to say. The creature looked like a dumb animal again—no more miraculous than a sleeping sow in a filthy pen.

He rounded on the woman. "What the fuck are you doing here? Who let you out of your cell?"

She didn't flinch. She stood up and walked toward him, and he deflated a little further.

"Mr. Wantyard," she said. "He's a very kind man. He seems quite taken with me."

"What? Wantyard?"

"Your boss, isn't he?" She smiled. "I told him I wanted a bit of a walk, and here I am."

She shivered. "It's cold down here, and this thing's boring. Come on, Maury, you can escort me back to my cell."

On the way back upstairs Maury realized that she'd had no light of her own; she'd been talking to the thing in the dark.

"Good night, Inspector." She stepped into the room that was supposed to be her cell. She sat by the window, in the moonlight. "Good *night,* Inspector."

He had too many questions and he didn't know how to begin. She scared him—that was the fact of the matter. *Tomorrow,* he told himself; *tomorrow, when it's light, we'll have a few fucking words, her and me.* He went in search of a stiff drink.

Ruth

Ruth walked Mrs. Rawley home after the meeting, through a cold rain, under the moonlight. The old widow was terribly fat, and she had a bad leg; she wheezed with every step over Carnyx Street's wet cobbles. "You're a good girl," she said. "Very kind." A factory over toward 120 vented steam and grit, and the sour smell of dust. "Streets aren't safe these days." There was a storm brewing over the

Mountain, and distant lightning flickered in the night. Rawley swigged whiskey from a hip-flask and cursed. The only thing she feared more than ghosts were the Know-Nothings who were supposed to protect against them; she was drunk, and lonely, and full of vague fears.

She slipped on a drift of wet leaves and nearly pulled Ruth down with her. She sat there cursing and laughing. Ruth sat cross-legged beside her. Her skirts quickly soaked with foul water, and she shivered.

"You're a good girl, Ruth. Strange, mind." Rawley sighed. "Forget about that thing. Nothing we can do about it now. Keep chasing after that sort of thing and you'll end up like your father."

Ruth stiffened. Rawley shook her head, mumbling, *oh, sorry, sorry dear, I didn't mean to say that, it's the drink . . .*

"I want to talk to the Black Masks, Mrs. Rawley."

The old woman shut her mouth. A shrewd expression crossed her face. "What would I know about that?"

The Black Masks—like the Know-Nothings, they were everywhere in the city, from the slopes of the Mountain south to the unimaginable borders. Like the Know-Nothings, they had their badges, their rituals, their meeting places, their secrets and schemes. Like the Know-Nothings, they were something to do in the cold evenings. In ordinary times Ruth didn't think much of any of them—they were all stupid boys.

Unlike the Know-Nothings, they operated from hiding, in masks, under false names.

They said they stood for the workers. They said they stood for freedom. Every so often they shot an executive, or kidnapped an executive's wife. Sometimes they blew things up—factories, warehouses, Chapterhouses, executives' motorcars. Their weapons were the suspiciously laden horse-drawn wagon, left inconspicuously beside Company buildings, stuffed with stolen dynamite and iron scrap; the letter bomb, wrapped in pamphlets; the sniper rifle.

They had no demands. If they had any particular goals, Ruth didn't know what they were. They'd been around for decades, and they never seemed to accomplish anything much. She'd heard that they were spies and saboteurs for the Mountain; she'd heard that they had leaders down south, in a zone where the Combines held no sway. More likely, she thought, they had no real leaders at all.

Ruth thought of them as a kind of escape valve. When the grinding pressure of the city got too great, it was time for the lads to put on the Masks, and go start a fire; and the great machine kept rolling . . .

In ordinary circumstances, she thought they were useless at best, and maybe dangerous. But this was an emergency. For the first time in her life she was almost desperate and frustrated enough to put on the Mask herself.

Ruth knew, because Marta knew, because Rawley had blurted it out once, drunk and drowsy with medicine, that Rawley's younger son, who worked by day shifting cargo at the Terminal, was a Masker.

"The Masks," Ruth said. "If we're going to get anything done, we need someone who's not scared of a little—you know."

Rawley shook her head. "Who says I know anything about the Masks?"

The Mountain loomed. A harsh rain was blowing down.

"Your son, Mrs. Rawley. Henry—I know."

Mrs. Rawley was silent for a moment.

"This city isn't right, Ruth," she said. "It's all broken."

"I know."

"It's hard on families—*you* know that."

"Tell Henry I need to talk to the Masks, Mrs. Rawley."

"All right, Ruth. All right. You're a good girl to care. Help me stand, will you?"

Arjun

In Cendylon Arjun met an old acquaintance. The waters below bloomed with rust-flowers; the iron bridges were twined with ivy and magnolia; the domes above them were copper-green and the torchlight golden; in the fragrant and lazy air the Mountain was the deep green of something sunk beneath tropical waters. As they passed by the flowered archway of the Traitors' Garden, where spectators and tourists watched the condemned men hang and writhe in the embrace of strangling vines, a man stepped out of the gloating crowd and called, "Arjun!"

It was St. Loup. Arjun recognized the man at once, and tensed.

"Ready your weapons, Brace-Bel," Arjun whispered. Then he smiled and shook St. Loup's hand.

St. Loup's smile, as always, was dazzling. At the moment it seemed he wore long and snakeskin-colored robes, like the locals. When he could be bothered to use it, St. Loup had a gift for looking as if he belonged. His glasses were round, gold-rimmed, and bright; his long blond hair, oiled and elegant. He was a little older than he'd been when Arjun saw him last—there were the beginnings of crow's feet around his eyes, a certain hardening of the skin.

"How long has it been, Arjun? Since the Hotel? Since the *Annihilator*? Were you there at that Coven in . . . ? May I ask who your friend is? Is he new to our peculiar brotherhood? Shall we have a drink? Oh come on."

In a half-lit underground bar they drank pungent aniseed liqueur out of tiny brass cups. Not the bar St. Loup first suggested—Arjun insisted on choosing the spot. St. Loup was charming but he was not above the use of poison.

"How goes the search for your God?"

"Not well, St. Loup. And your own search . . . ?"

"Sad, sad; no happy news."

St. Loup—who was he? Who had he been before he'd Broken Through to the City Beyond? It was impossible to be sure and it hardly mattered. At various times he had told Arjun that in his former life he'd been a prince, or a university instructor, or a prisoner in a mental institution; once he'd claimed to have lived in a part of the city full of tall buildings and motorcars and television advertisements, and worked in investment banking. One day he'd walked through a crowded department store and stepped between two bright mirrors, and in each mirror, over the heads of the surging and squabbling crowd he'd seen the face of the most beautiful woman in the world, walking away, left and right, and into a maze of gold-lit reflections. And he'd followed; and he'd followed her ever since, and never found her. Sometimes he said that she was a Queen, and she must be on her throne, on the Mountain, in the perfect golden light of the upper air; sometimes he said that she was too beautiful to be allowed to walk the streets freely, and that she must be held a prisoner in the harems of the Mountain's rulers, and it was his desperate dream to steal her away . . .

Was any of that true? Probably not. St. Loup never seemed much of a romantic. At other times he'd claimed to be searching for the secret of eternal youth, or for money. Once—with the air of a man confessing to a shameful secret—he'd told Arjun that he'd been lying on the dirty bed of an anonymous hotel and dying by his own hand of an overdose of pain medications, when the old man Shay had come to sit by his bedside, and had made him an offer . . .

It was certainly true, however, that for St. Loup the path through the city was marked out in mirrors, light, diamonds, clear puddles, bright eyes—and that he liked to surround himself with beautiful women. Every so often Arjun crossed his path—they chased the same rumors of the Mountain through the same strange places. Sometimes older, sometimes younger—it was confusing at first, then one stopped caring, became indifferent. In the Meta-context, people were split from their own lives' narratives, they neither progressed nor regressed; the only thing stable about them was their particular obsession. For a year or two Arjun and St. Loup had had a partnership of sorts, back at the Hotel, that had ended in acrimony after one betrayal too many—not all of them St. Loup's. Theirs was a small community, and not a close or friendly one. St. Loup was prone to suicide attempts and murders. He was quite mad. Perhaps they all were.

"What's your angle, then, Mr. Brace-Bel? What draws you from your home, into the great Beyond?"

Brace-Bel sighed and didn't answer.

"You'll go mad out here without a purpose," St. Loup said. "Pick a God to worship, any God. Your friend here has an obsession with a God of music. Has he mentioned it to you? At the Hotel he rarely talked of anything else."

"St. Loup . . ."

"No offense. We can *all* be the most frightful bores. Arjun, I saw Potocki recently—he has commissioned the construction of yet another flying machine. A kind of complex screw-thing, all wings and vanes. Gyroscopes. Can't be blown off course, he says. Not this time. Not *this* time. He intends to launch himself at the Mountain."

"Again," Arjun said.

"Again," St. Loup agreed. "Always the same strategy. He's like a stopped clock, or a jammed gear, or some horrible thing. Machines, machines. I may be a monomaniac, but at least I display a little variety in execution."

"None of us are any closer to the Mountain, though," Arjun said. "Perhaps Potocki has the right approach? He's good at making flying machines. Why not stick with it? He's patient."

St. Loup shook his golden head. "You're too kind."

"So did you steal his plans?"

St. Loup grinned. "I *tried*." He knocked back his drink and ordered another. "He's beefed up security since the old days. Do you remember? Never mind. Old news. What else? I heard that the famous Mr. Shay had been seen in Kovno, at the shipyards, doing business under the name Cuttle." He sighed. "But when I investigated I found that the yards had been burned over, and the waters were black with oil. What about you—any interesting news?"

"Nothing much."

"It's been a long time. You look older—you've acquired a couple of interesting wounds. Where've you been? You know, your absence has been noted for a while now."

"I've been sick, St. Loup." Arjun held up his wounded hand. "A black dog bit me. What brings you to Cendylon?"

"I was here to hear the last words of a heretic, in the garden of vines." It was probably a lie; most of the things St. Loup said were lies. "You are passing through?"

"From nowhere in particular, to wherever the music leads me," Arjun said.

"We are returning to the most hideous place in the city," Brace-Bel complained. "In the shadow of the Mountain, because of a mad dream of a talking Beast . . ."

Arjun kicked Brace-Bel under the table and he howled. St. Loup's eyes lit up.

"It's always a pleasure, St. Loup," Arjun said. "But we must be going."

"One more drink, Arjun. Why not? It's a lonely city out there. Let's welcome Brace-Bel to our brotherhood."

But of course there was no brotherhood—none of them could be trusted, as St. Loup well knew. Everyone who Broke Through did it alone. They were all at least a little mad. Arjun sometimes liked St. Loup, but trust was impossible. And as it turned out, St. Loup had two thugs waiting to grab Arjun in the street outside—

big brutal men with round pale faces, not local—so Arjun and Brace-Bel had to flee through the kitchens, and out across the bridges. St. Loup laughed, and called after them: "Always a pleasure! When shall we meet again? We must have lunch!"

Arjun swore and clenched his fists in frustration. Now they had to take a circuitous route, lurching wildly back and forth across Time and the city, so that their trail was too confused for St. Loup to follow. A waste of valuable time—but the last thing Arjun needed was St. Loup competing for the Beast's secrets; and besides he'd already brought more than enough danger into Ruth's life . . .

One obstacle after another!

Slowly, slowly, they drew closer to the Mountain.

Ruth

So Ruth met Henry Rawley, in the shadows of an alley out the back of the Terminal, on his shift break. He smoked ferociously and shook his head. "My bloody mum and her bloody mouth . . ."

"Will you help?"

She waited another day.

They came to her at night, throwing stones up at her window like little boys. Six of them, out in the street, masked and dressed in black. Despite the masks, she recognized two of them—Pieter from the sewage reclamation plant, Goodge from the refinery—local lads. The others were strangers. Henry wasn't among them.

She went down into the street. She dressed in black; it seemed to be the thing to do.

They said nothing. They put a blindfold over her eyes. They spun her around. They led her through the streets.

There was some theatrical business with beggars and whispered passwords; with signals rapped on iron doors, messages left under bricks. They went in and out of alleys, up and down stairs, into tunnels, over wasteground. Weeds and rusty junk under her feet. Someone challenged them; they responded. Secret words—the names of Combines pronounced backward, she realized. Secret handshakes. They addressed each other as *brother* or *comrade,* and named themselves after explosives, or knives, or night-birds, or stars. They spun her around again. They led her up a rattling fire escape, onto a high roof, into a cold night wind. Someone whispered in her ear, "Can you keep a secret? Whose side are you on, Miss Low?" Someone else drew a knife. "What's your business with the Black Mask?"

She said, "Knock it off, Pieter. I know your mum."

It was all pointless play-acting. That was how the Black Masks did business. Whatever real and hard-edged purpose the Masks might have had was encrusted under a vast impractical weight of fanciful nonsense.

It reminded Ruth of her precious books. In the history books, yellow and fragrant with age, fragments of history themselves, there were accounts of all the cults and assassins' guilds and revolutionaries and anarchists and heretics and secret societies of the past—in fact she owned a single volume of the *Atlas,* dimly remembered as the work of a terrible cabal of radicals and seditionists, and though it looked dull enough to her, she kept it hidden away from the prying eyes of Know-Nothings.

It was a large and paranoid city and full of passwords and blindfolds and secrets. There was a terrible weight of history behind everything everyone ever did. The Black Masks, it seemed to Ruth, behaved the way they did because they sensed it was the way for a secret society to behave. Who knew where they'd absorbed the notion? Maybe in a dream. A conversation heard through the walls. Something that trickled down through the city.

She sighed. Nothing in the city worked the way it was supposed to. The dust of Ages settled on everything. Everything that should have been beautiful or purposeful was ugly and futile. Were these stupid young men really the only help she could hope for?

She tore off the blindfold—the Maskers gasped, one of them said, *Ruth, hang on, not yet!*—and from the top of the high roof she could see the yellow moon, and the vast shadow of the Mountain.

THIRTEEN

The Return–Playing the Magician–
Red Wine–Dawn Shift–Five Impossible
Devices–"He Has Laboratories"

Arjun

With an immense *thump* that echoed across a dozen streets and stopped all conversation, a blockage in the north chimney of the Patagan Sewer & Piping Thirty-first Smelting Plant finally crumbled, allowing a cloud of smoke and grit and ash and rust and feathers to burst out over Fosdyke. It smelled like the death of machines. There was cheering from the Plant, followed by shrieks and groans from the houses below. The cloud surged down the hill and flooded the streets, blacking out windows, ruining the laundry. It broke at the edge of Carnyx Street. Two men staggered out of the grey, one fat, one thin, both coughing and reeling. Their faces were painted with dust, their hair was thick and bushy with it; they looked like tragic clowns.

"Fuck you," Brace-Bel spat. "May you be fucked to death by minotaurs. May you be torn to shreds by drunken harpies. Why have you brought me back to this terrible place?"

Arjun clutched a lamppost for support and beat at his filthy clothes with his free hand. All around them the curtains were twitching; they were being watched.

✻ ✻ ✻

There was a cheaply printed poster on the inside of the smoky windows of Ruth's shop. It said:

DON'T LET THEM DESTROY OUR MUSEUM
PRESERVE OUR . . .
MEETING TOMORROW AT THE . . .

And it said some other things, too. But behind it, Arjun saw, emerging from the shadows, Ruth's face. She pulled the poster down so that she could see more clearly through the glass. She looked amazed, confused.

The face disappeared. A moment later the bells rang and the door opened and she ran out into the street. She wore trousers and a worn black shirt—work clothes. Her hair was tied back and she looked tired and red-eyed, as if she hadn't slept. She took his hand, gently, nervously. She seemed surprised to be able to touch him, as if he might only be something glimpsed in a mirror.

Arjun shrugged. "I came back again."

"I thought you'd . . . I don't know. Vanished."

"I nearly did. I had help."

She blinked wet eyes as if sun-dazzled, and she looked suddenly full of hope—then her eyes narrowed and her smile turned into a scowl, as Brace-Bel stepped out from behind Arjun. "What's *he* doing here?"

Brace-Bel was disguised in brown overalls, and Arjun had cut his hair short, and his various glittering rings and amulets were hidden in his pockets. His face hovered uneasily between a sneer and a smile of ingratiation.

Behind him the neighbors leaned out of their windows, watching curiously. A crowd was gathering. Mothers held curious children back at their doorsteps. The street remembered Brace-Bel all too well.

"May we come inside?" Arjun said.

There was no falling into each other's arms. No kiss. After that first nervous brush of Ruth's fingers across his hand that confirmed his reality there was no further touch at all, and she sat across the table from him and there was a great uncertain distance between them. It seemed unfair. Arjun felt somehow cheated and ill-used.

"I failed to bring Ivy back to you," he said. "The Know-Nothings took her. She was with Brace-Bel willingly, Ruth, and she did not want to come home. She wants never to come home again. She wants to escape from this Time. I've known others like her. She'll never be happy until she finds the way—probably not even then."

Brace-Bel snorted. "Ivy is worth ten of either of us."

Ruth looked skeptically from Arjun to Brace-Bel.

"Brace-Bel will help us rescue Ivy," Arjun said. "He and I have a deal. A man called Inspector Maury took her. Where would she be held?"

Ruth started. Silently she got up and walked to the counter. She brought back a copy of the Know-Nothings' poster, announcing the destruction of the Museum, *By Order of Inspector John Maury* . . .

"He's here," she said. "Maybe Ivy's with him? Why is he here, Arjun? What did you do?"

He read the poster over twice. "The Museum . . . ?"

I remember everything, Arjun told her—*nearly everything.*

She drew in her breath. Brace-Bel shook his head. *Must we listen to your pious lament again?*

He told her everything he could. Too much of it was still a jumble—fragments, glimpses, sudden moments of light and darkness. The kettle in the kitchen was on the boil, there was a smell of dust and rain in the air, and it seemed absurd to be talking about those things. The poster had panicked him deeply—there couldn't be much time left. He still couldn't say what had happened to him on the Mountain. "Maybe the Beast can, but . . ."

"I tried to think of a way to save it," she said. At his surprised expression, she said, "I remember it, too. It was beautiful and mysterious and I can't bear to see those bastards destroy it." Arjun began to shake his head *no,* but she kept speaking: "But so fucking what? I did my best and I don't even know where to start." She gestured at her black clothes. "I went to meet the Black Masks. Ridiculous, right? Stupid boys. They'll only get themselves killed if they try. Nothing here works the way it should. Marta was right."

Brace-Bel drummed his fat fingers on the table. "*That* is the first sensible thing you've said, young lady."

"Nothing here works right," Arjun agreed. "Everything's poisoned, and dies. But there are other places. I want to show you something. On the way back here I remembered something. Those ugly birds—those Thunders, you call them—where do they roost?"

Ruth had no idea—but Zeigler did.

They met him in an alley not far off the Square. The peculiar old man shook Arjun's hand enthusiastically, held it a little too long, looked deeply into his eyes as if hoping to see reflected in them some of the sights Arjun had seen. He looked Brace-Bel up and down as though he was something fascinating but monstrous, like a great horned toad. "Oh my word, the things you two could tell me . . ."

He hugged Ruth. "Courage," he said. "Courage—this, too, will pass."

He'd spent the last four days sitting in the windblown Square outside the Museum—"documenting the atrocities." He sheltered from the rain under an umbrella and scribbled sketches of the paintings and sculptures and weapons and altars and ornaments as they were dragged out and destroyed. He was a notably terrible artist—his angular black-inked cross-hatchings all looked roughly the same, blobs, whether they were of the sarcophagus of an ancient king or the preserved body of an extinct sloth. Twice, his notebook had been confiscated; once, one of the Know-Nothings slapped it from his hand and pissed on it, and he'd had to start again.

"The Thunders?" Zeigler said. "The birds? Really? Yes—actually—I've made a kind of study of them."

He'd always believed that there was something unnatural and uncanny about the horrid birds. He'd always had a sense that there was something in their hideous song that was close almost to speech, and might if decoded describe whatever distant part of the city they'd come from. "An alien species," he said. "Like an invasive weed."

So he'd followed them and studied them; he'd mapped their aimless ragged flights and discovered their stinking and slovenly roosts. He'd even tried to catch one once, and they'd chased him shrieking and hooting all the way home, and battered against his windows and shat down his chimney all night: which was *not* natural behavior for birds, he'd always maintained. "They don't belong here," he said. "Am I right? Are they from your city?" His eyes gleamed at the prospect of having his suspicions confirmed.

"Yes and no," Arjun said. "I don't know how it works, exactly. Brace-Bel has theories about the essences of things, and what persists and what's changed across Time. This city is hollow, full of cracks, riddled with secret veins. Things escape from their proper place—in particular weeds, birds, names, music, magic. At least in my experience. Things tangle oddly in the Metacontext. Everyone always forgets where they came from. I only know that I remember the birds when they were something better. I think maybe I can talk to them. I remembered who I am—why can't they? I think maybe I can show you all something about magic."

Zeigler came along, despite Arjun's warnings that it would be dangerous. Why not? He wasn't going to stop the man—it certainly wasn't Arjun's place to hold anyone back from indulging his obsessions.

Zeigler wore black. His jacket was worn, shiny, and too tight even over his skinny body. His white hair blew free in the morning's gusts and squalls. He looked like a hank of pigeon feathers stuck in a drainpipe. He carried a notebook and pencil; he was full of unanswerable questions.

Ruth came, too, in trousers and buttoned jacket and a scarf the same deep green as her eyes. Her breath misted in the cold evening air. It occurred to Arjun that this was the first time he'd seen her outside the dust and shadows of the shop. (Was it really?) He smiled and she smiled back. The brassy sunset light became her. It was somehow unreal to see her in sunlight—an unreal evening. He felt suddenly nervous for her.

And Brace-Bel brought up the rear. The pockets of his overalls carried the last of Shay's devices. He used his stick as a cane. The crystal atop it was camouflaged with a cloth tied round with string. He grumbled about his bad leg and his various illnesses. He held a handkerchief to his mouth and complained about the stench as they walked down by the canals, under the shadow of the gasometers and the waste reclamation plants; as they cut across an empty expanse of weeds and stones and then between the tanneries and the slaughterhouses. His spirits rose as they headed up Collier Hill, where the factories had closed ten years ago and now lay hunched and broken on the slopes of the Hill.

"It's subsidence," Zeigler said. "What ruined these factories—plain old subsidence. Twenty years ago these bloody great holes had opened in the earth. Overdigging. Shoddy foundations. Leaks of who-knows-what awful stuff. Some folk said that you could hear crying and moaning and this horrible cursing coming up from the shafts. I came as close as I dared. I camped for a night on the edge. I had my notebook ready. Never heard anything but echoes and wind and dripping water. Voices in the earth, folk said. Arjun, could that happen? Are there places where that happens?"

"Probably," Arjun said. He was distracted.

As the sun set behind the crest of the hill the spare silhouettes of the factories looked like the skeletons of crucified giants—or so Brace-Bel said. Giants who had assailed the peak and been blasted back down; blood-red and black with the sunset and their own rust and filth. Scenes of ruination cheered him, he said. "In this time the choice is between monotony and disaster—I choose disaster!"

To Arjun's eyes the flood of red light was a beautiful bright cymbal-clash, and those black silent structures were an orchestra waiting their cue. He felt the familiar rising of memory—some further fragments of that forgotten *Music*. He turned the memory this way and that and tested its weight. Meanwhile Brace-Bel loudly explained that punishment and the history of punishment was an area of his especial expertise, and crucifixion was . . .

"No homeless," Ruth said. "No paperless. No squatters. Never seen any empty place in the city so empty."

"The birds are territorial," Zeigler said. *"Vicious."*

"They used to be different," Arjun said. "When they were boys and girls. I remember them. Always vicious but not so *ugly*."

Ruth held his wrist. "Stop. Stop showing off." He opened his mouth to object, but it was true—with his memory restored, with the world opened to him again, he'd felt flushed with strength, puffed up with superiority to the Low sisters' shabby and belated world. He'd been cryptic—playing the magician.

"What are we doing here?" Ruth said.

"In the city where Brace-Bel comes from, there were children who called themselves the Thunderers. They were wild, and dangerous, and more than a little mad. Brutalized and brutal. But they were very beautiful. They flew, Ruth! Like birds. Ruth, I have a lot to tell you about the Gods. Zeigler, everything you suspect is true is true somewhere. They flew, and they loved bright things, and they couldn't bear for anything to be caged. I called on them once to break a friend free from gaol. If they were here, they'd free the Beast, they'd free Ivy, there'd be nothing the Know-Nothings could do to stop them."

He shrugged. "But they're not here. These ugly little monsters are in their place. A cruel spirit rules this place, here in the shadow of the Mountain. But what if they could be made to remember, Ruth, what they might have been? What if . . . ?"

Ruth put a finger to his lips. She was looking over his shoulder, and her eyes were wide with fear. She said, "How long have they been watching us?"

Arjun looked around, and sighed. There was no way of answering that question. When it suited them the birds maintained a sullen bitter silence and slunk and shuffled stealthily in the shadows. Now the birds were all around them, grey and shapeless as rags or heaps of rubble, roosting on rusted girders and useless cranes, peering from holes in the walls and down from the gutters. Everything was streaked grey-yellow with their shit.

The birds began to scatter and regroup. The dirty air was full of wings and cries of alarm and hate. They gathered jealously around the heaps of rubble in which they'd hoarded their treasures of thread and silk and bright metal. Some of them landed with a thud in front of Arjun's feet and hopped forward shouting. Others lifted their shiny keepsakes in their claws and took to the air, weaving nervously back and forth between empty towers and broken windows, looking for safe hiding places.

The birds gathered comfort from numbers and anger, and pressed in. They swept their heads left and right, slashing their beaks like little dull knives. Those uncannily near-human voices swore and taunted.

One of the birds darted past Brace-Bel's head and scraped blood from his temple; he shook his stick after it and cursed it. The bird made a sound like vicious gurgling laughter and as it rejoined the rest of the mob the near-laughter spread. Brace-Bel swung his stick in the air.

"Don't hit them." Ruth and Arjun at once. Zeigler turned to run but the path back downhill thronged with the birds, too; Ruth grabbed his skinny wrist and held him back.

Arjun stepped forward, arms open, palms up, and the throng closed around him.

"I remember you," he said.

He looked back and saw Ruth's green nervous eyes for a moment; then the birds swept across his vision and he was alone. Their wings and shouts beat out a mad rhythm. Feathers fell around him like ashes.

"You are much debased. I remember what you were."

They wheeled and tessellated in complex chaotic patterns. Bird-forms combined and spun and fell apart around him like the shadow-shapes of a zoetrope, and he was stuck in the middle. They battered their wings against his face and their claws ripped at his shirt. They had not yet begun to use their beaks; perhaps they remembered him, too, on some dim level . . . He fought to keep his voice level and calm. He spoke as if soothing a child out of a tantrum.

"Brace-Bel believes that though we may undergo transformations across the Ages of the city, something of our essence persists. When I knew you before you could not bear to leave anything caged. You were breakers of prisons; you even saved Brace-Bel. Do you remember?"

They closed so thickly round him that he was in shadow. Sometimes daylight flashed through like lightning.

"Do you remember Silk?"

The thrashing of their wings was deafening, but they'd stopped shouting. The louder their wings the quieter his voice. They hovered and glared expectantly. What they were doing could not be *listening,* exactly, but . . .

"Brace-Bel reminded me of a music from the old city. A *Music.* Since I heard it I have recovered more and more of myself. Do you remember this song . . . ?"

Brace-Bel lay fetal. Ruth yanked at his collar. "You must have some weapon, Brace-Bel, you know magic, do something."

In the next instant the birds lifted. They burst into the darkening air in all directions like dust vented from a chimney stack. They screamed and hooted as they rose. Was there a kind of music in it? Ruth wasn't sure.

Arjun sat on the ground, surrounded by feathers, bloody from a dozen scratches, thickly beshitted. He had a blissful and beautiful and infuriating smile on his face.

He got to his feet slowly and stiffly.

"We have our weapon," he said. "Our key."

The birds circled overhead. They shrieked at each other as if confused and startled by some fabulous terrifying news.

"Then we're ready," she said. "I'll tell the Masks."

Better to strike at night, of course, but the Black Masks wouldn't be ready until morning. Arjun and Ruth agreed that it would be madness to rely entirely on the birds, to assault the Museum without more mundane and predictable backup. "Anyway," Arjun said, "it'll be better in the morning. This should be done by morning light."

When they went home, Marta was there. She shook her head. "This is insane."

Ruth said, "Will you help?"

Marta sighed. "I'll be here to clean up and hide you when the Know-Nothings come looking for their revenge." And she shut herself up in her bedroom.

Zeigler went home to sleep—"more precisely, I think, to toss and turn and pace and *wait*."

Brace-Bel went walking. "Night. Solitude. Cold winds. To prepare myself for death and focus my energies. I shall find myself a whore."

And the grey birds that had followed Arjun home to circle and disturb Carnyx Street's sky had settled into sleep when the sun set. They roosted on every roof. They curled into their grey wings like sleeping children. They gave the Street a gothic and gargoyle-haunted appearance. Arjun hoped they were dreaming and remembering.

And he spent the night in Ruth's room, where she brought up one of Ivy's rattling and dusty record players, those rare and precious artifacts, and played music, and she brought up a bottle of red wine, an extraordinary luxury in that part of the city. She was oddly shy and intense about it. She washed his bird-scratches; her fingers lingered on his face. "I never thought you'd come back," she said.

Things were different now—she looked different to him. *He* was different. When he'd first seen her, he'd had no memories of himself. She'd been the first and only woman he'd ever known. The thin thread of his life had depended on her. He'd imagined her as a kind of Goddess—her and her sister—they'd loomed in his mind larger than the city.

Now he saw things with new eyes.

Now he realized how fragile she was. In fact she was very nearly as fragile and desperate as he was himself.

What absence, what loss defined her?

He realized that he knew almost nothing about her. Until now he hadn't known what to ask.

She said, ". . . what?"

"I was thinking."

"You had a strange smile."

"Did I?"

"Yeah. You're different, now, you know."

"How?"

"Less like a ghost; more like a person."

"Ah." Maybe. He *still* didn't know what to ask.

She poured the wine and adjusted the music every so often. She seemed to feel this was how things were done. Maybe it was. Every possible way for men and women to interact was the way it was done somewhere in the city.

What kind of lives did people live here? What kind of life had she lived?

After everything he'd seen, what kind of man was he?

He started to tell her about his God, the music, the Mountain, his travels. Then he stopped. He felt ridiculous, out of place. They discussed the weather. Later he told her about his God anyway and she listened with what seemed like interest. He didn't know what normal people talked about. There was a silence, which he found pleasant. They sat side by side on the bed, and moved closer. The music-machine required constant winding. They let it wind down. It hissed, scratched, stopped. The room was cold so they made love under musty woolen blankets. *Made love*—her words. Was that how things were described here? Outside a great and ridiculous weight of birds shuffled and scratched and shat on the roof, and pressed against the windows as if they wanted to be near, as if they were lonely and lost. They made a noise like rain.

The Know-Nothings started work before first light, as the first whistles blew. The Square was full of a cold fog that muffled the sound of boots stamping, men swearing, hammers crashing, glass smashing, and wood splintering. The dawn shift was low-ranking men who still had regular jobs to go to. They resented the work. They half-arsed it. Who'd have thought the old Museum had so much crap in it? They staggered under the unwieldy weight of a whole gallery of paintings—the moon, as seen over a dozen different skylines, blank or haunted by the faces of a dozen different Goddesses. They warmed their hands by the fire till it chased off the fog. A few cold and bored protesters from Carnyx Street watched them. One of the protesters knew two of the Know-Nothings from school and they shared cigarettes. The dawn shift could have been chased away bloodlessly—their hearts weren't in it. But by the time Arjun and Ruth were awake, and Brace-Bel had been slapped from the hangover he'd somehow acquired, and the Black Masks had rolled up at the Low sisters' door—five men, carrying a variety of guns, and three of them already half drunk—it was too late. Midmorning: the dawn shift had been replaced by harder men. Maury had come to take charge.

By the time Arjun came into the Square, Maury's men had finished with the paintings and were moving on to rocks—Moon Rocks, Mysteriously Carved Rocks, Highly Magnetic Rocks, Miscellaneous Rocks—which they sledgehammered to powder.

Half of Carnyx Street turned out to swell the protesters' numbers. Rumors had spread.

"Zeigler," Ruth sighed. "Can't keep his mouth shut."

Arjun stood at the back of the crowd, his face obscured under a borrowed hat. Marta moved among the crowd and led the children away, and the elderly.

The stone fingers of petrified saints, the ebony eggs of the phoenix, radioactive core-rods—all shattered and swept into the corner.

And by the time that was done, a man from Holcroft Municipal Trust was there. He wore a well-cut black suit, a bright green waistcoat, and gold-rimmed spectacles. He affected heavy black boots in a show of solidarity with the working Know-Nothings. He strutted back and forth giving orders and encouragement for a while. He took a couple of swings with the hammer, and received obligatory applause from the men. He kicked and swore at the handful of ugly ragged thunderers that came to squat on the rubble and peck for shiny remnants. Then he settled back to stand beside Inspector Maury at the edge of the Square watching the proceedings with a sour expression. Every few minutes he glared over at the protesters and muttered something to Maury as if calculating the costs and benefits of a massacre. On the one hand he would clearly be happy to silence the protesters; on the other hand he clearly wanted an audience for his very public display of destruction, and these dregs were all that was available.

"That's Wantyard," Ruth whispered. "He gave a speech a few days ago. He's a big man at Holcroft. I don't know why he's still hanging around here."

The Know-Nothings had reduced the rocks to dust and were starting to carry out the Museum's great heavy brass abaci and calculating-machines. Arjun's heart clenched as he saw Wantyard lean in to talk to Maury again. The two of them seemed to reach an unpleasant agreement. Maury called three of his men over and gave orders. Wantyard settled back against the wall of the Chapterhouse, and smiled in eager and bitter anticipation.

"They're running out of things to break," Ruth said. "They'll do the Beast soon. Now that we're all here to see."

"Yes."

"Then it's time." She was more confident than he was.

"It certainly is!"

They both started at the sound of Brace-Bel's voice. He stood behind them, fat and sagging in his borrowed brown overalls, but the expression on his face was resolute.

Ruth shoved his shoulder. "What are you doing here? Don't you mess this up, Brace-Bel."

"Just stay out of the way, Brace-Bel."

"I will not. I do not shrink from conflict or crisis. And I do not trust your mumbo jumbo. My precious Ivy's life is at stake. I shall search for her myself."

"Brace-Bel . . ."

Brace-Bel elbowed his way sideways through the crowd and a moment later was gone from sight, as if he'd vanished.

"I hate that man," Ruth said.

"Another reason to move quickly. Before he does something to give us away."

"Wish me luck, then."

Ruth crossed the Square, stepping through ashes and rubble. The Know-Nothings dropped what they were doing and watched her warily. She unwound her green scarf nervously from around her neck as she walked, and raised her hands to show they were empty.

Arjun watched her approach Maury and Wantyard. She'd wanted to give them one last chance. He couldn't see her face as she spoke. He saw Maury telling her to get lost. As she walked away her eyes met Arjun's and she shrugged.

Arjun turned away from the crowd and headed down the alley behind the building to the south of the Chapterhouse. He climbed up on boxes and up onto the rusting fire escape. He turned around and around up the iron stairs and ladders until he was out on the broad flat roof, which was like a thick forest of grey feathers and beady eyes. The chimneys and the ancient wire aerials groaned under the weight of the birds. The floor seethed and churned with them.

They fixed their eyes on him. As he stepped onto the roof they hopped aside to clear a path. They began to shout and babble. It was nearly human speech. Their aggression had been replaced by a desperate need. Their harsh throats piped; they tried to sing that *Music* he'd taught them. They made a dreadful cacophony. They fluttered around him adoringly as if they expected him to teach them something vitally important. What were they remembering? They reminded him more than ever of lost children.

"Are you ready?"

A shudder passed across the shrieking mass. Some of them took to the air and circled.

"Do you remember what you were? What you could be?"

The mass rose slowly, swelled into a dark cloud. There were distant cries of alarm from the Square below.

One of the birds hung in front of Arjun's face. Its ugly wings were hardly beating; whatever held their twisted bodies aloft was not natural. It held something sharp and bright in its grubby claws. Arjun was suddenly afraid; he had no control over the process he'd started. They had begun to remember their other selves—and there were places in the city where these dangerous creatures were better, but there were places where they were so very much worse, and who knew what they might choose to recall?

It cocked its head and made a hissing noise that sounded like *Silk*. Then the swirling mass carried it away.

Arjun looked down over the edge of the roof.

Far below, the Know-Nothings emerged from the Museum's towering double doors, dragging on ropes a wheeled pallet, on which the Beast's immense cage rested. It emerged agonizingly slowly. It must have weighed a ton; Arjun had no idea how they would get it down the steps. Inside something heavy and coiled flinched from the sun. In sunlight its scales were the hideous green of rot or mildew, of rusty pipes and flaking paint. A single great yellow eye stared out. It seemed to catch Arjun's gaze. He couldn't read its animal expression.

He shouted, "There's the cage! There's the prisoner. There are the gaolers!"

He gestured like the conductor of an impossible orchestra and the birds descended.

First they circled the air over the Square like leaves caught in a whirlwind, calling out to each other, sometimes breaking and recircling against each other in waves and sudden squalling back-drifts. They gathered numbers. They gathered speed. They seemed to be gathering their memories. They were still unsure of their purpose and some of them shrieked out affirmations and others negations. They scattered tattered shadows on the Square below. Their grey feathers caught the sun and *sparkled*. Many of them clutched scraps of bright fabric and metal—their knives and razors. They were a carnival crowd. Some of their shouts and caws were something like laughter.

Arjun turned and turned down the fire escape. He was still on the other side of the Hall of Trade when the first shot rang out, and he didn't see who fired. At first he thought the noise was the percussive clanging of the stairs under his own feet. Thoughts about memory and perception and magic and power occurred to him but he had no time to entertain them. He dropped into the alley from the foot of the fire escape and nearly broke his ankle.

When he came out into the Square again it was like looking into a blizzard, or into a kaleidoscope. The birds flocked to and fro brighter and brighter, and the Know-Nothings and the Museum were both barely visible.

The protesters had fled the Square; they sheltered in the alleys and watched in awe.

The birds called out in joy and surprise at their own beauty and strength and numbers. More birds joined the flock every minute as their brothers and sisters shrieked to them of freedom and memory and beauty.

Almost as an afterthought they tore into the Know-Nothings, they beat against the bars of the Beast's cage. The cage! The gaolers! They shrieked with righteous hate.

They flocked thickly past Arjun and shouted in his face but they didn't harm him. He shivered at the touch of their wings. He was thrilled and afraid; the perfect moment of recall could not last forever.

. . . and suddenly it was over. The birds broke apart like a reflection of the city in a dirty puddle, shattered in waves by a single step; when the moment passed it passed utterly. They scattered, as if suddenly embarrassed, into ones and twos, patternless, purposeless, squawking and shitting. They were too badly debased. Unable to bear the vision of what they might have been, they fled; down alleys, behind chimneys; they vanished over the rooftops, filling the sky for a second with strange clouds. It hurt to watch them go. Arjun thought: *if I were stronger, if I were wiser, I might have brought them fully through . . .*

Then they were gone, leaving the Square bloody and mucky and feathered; leaving the job half done and the prisoners not yet liberated.

The Know-Nothings sprawled on the ground, crouched with their arms over their heads, huddled together as if for warmth. Their hands were bloody and torn. Their faces bled, some from scratches, an unlucky few from blinded eyes. They stumbled as they rose. Some were still screaming. *I'm so sorry,* Arjun thought, *not again*; and *please forgive me*; and he felt sick at his own hypocrisy, because he remembered now that he'd done cruel things before on his path through the city, and always forgotten them and moved on.

And then he forgot his guilt, seeing the Beast thrash in its cage. The birds had somehow, between them, in their vast surging numbers, bent the bars, in an attempt to break the cage. It seemed they'd half lifted and then dropped it. It now lay on its side, halfway down the Museum's marble steps. The Beast was forcing its huge head through the bent bars. The Beast's huge shoulders violated the cage's unhinging structure and the metal groaned and snapped. The creature's jaw hung open and it made a constant hissing sound like steam escaping from an engine. Its long red tongue lashed the air hungrily. The creature was much larger and leaner than it had seemed in the cellar. Its thick neck stretched revoltingly and bulged with the effort of expansion and birth. Another bar broke noisily loose.

Brace-Bel

Later, as Arjun and Brace-Bel hid in the darkness of their bolt-hole, Brace-Bel would breathlessly recount his adventures in the Museum. He explained that he had always, in his strange life, been the villain, or worse, the laughingstock; but he'd ventured into the enemy's lair in search of his true beloved like a hero of the highest and most chivalrous romance. His purpose had been pure as the purest knight's, because he expected *nothing* from Ivy, nothing at all. He became what he was always meant to be. It was *laughable,* humiliating, but also superb . . .

So Brace-Bel wandered the dusty halls of the Museum. His feet scuffed the dust, which reassured him that he truly existed, notwithstanding the fact that he could not see his own feet. Whenever he looked down he felt as though he should fall. He touched his own face compulsively. He could not see his fingers. In fact he could not see any part of himself, nor could he (so far, touch wood) be seen by others.

He'd inherited no fewer than *three* invisibility devices from Shay. He'd kept them on his person and they'd survived the destruction of his household. One, which hung from a chain around his neck, was a grey pigeon's feather, which smelled of dry blood and smoke, and was distressingly cold to the touch. Shay had said that it held the power of a God of the city's unwanted and friendless and elderly, and imparted that God's gift of being forgotten. A second, clipped to Brace-Bel's belt and humming softly, was a little box of circuits and diodes that might one day be invented somewhere, but never here. Shay had explained—as if it "explained" anything!—that the box created a field that bent and scattered light. And last there was an inky black stone, shiny but unreflective, massy and somehow ancient-feeling, that Shay had refused under any circumstances to discuss. Brace-Bel kept it in his pocket and tried not to touch it.

He had no idea which of the three devices did the work of hiding him. Perhaps all of them did! He felt terribly uneasy. He felt remarkably brave and pleased with his own bravery and ashamed that in these last days, this alien city, he had been reduced to being proud of such nonsense. He wiped his brow and felt sweat that he could not see.

Because he was a scholar, and had had conversations with the leading students of optics of his day, he wondered how he was not *blind*. If he could not be seen it seemed to him that he should not be able to see. A puzzle. It was sad to think that he knew no one with whom he could share it.

Over the sound of the thrashing of wings he could hear men outside in the Square screaming. A little shiver of delight ran down his spine.

He had a device like a tin whistle that could throw, like a ventriloquist, various noises, and he used it to distract the Know-Nothings when he needed to pass. He had a device like a monocle that did *something* to people that left them sitting on the floor staring vacantly through their own pouring tears.

He found Ivy on the second floor, the only object in an emptied room, standing still at the window, watching the birds circle. She stared with a fierce curiosity as if trying to calculate their chaotic interweaving trajectories. She did not seem to be anyone's prisoner.

"If every beautiful thing in this Museum were destroyed," he said, "and you alone remained, this would be no less a storehouse of wonders." He was at least half sincere, which delighted and confused and appalled him.

She turned from the window. "Brace-Bel," she said. She did not seem surprised at his presence, or his invisibility. She sighed and said, "I might have known you'd interfere." Unable to think of anything intelligent to say, instead he went down on one knee, where he wobbled slightly, then cursed as he realized that she could not see him, and fumbled in his pockets for the relevant devices, which he was not sure now how to deactivate, and his hands were soaked with sweat.

She helped him stand, saying, "Never mind, never mind. Too late now. Let's go talk to the Beast." She gave him her arm and permitted him to lead her to safety.

Arjun

Outside in the Square the Know-Nothings got to their feet. Some of them were still in agony or in tears; two ran away into the alleys behind the Museum. The rest drew their weapons. They were scattered and panicked and confused; their clothes were torn and they looked like bloody scarecrows. Maury moved among them calling for order and it seemed to Arjun that he was telling them to stay calm and in control and knocking their guns from their hands. But in fact there was no one obvious to shoot anyway. The protesters had fled.

Where was Ruth? Was she safe?

Arjun peered from around a corner and as far as he could see the Know-Nothings hadn't yet noticed him.

There were only half a dozen of the Know-Nothings standing. It seemed like more, but he counted carefully.

One of the Know-Nothings aimed his gun at the Beast, still struggling out of its cage and into the city.

It was a violent birth; the broken bars gouged into its scaly hide. Blood oozed from the wounds in its throat.

Maury wrestled the gun from the man's hand, as if he'd decided now to save the Beast. (*Was* it Maury? Whoever it was still wore his torn and filthy black coat over his head as a shield against the birds.) The Beast's would-be executioner decided to run for it, slipping and sliding on bloody feathers. Maury—if it was Maury—sat on the steps, wrapped in torn black, and watched the Beast emerge.

There was a terrible explosion of noise in Arjun's ear, and he stumbled. His face was warm; he put a hand to it and felt blood, dust.

A bullet had hit the wall next to his head, sprayed him with fragments of brick. His ears rang with noise and shock. Who'd fired? He couldn't tell. He stumbled back into the alley, hunching for cover.

Ruth

As the storm of birds descended Ruth sheltered in an alley just off the Square. Marta was there, clutching Mrs. Anchor's frightened snotty children by their collars—where was Mrs. Anchor? Zeigler was there, an expression of utter rapture on his face. The alley was heaped with stinking refuse, broken crates. Mrs. Rawley was there, sitting on a crate, swigging from her whiskey-bottle, cackling. Schiller the dogcatcher peered from the shadows, baring his broken teeth into a snarl of joy. "Take that! Fucking Know-Nothings!" Shriveled old Mrs. Thayer leaned on her huge pale damaged son, who'd left his bedroom for the first time in years to see the miracle for himself, and was maybe bellowing, maybe laughing, and either way his round face was bright with tears.

At the back of the alley was a wire-link fence, at the foot of which were heaps of garbage, rank stands of weeds; over the top of which hung half a dozen children, fingers knotted in the wires, watching the miracle.

At the mouth of the alley the Square, the city, the sky were all utterly transformed. The beating of wings was loud as a train. Nothing was visible but bright feathers, flashes of color and light—and sometimes the chaotic thrashing *stilled,* and for a moment it seemed every bird swooped together, like a single white wing beating slowly. It was impossible to imagine that the world would ever return to normal.

Ruth stepped out into it with her eyes wide open. She heard Marta's voice calling *stop* . . . and then she could hear nothing but the thrashing of wings, the cries and song of the birds. They left her unharmed. They resembled illustrations of angels torn from an old book, set loose on the breeze. She couldn't stop laughing . . .

. . . until suddenly they rose, all at once, their song tapering off into cries of dismay and confusion, their flight becoming unsteady and uncertain. She reached after them; they were gone.

The Square was a bloody, filthy mess. A Know-Nothing with his eyes torn from his face staggered past her, fell at her feet. At the far end of the Square the surviving Know-Nothings were regrouping.

After the miracle was over the world was unchanged.

Now the Black Masks came into the Square, from the east and west sides, as arranged, guns at the ready, to demand the Know-Nothings' surrender.

Ruth wasn't sure who started the shooting.

She walked forward across the Square. Marta was calling, *get back here, Ruth, come back.*

On the steps of the Museum the Beast was forcing its way out of its cage.

It was so much larger than she remembered, so much uglier and wilder. Its savage jerking motions as it thrashed at the bars were nothing like the gentle creature of her memories. Only its huge yellow eyes were the same.

Its neck seemed to stretch, snakelike, as it squeezed out into the world.

It terrified her. What would it do when it escaped into the city? *What have we done?*

Then she saw the scars and stitches that covered every inch of its hide. She saw how badly put-together it was, and she was full of pity for it.

A shapeless black figure approached the monster, stumbling, half on its knees, half upright—Inspector Maury, who it seemed had sheltered from the birds with his long black coat over his head. He knocked aside another Know-Nothing and kept stumbling forward. When he reached the cage he threw the torn and filthy coat aside, and stood up. He barely came up to the Beast's long scarred throat. He lifted up his hands as if seeking the Beast's blessing, and its head, madly thrashing, swooped and snapped shut over his left arm—and tore, and twisted, so that Maury jerked like a puppet—and it swung its head and threw him aside, bleeding, broken, to roll down the Museum's steps.

Ruth stepped over him. She was running, now . . .

Mr. Wantyard had staggered to his feet. His waistcoat was torn and his belly protruded; he looked like an unraveling scarecrow. He snatched a long rifle from the limp frightened grip of his bodyguard. He sighted and fired into the Beast's open and slavering jaws. Blood sprayed. He fired again. Before she knew she meant to do it, Ruth found that she'd lifted a truncheon from the belt of the unconscious Know-Nothing at her feet, and run up the slick and feathered steps, and struck Wantyard with all her strength on the back of his bald head.

Wantyard stumbled, cursed, dropped the rifle, and put a hand to his head. He rounded on her, snarling.

Arjun

Arjun's head rang; he could hear nothing in his left ear but the droning echoes of that shot, like an airplane circling in his skull. In his right ear he could hear dim and muted sounds of gunfire, screaming. He felt sick.

He staggered back out of the safety of the alley and into the chaos of the Square. One of the Black Masks had been shot and lay writhing. Arjun couldn't hear—was he groaning or screaming? At the south end of the Square a group of Masks was accepting the surrender of the last of the Know-Nothings, or perhaps it was the other way around.

Soundless, the scene was unreal, dreamlike, meaningless. The Beast opened its bloody jaws in a silent roar. Feathers still drifted in the air.

Up on the steps a fat man in a torn green waistcoat was wrestling with—Ruth?

Arjun ran up the steps. He slipped on something and fell, bruising his shins. When he got up again, he saw that Ruth and the fat man—Wantyard?—both stood still, watching the door to the Museum, from which Ivy was now emerging.

Behind Ivy there was a faint shimmer in the air—Brace-Bel.

Ivy wore a simple black dress. She appeared quite calm—almost amused at the strange scene before her.

The Beast stilled its thrashing and watched her.

Ivy reached out and took a drifting feather from the air. She examined it, and smiled.

Wantyard let go of Ruth.

Wantyard said something; Ruth said something; Ivy said something. Drone and buzz; silence.

Ivy walked straight past Ruth. She took Wantyard's hands in hers and whispered something in his ear.

Did they know each other? Apparently they did—because Wantyard attempted to kiss her, and when she stepped deftly aside, he followed her eagerly over to the cage, where the Beast waited.

The expression on Ruth's face—confused, upset, angry? Arjun moved next to her and held her hand. He pointed at his ears and mouthed, *can't hear*. Her eyes were wide.

Ivy and Wantyard stood together before the Beast's cage. Ivy turned and smiled at Wantyard, whispered in his ear, and he swallowed, leaned forward, and reached into the bars of the cage.

Instantly the Beast lunged and clamped its jaw around Wantyard's arm. Wantyard reared back—and then Ivy was standing behind him, holding his shoulders, and she was shouting something at him, or at the Beast—which bit again, and then again, in Wantyard's shoulder, in his belly, in his leg, opening shallow precise wounds . . .

The Beast worked on Wantyard with the delicacy of a surgeon. With a swift slice of its claws it removed the man's genitals; raking deftly back and forth it opened the man's throat like an accordion. It was a complicated operation. It seemed to go on for some time.

Ivy stood beside Wantyard, talking, gesturing—as if she was giving the Beast instructions.

Ruth buried her head in Arjun's shoulder and sobbed. Brace-Bel, visible now, blanched and looked away.

As the Beast worked on Wantyard its own stitches began to open—the scars of the surgery that had made it. At first they bled, a thick black ooze. Then they began to leak dust. They snapped open and dry sheets of hide and scale fell away, exposing wet mus-cle and bone. The creature's movements became slow and painful. The light in its yellow eyes faded. Its haunches sagged. At last it slumped to the floor and lay still.

After a long moment Wantyard got to his feet.

He was bleeding from a hundred wounds, small and large. His clothes were torn and he was nearly naked.

He smiled, and his smile was too wide. His eyes had an ugly yellow shine to them. His tongue flickered.

Ivy wrapped Maury's discarded black coat around Wantyard's shoulders. Wantyard struggled to get into it, jerking and twisting, as if unfamiliar with clothing. When he was done he smiled again, and began to stroke the coat's leather, preening himself.

Arjun realized that the hearing in his right ear was returning—his left ear still buzzed and roared. He could hear Ruth crying. He could hear distant alarms.

The creature wearing Wantyard's flesh stopped its preening, and came toward Arjun. He stood his ground. He was very fright-ened; but all it did was stand in front of him and look him curiously up and down, and smile, and sniff, repeatedly, obsessively, as if puz-zled by the sensory deficiencies of its new body.

It grinned again, and spoke, and Arjun strained to hear the dis-tant buzzing words: "He has laboratories. He made me. I made myself anew. He no longer owns me."

Ruth still kept her head turned away, as if she couldn't bear to look at the bloody creature.

Arjun said, "You promised to tell me my past. I haven't forgot-ten. How did I find my way up the Mountain? What happened to me there? Did I find my God?"

It said, "He made me and sent me out in the city as a sign. That unkind father Shay. The young one, not the old. I was made to send fools like you to your deaths. Why should I do it any longer?"

"I don't understand."

It said, "There is a door on Pandora Street. Once you begin it will be like falling. He will be waiting for you. He is always wait-ing for his enemies. Now—I have unfinished business with the woman." And it turned and walked over toward Ivy, who reached out and adjusted its collar, and whispered to it.

The alarms were getting closer. There was the sound of running feet in the alleys. Marta stood at the foot of the steps calling, "Come on, come on!"

Below, in the Square, the surviving Black Masks and the people of Carnyx Street and whoever'd simply wandered by and been curious stood confused and nervous, uncertain of their lines. And the alarms came closer. And Ruth took Arjun's hand and said, "We have to go—we have to go now."

Ivy and the Beast ran in one direction. Ruth ran in another. After a moment's uncertainty, Arjun followed Ruth. Brace-Bel, huffing and puffing, ran after him.

FOURTEEN

The Bolt-Hole–Gathering the Expedition–Good Riddance–An Act of War

Arjun

Over the next few days the Know-Nothings searched every house on Carnyx Street twice over, and questioned every last man, woman, and child until they were tired and dizzy and desperate. There were beatings; doors got kicked in.

They demanded answers about the "Incident." There *was* no monster in the Museum, they insisted, and they took the fact that so many people claimed to have seen it as evidence of conspiracy; or perhaps of some mass-hallucination weapon devised by the unnatural science of the Mountain to aid their assault on the city below. They simultaneously insisted that Wantyard and Maury had not gone missing, that they were perfectly fine, that it was unthinkable that terrorists or saboteurs might have laid hands on such important men—*and* that they had been murdered, and the people of Carnyx Street were hiding the killers. Their orders and strategies seemed confused.

The city's vestigial official police force poked around briefly, until the Know-Nothings chased them off.

There were only two casualties. When the Know-Nothings barged into Thayer's dank room, shoving his old mother aside, and accused him of being in league with Brace-Bel and whatever uncanny powers backed him, Thayer became violent. A Know-

Nothing was hurled from the window and broke his back on the potting sheds below; Thayer got shot. His mother, distraught, was sedated with Marta's herbs and installed in the bed in the Low sisters' attic.

The Thunderers came and went in the skies, and perched on the washing-lines shifting uneasily. They no longer stole or menaced. They called out plaintively. They seemed unsure what to become.

All this was related to Arjun and Brace-Bel in whispers, by Mrs. Rawley, through the cracks in the hidden door to the secret room behind the barrels in the cellar of Rawley's public house. She came down to share the gossip every evening. Otherwise they were alone.

Of course Arjun had tried to flee—to open a door into some safer part of the city. He'd led Ruth and Marta and Brace-Bel and Rawley and Zeigler out into the streets, saying, *Come with me. No one has to stay here for this.* Then he'd spent an hour blundering down alleys and shoving at locked doors. His hearing—his hearing was still a mess. The buzz and drone had subsided a little, but now he heard everything as if from a great distance, through a thick wall. All music sounded like the same dull tones—he was trapped. He rapped at windows and yanked at rattling wire fences and kicked on corrugated iron walls; nothing. It became humiliating. Eventually Marta said, "We need to hide you. Rawley's place, Ruth, what do you think?"

So Rawley's place it was, then. A tiny and increasingly unpleasant bolt-hole that some previous owner had apparently once used for hiding contraband, and that Rawley used for hiding ghosts.

Rawley came in the afternoon, slid the door back, shoved in a tray of food. "You stay there, you two, another night. This new Inspector's a bastard. He's not going anywhere yet."

Arjun, shamefaced, handed over the waste-bucket. She took it without embarrassment.

He said, "Where are Ivy and the Beast?"

"Don't know. Clever girl, that one. She's found a nicer hiding place than this, I bet. Hah! We do our best."

"Is Ruth still safe?"

"They questioned her again. She's all right. Bit shaken."

"Does she have a message for me?"

Rawley shook her head. "You get some sleep, now. I have an appointment. I'll be back soon." She slid the door closed again.

Ruth

In the evening Ruth slipped away from the shop, and away from Carnyx Street. The patrols were starting to get lazy—they didn't notice her. She cut across gardens to avoid the checkpoints. It began to rain lightly, and she hunched into herself. She slipped past the stables, past factories, through a tangle of little houses, down by the edge of a black and freezing canal, and across a little waste of muddy ground to the half-open door of an old concrete slate-roofed building.

The windows were broken, and the door was rotten. There were soft lights behind it. Cold water dripped and gurgled. A rusted sign read PATAGAN SEWER & PIPING—PUMPING STATION 300.

She knocked on the door. Voices inside went silent.

"It's me. I've brought food."

Inside, amid rusting machinery, in the light of stolen gas lanterns, Ruth and the Beast held court.

They sat on half-rotten furniture. Dead valves and pumps loomed behind them. Ruth wore black. The Beast wore an old coat, and nothing much underneath except bandages. Its wounds were still raw and seeping. Its eyes were bright.

A half-dozen people sat around them on the floor. The Beast was telling them a story, something unpleasant about a Hotel and various scheming madmen.

Ivy waved Ruth over. "Good. Here. Did you bring paper and ink?"

"Yes. That, too, Ivy."

Ivy had scattered maps and calculations all over her hiding place, her notes of the Beast's mad stories and prophecies.

"There aren't as many patrols today. You can come home soon."

"Don't be silly, Ruth."

Someone in the Beast's audience hissed at Ruth to be quiet.

For days now, people from Carnyx Street had been slipping down to the ruined Station, by ones and twos, under cover of darkness. They came to see the Beast, to listen to its stories. They came to hear about the Mountain. Ruth recognized two of the Black Masks. She recognized Mrs. Rawley, sitting on an old box in the corner.

"Mrs. Rawley? What are you doing here?"

Rawley shrugged. "I'm an old woman, Ruth. There's nothing left for me down here."

Ivy's hiding place was becoming an open secret. It was only a matter of time before someone gave it up to the Know-Nothings. But Ivy didn't seem to care about the Know-Nothings anymore. Her attention was fixed on the Mountain.

"Marta says . . ."

"Marta can come herself if she wants to talk."

Ivy dipped her pen and began scratching again—numbers, maps, geometry. Designs like the gears of a great machine.

"Don't go, Ivy. You won't come back."

"I certainly hope not."

The Beast was lying with gusto about mad Gods called Builders, who hated humanity and made the city as a cage. Its audience shuffled closer. Ruth noticed Zeigler among them, listening with a little smirk of fascination.

Ruth whispered, "You're not going to take these people with you, are you, Ivy? They're not like you."

"They might be useful."

"I forgot what you were like, Ivy."

Ivy kept writing. "You fooled yourself, then, Ruth. You wanted to believe we were happy once, I expect. That was always important to you."

"You're like *him*."

"We'll see about that, won't we?"

The Beast stood and clapped its bandaged hands. "And *that* is the truth of the Mountain." It looked Ivy's way. "Are we done here? Is the debt paid?"

Ivy nodded. "I have all I need."

"Enjoy the Mountain, then. Give my regards to you-know-who. Oh won't he be surprised to see *you*? Oh this will hurt him. It almost makes me want to go with you. But I have a life to lead. At long last, I have a life to lead. I think I shall find a mate . . ."

The Beast walked toward the door, talking over its shoulder.

"Aren't you coming? Sir?" Rawley called after it. "Aren't you coming with us? You know what it all means."

"All *you* need to know, old woman, is that you will die on the Mountain. The old man's defenses will tear you apart and hollow you out. You will get as far as the gates of his house and a shadow will descend from black skies and you will not see it coming. I expect it will hurt. Good-bye."

Then the Beast was gone.

Ruth leaned forward, putting her hand on Ivy's papers, stopping her pen. "Don't go."

Ivy forced a smile. "I'm not ready yet anyway. Come back tomorrow. We can talk then."

Arjun

They had Brace-Bel's crystal for light. It filled the bolt-hole with a wavering honey-colored glow. Brace-Bel, cross-legged, held the stick in the crook of his elbow, clutching paper and pen in both shaking hands, scribbling endlessly. Meanwhile Arjun sat in the shadows and turned over his memories.

Pandora Street? That meant nothing to him. How had he approached the Mountain before? Perhaps there were as many routes to the Mountain as there were facets to the city.

Brace-Bel shifted and adjusted the stick. The light brightened a little, and darkened again.

Shay, the Beast had said. *The young one, not the old*—as if there were two of him. And the Beast spoke of Shay as if he were not only the Beast's maker, but also the ruler of the Mountain. Brace-Bel had believed that Shay wanted him to *assault* the Mountain. And then again when Arjun met the man—as Shay, and then again as Lemuel—he'd been the ruler of nothing, only a wanderer, a schemer, a crook, a snake-oil salesman . . .

Who ruled the Mountain? What was it? What did Shay have to do with the Mountain, what did the Mountain have to do with his God, with the city, with Ivy and the Beast, with Ruth, whose dreams, like his own, were simple and innocent, who did not deserve to be caught in this web of madness and cunning and cruelty . . .

He had no head for puzzles and paradox. He craved simplicity, and the peace of music and worship. It made him angry—the city was perversely constructed. He wallowed in self-pity for a while, he worried about what might be happening up above to Ruth, he banged his head against the impossibility of the Mountain, and he was full of self-pity again, and again, until suddenly Brace-Bel interrupted.

"My musical friend! Give me a word for the continuance of a theme in restricted circumstances. Something that speaks of resilience, persistence, if you please."

"What are you writing, Brace-Bel?"

"This? This awful hole is only another kind of prison," he said. "I shall continue my memoirs. It's a comfort," he added. "You may borrow my pen."

"I have no gift for words."

"A musician. A monk. A pilgrim. Thinker of simple passionate thoughts. A man who lives in the moment of ecstasy."

"I've never thought of myself as passionate."

"I would hate to see what bloody and mad things you'd do if you ever *were* passionate."

"What do you mean, Brace-Bel?"

"Not an introspective man. No compulsion to apology or self-accounting. No urge to spin theories or excuses. I admire you. But *I* must write. Moreover, I am compelled to leave behind some record of myself in the event that we do not return from the Mountain."

"*We?*"

Brace-Bel was thoughtful for a long time. Then he said, "I mean to see this through to the end, now. Besides," he smiled, "Ivy will need my counsel."

"Ivy?"

"She will take me, she will need my counsel, she will need someone to tell her story. I would not serve Shay but it would be my pleasure to serve her."

"No, Brace-Bel. *I'm* going up the Mountain. My God is there. I've spent years . . ."

"Well, but here you are in this horrible cellar with me, and *she* is out there with the Beast and his secrets and planning the way up the Mountain, so perhaps you have not played your hand as well as you might."

Arjun sat in scowling silence for a minute. Then he moved suddenly, and crept toward the door panel, and slid it open a crack.

The voices of Know-Nothings echoed and boomed in the bar just outside.

"I think it's the afternoon," Brace-Bel said. "Try again at night."

Ruth

Why hide in the Pumping Station? It fitted the Beast's nature, but not Ivy's. She was always fastidious about cleanliness—and Fosdyke offered a hundred other less damp hiding places. Cellars, bolt-holes, conspirators' hidden rooms, the city was riddled with them. Ruins, abandoned buildings, warehouses that even the Combines that owned them had forgotten existed, lost in a fog of bureaucracy.

Ruth slipped through the streets, down to the Station, again, another moonlit night. The route was becoming familiar. She wondered if the Station *meant* anything to Ivy. If she remembered.

Because in the years before the Dad left, when the sisters had been small, and the Dad was always going on longer and longer journeys, leaving them alone, they'd had a game. They'd gone exploring the streets, creeping out of the house at night. All three of them together. (They had been strange children.) Exploring, conquering, naming and renaming waste grounds, inventing history for shuttered ruins. Declaring themselves Princesses of abandoned spaces. They had followed the canal as far out as Walbrook. They had broken into Pumping Station 300 and claimed it as theirs. It had been one of their favorites for a week or two before they found the stables on Crow Street. It was still active in those days—the pumps heaved and roared and rose and fell. Ruth had imagined the machines were an army, shifting in centuries-long fairy-tale sleep, waiting to be woken. Marta had declared the place a ruined castle, left over from forgotten Ages of the city, disguised in concrete and slate.

Did Ivy remember? Was that why she'd gone to ground there? Maybe. Maybe not. In retrospect Ruth thought little Ivy had been less interested in their childish fantasy than in the machines, the processes and systems they represented.

Ruth knew something was wrong as soon as she turned the street corner and saw the Station, down by the water. At first she couldn't say what it was. But then, of course, she realized that the Station's windows were dark, again.

She stopped, and she waited, and the lights did not come back. She approached slowly, already knowing what she would see: the ruined building returned to disuse, cold and silent again.

Scraps of Ivy's notes and calculations were scattered on the damp floor. Numbly Ruth picked them up and scanned them. She didn't understand any of it.

They'd taken the lanterns. Perhaps the Mountain was dark, or the path to it. They'd left most of the food for the rats. Maybe you didn't need food on the Mountain.

In the muddy ground outside the Station there were footprints. Were they fresh? Ruth wasn't sure. A dozen people or more, walking together, down along the water—and the tracks were lost in the weeds.

Who'd gone? Who'd been left behind?

Suddenly she thought of Arjun, in the dark of Rawley's bolt-hole. Was he still there?

She ran back to Carnyx Street.

Arjun

All evening the Know-Nothings in the bar outside had been making noise—drinking and shouting and arguing. The bolt-hole echoed with muffled voices. Where was Mrs. Rawley? Arjun hadn't seen her since the afternoon of the day before, and in her absence the Know-Nothings seemed to have moved in permanently. They seemed to be drinking her cellars dry.

Arjun was hungry. Brace-Bel had fallen asleep.

The Know-Nothings all went silent, very suddenly and all at once. Brace-Bel muttered in his sleep.

There were footsteps in the corridor outside. Arjun picked up Brace-Bel's stick and held it like a club, waiting in the dark.

The door slid back. Framed in the lamplight that poured in, glowing like an angel, was a head of curly blond hair, and a brilliant smile.

"Arjun? *There* you are."

"St. Loup?"

Behind St. Loup stood a little round man in a brown suit, with an egg-shaped head and mild bespectacled eyes.

"Turnbull?"

Behind Father Turnbull, lying in the corridor, was what appeared to be at least one Know-Nothing, possibly deceased.

St. Loup vaguely waved the needle-gun in his hand.

"I think at this point you should probably regard yourself as our captive," St. Loup explained.

Brace-Bel rolled over, snoring.

"And I suppose we'll take the fat one, too."

Ruth

Ruth went to bed that night without a word to anyone. Marta tried to say something to her; she didn't listen. She slept most of the next day, and most of the day after.

Who was gone? Ivy was gone. Rawley was gone—when Ruth had gone running panting into Rawley's pub, she'd found it empty, except for a half-dozen Know-Nothings who appeared to be passed out in a dead drunk, so total that they might in fact have been drugged. Arjun was gone—the bolt-hole was empty. Had Ivy come to Arjun, had Arjun gone to her? Had they all left together? She couldn't know. Who else was gone? She didn't care.

"Ivy's gone," Marta said. It wasn't a question.

"Yes."

"Huh. Well, good riddance."

But Marta was tough. *Good riddance* was what she'd said when the Dad disappeared, too.

Ruth couldn't stand to be alone in the house. She went walking, on the streets on which she was trapped. The Know-Nothings hung around for a few more days, inquiring after the mysterious disappearances of the following individuals of interest to their inquiries: Mrs. Rawley, Mr. Zeigler, a Mr. . . . Then they went home. The patrols were recalled—the state of emergency was relaxed. Carnyx Street was quiet again. Hours were increased at the local factories to compensate for the lost productivity of the past week. The weather got a little worse. The Mountain looked the same. The lights of distant streets were scattered on it like nameless constellations. The peaks were a void, coal-black.

One night there was a storm over the Mountain, a real shocker, slashes of violent white lightning and lurid clouds, nets of rain sweeping and surging across the city, and maybe that storm meant something and maybe it didn't. In the morning everyone slogged to work through the puddles, same as every day. Whatever Ivy had done on the Mountain had made no difference to anything, except that she was gone, and Arjun, and everyone else. The city felt the same as ever, only slightly less so.

One night, as she sat in the upstairs window smoking *xaw* and watching the unchanging Mountain, she saw three bright specks appear against its dark mass. At first she thought they were stars. Then she wondered if they were birds.

She watched them as they approached, fanning out across the city. As they spread out it became clear that there were more than three—six, twelve, twenty-four points of light.

They appeared to have come from the Mountain. But that, of course, was impossible. They might as well have come from the moon. Was she hallucinating? She stubbed out the cigarette.

The lights continued to move across the city. Most of them drifted off to east or west, but one came closer and closer.

It was hard to judge perspective—how large was it? It appeared to be a sort of flying machine. The mass of the thing was a dark grey balloon, long and bulletlike and ugly. The light was just something that hung from a cage below it—a cold, hard artificial light of a kind that she had not seen for years, not since the Dad's experiments with electricity.

The thing droned. It had engines.

The light beamed down across the darkness of the city, freezing flashes of white rooftops and chimneys and fences.

Was it looking for something?

"Ivy?" Ruth said. She leaned out of the window.

The thing passed overhead and two streets away. She ran to another window to try to see where it went, but the angle was bad; all she could see were the edges of the light as it passed. All she could hear was the drone of its engines.

Did it have a pilot? Did it have a mission? Who sent it?

Moments later there was an impossibly loud and earth-shaking crash, and a flash of red flame from over on Ezra Street, and the window cracked and the house shuddered.

An explosion? A bomb?

Ruth ran downstairs, pulled on a coat, and went out into the streets.

BOOK TWO
After the Second Expedition

FIFTEEN

Wake Up!–Inquiries, Cryptozoological and Otherwise–News of the War and a Dialogue on Faith–Fragile Alliances

Arjun

"W ake up."

"Wake *up*."

"Is he dead? He'd better not be dead, Turnbull."

"We can know very little in this life, St. Loup. We are but mortals stumbling in the dark. But I *do* know poisons. He is not dead, and he *will* wake up."

"He'd better, Turnbull. He'd better."

"Are you threatening me, St. Loup?"

"A man of the cloth? Perish the thought."

"His eye just twitched."

"Give him another shot. More electricity, that's the ticket."

"Be quiet, St. Loup. Did you just hear him moan?"

"That's scintillating conversation by his standards. I'll give him a kick."

"Ah, there we go. There we go."

"Finally. Wake up! Wake up! It's your old friend St. Loup and good old Father Turnbull. We have questions for you."

They held Arjun in a small suite of rooms, somewhere in a tall building. It appeared to be anonymous commercial office space.

Perhaps St. Loup had rented it—he had business interests all over the city. Perhaps it belonged to one of Turnbull's people—Father Turnbull operated in a number of districts, working with young people, in churches, seminaries, universities, and temples, undermining and corrupting naïve faith, and a surprising number of his protégés later became great successes in the business world. Perhaps it was neutral space.

The walls were grey and the carpets blue. There was a room with an ivory-white conference table, a small bathroom, and an office with a typewriter, on which he was encouraged to record his experiences. (He refused.) The conference table was covered in rows of bulky black telephones, all disconnected. The windows were all barred, and the door onto the corridor outside was locked. There were faint sounds of typing and conversation and elevators from the rest of the building, but no music, and certainly no doors out into the Metacontext.

It was high summer, and not air-conditioned.

They had drugged Arjun to bring him into the building, and he had no real idea where he was. Nowhere in particular, he supposed. Somewhere far distant from Fosdyke, certainly, in time and space and other respects. They had drugged him twice since then, once with something that Turnbull claimed was a truth serum, and once—apparently out of spite—with a hallucinogen that had caused him to imagine that the telephones were all ringing at once, and their black shiny bodies were like children burned in some horrible war, wailing for the death of his God; that was unpleasant.

Otherwise they hadn't tortured him much yet. Once St. Loup had petulantly stamped on his wounded hand, and sometimes Father Turnbull rapped his knuckles or twisted his ears. Mostly they tormented him with endless questions. They were convinced that he knew more than he was telling them.

Arjun wasn't sure how they'd come to be allied—they'd never been fond of each other. St. Loup was decadent, materialistic; Turnbull ascetic, intellectual. Probably Turnbull's spies and St. Loup's spies, both watching Arjun, had gotten tangled together, and now the two of them had reached a kind of wary *entente*. They were like two predators facing off over the same downed prey. They questioned him separately, taking turns. Apparently despite their new arrangement they still couldn't stand to be in the same room with each other.

He expected they might kill him eventually. He'd asked St. Loup what they'd done with Brace-Bel, and the man had waved a hand vaguely and said, "He was useless. We got rid of him."

That was days ago now. The beard he'd started to grow in the bolt-hole was coming in thick and scruffy.

What a stupid, humiliating way to go! There was still so much left to do.

St. Loup sauntered in. One of his thugs locked the door behind him and stood mute, arms folded, scowling like a bouncer.

St. Loup sat on the edge of the desk, took his sunglasses off, and smiled.

"Are you well? Are you getting enough to drink? You look tired."

"Well enough." Every day one of the thugs brought him greasy noodles wrapped in white paper, bought off the street below, and bottles of water. It gave him indigestion.

"If there's anything we can do to make you comfortable."

"The silence is oppressive. A record player might be nice."

"Ha. Perhaps not. Speaking of music, I visited the opera in Maliverne last night. Some thousand years forward and leagues clockwise of this place. Do you know it?"

"I don't think so."

"They engineer their sopranos from birth for fat. They make their fat ladies almost literally spherical. They think it's important. One of those misunderstandings that gets passed down that buzzing telephone-line of the city's history. It looks rather remarkable. Shining in stagelight, a chorus of perfect spheres, like people sometimes imagine angels. Except sweating copiously into velvet dresses. And the noise is very loud but not very good. My date was unhappy, I had to leave early. But this reminds me: how was the *Beast* engineered? Describe its scars. Describe its *shape*."

"It was a very big lizard."

"Oh, don't be tiresome. What was it took your fingers off, by the way? Does the thing bite?"

"A machine. I got caught in its gears."

"Did it have *very* sharp teeth?"

St. Loup wanted to know everything about the Beast. Again and again he questioned Arjun—what had it said? How was it made? Bird, reptile, mammal, or indeterminate? What had it said about the Mountain? What had it said about Shay?

Because Shay's Beasts were rare, and precious. They were the most extraordinary game in the city. Shay made them and used them and discarded them, scattered across the city in freak shows and sewers and temples and ruins—whispering Shay's secrets, babbling prophecy. Rumor had it that they knew what Shay knew of the Mountain, which was likely considerable. Most of them didn't last long. Hunters caught and beheaded them. Churches burned them, mistaking them, not unreasonably, for demons or lycanthropes. Sometimes they died of their own surgical wounds, or simply relaxed into nonexistence. Sometimes one or other of St. Loup and Arjun's fellow-travelers caught one, squeezed its secrets out of it, and killed it quickly so it could speak to no one else. The magus Abra-Melin had a glass jar containing a dead cat that had borne the marks of Shay's manipulations, but didn't dare open it for fear the little thing would turn to dust. Once St. Loup had fought a duel with Lord Losond, up on the roof of the Hotel, in the glass and sunlight and murmuring bloodthirsty antennae, over the ownership of a recently discovered Sphinx; and both of them had cheated, but Losond cheated better, and St. Loup ended up in the hospital, and Losond listened to what the Sphinx had to say, and vanished soon after and was never seen again.

"Where did it go? After the Museum, where did it go?"

"It took on the form of a prosperous local businessman and I believe it went to start a new life for itself."

"Oh, Arjun, haven't we been through too much together for you to tell me such ridiculous lies?"

Turnbull pulled up a chair and sat down opposite him, folding his hands neatly in his lap, leaning forward as if slightly concerned.

"Has St. Loup been mistreating you?"

"I think you were the one who drugged me."

"You were talking to him for a long time yesterday."

"I told him nothing I won't tell you: that I don't know anything useful."

"Well, now, don't sell yourself short. You found one of Shay's Beasts. That's not bad work, even if you did manage to lose it again."

There were two thugs at Turnbull's back—a big low-browed man in a cheap suit, and an even bigger man in janitor's overalls. They glared at Arjun, they glared at Turnbull's back, they kept glancing warily at each other, braced for action. Arjun guessed that one was Turnbull's man and the other St. Loup's. When would they betray each other?

"But frankly the Beast interests me less than the place where you found it. Shay's Beasts lie. There is no such thing as prophecy. But the Age it was hiding in . . . For such a drab little backwater, it has some remarkably unusual properties. 'Ghosts.' The proximity of the Mountain. Very unusual. Very unusual place. So tell me more about the Combines. Who owns Holcroft? Who owns Patagan?"

"I have no idea."

"You must. You were there for weeks."

"I ended up there by mistake. I know almost nothing about the place. It wasn't very nice."

"What are the Hollows?"

"I don't know."

"What do you know about their war?"

"What war?"

"Don't tell me you don't know about their war."

"They weren't at war."

"But they will be. You must know that. I refuse to believe you went there without doing any research. Stop lying to me."

"What war? Turnbull, what happens to them?"

"Why don't *you* tell *me*?"

At night Arjun dismantled the typewriter and the furniture to make approximations of crowbars and chisels, and worked on the window-bars. The moon was full and the sky was full of stars, and there were people working late in offices across the street, but they didn't see him waving, or if they did they didn't care. The pigeons

on the windowsill resented him. The Mountain was distant, here—
just a thin starless spike on the horizon. The bars didn't give.

S t. Loup paced.

"What *were* you doing there? Why there, of all places? It's a
backwater. We all overlooked it. What drew *you* there?"

"I was lost."

"Hmm. You know, we all noticed your absence at the Hotel.
You left without so much as a note, which I consider bad manners,
especially since you and I had been such close allies once. People
asked questions. A lot of people assumed you were dead. Some accused me of foul play. I said you'd simply wandered off somewhere,
the way you always used to, you'd heard of a new choir or orchestra
or a new bird with a particularly pretty song or something and gone
chasing music. God. Whatever. Is that what happened?"

"More or less."

"Maybe. Or maybe you learned something that actually matters. You always were a secretive type. You always did have more
courage than sense. Did you try for the Mountain?"

"Not yet. I'm not ready yet."

"Because you see, Arjun, we questioned some of your associates.
We tracked you down to that Fosdyke place because of a newspaper
story about the incident at the Fosdyke Museum, and we tracked
you to your bolt-hole the old-fashioned way: bribery, threats. It
wasn't all that hard. The locals seemed to be under the impression
that you had come down to them from the Mountain."

"They're superstitious. They blame everything on the Mountain.
They're almost as bad as us."

"Hmm."

St. Loup paced. One of the thugs—the one dressed as a janitor—watched him intently. The other stared blankly out of the
window.

"Turnbull was asking me about the war."

"Yes. The war. One of a number of oddities about that place,
that time. What about it?"

"Some of the people there were kind to me. I want to know
what happens."

"Bad news for them, I'm afraid. Shortly after we picked you up and we pulled you out, there's what appears to be the most appalling war. Bombs. Ruins. Starvation. Collapse of whatever passes for government there. The whole horrible show."

"Why? How?"

"No idea. We searched in all the usual libraries. You know the places. The ones that cater to our peculiar demands. The *best* libraries, the deepest networks. But we could find no news of that district past the first few days of the bombing. Airships. An unknown enemy. Why? Who knows? History does not record. A cul-de-sac in Time, an appendix. That part of the city ends there. The city continues elsewhere. Who cares? It's just statistics; everything is always ending somewhere. It never would have occurred to us to explore in that direction had you not tipped me off. Had we not chanced to meet. But here's the remarkable thing. As you get closer and closer to that moment, that fracture, that particular end of the city, it becomes harder and harder to travel. Maybe you noticed. For me the key was always lights, beauty; for you it was music. Both are in short supply at the end. The doors are locked, one by one, as the hours go by. Which is why we came late, unfortunately; we would rather have joined you at the Museum."

"What happens to them, St. Loup?"

"I don't know. That part of the city seems to separate itself from the Metacontext. As if the war cuts it free. It's very odd. After those first few days no news escapes, and no traveler who has visited has returned. How is this possible? Well, I was hoping you could tell *me*."

"Turnbull seemed to have a theory . . ."

"He did?"

"I don't know. He seemed to have a theory about it, something to do with the Mountain." Arjun improvised: "He was asking a lot of questions about the weather."

"What? Why?"

"I don't know, St. Loup. You'll have to ask him."

Turnbull stood with his hands folded behind his back. There was just one thug in the room, the janitor. Turnbull himself appeared to be fidgeting behind his back with a weapon.

"What's on the Mountain, Arjun?"

"I don't know any more than you, Turnbull."

"It's so *close,* there, in that place where we found you. You were there for ages. You must have seen something."

"Go yourself."

"I'm not ready. Not ready yet. Why do you want to go to the Mountain, if you don't know what's there?"

"I've told you this before, Turnbull. My God is there."

"How do you know, if you don't know what the Mountain is?"

"I don't know. I believe. I don't have any other choice."

"*I* know what the Mountain is, Arjun."

"No one knows."

"It's nothing. Just rock. Just black rock. It isn't the seat of the Gods, it isn't paradise. God isn't there, whatever silly little thing *you* call God isn't there either. St. Loup's palace of beautiful women, Potocki's perfect machine, none of it. It's just rock. A million tons of nothing of significance. It isn't the heart of the city in any sense except that that's where it happens to sit. We've woven the most ridiculous delusions around it."

"Maybe that's true. I don't know."

"You know, for years I was like you, Arjun. I didn't earn my title dishonestly. I was a very devout and humble reverend. It only slowly became apparent to me that there was no God, and the Mountain, which the nuns at school had always assured me was His Holy Seat, was empty. It was a painful realization. In fact I was in the process of committing suicide when Shay first found me and retained my services. He pulled me from the gas-filled car. He never tired of reminding me that I owed him my life. But we all must face the truth sooner or later. There is nothing there. I must find the way to the Mountain so that I can show the city: there is nothing there. Nothing. You can be liberated from that obsession of yours. You can give up. You can be free. Wouldn't that be a relief?"

"It might. It certainly might."

"Give me some straight answers, then. Help me. Better me than St. Loup, wouldn't you agree? In our different ways we are both men of religion. St. Loup is a sensualist, he'd turn the Mountain into a brothel. Let's begin again: who owns the Combines?"

"I already told St. Loup . . ."

"What? What did you tell him?"

". . . Nothing. I told him I don't know anything."

"No. You were about to say something else. *What* did you tell him?"

"Nothing. I'm sick of both of you. Ask him."

St. Loup was drunk. His sunglasses were pushed back on his head. He staggered and fell into a chair. He held out a bottle of something yellow that smelled like whiskey. It had what appeared to be an extraordinarily tiny human fetus floating in it. "Drink?"

"No thank you."

"Hotel's rarest stock. Thousand-year-old vintage. Only a hundred bottles made before the mob hanged the brewer. Hung? Hanged."

"No thank you, St. Loup."

"I was just back at the Hotel. Have to keep up appearances. Have to be seen being seen. You know how it is. Li-Paz was flirtatious—she must suspect something's up."

"Nothing's up, St. Loup. It's just the same old game. I don't know anything and nor do you."

"It always feels like the walls are watching you. Someone always *is* watching you. Microphones in the plants. Cameras in the mirrors. You had the right idea, your little holidays, your music, your what-do-you-call-'em, pilgrimages. Get away from it all. Not my idea of a good time. I'd rather be on a beach with a beautiful woman, but to each his own."

"Do you want my advice on your life, St. Loup?"

"In real life I was something special, Arjun, you should have known me then. Before Shay found me. I won't say I was always happy but I was, I was the other thing. Rich. Important. Young. Master of the universe."

"And the universe turned out to be bigger than you knew."

"Yes. Yes. And all this beauty in it; this extraordinary gift we've lucked into; and *this* is how we spend our days. Spying and scheming. Torture and murder. Doesn't it make you sad sometimes?"

"Constantly."

"Me too. Me too! I'm not a monster. You're not the only one with feelings. It's not our fault. It's the situation we're in. Sometimes I blame Shay. He should have chosen someone else. We're the wrong sort of people for this."

"So let me go, St. Loup."

"Sometimes I blame the Mountain. All this time, living in its shadow. Always knowing that whatever we do doesn't mean anything, because the real action's somewhere else. Up there. It's cruel, it's not fair. It, it makes us *smaller*. We can't grow up. I don't *care* what's up there, I really don't, I just don't want to be out here anymore, with the nobodies and the second-raters. Aren't you sick of it, too? So help me. Let's put an end to it all. You and me together, on the inside at last. Tell me what you know."

"I've heard this speech before, St. Loup."

"Yeah, so? How many times have I had to listen to your speeches about your bloody God?"

"I wouldn't help *you* anyway."

"What's that supposed to mean?"

"Nothing."

"What do you mean, *me*? What have you been telling Turnbull?"

St. Loup and Turnbull turned on each other with satisfying inevitability. They were paranoids, obsessives; cunning but predictable. Having never been able to work out which thug belonged to which man, Arjun wasn't entirely sure who would strike the first blow, but otherwise it happened just as quickly and surely as he had expected. As St. Loup was questioning him one morning Arjun stood, shook his head, and said: "That's enough. All right. All right. I'll help you. Better you than Turnbull. I'll tell you what I saw on the Mountain . . ."

And on that cue the thug dressed as a janitor lunged with a knife for the thug dressed in a cheap suit; but cheap-suit was ready, and took the blade glancingly on his arm and grappled for the other man's throat, and the two of them went down. Presumably then the janitor was Turnbull's man, and he had been instructed to act quickly in the event that Arjun seemed about to let valuable information slip to St. Loup. Maybe it was the other way around. Not that it mattered. St. Loup turned to look at the wrestling men on the floor, then turned back, and Arjun hit him in the head with a telephone, breaking his sunglasses and bloodying his golden curls, and took the key from his hand.

Arjun was out into the corridor moments later, and even as

Turnbull emerged from the adjoining suite and blinked in shock and put his spectacles on and fumbled for his gun, the elevator doors were already closing behind him.

It was easy to move away from that place, out into the Meta-context. He had his hearing again and the subtle keys and paths through the city's music were audible to him again. He found a clothes-store playing cheerful repetitive muzak and stepped through the dressing-room doors onto a distant Square full of brass bands and equestrian statues. If Turnbull and St. Loup were following him, he saw no sign of them. With a bit of luck they'd decided to kill each other instead. From the Square he went forward, and forward again, until he found a music he recognized—a funeral march down a narrow wooden street—and from there he worked his way forward again, toward Ruth Low's city.

It *was* hard to find his way back. St. Loup hadn't been lying about that. There were fewer and fewer doors as he came closer. There were dead ends, and obstructions, and paths that curled back on themselves. He probed and pushed for hours, maybe days, insofar as days meant anything where he was. Frustrated, he sat on a stone bench by the banks of a river full of gliding swans and striking phosphorescent jellyfish, and considered giving up. He sat there long enough for more than one passerby to throw him some change.

Was what St. Loup said about the war true? What had happened to the city? What had happened to Ruth, and Marta, and Ivy?

If he found a way through, would he ever be able to come back?

Was the way to his God closed to him now?

The prudent thing to do would be to wait, to prepare, to plan and research and gather his forces. But he never was prudent.

One of the swans came too close to a jellyfish. There was a soft splash. The bird's long neck went limp and it turned over slowly in the water like a sinking ship.

Arjun gathered the small change off the ground and bought himself a sandwich. He kept looking for a way through.

SIXTEEN

The Ruined Zone–Searchlights–
The Order of the Rope Factory–
The New Territories–Captured

Arjun

No building stood unbroken anywhere in sight. He stood on an open waste of shattered concrete and brick—residential flat-blocks blown open by bombs. All this had happened days, maybe weeks ago—the rubble was cold. The ground was carpeted with dust and ash and plaster. Underfoot were dented pots and pans, twisted bedframes, torn sheets fluttering ghostlike and grey. Strange metallic growths sprouted, twisted and molten—exploded bombs? Beggars and blank-eyed children sat in the rubble. Collapsed chimneys lay across the edge of the Square like storm-felled trees.

What had happened to the city?

If there had been a war, as St. Loup had said, it was over now. This was the aftermath of war. This was defeat.

This wasn't Fosdyke—thank the Gods for small mercies. It was the closest place Arjun had been able to find to Fosdyke, somewhere off to the south. He was unsure of the date. It was probably weeks, at least, since the events at the Museum. It felt like a hundred years. Long enough for a civilization to fall to ruin.

There was a kind of market nearby, in a vacant lot. Men at work.

Someone had hung a great red banner over it: SOUTH BARA DISTRICT RUINED ZONE RECLAMATION PROJECT. What had been homes and factories were now waste-ground, what had once been empty ground was now a center of activity. Armed men stood on watch at the corner, on the broken rooftops. There were refugee tents, and a smell of cabbage, canned beef, bad beer. Arjun went the other way. He'd had enough of armed men for the time being.

It was night before he knew it. The sun set behind the Mountain, and for a few minutes that dark mass was limned in fire, like the light creeping around the edge of a locked door. The clouds around the Mountain's peak seemed to blaze. Then the city was plunged into moonlight. The sky was full of sullen black clouds; the Mountain was only an absence of stars.

Something rose from the Mountain and approached.

At first they were specks, and Arjun thought perhaps they were clouds. Then, adjusting his sense of perspective, he thought they were birds—their progress was too rapid and too purposeful to be clouds. There were at least a dozen of them. As they approached the city they grew farther apart from each other, so that it seemed that they were setting out on divergent courses, like the spokes of a wheel, like the thorns of a crown. If that were the case, some of them must have been very far away, and therefore very large; not birds, then. Dragons, or Rocs, or some other exotic creature from remote Ages of the city?

Some of them were coming closer and he began to make out their shape; something rounded and immense that made him think of whales.

The slow outward radiation continued. Then all of the dark shapes at once began to sparkle like stars.

As the nearest shapes came closer, Arjun realized that there was a column of light depending from each of them, flickering down on the ruins below. *Searchlights.* He began to get nervous.

The first explosion sounded a couple of miles away. There was a flash of red flame and a distant *thump*. In what seemed the same in-stant the searchlight passed over his little corner of the ruins and everything in the world was suddenly blindingly bright like bleached bone. He threw himself to the ground and covered his

head, but the light passed on. There was an explosion nearby and
the sound of a building sliding into wreckage, but Arjun was un-
touched.

As the shape in the sky passed he saw it: an *airship.*

An airship of unfamiliar design. He recalled the *Thunderer,* and
indeed the airships of another half-dozen eras: all of them had been
beautiful things, winged or sailed in one way or another, elegantly
curved, brightly painted. Everywhere else in the city, flying things
were *sacred* things. But these were almost willfully ugly—soulless
and functional. A long grey balloon like a blunted or spent bullet,
from which something like a cage hung.

Here and there a crackle of distant gunfire and flashes answered
the airships. They drifted on implacably. Serene, untouchable, un-
caring.

After a while it was over. The airships turned back, closing in
like the fingers of a fist. Their lights went out and they vanished
into the shadows of the Mountain.

In all his years wandering the city Arjun had never seen anything like it. The Mountain was always there in the far distance;
he'd never seen it *reach out* . . . He felt violated. It was unnatural.
The fact of *contact* scared him worse than the bombs. What had they
done?

Had Ivy—had Ruth, too, perhaps, and the Beast—had they
gone onto the Mountain? Had they caused this, somehow—had
they provoked the Mountain into reaction? Or, worse, were these
airships under Ivy's command, or the Beast's? Were they capable of
this?

Was this his fault?

But under the shock and the sick crawling beginnings of terror
and guilt there was a part of him that was excited. If the Mountain
had reached out to touch the city then it was *wounded.* No longer
aloof, unattainable. They'd opened a pass in its borders. Through
every change in the city, every aching turn of its gears, he came a
little closer to its heart.

In the morning Arjun met a group of women who lived in what
was left of a rope factory. They came out of their hiding places as he
passed to tell him to *move along, fuck off, their husbands were coming*

back soon and they'd kill him if they caught him. They said, *whether you're Night Watch or Lamplighters you can fuck off either way.* When he asked them who sent the airships, they decided he was a harmless fool, took pity on him, shared some water with him, and a tin of pink unpleasant meat paste.

"The Mountain," they said. "The airships come from the Mountain. Where have you been all this time?"

"Why?"

"Why? Who knows. There's a War on. It finally came."

"Who rules the Mountain?"

They shrugged. He asked them if they knew the name Shay, and they shrugged again. They didn't know much.

He asked them what the South Bara Ruined Zone was. They said, "Is that what they're calling us now?" He asked them about the Reclamation Project and they laughed bitterly. They hadn't been outside their factory much in the last few weeks.

They admitted that their husbands were mostly dead. A bomb had hit the shed where the men worked. The survivors had joined up with the Know-Nothings to go off to the Front. Where were they now? None of the women knew.

He was too full of questions—where to begin?

He ate gratefully. They hovered over him, watching him closely. "I have no news of the outside world," he admitted. "Perhaps I was hurt in the fighting," he lied. "I have lost much of my memory."

He asked them how long the War had been going on. They looked at each other; about three, four months since the airships first came? It was hard to keep track of time—now that the Combines were gone, and the police, and there were no shifts, no whistles and bells, no orders.

Who was winning? They didn't know.

How had they survived? They glanced at each other, smiled, and said, "Our God keeps us safe."

"Your God?"

They looked at him pityingly.

"The Gods have returned?" Another transformation in the city! "Do you mean . . . Have you *seen* this God?"

"What do you think? Do you think we've gone mad?" If he thought they were just a bunch of scared women going mad in the

ruins, they said, he had another think coming: they were an *Order*.
They'd seen God, walking down the streets on feet of fire, head
wreathed in flames, body pouring smoke like a fabulous engine.
Right in the street out the back of the factory! (Where previously
there had been a rubbish heap.) The rope factory ruins were His
temple.

They got excited, talking about it. They were unwashed and
dirty-faced and hungry. Some of them had burns on their raw and
bony hands; had they tried to touch their new God?

There were other Gods in the city now, they said, but He was
the best. Some of them were just lights. Some were just shadows. A
lot of them were just noises. He was Fire—who better to keep them
safe from bombs? He was *theirs*.

The women made Arjun nervous. They had a feverish zeal.
They were new to the business of Gods.

"You can stay awhile," they said. "Sometimes He comes at
night."

"I'm sure it's a wonderful God. It sounds magnificent. I con-
gratulate you on your good fortune. But I have to move on. I've
wasted too much time already. I had . . ." He realized that he had
nowhere to go. Another path to the Mountain had failed. Did he
have the strength to start again? "I had friends here, before the
War," he said. "In a place called Carnyx Street. Do you know it?"

The women looked at each other, unsure. One of the older ones
said, "In Fosdyke, right? Patagan and Holcroft used to own things
up there—before the War."

"Yes!" He leaned forward, eager, relieved. Until then, he realized, he'd not been entirely sure he was in the same city as the one
where he'd met Ruth, and Brace-Bel, and Ivy, and the Beast; but if
there was a Carynx Street here, and a Holcroft and the rest, then
this was still the same place; only time had passed. What had happened?

What if Ruth was dead?

"How do I get there from here? North or south? I have to find
them."

They told him, *north—northeast*. He thanked them and moved on.

Five minutes and a few ruined blocks away from the rope factory, he noticed three of the younger women following him. He
stopped to let them catch up.

"You said there was a Reclamation Project, yeah?"

"Yes. So the banner said."

"Are there jobs there? Food? They're rebuilding?"

"I suppose so." He pointed the way. They walked together for a few blocks, then the women turned left and he turned right. They seemed strangely optimistic. They said *rebuilding* and *reclamation* like the names of Gods. At the crossroads they wished him good luck.

He wasn't sure what to feel. The women had adapted to life after the War, but the ruins were still new to him—at every street there was a new scene of devastation, and it left him numb and shocked.

At least now he had a goal: to find the Low sisters. If they were still in the city to be found. If they weren't dead, or on the Mountain, which amounted to much the same thing. Retrace his steps—Fosdyke, the Low sisters, the Beast, the Mountain, his God. Begin again.

The Low sisters! He imagined them dying in a hundred ways. Bombs; fire; falling masonry; looters; madmen. He got his hopes up and cautiously depressed them again. He imagined himself standing over Ruth's body and being unable to say any suitable words. His nerves froze and he found it hard to keep walking, so he hummed that fragment of the Music that was all he had of his God, and soon enough his spirits lifted. In a little while he found himself, rather embarrassingly, daydreaming how he would find Ruth at the moment of some peril and heroically save her.

Far behind him there was a distant glare—the God of the rope factory? It flickered and burned and faded.

Arjun walked north, through the South Bara Ruined Zone.

There were whole streets where the bombers had passed over harmlessly, but every building was empty anyway. There were bare blasted fields of broken brick and cratered earth. A few fortunate streets remained intact and inhabited and even well lit. They looked well guarded—he avoided them.

All afternoon he passed through a district of warehouses and storehouses in which every door had been smashed open, every crate and box looted. He stumbled over the rubble of old riots. There'd

been fighting, on a petty scale—squabbles between looters and security guards—and there were still uncollected bodies, half rotted
in the doorways, drooping out of broken windows.

He passed a row of grey gasometers, all deflated, their domes
close to the ground like mushrooms, their skeletal frames empty.
He found them strangely upsetting.

There was a warehouse on 117th Street. It was painted on one
wall, in huge red letters, CARLYLE SYNDICATED NO. TWELVE. The
other wall had been scythed clean away by bombs. When it started
to rain Arjun sheltered in the building's open guts. There he found
a case of tinned beef that looters had apparently missed, and a
jagged knife of broken piping to open the tins with. The meat was
tasteless but not rotten, and the discovery delighted him. The tins
were small enough to fit in a pocket; he took four. A fifth was
dented, so he threw it away.

When he passed a family going south, he gave away a tin in exchange for information. There were four of them—two children,
grubby and ginger-haired. The mother held the children nervously
while the father spoke. A slight man, freckled, balding, in a dirty
white shirt. He said, "This is the South Bara Ruined Zone."

"I know."

"Where are you going?"

"Fosdyke," Arjun said. "Carnyx Street. I have friends there."

"Don't know how things are in Fosdyke. We came from Fleet
Wark."

"Fosdyke might be intact?"

The man shrugged. "Might be, might not be. Bara, here, you've
seen what happened here. Fleet Wark got off pretty light. It's a big
city. Some places the airships pass over. Some places got fucked.
You got an opener for this?"

They levered the tin open with Arjun's bit of sharp pipe, and
the man divided the food among his family.

Arjun asked, "Where are *you* going?"

"South. They say south of Bara there's a district called Anchor,
where they've got some local boss, they've set things up, got some
of the engines running again, they're Reclaiming things. Fleet
Wark—things are falling apart in Fleet Wark."

"But you said the bombers passed over?"

The man shook his head. "Where've you been? What's wrong with you?"

"I was injured in the fighting, and my memory . . ."

The man put a hand on Arjun's shoulder. "Don't worry, mate. No one cares if you're a ghost now or what you are or where you're from. The worst happened already. We're all ghosts now, that's what people say. I'm a fucking deserter, so who cares what you are?"

One of the children started crying.

The man—his name was Fallon—told a long confusing story about the end of the world and life after the War. The child kept crying, and soon the other one started up, too, so Fallon and Arjun walked a little way away, and sat on a broken wall, and Arjun tried his best to follow Fallon's account.

The War! It was too large and terrible to imagine.

One night, six months ago, there had been a terrible lightning storm over the Mountain. Thunder and driving rain had woken everyone for a hundred miles. Windows shattered, laundry whipped loose, cellars flooded. The next night, and for the rest of the week, it happened again. If you asked the foremen or the Know-Nothings what was happening you got a clip round the ear: the official story was that there were no storms. But in the night the Know-Nothings could be seen massing at their Chapterhouses and drilling in the backyards and readying as if for War . . .

"Strangest thing," Fallon said. "Strangest thing—you don't have a cigarette, do you? No?—was that sometimes it looked like it wasn't really lightning. It looked like it was the Mountain shaking, sort of flickering, like a candle—and there was this light escaping. Like a broken furnace with the door banging open. Don't tell the wife I said that, she'll say it's mad."

One night the storms stopped. The Mountain sat there, still and dark. One week later the airships came.

At first they came every night, and they reduced whole districts to rubble. Now they came only occasionally, and their bombing was haphazard, casual, desultory. It seemed they'd made their point, they'd satisfied whatever urge for blood had driven them.

"What if," Fallon had said. "What if the storms were the folk on the Mountain fighting—what if they're only people, too, like us, they have their own Combines and things at each other's throats, and there was a fight, and whoever won decided it was time to get rid of us down here? Change of policy sort of thing."

Arjun had shrugged. "Perhaps."

"It couldn't be anything we did."

"Perhaps not."

In the first two weeks Holcroft and Patagan and Carlyle and Burgess and Frick and all the other Combines collapsed. It was unthinkable, but they simply ceased to exist. They were only ever paperwork, a shared delusion. The airships destroyed their offices, broke their supply chains, scared the workers away from what was left of the factories. "One good smack and they burst like balloons," Fallon said. "There never was anything in 'em but hot air."

And it wasn't just the physical shock of the bombers: the Combines devoured themselves from the inside. In the last days there were conflicting and nonsensical orders, shutdowns and lockouts, supply chains tangled, warehouses thrown open and others burned down, as if the owners had gone insane, as if some malign influence at the top of the chain of command were determined to drive the great corporate organisms mad. When no one took them seriously anymore they ceased to exist.

"Now instead we've got *Gods,*" Fallon said. "Like in the legends, like in the old days. You, in the city you're from, were there Gods?"

"There were."

"How did you not go fucking mad?"

"Hah. I'm not the best person to ask about that."

At the end of the first week the Know-Nothings went to war. "I always used to hate them," Fallon said. "But they did good back then. We didn't know, you know—we didn't know which side they'd be on. Us or the Mountain. We weren't sure. But they did their best. It didn't do any fucking good, mind you."

Four hundred Leaguers met at the Omnibus Terminal in Fleet Wark North. Fallon had heard that another four hundred met at the Terminal in Rookgate. If their wives and kids were still alive they said good-bye to them there. They carried rifles and packs and wore grey-black camouflage, from emergency stores. They packed themselves on the back of buses and whipped the horses north.

"I know they were seen as far north as Kellham," Fallon said. "Still going strong, singing a song. The streets were all fucked up there by bombs so they had to march. North. Never came back. The airships kept coming."

"It's always dangerous to approach the Mountain without knowing the path."

Fallon looked at Arjun suspiciously. "There are legends of the Mountain everywhere," Arjun said.

"Ah." Fallon sighed. "It's a big place, the city, isn't it? I never spoke to one of you before. I never dared. I'm not brave—I'm a bloody deserter. We sent *more* men, you know. From all over. You don't realize how big the city is until . . . You live in your own little parish with your own chapter or your own street or factory or whatever, you know, and you do your job, and you don't know how much of a city there is out there, you don't know what forces the men running it can bring to bear, when they get all the gears up and running. They gathered another four hundred men in the Seventeenth, I heard, and they lost them, too. And three hundred at Quay Street. They ran out of regular Leaguers, so they sent the Junior Auxiliary, and the Veterans' Lodgers. They sent the cripples and the mental defectives. They recruited regular people, let them have guns—I mean by the third week all the old differences had broken down, Know-Nothing, civilian, who cares? *All in this together,* right? Like those old posters. I never went—wife and kids, you know? Sent 'em up and they never came back. Hundreds. *Thousands.* They all went up by different routes but it doesn't look like anyone ever found a safe one. By the end they weren't sending up the big forces, they were just taking tiny little stabs at the Mountain: twenty men, ten men, five men, one man. Nothing."

Fallon's eyes were distant, haunted; he stared vaguely north. The Mountain was hidden behind tall buildings.

"I read a book once," Fallon went on. "About all the battles in the bad old days of kings and princes and dukes and all that. Against the law but I found it and I read it anyway. In the old days they drew lines in the city and said, this is mine and this is yours, and sometimes they sent soldiers. There was a *line* where the soldiers fought. A *Front,* they called it; you could say, these streets, this park, here on the map, this is the Front. But not this time: there was no Front. Just shadows."

"I'm sorry," Arjun said. It was too much to take in; it was like reading a historical account of some long-forgotten war. Was it his responsibility—had he somehow provoked the Mountain to this? It was impossible to imagine. "Is anything left?"

Fallon shrugged. "Like I said. Fleet Wark's not done badly for itself. Bara got *fucked,* but south of Bara, in Anchor, they say they've got order, water, power, they're Reclaiming things. That's where the survivors are going. All packing together, leaving these Zones empty. Don't know what happened to Fosdyke. The Combines are gone, and the Know-Nothings, but there are all these new things now. New ways of running things. Like the cults—the temples— the Orders and things. With all these new Gods, there's a whole lot of churches. I don't like them much myself, any of them. In Fleet Wark there's a man called Berkman, calls himself the Mayor now, used to be an executive for Patagan—he runs Fleet Wark. I've heard in some places there's Workers' Councils, or little people like us running things—committees and things. I don't trust them, frankly—I don't trust people like me to run anything. The whole city's a bloody mess. *Territories*."

Fallon laughed. "You know what they do—here in the Ruined Zone it's all empty now, but if you go north you'll see—they cut up old bedsheets and they make *flags*. Like in the old books, fucking flags, hung over every street. Green or red or blue. What's that, painted on it, looks like a deformed cat? Right? You're in Church of the Dog territory now, better say your prayers. Look, someone's painted a green line on the road, well, you're on the Seventy- seventh Street Committee's turf, better not make trouble. Better pay your tolls, or your taxes. Who runs anything? Who bloody knows. None of it makes sense anymore."

Fallon scratched his nose. His pale skin flushed. "Well, you know. Things are weird, now."

"Why did you leave Fleet Wark, if Fleet Wark's still intact?"

"The Hollows," Fallon said. His voice dropped, chilled.

"The Hollows?"

"You don't know that either? After the airships—at night— there's still fighting, and I'm bloody sick of it. The Hollows . . ."

Fallon's wife called out to him. "It's getting dark. The kids are hungry. Get a move on."

Fallon got stiffly to his feet. "Thanks, ghost. Steer clear of Fleet Wark, that's where the fighting is. Hope the Hollows aren't attacking Fosdyke. Go back to your own city, if you can. I'm moving on."

Arjun put a hand on the man's skinny arm. "Wait," he said. "I may be able to . . ." His voice trailed off. He wasn't sure how to explain without saying too much. "I can take you somewhere far away from this. Your children . . ."

A look of mingled hope and fear and disgust passed over Fallon's face. He shook his head. "Ghost tricks? *Your* city? No thanks. We'll stay in ours. Things are bad enough as they are. Keep whatever tricks you've got to yourself, all right?"

He must have seen the look of hurt and confusion and rising guilt on Arjun's face, because he softened, put a hand on Arjun's shoulder, and said, "Anyway—down south, they're Reclaiming. That's work worth doing."

Later, Arjun sat on the edge of a hill, chewing dry salty meat, wishing for water, watching night fall over the city.

No airships. No bombs. Not tonight. All the vast expanse below was dark, and he was alone on the hill.

. . . no; it wasn't all dark. There were occasional glimmers of fires. Somewhere in the ruins behind him, Fallon and his family must have been camping—which one was theirs? There were lights in the distance, still, that gentle nebulous haze on the horizon that the city always made; perhaps the bombers had not yet reached out that far.

And in the ruins below, there were distant trails of ghostly light that crept through the darkness of the city. To the southwest something progressed through the streets that was sometimes blood-red and sometimes the color of orange peels, and sometimes faded to gold. To the southeast something drifted over an open moor that was the deep blue or green of undersea life, and moved with indifferent undersea grace. Lights in the darkness! A pattern of slow sacral processions. It seemed the lights might interweave but they never did; they remained aloof from each other.

They must have been very distant. From the side of the hill,

Arjun could not make out their details. If they were Gods, as he suspected, they would have certain accidents and incidents; they would be symbols of something or other. The city would shift and change with their passing. Perhaps flowers would grow from the rubble. Perhaps even the weeds would die. There would probably be a crowd following after them in the dark, chanting or clanging bells or whipping their bloody backs or whimpering in fear, dreading the presence but unable to turn their backs on it, and at last scurrying closer to touch it and be driven mad.

If the Gods had returned they'd have brought all that back with them. Arjun remembered it well. But from the hillside all he could see was the distant crawling glow, and maybe he misunderstood what it signified.

In the morning he began to try to open doors into the City Beyond, hoping to cut short the trek back to Carnyx Street—and hoping to remind himself that there was still a city of infinite life and variety beyond those ruins.

A blackbird settled on a broken tree and sang, and there was a door in the mouth of the alley beside it.

The wind made chimes out of a broken fire escape, and there was a door in the muddy oozing crater in the street below.

But neither opened anywhere outside the confines of the city in which he stood, the ruins in the shadow of the Mountain, after the War. They spanned distance, but not time. He could feel it.

It was as if there was some dull obstacle in his path—a wall of grey muffling shadows. As if somehow every door out of the city had been *locked*. As if the gears were jammed. As if some unimaginable mechanism had shifted beneath this aspect of the city and wrenched it out of alignment with the brighter possibilities beyond. What St. Loup had said had been true: there was no way back.

Had the Mountain done this?

Among the handful of madmen and seers and obsessives and paranoids who shared Arjun's gift, who'd learned how to pass Beyond, there were a thousand rumors about the Mountain. They called it a machine, a weapon, a great sorcery discarded by the city's makers . . . Could the Mountain do *this*?

It was irrelevant, for now. He was far from the Mountain, and there was nothing he could do about it. Meanwhile there was no avoiding the stark fact of the world around him. The City Beyond was out of his reach again. The City-to-Hand would have to be reckoned with.

He found a door in the ruins of someone's home, where the broken pipes whistled and sang. It was a valuable shortcut; it took him out of the silence and devastation of the South Bara Ruined Zone, and a couple of days' walk north. He stumbled out into the heart of a busy drunken market crowd, at evening, under torches, and black and scarlet flags, and the din of a half-dozen competing buskers. For a moment he thought he was *elsewhere*—but then he looked around, and he saw that on the wall behind him there were old Know-Nothing posters, BE VIGILANT! and WE'RE ALL IN THIS TO-GETHER. And above him, above the rooftops where riflemen stood on watch for airships, there was the Mountain.

He was in a place called Clay. ("I'm looking for work," he told people. "I'm a refugee from the Ruined Zone.") Before the war Clay had been dominated by the Burgess Ironworks. Now the Ironworks were in the hands of deserters from the Know-Nothings, and a committee of the workers, and former members of the Black Masks; and this makeshift Court was ruled by a makeshift king, a recently promoted stable boy, a big lad in a heavy iron crown. The machines pumped out crudely mass-produced swords and spears, now. Clay was at war with the cultists of the Horned Man, who held the next district over, in Salisbury. At stake were the breweries in the disputed border zone. And in the northwest and the east there were rumors of aggressors called *Hollows* . . .

The crowd cheered and drank and shouted with the mad energy of people who were making the world new. A huge bare-chested man with a blacksmith's build and burn marks all over his back held Arjun's shoulder and said, "You want work? You think you can handle a weapon? Swords, like in the old stories—that's what it's come to." He seemed happy enough at the prospect. "Beats working in a fucking factory!" He slapped Arjun on the shoulder hard enough nearly to knock him over, and laughed. "You want to join up?"

"I'll certainly think about it," Arjun said. And later, when no one was looking, he ran. He went north through Salisbury by night, where the cultists of the Horned Man banged a wild echoing rhythm on the broken-down machines of what used to be motorcar factories. In the morning he crossed the cratered wasteland that was the Walbrook Ruined Zone—no sign of Reclamation there yet, only looters, bandits, refugees. In the evening he stood on a hill and looked down over Fosdyke.

Fosdyke's factories were silent. The buildings, however, were largely intact—though here and there he saw a gap in the skyline, a street wiped from the map. Away across the uneven rooftops Arjun recognized the Fosdyke Museum of History and Natural Wonders. Still standing! The angelic statue that stood atop its dome caught the red light of fires in the Square below, and turned demonic. When Arjun first saw it he thought for a moment it might be a God. Beyond it he could make out the roof of the Know-Nothings' Chapterhouse, which was irregularly shaped, as if a bomb had ruined its upper floors. Shadowy things like flags or ravens fluttered on its rooftop, and made him uneasy.

The streets were quiet, but there were lights in the windows, and in places there were dark clouds of chimney smoke. The bombers had shaken Fosdyke but not destroyed it. Life of some kind went on.

Where was Carnyx Street? What sort of condition was it in? Arjun couldn't quite make it out. He couldn't exactly remember where it was. Had the streets changed—had the bombs rearranged them—or were his memories uncertain again? He decided to make for the Museum, and retrace his steps from there back to Carnyx Street.

No one challenged him. He slipped through the shadows of unlit streets. He was aware of being watched from the windows. No flags, no banners, no signs—there were no marks of territory. Who controlled Fosdyke, now that the Combines were gone? What kind of place was it now?

He passed an empty fenced lot behind a dark factory, and set two dogs behind the fence to barking madly. He walked briskly away before the noise attracted attention. Had he caught a glimpse of vegetable gardens? The sparse beginnings of farmland?

In the quiet red-brick streets old men sat out on the porch as the light died. From the door of what looked like a warehouse there was light, and laughter. A fragile illusion of normality—if not for the silence of the factories, Fosdyke might have seemed unchanged by the War. If not for the fires in the Square.

Once Arjun stepped onto Holcroft Square, he could see that it had in fact been hit by the bombs. The Museum had lost its west wing, and something had taken a bite out of the side of the dome, leaving the angel's position precarious. There was a crater in the middle of the Square, half flooded with dark rainwater that flickered red in the light of the bonfires that were stacked high around the edge of the Square and on the steps of the Museum. High on the steps there was a kind of statue—made out of wood and lead pipes and bedsheets—of an immense bird. Beside it was another statue, of an equally immense lizard. Two dozen people stood or kneeled before the great idols.

Arjun sighed. It was all beginning again. In ten years, if the city survived the airships, there'd be temples everywhere. The usual cacophony.

From the end of Holcroft Square opposite the steps was the alley past the ruined Chapterhouse, and a left turn at the end of *that* would put him on the route back to Carnyx Street, and then, and then . . .

He hadn't taken two steps down that alley when four armed men stepped out of the shadows around him, and a firm hand grabbed his shoulder. An ugly face shoved into his demanded, "How many times have we told you idiots about those fires?"

He tried to remain calm. "I'm not with the people in the Square. I'm lost. I came here out of the Ruined Zones looking for work . . ."

The man holding him wasn't listening. He was looking closely at Arjun's face, as if he recognized him.

Arjun's heart sank. What if these men were Know-Nothings, what if they recognized him from the incident at the Square? He prepared himself to twist and run.

The man turned Arjun's wrist to get a closer look at his hand—

his maimed and marked hand. The other three stared at it, too. Apparently the wound had some significance for them. Arjun consulted his memories; what cults in the city attached significance to wounded hands, missing fingers? Too many, too many. The Order of the Plough and the Worm. The Scriveners of Tagore. The Maimed Servants of Saint . . .

"Hey, you. Do you know a man called Maury?"

"No." He said it too quickly, too firmly—the man clearly didn't believe him.

"He said, a dark little bugger, missing fingers. Arroon, right? That your name? Something like that?"

"No. You have the wrong man."

"Do we? Do we?"

They whispered among themselves. He heard expressions of surprise and disbelief. Then they reached a decision.

"We're the Night Watch. You're coming with us. The Inspector's been fucking *dreaming* of getting his hands on you."

SEVENTEEN

The Blast–The Closed Circle–
The Committee for the Emergency–
King of This City–The Jealousy of
Shadows–A Monster Story

Ruth

Having been left behind, again, Ruth had been there to see the first bombs fall. Even now, months later, she still woke sometimes and thought: *had that really happened?* The blast. The shaking of the earth, the breaking of windows and mirrors. The noise, the fire, energies unleashed into the city that seemed creative and destructive at once. She had pulled out her coat and run out into the streets to see what had happened, maybe to see if there was anything she could do to help. The searchlights had drifted over her head, and for a moment the city around her was bright, and frozen, stark white and beautiful. Then the bombers passed over. As it turned out there wasn't anything she could do.

What had happened? The south end of Ezra Street was in ruins. How many dead? Too many. The sewage treatment plant on Forty-ninth was gone, too. Rumors flew in the night: it had been worse to the south, in Walbrook. The airships had come from the Mountain. The War had finally begun.

The Know-Nothings formed fire-fighting teams as if they'd

been drilled for this, as if they'd always half expected it. They told her, "Move along, Miss Low, move along—we've got this under control." They seemed almost relieved; after the humiliation of the incident at the Museum, they were glad to throw themselves into work. They were glad the War had finally come. Confident and competent—Ruth had never seen them that way.

No one went to work the next day. Men stood out in the streets in the afternoon sun, as lost and confused as lifers released from prison. They scanned the skies for bombers. They swore and cursed the Mountain. They got drunk. Their wives waited nervously indoors for them to come home reeling and fall into bed. In the evening there was music and dancing in the streets, and a great mad joy—the world had changed, at last. In the night the bombers drifted over again and cratered the Square out front of the Museum, and wiped out the factories all along the Walbrook border. John Beecher, from the house on No. 47 Carnyx Street, hungover, hysterical, killed himself and his wife and his three children, and left a note saying: *the end's come for us all*. He wasn't the only one.

Ruth didn't know what to think. It was unreal. She no longer belonged here. She waited skeptically for the next revelation as if she was watching a stage magician's show.

"The cellar," Marta said. "The Dad's cellar. We need shelter." So Ruth and Marta spent the day clearing out the old junk down there—the radios, the maps, the exotic taxidermied birds and street vermin. Everything was covered in a thick layer of dust. Unusual experimental molds still grew down there, in the cracks in the walls. Painful memories—it was always painful handling the Dad's stuff. The dust recorded the years of his absence. These were the things he'd abandoned, and now they were broken. "About time we got rid of this shit," Marta said.

But there were happy memories, too—under the pipes in the south corner there were the Dad's old charts and maps and models of trains and trams and tracks. Ruth had been maybe nine years old when he'd turned his attention to the trains. He'd built the tracks and drawn up the charts to puzzle out the mystery of the inputs and outputs of the city's factories, to determine what kind of business the city did with the Mountain. Of course, Ruth hadn't understood much of what he was doing; but he was jolly about it, as he sometimes was when he was on the edge of a breakthrough. He laughed and encouraged the girls to admire the little trains, which he made himself, and to come with him on weekends to spy across wire fences and weed-strewn lots at the hidden railway sidings. An adventure! Ruth remembered how they'd once run away hand-in-hand from the station guards . . .

And the clocks, heaped in the corner! Ruth remembered how the Dad's fascination with the times of trains and trams had given way quite naturally to a fascination with time itself. He'd scavenged quite a collection of old timepieces, which Ivy proved to have a talent for repairing. The cellar ticked and hummed and frequently buzzed, rang, or chimed. He would sneak around at night, avoiding the Know-Nothings, to nail up his clocks in odd places, at either end of Carnyx Street, and then Fosdyke, and then farther afield; and he checked them nightly and came back to the cellar and made notes of anomalies. That lasted a few months; at its height, Marta had to remind him to eat. When he worked on the clocks he'd been mean and cramped, complaining that the girls distracted him. Time was a burden to him.

It felt good to clear out the cellar. It was good to sweat, and ache, and work. It was good to be done with the ghosts of the past; it was a new world, now.

They kept the old stills, and the dusty bottles of home-brew. That night they welcomed their neighbors into the cellar, and they drank together while the bombers went over. In the morning, when they emerged, Mrs. Rawley's vacant house was reduced to shattered bricks and timbers, and the street was grey with ash and cinders.

No one went to work, and the factories were silent. The Combines that had dominated everyone's lives for as long as anyone could remember suddenly seemed irrelevant.

While they huddled in the cellar, Marta said to her neighbors: "This isn't going to be over anytime soon. We need to fend for ourselves. We need to start stocking up food."

Thirty men and women marched on the Holcroft Packing & Bottling Plant on R Street, Ruth and Marta in the lead, Marta carrying a list of demands, and a petition demanding that *in light of the crisis, Holcroft recognize the legitimate necessities of the public and release sufficient food from stores to* . . . Ruth expected a tense scene; she was half ready for violence. As it turned out, there was only one guard left at the Plant, and he'd received no orders for days. Marta shrugged: "How are we going to do this, then?" The guard's face broke into a grin and he unlocked all the doors for them. They left with wheelbarrows full of flour, rice, tinned and dried meat. The guard was so relieved to be told what to do that he followed them home.

The Museum had been cut in half, its west side smashed open. Its cellars were exposed to the sky, then flooded. No magic left there. Those childhood dreams were erased all at once. Half of the places where Ruth and Marta and Ivy had played were gone. As children they'd reinvented those streets, renamed them, made them fabulous. Now they were broken, reconfigured, and the new map held no meaning for her.

Ruth could have just walked away and kept walking. Only Marta kept her anchored there.

Meanwhile the Know-Nothings drilled with rifle and pack in the ruins of Holcroft Square. They'd gotten new uniforms from stores—black and grey, blotched for camouflage. They looked very serious and dangerous.

They looked *happy*. Suddenly they were needed; suddenly everyone loved them.

When some one hundred of them gathered at the Terminal to pack onto the omnibuses and go north, to strike back at the Mountain, even Ruth joined the cheering crowds. She watched them go, trailing off up the hill, the bus rattling and bouncing on the cobbles, the horses straining, and she thought how *young* the soldiers looked, how handsome.

For a moment she allowed herself to believe they might succeed. But they never came back. Nor did the next lot.

When they started recruiting regular folk, Ruth cornered her friends and said, "Don't go. It's not so easy to find your way to the Mountain. You won't come back." They didn't listen. They didn't come back.

She'd seen those grey-black uniforms before—the new uniforms the Know-Nothings went to War in. Those nameless and haunted ghosts who'd come wandering down the Mountain, year after year for as long as she could remember, lost and confused and scarred, mumbling or sobbing about the War that was to come—they'd worn those same uniforms.

What happened to those who went up on the Mountain? The Mountain stood outside of time, outside of the city—she'd always understood that. Those who were thrown down might fall *anywhere*. Ghosts, loose in time, haunting their own lives. The War was a closed circle. It was hopeless to fight back.

She wasn't sure whether anyone else understood that or not. She didn't like to talk about the War much. It was over soon enough, anyway. There were no more Know-Nothings to send, and no one who was left wanted to go. The bombers came every other night, then once a week, and then hardly at all. They'd made their point. Walbrook, to the south, was in ruins, but Fosdyke was mostly intact; it could have been worse. It was time to start rebuilding.

The Combines were gone. And the Know-Nothings were gone, and the police, and even the post offices. The omnibuses no longer ran. The factories sat uselessly, with no one to operate them. People hid in their homes. They went pointlessly to their old places of work, and hung around outside the locked gates, waiting for . . . what? They didn't know. Someone to tell them what to do. That was the power of habit; that was the weight of the city's long history.

Marta and the others re-formed the Carnyx Street Committee. Zeigler's place was taken by old Mr. Sedrich, who'd worked in the brewery, and young John Coulter, who'd been with the Black Masks, before the War. The Committee worked out a system of rationing for the food they'd taken from the packing plant. The Committee incorporated Ezra Street and Capra Street and Leather Street, which had no leadership of their own—and so they took over the warehouses at the end of Capra Street. What saved them from starvation in the first months was the vast and pointless overproduction of the city before the War; the warehouses the Combines had left behind were stacked high with canned food. Water was more difficult—they incorporated R Street, and took over the canal that ran along it. At night Fosdyke's people huddled like moles belowground; the Committee worked out a rota for use of the cellars and sewers. The Committee cut a deal with the workers who'd seized the tannery at the end of Leather Street, the refinery on the hill, the stockyards at T Street. They took over the armory the Know-Nothings had left behind on 220 Street. They carved up the waste-ground and the vacant lots and the backyards and the scant scrubby parks, and they began tentative experiments in farming.

Fosdyke hadn't been much troubled by Gods. They heard rumors. Refugees from the Ruined Zone said that the wastes of Walbrook were haunted by the howling of the Dog. Salisbury, to the south, was said to house the temple of the Horned Man, in an old brewery, and the streets were said to run with whiskey—a few brave souls struck out from Fosdyke south across the Ruined Zone to join the revels. Bargees came down the canals from Thibaut, in the northwest, and reported that the waters there were now . . . *strange,* and that some of the barge families had given themselves over to the worship of the thing that lurked in the depths. One day a white Bird of immense impossible size and beauty came curving in a lazy arc over Fosdyke, and the morning sun sparkled through its white feathers, and left light like snow all through the rain-wet streets . . . But Ruth was working down in the storage basement of the old Holcroft Infirmary on 109 Street, cataloguing the abandoned medicines and supplies, and missed it. "Story of my bloody life," she said.

By the end of the second month, the Committee (now the Committee for the Emergency) ran pretty much everything in Fosdyke. People spoke of it in the vague terms they'd used to speak of the Combines—"The Committee'll take care of it." It was a sprawling, complex thing, hastily engineered, an unstable coalescence of all the fragments of power left behind by the collapse of the old order, and it was hard to say exactly who ran it; but it worked, up to a point. Marta had been named the Secretary of Minutes, and buried herself in meetings and paperwork at the Committee's Temporary Headquarters, in the old Terminal building on S Street. She appeared to be as much in charge as anyone was.

By the third month, the new world had started to seem normal. The bombers came infrequently—and there were now watchers on the tallest rooftops, and a system of bells and alarms to warn people to go below. Sometimes some mad cult out of the Ruined Zones—the Night Watch, the Dog's Men, the Lamplighters—would make small annoying incursions, but not often—Fosdyke was well defended. The rebuilding had become routine. A few of the factories were running again. The farms showed promise. People went back to work. In the first days after the War Ruth had gone scouting with lamp and knife in hand through dark abandoned warehouses in search of food and supplies. Now she worked in an office, bookkeeping, cataloguing the Committee's food distribution efforts. It was tiresome work. At her desk her mind began to wander again.

She kept glancing up at the Mountain. That name Arjun had spoken—*Shay*—kept running through her head. Before they went up some of those doomed soldiers—drunk, proud, hysterical—had let that name fall from their lips. *Shay. Big secret. That's what the higher-ups say. King of this City. Been too long in the shadows, pulling strings. Gone too far. Time to settle the fucking score. Big secret, that's what they say. Give us a kiss, love, come on, we go up tomorrow.*

Do you ever think about the dead?"

Marta sighed and rolled her eyes. Ruth put a hand on her arm. "No—I mean it." They sat across from each other at the table in the kitchen of the old house. It was dimly lit; candles and oil were rationed. Marta rarely came back to the house, and when she did they were rarely alone—Ruth now shared the house with four refugees from Walbrook. Marta looked severe, tired. She was starting to get fat—stress, desk-work, bad food. Ruth was drunk, Marta sober.

"I *mean* it," Ruth said. "Out there—in Walbrook, how many thousand? In Bara, how many? Those were places where people lived and worked. Now they're dark all the time, and they're fucking haunted. How many people?"

Refugees came to Fosdyke. The survivors of the Ruined Zones. In their fear the city's people packed together for warmth like cattle, leaving great stretches of the city bare of life. They told horror-stories. Streets on fire, men and women like puppets jerking in the red light. Streets where white dust still hung in the air, weeks after the bombs, making ghosts out of everyone who stumbled through. Bodies in a bomb-crater plague-pit. Hunger and madness. They never told their stories twice—they quickly learned that no one in Fosdyke wanted to hear that stuff.

Marta put her hand on Ruth's. "Let it go, Ruth. Let it go. We're rebuilding as much as we can."

That was what the Committee always said—that was the Committee speaking. Rebuild! Eyes front, face the future! The catastrophe was kept at bay, outside the borders. The wound was denied. The horror, the loss of it, surfaced only in nightmares, in the black jokes that Fosdyke's workers made, constantly, almost obsessively—because *everyone* was sophisticated now, everyone understood irony and absurdity and the shortness of life.

"All that darkness out there," Ruth said. "We can't make it right. We can't bring them back."

"Whoever said we could? We have to look after ourselves, now. We're still living in the surplus of the old world. It can't last forever. We have to build, we have to . . ."

"You *like* this."

"I'm good at it, Ruth."

They sat in silence for a while.

Ruth said, "Do you ever think about *why?*"

"There aren't any answers down here. What happened, happened. We just have to live with it."

"Don't you ever wonder what happened up on the Mountain"— Marta winced at the word—"whether they did something up there, made something angry—Arjun, Ivy. Marta, what if Ivy did this? What if we did this?"

Marta snarled. "It's not *my* fucking fault." She hit the table. Breathing deeply, she avoided Ruth's eyes. "Let it go, Ruth. Let it go."

"I can't, Marta. I need to know. Who'd do something this cruel? What kind of world works like this? It's too cruel—it doesn't make any sense. I need to know what happened."

"You sound like the Dad. You sound like Ivy. Before they *left.* Fucking go *on* then."

Marta's bodyguard came into the room and coughed discreetly— she had business back at the headquarters of the Committee for the Emergency. Marta left without saying another word.

*　*　*

Ruth went walking alone through the city at midnight—down silent and subdued Carnyx Street, across the waste-grounds, the new farms, where the beanpoles stood in rows like ghostly soldiers, and then along 221 Street. The cold sobered her. The *xaw* she'd smoked sharpened her senses, silvered the lights, deepened the shadows.

In the first weeks after the War the city's night had been dark: unthinkably, utterly dark. The gas was disrupted. There was no one to light the lamps—and no one dared, for lamplight might draw the attention of the bombers. The factories stood empty, the pubs were deserted, and people huddled in their cellars. Light, Ruth had realized, was what distinguished the city from wilderness. Now the light was creeping back—despite rationing, despite broken gas lines, despite the best bloody-minded efforts of the fucking Night Watch! A few lamps lit the farms—guards stood beneath them. Some of 221 Street's windows had light. There was a pub on the corner, Peake's Place, in what used to be a house—strictly rationed, but still noisy and warm. It was very important, Marta said, to make sure there were a few luxuries for the rebuilders . . .

Ruth didn't go in. If she'd gone in, she would have been drawn into conversation, and it would only have depressed her, reminded her that she, too, was stuck here, same as everyone else. Outside, in the cold, in the faint light, her mood was getting better. How could it not? The rebuilding. The return of the light. The noise of laughter and singing from the pub—a couple fucking in the alley behind it, and why shouldn't they?—the sound of distant factories, running again, against all the odds. It was an extraordinary achievement. A *shared* achievement. The old Know-Nothings used to put up posters saying, WE'RE ALL IN THIS TOGETHER, by which they meant, *snitch on your neighbors* and *do as you're told*. Now the old slogan was true. She felt a huge vague affection for Fosdyke and everyone in it. She felt the age and the vastness of the city, and its resilience. The city *endured*.

Between the rare working lamps and the windows lit with flickering candles the shadows encroached as if jealous. Behind the rooftops the dark Mountain loomed over everything—bitter, cold, resentful. She stared at it; for a moment she had a sense that it might come rushing forward out of the night, made of the night, and flood everything, destroy everything that had been rebuilt; but it just sat there, sulking. *Fuck you,* she thought, jubilantly, *we don't need you, we never needed you, we're better off without you.*

Two men were watching her from the street corner. As soon as she saw them she felt ashamed.

W hat were they?

She knew at once that they weren't exactly human. They came forward toward her, and as they passed under the streetlamp they remained in shadow. Their shoes clicked on the cobbles—a hollow, anxious sound, like the ticking of a clock, like being late for an appointment. Their features were vague—pale shifting faces under black hats. Their heads flicked birdlike up and down the street, taking in the lights in the windows, radiating sour disapproval.

For a moment she thought perhaps she was dreaming them— her sleep had been disturbed by dreams for as long as she could remember—or that the *xaw* and the night had confused her waking mind.

Then she recognized them. She remembered them: they'd come hunting for Arjun, long ago now, infinitely long ago, because it was before the War . . . *The men from the mountain,* Arjun had said. *My pursuers. The Hollow Men. The unhappy men.* They'd come hunting through her shop, and terrified her, and somehow she'd forgotten them. Even now she struggled to remember how they'd questioned her, their silent monotonous voices . . .

What were they? They moved at odd angles to the world, and limply. Their shadows weren't quite right. They wore the shadows like an ill-fitting suit. They were poorly made, mass-produced.

Spies?

An invasion—foot soldiers, following the bombers?

They glanced at the open door of the pub. It seemed to annoy them. *We weren't meant to rebuild,* Ruth thought. *We're only making more work for them.*

They turned toward the pub door and toward Ruth at the same time. There was a faint rustling and sense of strain, and then there were four of them. Two went into the pub, and first the conversation fell silent, then there was screaming. Two came slowly closer to Ruth. *Too much,* she thought. *It isn't fair. What did we do to deserve this?* And she couldn't quite make herself run. Her legs were weak with fear and shame. They reached for her with pale hands—scarred hands, the fingers not quite right, as if broken and reset, as if subject to dreadful surgeries, *who made you, you awful pitiful things?* She stumbled back, and for a moment the light of a street-lamp fell on her.

The black eyes of the Hollow Men fell on her face—and they drew back. They looked at each other in apparent confusion; their eyes flickered back again and again to her face. Was it possible that they recognized her?

They fluttered their broken fingers at each other, and a silence passed between them that was like conversation. They shifted from foot to foot as if they weren't sure what to do—as if Ruth's face were an impossibility not accounted for in their orders.

Ruth's terror began to turn into contempt.

One of them nervously scratched his pale scarred scalp, and clumsily knocked his black hat from his head. It rolled into the shadows and he went stooping bandy-legged after it. The other one scowled at her, then offered a small bow, then scowled again, backing away, fading into the shadows.

Ruth shook with rage and loathing. From the half-open door of the pub there was the pathetic sound of grown men shouting and screaming. She stamped down the steps and threw the door wide. The drinkers were backed up against the far wall, two men lay stiff and dead on the floor, and the Hollow Men stood over them. Their heads flicked back owl-like to look at Ruth. Her finger quivered as she pointed at them, saying, "Fuck *off,* fuck *off* and leave us *alone.*"

To everyone's surprise, they did.

A week later, two of the Hollows were seen poking around the ruins of the old Chapterhouse, the steps of the Museum. They interrupted an evening service of the Bird cult and made everyone there feel ridiculous.

A few days later another pair were seen standing on the roof of Warehouse Seventeen on Leather Street, patiently watching people go by below, like foremen supervising the production line.

Two of them walked insolently into the headquarters of the Committee for the Emergency in the middle of the afternoon, as if they were there to file a complaint. A guard tried to get them to leave and they shredded him to dust and dry leaves. They inspected the paperwork and left.

Refugees and deserters came from Fleet Wark and said that Fleet Wark was at war. There the Hollow Men were cleaning up the last of the mess left behind by the airships. Fleet Wark had rebuilt itself, strong and free, better than before—and the Hollows wouldn't permit it. Regiments of shadows gathered in the jags and pits of the Ruined Zones. They massed against Fleet Wark's borders, appeared in the corners of bedrooms at night with murderous intent. They couldn't be hurt, exactly, but they disliked noise, and fire, and light, and crowds, and music. In Fleet Wark the border patrols carried torches and bells.

The Committee for the Emergency doubled the patrols along Fosdyke's streets. There weren't enough bells in Fosdyke but there was a massive overabundance of pots and pans, and sticks to beat them with.

The Hollows were seen on Capra Street, and in the bomb shelters at night, and in the fields. Two of the patrols vanished. A child was taken from her bed, leaving only dust behind. Fosdyke waited for the invasion.

The Committee for the Emergency questioned Ruth in a room in the basement beneath their headquarters in the Terminal. Bare table, an oil lamp smoking and glaring just beneath Ruth's face, half a dozen men and women ringed around her in the shadows. That was how the Know-Nothings used to question you, when they'd decided it would pay to be brutal. Now, it didn't mean anything much. Nearly everyone on the Committee had sat there once or twice—in their panic they reached for the old way of doing things.

She didn't know, she told them, she didn't know why the Hollow Men had run from her. She didn't understand anything. They didn't seem to believe her. "Fucking beat me, then," she said. "Get it over with."

"We're done here," Marta said. "She doesn't know anything. Go home, Ruth."

Marta and Ruth walked out together through the corridors under the Terminal building.

"Ivy," Ruth said, when they were alone.

"Ivy?"

"My face—they stopped when they saw my face." Ruth looked into her sister's face, careworn, solid, but so much like her own. "It was like they knew me. *Ivy*. Marta, what do you think happened up on the Mountain? What do you think she did up there?"

Marta touched Ruth's face, gently, as if reminding herself what it looked like. Her fingers were rough and ink-stained. "Why didn't you say anything in there?"

"Everything that's happened is all about *us,* Marta. Ivy. Arjun, too. I don't know, our father, everything. Everything that's wrong with us. How can I say that and not sound mad? You tell them if you like. It won't help. They can't fight the Mountain. If they beat back the Hollows it'll just be some other bloody thing. This whole city is made all wrong. We have to find Ivy, Marta. We can't stop this from down here."

Easier said than done—where else was there to go? *Wanting* to ascend the Mountain wasn't enough. You couldn't just walk there, any more than you could walk to the moon. It required a cunning, a vicious disregard of the world and its logic, that Ruth simply couldn't achieve. She was no Ivy. She wasn't her father's daughter. And besides, she was never alone—with the Hollow Men abroad in the streets, no one was ever supposed to be alone. She was accompanied everywhere by colleagues, refugees, armed men and women. She couldn't think. She couldn't see. When she tried to explore the borders of the Ruined Zone, the dark alleys, friends held her back—they asked her if she was mad.

At night the bombers went over, and though these days they usually passed over harmlessly, bound for southern districts, everyone still went below, into the cellars and tunnels. The new life of Fosdyke was half in the light, half subterranean. In the cellar beneath the old Low house there were now cots and oil lamps and homemade shrines to the new Gods of the city. It was home during the day to two refugees, and it was night shelter for half the street.

Ruth was Ward Coordinator for Carnyx Street; it was her job to count her neighbors in, to bang on doors and help out the elderly. Tonight there was one man too many clamoring for shelter.

He was a dark-skinned man in a red shirt and spectacles. He was thin, dirty, and bruised. Ruth stopped him with a hand on his shoulder, and asked who he was. These days you couldn't be sure—it was tempting to think that everyone in Fosdyke was on the same side, but there were maniacs from the Night Watch out there, there were raiders from the Ruined Zone, there might be spies from other districts.

He flinched from her touch and she wondered what had happened to him to make him frighten so easily. He said his name was Hatch; he was from Walbrook; he didn't have a home anymore. His eyes were pleading—the searchlights were coming slowly closer, over the hills, covering the peaked rooftops and the tall chimneys in white ice. "Come on," Ruth said. "Come on, get down, don't make any trouble." She closed the door firmly behind them both—it upset the children to hear the drone of the bombers going overhead.

Mrs. Watts lit two oil lamps and a warm convivial glow suffused the darkness. Joanie Crick shared out the playing cards. The children began to play a game among the crates in the corner; one of them would stand on a crate and announce himself the ruler of the Mountain, and the others would try to knock him off and claim it for themselves. Mr. Titus Schott, who'd joined the cult of the Bird, decided it was a good time to make converts, and got shouted down and laughed into a huffy red-faced silence. Hatch smiled and tears sparkled on his dirty cheeks. "They said there was still real life, real people, here in Fosdyke, but I couldn't believe it."

Ruth blushed—her hospitality seemed poor enough to her. "Where have you been, Mr. Hatch?"

He shook his head. "You don't want to know." He got up and paced. Joanie Crick pulled the children away from him, by ears and dirty collars.

He saw the nervous expression on Ruth's face and smiled as if to apologize for his oddness.

He began to sit down—and then something in the corner of the cellar caught his attention, and he darted across to it, scattering the playing cards.

In the far corner they'd heaped the last of the Dad's stuff they'd never gotten round to clearing out of the cellar. There were a couple of peculiar clocks, a few things with dials and wires and black tuberous growths that the Dad had called *telephones,* some boxes, some books, half a dozen stuffed birds and vermin. These last seemed to horrify and fascinate Hatch. He picked them up by their stiff limbs and lacquered wings, and turned them over and over.

Ruth put a hand on his shoulder. "My father's," she said. "It was a hobby of his. Are you all right? Did you lose someone who . . ."

He held up a kind of—well, Ruth supposed it was a kind of lizard. It was oddly brightly colored—shiny in an oily way. She was never sure where her father got those creatures—she was very small during his fascination with taxidermy. She remembered visits to the house in the middle of the night by shifty-looking people. She remembered Marta explaining sourly that they were going hungry that week because the Dad had bought a rare parakeet or something. He'd been a terrible taxidermist, anyway; the creature was scarred and hacked about and ruined. The scars reminded her of . . .

Hatch took a deep breath and put the horrid thing down. "Where I've been—it reminded me of something. The man I ran away from, he did this sort of thing, all the time. Those of us who followed him, he had us picking through the ruins for vermin. He was bloody *mad,* he was."

Ruth squeezed his shoulder. "It's all right now." There was a muffled thump from the streets above, and one of the children shrieked. Hatch flinched; she held his shoulder firmly. "In the morning we'll get you a billet and a job. But where have you *been,* Mr. Hatch?"

"Out in the Ruined Zones—out east of what used to be Walbrook—out in Juno, where the quarries were—and all around. We followed him, all around. Through the ruins, the quarries. Like he was a God. He made us call him Beast. He made things like this, all the time. We brought him rats and cats. He was scarred like he was one of them himself. Sometimes he did it to one of *us* . . ." He shuddered; then he recoiled from the intense interest in Ruth's eyes.

She wouldn't let go of him. "Where is it? Mr. Hatch, where is the Beast?"

☆ ☆ ☆

She left the cellar at first light. She gave Joanie Crick a message for Marta. With a smile and a wave it was easy to steal a pack and a rifle from one of the Committee's storehouses—"Morning, Miss Low, you go ahead, don't hurt yourself with that, now." She stuffed the pack with food and filled the leather canteen that was strapped to it. There were too many straps and she wasn't sure she'd buckled them right—the pack shifted uncomfortably. She went out of Fosdyke alone, and into the Ruined Zones.

The Beast! It lived! Well, after a fashion. It would tell her the way to the Mountain. It would tell her how to put things right. It would tell her who made it. It would tell her what was wrong with the world. She had so many questions to ask it. It would talk to her, she knew. It was suffering—she could feel it. It was like a sister to her.

EIGHTEEN

The Night Watch—Maury at War—
The Lamplighters—Brace-Bel at War

Arjun

There were two chairs in the office, and a desk. There was no
light except the moon outside. Arjun sat in one chair; Inspector
Maury sat facing him. The office was raised on a mezzanine of iron
walkways and platforms above the floor of an old cattle-pen or
slaughtering-house, from which all the cattle seemed to have fled.
There was a disconcerting crack in the concrete ceiling, which
leaked. The timbers creaked, the pipes shrieked, the shutters
banged, the obscene tubes and clamps of the old pre-War milking-
machines clattered. In the darkness below the men of the Night
Watch slept, paced, cleaned their boots, prayed. No lights—no
lights anywhere. Arjun coughed and Maury swore. There was a
strange intimacy between them, and neither of them was sure what
to say.

"What . . ."

"Do you . . ."

"No, you . . ."

"Sorry—you go on."

Maury swore again. He hunched in his chair. His maimed left
arm was bound in a sling across his body; otherwise he looked unchanged. The battered black leather coat, the shabby suit, the neck-
tie loose and frayed. A little older, more tired; a grizzled white
growth of beard like mold on old food. He swore and growled,
"Still alive, then?"

"Apparently."

"Still stuck here in this shit-hole?"

"I seem to be."

"We're all just circling the fucking drain, aren't we."

"Fosdyke seems to be weathering the crisis well enough, Inspector—are you still an Inspector? Maury, do you know if Ruth and Marta Low of Carnyx Street are still . . ."

"Fosdyke!" Maury grunted. "They'll get theirs soon enough."

"Maury, are the Lows still alive?"

"How would I know? Probably. We're at fucking war with Fosdyke, aren't we? Bastards."

"Maury, where are we?"

The men of the Night Watch had dragged Arjun through the streets, in the dark. They'd ducked and dodged as if avoiding patrols, and he'd lost his sense of direction. Periodically they'd stopped to smash streetlights, break windows, and extinguish the lamps inside, confiscate the candles from the hands of lone pedestrians. Their behavior had struck Arjun as peculiar, though he reserved judgment; the city had changed, again, and perhaps what they were doing made a kind of sense. They'd dragged him out through empty ruined places, through wide open spaces under the dark clouds, and into these abandoned and unpleasant stockyards. Arjun had no real idea where he was.

Maury grunted. Apparently he didn't intend to answer.

"What's happening here, Inspector Maury?"

"Where've you been?"

"Elsewhere."

"Elsewhere? What's that mean? Where's Ivy?"

"She went to the Mountain. I didn't. I don't know what happened to her."

Maury sagged. Then he jumped up, and Arjun braced for violence; but instead Maury went to the door and yelled out, "Pike, Drummond. Get us some fucking coffee."

Maury slumped back down. "If there's one thing we've got here it's coffee. The warehouse next door used to store it and ship it. Boxes and bloody boxes of it. Coffee, salt beef. Spoons, for some reason. You really don't remember?"

Arjun told Maury how he'd woken to himself in the ruins of the Carraway Estates, in the South Bara Ruined Zone. One of

Maury's men—Pike? Drummond?—brought in coffee in two black mugs. Maury gestured Arjun to shut up. When Drummond—Pike?—was gone, Maury said, "They don't know. They don't need to know about that monster, about the Museum, about Ivy. I told them to look out for you, you had valuable intelligence. Didn't say what. No one needs to know that. Who knows what the boys would say if they knew this was all our fault? All right? Maybe I should just shoot you now, shut your mouth, that's what'd be safest. Was it our fault? None of this makes sense. That woman, that monster, the Mountain. I should shoot you now but this is all about you, isn't it? Last chance. Last chance to put this right. Only lead in my inquiries. What's going on? What do we do?"

Maury said this in a monotone, while he held his coffee near his lips in a shaking hand. Then his eyes settled on Arjun and he said, "Yeah, I tried to kill you, but you tried to kill me. With the birds and all that. No reason we can't be friends now. We saw some things together. That changes a man. I'm being serious. It's a different city. Everything's different now. We have to work together. Between us we've got just about enough hand for a handshake, right?"

So Maury was mad, then, Arjun thought. How mad? A little madness, under the circumstances, was understandable. How dangerous was he?

In fits and starts, swearing and snarling, Maury told his story.

"I missed the War. After what happened at the . . . after what happened I was pretty much nearly dead. You did a good job on me, you little bastards."

He paused to fumble one-handed with a cigarette. "We've got about a million of these, too," he said. "Warehouses stacked high." Arjun helped him light it—Maury flinched at the fire and glanced nervously at the window.

"I suppose I don't know who took me in. My guess is they didn't know who I was or they'd probably have slit my throat. More fool them, right? Someone put me in a hospital bed. No name, no papers. Death sentence, anyway, they might as well have left me in the gutter. Someone sewed up the arm. Then they leave you to sweat and shit out the fever. I didn't die. I didn't. I wouldn't. Do you think something kept me alive for a purpose?"

"I don't know."

"Me neither. I think I was just too fucking angry to die. The first bombs fell and I slept through it. They left us alone in the hospital and we had to fight for what food was left, too weak to crawl. I didn't die then either. I didn't even know who I was for a long time, all I knew was that everything was wrong in the world. I went out into the city and everything was different, I didn't know who I was or where I was and maybe I went mad for a bit."

"I'm sorry. I know how that feels."

"I'd missed the War. Waited all my life and I missed it. Went walking. Turns out the hospital wasn't far from Barking Hill—where we met, remember the good old days? We had a laugh, didn't we? Empty now. Rich folk lived there, they went to shelters. Evacuated. Don't know what happened then. Walked through the ruins. Learned a thing or two—saw the airships. Light calls to them. Light brings the airships, noise brings the Hollow Men. World's over. City's over. Trying to start again—that's madness. Hide in the dark—all we're good for now."

He went quiet for a long time. Suddenly he said, "Anyway. Met up with some of the lads. Guardpost south of the Hill. Not bad lads. Deserters, I suppose, in a way, but that's all past now. They didn't recognize me at first. I thought, maybe *I'm* a ghost now, too."

Maury lit another cigarette. Clouds passed across the moon and the red tip was the only light. "I understand something now. All my life those ghosts who came down and talked of War. Soldiers. Bombers. Ruins. Fifty years of fearing what was coming. I was only a kid when I looked into that alley and the man in it who I'd thought was sick dragged me in and said: *all you kids die in the War.* Hands all filthy with soot. Not my fault, is it, if I was frightened? I know who they were now, all them poor lads. Our lads, who we sent up to the Mountain, and the Mountain threw 'em back down, higgledy-piggledy, all over the years. Minds gone. Just did it to scare us, I reckon. Not our fault. Someone played a nasty game with us. If those ghosts had left us alone we'd all have been kinder people. I really believe that."

Softly, Arjun said, "Maybe that's true, Inspector. There's something cruel in the Mountain. It's taken from all of us."

"Maybe. Maybe. Too late for mending now. Anyway." Maury waved vaguely. "The lads recognized me in the end. We met up with a few others. People need order, now. They don't know what's good for them. Trying to pretend nothing's changed. No sense. No sense to *fear*. We're a kind of police, I suppose. Night Watch. Going from door to door, reminding people to put out their damn lights, *hide*. Making 'em see sense, if they won't do it for themselves. Here in this House we've got twenty men, but there's lots of us, all over. Mad gangs, now, and worse, Lamplighters and things. One big stupid war turns into lots of stupid little wars. Something has to be done. It just makes sense, you see."

"That's good, Inspector. These people *need* help. What are Lamplighters?"

Maury ignored the question. "What happened on the Mountain?" he said. "What did she do? Ivy . . . I shouldn't have trusted Ivy. Bad things happened and I don't know what. But,"—he jabbed his finger at Arjun's face—"I remember this. At the Museum, on the steps, there's me lying there with my arm all bloody, everything numb or cold or burning, dying maybe, and I saw that *Beast,* I should never have tried to talk to that thing, I saw it changing. And it said something I remember well—it said *Shay*. It said Shay rules the Mountain. It said Shay made it. Whined about it. It said Shay made it to show the way. You know about this stuff. What's Shay got to do with all this?"

Arjun nearly jumped out of his seat. "You know Shay?"

Maury banged the table and roared, "Sit the fuck down!" In a calmer voice he said, "Yeah. I know the name. He was a ghost we saw a lot of—us in the League. Troublemaker. It's in the files. I don't remember now. Nasty magics. Skulking around the shadows, making deals. Asking funny questions about the Mountain. Bunch of different names. Sometimes he looked like an old man, sometimes he looked young. Always got away, came back over the years. Well connected. Knew people. Don't remember the details. Never thought much about him. Name stuck in my mind, is all. What's he got to do with all this?"

"I don't know," Arjun said. "I don't know. Where are these files?"

Maury shrugged. "Don't know. Any Chapterhouse."

Arjun sighed. "Secret files, ruins, buried intelligence. Ghosts and criminals. Inspector—I came here to this city, so many years ago, thinking things would be simple. I came naïvely, in search of music. I dreamed I would wander down broad sunlit boulevards, find my God singing in golden temples, and bear it home. But everything is very complicated here. I am trapped in some horrible game I do not understand. We all are. I'll tell you everything I know about Shay, and it won't be enough. The answers are on the Mountain. Help me get there, Inspector—do you want answers?"

"Fuck answers," Maury said, with finality—and Arjun, who'd found a passably sharp pen on the desk, and palmed it in the dark, readied himself to strike at the Inspector and run. "Fuck answers," Maury repeated. "It's too late for answers. The city's dead. I want revenge on whoever did this. Not *my* fucking fault."

Maury stretched out his hand. They shook on it.

"First we find the Low sisters," Arjun said.

Maury sneered, looked sick, but didn't say no.

Arjun felt himself sag with relief—had he ever in his life been so tired? He added, "And I need somewhere to sleep tonight."

Brace-Bel

And what had happened to Brace-Bel? He wasn't dead, not yet; in fact he was very happy to say that he was more alive than ever. He had landed in the aftermath of War, and found beauty in the ruins. He'd personally shot and killed at least three or four people and the men under his command had detonated a number of bombs, and he had a new appreciation for the speed and power and thrilling aesthetic purity of rifles and bullets, the glories of rockets. It occurred to him from time to time that he might have lost his mind, but could he really be blamed for that?

What *had* happened to him? He'd been dragged from the bolt-hole on Carnyx Street, drugged, transported *elsewhere* in a packing crate like a slab of meat—slapped awake, strapped to a chair in a bare white room, subjected to Father Turnbull's strict inquiries, to St. Loup's aimless sadism. Brace-Bel had roared and spat defiance and dared them to do their worst, which perhaps wasn't the wisest way to handle them, but Brace-Bel was what he was. They questioned him. He didn't understand anything they said. It wasn't in his nature to admit ignorance so the questioning went on and on.

St. Loup tortured him with cigarettes, Turnbull with poisons and fevers and hallucinogens.

"This is a waste of time," Turnbull said.

"He's nobody and he knows no one," St. Loup agreed.

"How dare you," Brace-Bel said. "I am Brace-Bel, my crimes are legend, how dare you, you specters, you nameless drifters."

"Gods, can't we just shut him up?"

"Fat little fish," St. Loup said. "We're throwing you back where you came from."

They ejected him from the backseat of a black motorcar as they sped down a narrow twisting street. The scenes from the car's windows had been monstrous, unnatural. A sprawl of slave markets, idols and minarets, the shores of a hot and blue lake, tall golden glass buildings, ruins. Gods crossed their path like cattle—many armed, refulgent, tenebrous, beautiful, hideous, howling or drumming or resounding like a clash of cymbals. St. Loup tapped his gloved finger on the steering wheel as he waited for them to pass. Factories, smokestacks, concrete. Grey skies. Color bled from the city. "Out, here." And the door opened and someone shoved Brace-Bel, hard.

Free again! In a manner of speaking. He rolled and rolled, and ended spread-eagled on his back in a puddle, in the gutter. The car roared away, into better futures, gentler pasts. Brace-Bel lay shivering in the rain, back again at the end of time, in the shadow of the Mountain.

They had stolen his remarkable stick, with its precious crystal.

He lay there for some time. He had no particular inclination to move. He was weak, exhausted. His veins were full of Turnbull's drugs and his head still buzzed and hummed. People stepped over him. His left eye, which St. Loup had mistreated, went dim and then blind. Oh well, he had another, and he'd always been ugly. He crawled into an alley and drank rainwater. A day passed, and another. Night fell. A droning sound filled the world, and at first he thought it was in his head, and that he was dying at last. Then stark white light broke over the rooftops, and it was the most beautiful thing he had ever seen. An airship passed overhead and bombs started to fall.

＊　＊　＊

Brace-Bel's memories of the following days were hazy. He was not well. He remembered standing in bread lines. He remembered being turned away from the armies that went up on the Mountain, for his flat feet and his blind eye and his fat gut and his other deficiencies—physical, moral, and hygienic. He could not remember volunteering. He remembered the girls throwing flowers after the soldiers as they marched, off to their doom in the shadows. Red roses in the gutter. Where did they get roses?

The soldiers didn't come back. The bombers came again, and again. The world fell apart. There were riots, starvation. New wreckage sprung up every morning. Ash and dust made everything grey. Thousands and tens of thousands died, but Brace-Bel survived. He saw chaos, hunger, despair. He formed plans.

As it happened, Turnbull and St. Loup had discarded Brace-Bel not far from Jubilee Hill, where numerous executives of the Patagan, Holcroft, and Blackbridge Combines had kept their mansions. And though the Combines were gone now, and Jubilee Hill was fallen far from its former glories, still Brace-Bel naturally gravitated upward. The memory of wealth and luxury called to him.

The place was in a dreadful state. It had suffered terribly in the first wave of bombing—the enemy, it seemed clear, had struck hardest at the city's head. Mansions lay in ruins. Trees were blasted and burned. Marble statuary was scattered limbless and headless across lawns that were now wastelands of mud. The Combines were gone. Looters prowled, and lapdogs had gone feral. There was no security anymore to stop Brace-Bel simply wandering up the Hill's once-exclusive avenues, across its formerly lush lawns, into what was left of its stately structures.

What he found, huddled in the hollowed-out wrecks of their homes, were executives' wives, executives' children. Nonessential personnel, they had not been evacuated. Though a few still wore pearls or furs, the women were haggard and unwashed and rake-thin. The children were already starting to look like animals. Many of them still wore tennis whites, blotched with mud and blood. They took Brace-Bel for a looter at first, and screamed. The children hid beneath rain-warped dining tables and grand pianos, the wives brandished carving knives and letter openers and candlesticks. Their eyes were blank, confused. The world had moved on, and there was no place for them in it.

"Do not despair," he told them. He stood with his arms out-stretched. His voice echoed in the ruins, sonorous, commanding. "The world has changed, that's true. All your lives you took the way the world was for granted, you thought you were blessed. Now you know that no one is blessed, that nothing can be relied on, that the cruel engine of the city does not care who it grinds. I had to learn the same lesson once. And then again, and then over and over again. Like you I was cast out, left behind, purposeless, ridiculous. I re-made myself. You will, too. Dark and ugly and impoverished and mean-spirited times are coming. The city will need those who can appreciate beauty."

They stared at him. They were too desperate to laugh.

"Bring me light," he said. "And wine, if you have it."

One of the ragged children ran wordlessly up the stairs.

"And a patch," Brace-Bel said, prodding his swollen eyesocket. "Silk, if you please."

Within a few days he was the undisputed master of Jubilee Hill. He could not have fascinated the children more if he had been an actual ogre. He was pleased to welcome a number of the wives into his bed (he had taken over a master bedroom that once belonged to a senior vice-president of the Blackbridge Combine). He dressed in very expensive suits that did not fit him, accented with a red silk eyepatch and scarf, and a substantial amount of gold jewelry.

His motives were not selfish—or rather, he pursued a higher form of self-indulgence that, he believed, was rather like altruism, only less dour. The people of Jubilee Hill needed someone to orga-nize them, to shock them out of their stupor. A living spirit. He se-cured food and guns from the emergency supplies at the peak of the Hill. He arranged repairs of some of the more beautiful buildings. He had the fireplaces stoked with broken furniture and dead trees, he put lanterns in the windows. "Warmth! Light! Let us blaze, let us be a beacon to the city below!"

The city below went mad. Cults and scavengers and bandit mobs took the place of the Combines. Ordinary people hid in their homes and waited in despair for the bombers. It was clear to Brace-Bel that the city craved leadership. Accompanied by women who were beau-tiful again, by children who were strong and pink-cheeked (not to mention well armed), Brace-Bel went down into the low places. He went into the Ruined Zones, into the places where dour committees of local busybodies and do-gooders imposed rules and rationing and the dull slog of rebuilding; there he gathered to him people who'd never known luxury or beauty, but hungered for it. Down in the low places the Night Watch and the committees and the local bully-boys said: *put out your lights—the airships will see you.*

Brace-Bel quickly diagnosed the city's problem as: darkness. Darkness, fear, and a meanness of spirit.

"The city is ours to create anew," he told his followers. "The question is, are we to cower in the darkness like mushrooms, always in fear, always cold, building nothing, writing nothing, singing nothing, abasing ourselves, or shall we blaze to the heavens? Let us say, *damn* the airships and *damn* the Mountain, let us shine! Let us be beautiful! Let us be no longer prisoners of fear! If the bombs come they come! And what do we care, so long as . . ."

The Mountain, or whoever or whatever sent the airships, had decided to bring death to the city. Out of sheer bloody-mindedness Brace-Bel decided to defy it with *creation.* He would work in the medium of light—which was to say, generally, fire. Occasionally, bright paint, wine, shattered glass. His followers, who became numerous, too numerous and far-flung for him to count, came to be called the Lamplighters.

The mania spread. New cells formed. Signals and emblems and secret codes, not all of which even Brace-Bel understood: lamps in windows, bright flags, drunken half-naked dancing around night-fires in the ruins. The Lamplighters were a kind of loose and louche army, formed from malcontents, suicides, teenagers, the reckless. The world was ending: they wanted to be drunk.

In the Night Watch the Lamplighters found their perfect opposite—their reason for being. The mean-minded thugs of the Night Watch, most of them, frankly, *policemen,* whose fear of the airships had driven them quite mad, who kicked in windows and smashed down lamps and put out fires and crushed all efforts at rebuilding. They had splendid battles!

"A man should be involved in the struggles of his Age," Brace-Bel told the beautiful women. They were mostly formerly rich widows. He forgot their names. He addressed them all as *Ivy*. He liked to imagine that she was watching, up on her Mountain—that she was giving meaning to what appeared, he had to admit, to be somewhat meaningless actions. Sometimes he worried that he was a little mad, sometimes he felt that he was caught up in the gears of a great machine and his actions were not quite under his control, but he kept talking and talking and the doubts went away. "The struggle between darkness and light, surrender and resistance, fear and joy, Night Watch and Lamplighters, is the defining contest of our age. A man who abstains from such contests is something less than a man. The passionate grapple of ideas is what it is to be human! What can we make of a man who walks unconcerned through the battle, eyes fixed on the Mountain, ears full of music . . . ? In a former life I wasted my time trying to fight the battles of the long-forgotten Age of my birth—uttering blasphemies against long-dead Gods. I was outrageous and daring and no one very much cared. Broken free from the prison of my life, I set laboriously about reconstructing it, so that I might reenact my rituals of escape. My escape was my prison; I made it myself. I did not see freedom for what it was."

A series of skirmishes culminated in a great battle between bright-clad Lamplighters and the grim Night Watch at the Hogue Point glassworks. The Night Watch had guns, but the Lamplighters had numbers, ingenuity, and broken bottles—not to mention they had dug up a half-dozen unexploded bombs, which they deployed with a combination of cunning and gusto. And the dismal forces were routed. Brace-Bel received a flesh wound. At Forty-ninth the Watch routed the Lamplighters in turn and another happy street went dark.

"The one pleasure I never tasted in all my long life," Brace-Bel said, "was the pleasure of *War*! I may never pick up a pen again."

NINETEEN

Closing Time–The Battle at the Elton Street Brewery–Under Observation–Silence

Arjun

In the morning Arjun met Maury's men, out in the cattleyard. There were thirteen of them. If what Maury said was true—a doubtful proposition—the Night Watch was a city-wide movement. This little mob was Maury's fragment of power.

A misty rain blew in through the cracks in the concrete and corrugated iron. The men—they were all men—were a mostly thuggish-looking bunch. The youngest was a greasy teen; the oldest grey and wrinkled. They'd slept in the cold on the floor of the cattle pens, and they ached and stumbled and swore. They smelled stale. They wore expressions of despair, fear, anger, low cunning.

Arjun offered his hand to them and they looked at him like he was a snake. They asked Maury, "Who the fuck is this? Why's he coming with us?"

"Shut your fucking mouth," Maury said. "And do as you're told."

The men armed themselves, drank cold coffee, discussed plans and grudges and the movements of their enemies, who seemed to be more or less everyone and everything. Even more than they hated the Mountain, or the rival cult they called the Lamplighters, or the new and strange Gods, they hated the people who were rebuilding Fosdyke. They seemed to regard other people's hope as a kind of personal affront. Light only brought down the bombers—

wasn't that fucking *obvious*? They were the bleakest and most bitter nihilists Arjun had ever met.

"You're in the Night Watch now, son," Maury said; and he shoved a rifle into Arjun's hands. "These are your people."

The men of the Night Watch nursed their resentments all afternoon—with a brief break for target practice. In the evening they moved out across the muddy fields and waste-grounds of the stockyards. "Used to belong to the Blackbridge Combine, all this," Maury said conversationally. "Big agricultural concern. You won't have heard of them. Gone now. Fosdyke's looking to take this over for farmland. Not going to happen, if we've got anything to say about it." He waved at his men, at their rifles, at the great cresting waves of barbed wire with which they'd fenced the fields. Escaped cattle and the monstrous engineered horses of the last days roamed the wastes, bony, immense, remembering long-buried instincts of herd and territory, caught on the wires, drowned in ditches, lowing and shaking their heads like things of the primordial plains. "We'll get you back to Fosdyke. Stick close. We've got a bit of business first."

"But . . ."

"Nest of Lamplighters. I told you about them, right? Now you'll see. You'll see what has to be done."

Arjun watched for the first opportunity to slip away. The Inspector was mad and dangerous, his Watch were depraved. No doubt the Lamplighters were just as bad. Arjun had seen enough mad little cults like this—they sprang up in the wake of every one of the countless disasters that had hit the city. He had no intention of joining one.

They went north, then northeast, through ruined streets, through living streets. "Where are we going?" Arjun asked, and they hushed him. In places where people were still living, the men of the Night Watch split up into twos and threes, pretending not to know each other, keeping their heads down and their weapons under their coats. They smashed the odd lamp, they broke the odd window—less like a military force, more like a vague migration of thugs through the streets at closing time.

The battle was joined before Arjun even knew it was coming. Who was shooting? He realized too late that it was his own loathsome comrades. He noticed too late the blazing lights in the windows of the factory at the end of the street—the torches burning golden and crimson, the bolts of bright cloth fluttering from the sills and draped from the wire of the fence, the cables hanging lanterns from the chimney like festival trees. Lighting the city's darkness. Recklessly burning through the last of the city's stockpiled oil. Were these the people Maury's men called the Lamplighters?

The Night Watch, enraged, fanned out around the fence, crouching in the shadows, darting across the factory's lot, firing wildly at the windows.

Maury held a small staff revolver and gestured with it, left and right, forward—*quick, go on, while they're still too drunk and stupid to know what's happening to 'em*. He hung back outside the factory gates with a couple of his men.

With the dull muzzle of his gun he beckoned Arjun to stand by him. "Look at these bastards," he hissed, pointing at the glowing factory. "If that doesn't bring down the bloody wrath of the Mountain what will? What's wrong with them?"

From inside the factory—what was it to them? A church? A festival-hall? A work of art? The plan of a new city?—the Lamplighters returned fire. Wine bottles filled with oil and burning rags arced over the empty lot. When they smashed they unleashed crests of red flame; they spilled a poisonous lime-green luster; they roared gold across the night. They left glittering volatile slicks. A man of the Night Watch danced like a dervish over the flagstones, burning, spinning, and stooping, fire transfiguring him, making him immense, a dozen feet tall, his shape diffusing into light.

The Night Watch kicked down the door and went inside.

Maury took a couple of vague and pointless shots at the windows. The two Watchmen standing beside him kneeled and fired, reloading with grim efficiency. He elbowed Arjun in the ribs and said, "Go on, son, we gave you a gun."

"This is mad," Arjun said. The fires reflected in Maury's eyes made him look like a devil. The two men of the Watch who knelt beside him looked back angrily at Arjun. The night sky above was rendered grey and milky by the haze of firelight; in it Arjun saw a flock of distant black specks, slowly approaching.

He lifted the rifle to his shoulder. Another bottle exploded not far from him and he nearly dropped the weapon on his foot. Maury was shouting orders. On the roof of the factory, two men struggled barehanded, silhouetted against the grey sky, and it was impossible to tell who was who. One of the cables snapped and the lanterns fell. They burst like fireworks. Behind the factory the bombers approached.

Arjun gave up fumbling with the rifle. Instead he turned it and slammed the stock into the back of the nearest Watchman's neck. The other, turning, got it in the face. Swinging the rifle, Arjun hit Maury hard in the stomach so that he fell gasping on all fours.

Arjun dropped the rifle and ran.

He headed down the street, away from the factory. The street was a row of concrete warehouses on either side, and it offered no hiding places. Behind him he heard running feet, shouting and swearing—the Watchmen had recovered quickly.

He heard three shots, in quick succession.

He heard Maury calling, "Wait! Arjun! Stop!"

He dared to turn around for a moment.

The two Watchmen lay dead on the street. Panting, Maury came running up behind, his revolver still in his hand. "Arjun! Stop! Take me with you!" He fell to his knees and gasped for breath.

It was a weakness in Arjun's character that he was too easily moved to pity. He was well aware of it. He'd been in fear of his life too often; he was painfully conscious of his own life as a fragile and contingent thing. Maury was mad, of course; but who wasn't? That was the sort of person Arjun had chosen to live among. He helped Maury stand. "Are you all right, Inspector?" Maury gasped and clutched Arjun's shoulder with his one hand. Arjun felt that familiar involuntary surge of pity. "Come on, Inspector. Quickly."

They staggered together into the shadows, and away. The battle at the factory burned itself out—everything went dark. A few men came hunting down the street—were they Night Watch or Lamplighters? Who'd won? It didn't matter. The bombers passed overhead, three of them together in a slow solemn formation. Their distant drone filled the night like the sound of crickets. They passed harmlessly over the smoldering factory—a few miles south they dropped their bombs over a dark and unoffending patch of city. They didn't seem to care what was happening below.

Brace-Bel

Brace-Bel was no fool. He took it for granted that St. Loup and Turnbull had not set him loose out of kindness or mercy, that they had not gone to the trouble of sending him back to that Age without an ulterior motive. Nothing they did was unselfish. He had spent long enough at Court to know their type. He assumed they were watching him, waiting to see what he would do next, where he would go. Shay had had scrying and spying devices that one could hide on a man's person without his knowledge, and maybe Turnbull did, too—Brace-Bel scrubbed fastidiously and changed his clothes frequently, but he could not be sure he was not, what would the word be, *marked*. Perhaps, like Shay, St. Loup could watch him through the eyes of rats or snakes or birds. Perhaps their agents were mingling among his troops. Sometimes he thought he saw their faces on street corners or at windows or in his nightmares. No matter. He was used to being watched. Censors, jailors, spies; his audience, his readers, his admirers. He would put on a show for them!

The headquarters of the Lamplighters moved from place to place—usually to avoid enemies, once or twice because the Lamplighters had accidentally drunkenly burned the building down. When Brace-Bel received the news of the loss of the Elton Street Brewery, their headquarters was in a mansion on Meadow-grass Hill. They had painted most of the mansion red, and hung the dining-room walls with lanterns and brightly colored trophies. Brace-Bel was pacing around and around the dining-room table, studying his maps of the city. "I should thrash you," he told the messenger, brandishing his new cane. "But I won't, because you are a very handsome young man."

On the maps he marked his own forces with silverware, and his speculations as to the Adversary's whereabouts with chunks of coal. Actually he was uncertain of the whereabouts of his own forces, as well. He wasn't sure whether any of his orders were obeyed. The thing was out of his control. He was a better artist, he had to admit, than general.

"No matter," he said. "If we lose one battle, or a hundred. We are fighting splendidly, beautifully. Better to burn in a last glorious flame than to, ah, um."

For the sake of morale he ordered a party, which turned as such things generally did into a sort of orgy, out on the lawns. They polished off the last of the mansion's wine cellars and they burned most of the furniture in a gigantic bonfire, and they burned the hedge maze, too. In the shadows, in the firelight, among the dancers, was that St. Loup watching? Golden-haired, smiling, handsome, mocking? The shifting wind drew down a curtain of black smoke and the face was gone. Was that plump little Turnbull sitting on a tree stump, taking notes? Surely not. Perhaps. Brace-Bel cupped the breast of someone's widow in his hand and swigged stolen wine. Who was that bearded giant in black robes and skullcap, hefting that unlikely staff? Brace-Bel had seen him at the last party and didn't know his name. All of his Lamplighters were freaks and misfits; it was hard to know who belonged and who didn't. No matter. Nothing down here mattered.

Behind the fire, behind the smoke, behind burned trees and jagged ruins, loomed the Mountain; and that, too, was watching him. *Ivy* was watching him. He felt her eyes upon him. She had gone to the Mountain. She had been translated into divinity. She had gone where he was not brave enough, strong enough, daring enough to go. "For you, my dear," he muttered. The woman in his arms smiled happily, misunderstanding. "This beautiful struggle, for you." Could she see it, where she was? Was it enough? Was it enough to show what he was worth?

He had the last two casks of very expensive whiskey rolled out of the mansion's cellars and thrown onto the fire. The explosion blew out the mansion's windows.

Ruth

Ruth, alone in the Ruined Zone. A high wind whistled through the broken towers, the shattered windows, across the wastelands of rubble, down the unreal streets. Houses were reduced to facades. The world was moth-wing grey, streaked with red rust. There were wild dogs in the ruins, and sometimes they barked and howled. Birds roosted in the wreckage. Otherwise the Ruined Zone was silent. The devastation there had been too great—the shock of the War had killed the organism. The people who'd lived there had fled: north to Fosdyke, west to Fleet Wark, south to whatever was south.

Those few who remained hid in their holes and kept quiet. Stone and plaster and concrete and dust everywhere—walking in the Zone was like a dream of walking on the moon. The air was clear and smokeless and cold. Vast heaps of bricks and timbers like the bones of long-dead monsters blocked the streets. Ruth's stolen rifle made a passable climbing-stick. She ascended the shifting slopes. Windowsills and buckled rusting fire escapes gave her handholds. At the peak she looked south across the Zone. It reminded her of things she'd only read about in books. Moonscape? Tundra? Mountain?

It was her fourth day in the great clear, cold silence of the Ruined Zone. The city was far behind her now. At first the silence had been oppressive, unsettling; she'd felt she was being watched. Now she was at home here. Last night she'd slept in a half-exposed cellar, like a wild thing in a cave. She was learning self-sufficiency. She drank from broken and leaking water pipes. Could she hunt the wild dogs, bring down a bird? In a few days she might have to try.

She got thin. Bone and sinew. When she caught her reflection in broken windows, muddy puddles, she looked like a feral child. She didn't mind.

On the second day she'd chased off a pack of bandits with a single wild shot. On the third morning she'd stumbled into a ruin claimed by displaced and confused Thunderers, and had to flee for her life. In the evenings she'd watched the distant lights of Gods moving stately among the ruins. By day the skies were blue, unpolluted. At night the stars came out.

Slowly, shyly, as the days went by, she'd realized that she was happy. In a way. She felt guilty about it. She'd seen no shortage of terrible things—gnawed skeletons and the stain of human ash became routine. Part of her wanted to scream and sob at the outrage and cruelty of it; part of her wanted to stand on the peaks and yell for the sheer joy of breaking that silence, of being alive and free. The world that had ended was over, and there was no one here with time to mourn it. Every muscle in her body ached. She felt hungry but strong. That cold fierce freedom—was that how Ivy felt all the time? Was that what their father had felt when he'd finally broken free of the mediocrity of his life, when he'd left them all behind?

☆　☆　☆

A man came walking down the road toward her. He clambered over wreckage. She trained the rifle on him, but he didn't seem to be bothered by it. When he got closer he waved. Was he real? He was the first living person she'd seen in days. Certainly he was peculiar enough to be a hallucination.

"Good afternoon! You look a long way from home."

His voice was confident, friendly, cultured—an unusual but pleasant accent. He had a tan. Long blond curls spilled down his shoulders. He wore dark glasses, a crisp white shirt, and linen trousers. He carried no weapon, and apart from some neat stitches and a purple bruise on the side of his head he was incongruously clean and healthy looking.

"That's close enough. Who are you?"

He shrugged and sat on the steps of a ruined house. "No one in particular. Who are you?"

"Ruth Low. What's your name?"

"Ruth Low. What brings you out here?"

"Maybe I'm from here. Who are you? Why are you here?"

"I'm a bit lost, actually. That's the honest truth. There's somewhere I need to be but in the meantime here we both are."

"Have you been following me?"

"No." He smiled. He was lying. "Why? Are you the kind of person who gets followed?"

"I didn't think I was but maybe I am. I don't have anything worth stealing."

"Of course you do. But I'm not a thief." He leaned back, legs crossed. "Would you like company? I find myself with time on my hands at present. I used to have a job and a life in the world before this one but now I'm the most awful sort of idler. I could go with you."

"I'm not going anywhere."

"Nor am I! Just circling and circling."

He focused his smile on her again. It was strikingly handsome, and would have been charming had it seemed less practiced. In any case she had no intention of being charmed by handsome smiles. "I'd rather be alone."

He frowned, comically. "How sad."

"Who are you? Are you a ghost?"

"Very much alive. Well," he looked thoughtful, "more or less.

Good-bye, Ruth Low. Don't keep going the way you're going. There are some unpleasant people ahead of you. Bandits. Cannibals. Sad, really. Take a detour. I'd like to see you get wherever you're going. Good-bye."

He walked away.

"Stop."

He kept walking.

"Come back."

He turned a corner, and was gone.

After some thought, she decided to take a detour.

So much for solitude. You were never alone, not even now. Was he following her? She couldn't tell. She didn't see him again. She didn't see anyone again for days, and by that time she'd almost forgotten she'd met him at all.

She saw them in the far distance, far away over the ruins of the Zone. First their motion caught her eye; then she noticed their smoke. An antlike procession down an empty road between shattered buildings. She couldn't quite make out the ones who went on foot, or horseback, but the black specks of motorcars were visible if she squinted. The procession that the Beast led through the wasteland, just as Hatch had described it. The buildings around them were tiny as matchboxes, thimbles, scattered dice. There, crawling, was a miniscule flash of red—was that the Beast's palanquin?

It was days before she caught up with the procession. It moved slowly—rubble blocked the streets and had to be cleared before the motorcars could pass—but so did she. And perhaps she hung back a little—out of fear, out of a desire to prolong her solitude. She went to sleep in the evenings, when she could have pressed on. Once she was on its trail there was no losing it. Now that she knew what she was looking for, the tracks the procession left—cleared roads, rubble heaped at the side of the streets—were obvious. Animal bones and human waste. Oil—one of the cars had a leak. Round and round the procession went, circling the Ruined Zone. If they'd gone south, or west, or east, or north, they'd have found themselves, eventually, in Fosdyke, or Fleet Wark, or any of those places over the horizon where the lights were coming back, where the city was rebuilding. But they didn't. They turned back again and again into the wasteland. They passed south out of the Walbrook Ruined Zone, and into Juno, a blasted and barren landscape of quarries and mineshafts. The procession wove through slag and gravel, around the yawning violent chasms of the granite quarries, the stark white glare of the chalk quarries. Round and round. Why? Ruth began to imagine that the procession's spiraling path through the ruins had some significance—was like some careful surgical procedure, enacted on the wounds of the city. She hung back, waiting to see what would happen. Sometimes, when she climbed the echoing unsteady staircases of vacant buildings and looked out from the broken rooftops, she could see the procession crawling on ahead. Five black motorcars, adorned with flags, skulls, ivy, wire, and groaning under the weight of the excess passengers who sat on the roof, who leaned from the windows. A flatbed truck, bearing a folded scarlet tent—shiny, thick, like a tongue. The shufflers coming behind. Down into the quarries and out again.

When they stopped they erected that scarlet tent—huge, a marquee, like something an executive's daughter might marry in. It took hours. Tiny men scuttled around beneath it. What were they doing?

That was as close as she chose to come. When she finally made contact it was by accident.

She'd been looking out over the quarries from the roof of an abandoned office block—what used to be an office of the Juno Mining and Mineral Combine. She came down the stairs, where the filing cabinets had shaken open and pointless paper blew in the dust, and out by the back door, where weeds reclaimed the parking lot, and she stopped short in shock.

Two men knelt in a thicket of nettles and ragwort, under the fire escape. For a moment she forgot how to speak.

One of the two men wore filthy rags that might once have been a smart business suit. The other was bare to the waist, and his chest was scarred and badly stitched, in a way that made Ruth think of the Beast's poor hide. He looked half starved. They didn't notice her; they were intent on something in the weeds.

"It's coming toward you! To you, to you!"

"Where did it go?"

"No, you idiot, grab it . . ."

The bare-chested man suddenly lunged, sprawling on his belly in the nettles. Something shrieked.

Grumbling "Bloody thing got me!" he stood. He held a black and white cat by its neck against his scarred chest. Its yellow eyes were wide and it hissed and squirmed.

The man in the suit poked at the creature's patchy underbelly. "This'll do. This'll do."

The two of them turned slowly, as if suddenly noticing Ruth. Wary eyes regarded her—four bloodshot, two yellow.

The man in the suit drew a knife from an inside pocket—it looked like it had been a gilt-edged letter opener in a previous life.

In the sternest and most scolding voice she could muster, Ruth demanded, "What are you doing with that cat?"

She'd caught them off guard. Blushing, the man in the suit lowered the knife.

"Let it go *at once*."

The man in the suit glanced over at his bare-chested companion for support—but he was staring at his feet, at the blue sky, his eyes averted from Ruth, and from the spitting mangy thing in his arms.

"Poor thing—it's scared. What do you think you're doing?"

The man in the suit finally opened his mouth. "Don't you know? The Lord of these ruins needs these for his experiments. He's making . . ."

"I know what he's doing with them," Ruth lied; and she kept lying. "He's wasting his time. Let that poor creature go. I've come to find him. I know who made him—I know what he's for. That's worth more than any mangy stray. Take me to him."

TWENTY

Strays–The Quarry–Theater–
Scarlet and Gold–Sisters Under
the Skin–Shay's War

Ruth

The two interrupted hunters of cats were called Flitter and Silt—Silt being the grey-haired man in the ragged suit, Flitter the one whose bare and malnourished chest was now purpling from the nettles and the cat scratches in a way that made Ruth wince to look at it.

In the old world Flitter, as it happened, had been a rat-catcher. Sewer-diver, dark-delver, bloody-handed, and solitary. Silt had been a lawyer at the head of the Claims department of Juno Mineral. Now they were, Flitter said, easily the best and most valuable of the Beast's servants.

"We are high in his regard," Silt agreed.

"Fucking right!" Flitter said. He frowned. "He would have liked that cat."

Cats? Not just cats! Flitter, energetic now, in the tones of a working man delighted to explain his trade, his *craft,* told Ruth how they'd hunted rats, bats, dogs, a tortoise once, some lizards. How, on one memorable occasion, they'd acquired a tawny owl up in the rafters of a ruined office building . . .

"Spotted," Silt said. "It was a *spotted* owl."

. . . *spotted,* then, and Flitter'd taken a few good scratches getting it in the sack, but he hardly felt scratches those days. And the

Beast had drawn it from the sack with his great scarred hands, and looked the fierce bird in its yellow eyes with his own terrible eyes, and made it afraid; and then with his little knives and his sharp strong nails started cutting and slicing, reknitting guts and veins and muscles and . . .

"Tendons," Silt said. "Tendons are very important." He tapped the side of his nose. "I watch the master work."

. . . *tendons,* right, Flitter agreed, and bones, the bones re-arranged, even the little fiddly ones in the wings, and the Beast get-ting his fingers all covered in blood and feathers, and sometimes, when he forgets people are watching, slipping a little bloody bit of meat into the side of his mouth and licking his lips.

And then the owl *flew*. Remade, it flew on wings of shadow. It was only intermittently visible. It had followed the caravan ever since, flitting in and out of dreams and memories. It asked meaning-less questions, in something that wasn't quite language. The Beast had judged it a horrible failure, and gone into one of his black rages.

The owl, Flitter said, was his proudest accomplishment. He'd never had any children, back in the old world, and the owl was like a daughter to him.

"Mr. Flitter doesn't understand the theory," Silt said. "Or the significance of our work. He's a simple man."

"Too fucking right!" Flitter laughed. "Fair enough!"

Throughout this conversation, the two men led Ruth through the little grove of office buildings, and out over the stony wasteland of the mines and quarries of Juno. They stood on either side of her. When they thought she wasn't looking—neither of them seemed very bright—they flashed little hand-signals and eye-signals to each other. They appeared to be under the impression that it was necessary to herd her—as if she hadn't come hunting for days across the Ruined Zones just to meet their master! They brought her back to the Beast as if she were some kind of exotic stray. It could have been worse. At least they didn't try to put the sack over her head—though she could see them gathering their nerve for it.

The Beast had led its caravan down into a deep quarry. What, in the old days, had the Juno Combine dug up there? Ruth wasn't sure; the sign at the gate had fallen from its post. The sheer walls of the quarry glittered in the afternoon sun, rust-red, wine-purple. There was a faint mineral scent of electricity. The far wall of the quarry shifted to blue in the distance.

A broad and steep path spiraled down into the depths. Old earth-moving machines lay abandoned on it.

Down on the flat earth at the quarry's heart, the Beast's followers and vehicles were tiny, toylike.

Round and round, down and down. Silt surreptitiously lifted the sack above Ruth's head, and she slapped him in the face, making Flitter laugh and Silt sulk. Round and down, the Beast's vehicles and tents and immense crimson marquee growing larger and larger, like a little fairy-tale town in the wilderness.

She walked faster and faster, down unsteady slopes of purple flint. Silt, complaining of a twisted ankle, fell behind, and Flitter stayed tenderly with him. Ruth pressed on alone.

By the time she reached the depths of the quarry it was evening. Torches burned between the tents. A few square prefabricated offices hunched in the shadows. Gravel crunched underfoot. Cranes leaned overhead, looking down into the quarry like children leaning over a rock-pool. The motorcars gleamed in the dark, black and sleek as panthers. Their hoods and fins were adorned with skulls and furs.

A circle of bony and ragged men and women sat cross-legged on the dirt, around a low wooden stage, where once the local foreman of the Juno Combine would have stood to supervise the quarry-workers. Now the Beast paced on the stage in the firelight, gesturing madly with its hands. It wore the scarred flesh it had stolen from Wantyard, and nothing else. It was a white map of stitches. Between its legs was a sealed wound. It lurched from side to side of the stage, speaking in different voices. Its hungry followers watched silently, adoringly.

It seemed some kind of theater was under way. Ruth sat down at the back of the crowd and watched.

Crouching, rubbing its stolen hands together in a cruel parody of fear, speaking in a wavering and ethereal voice, the Beast said:

—What crime am I accused of? What have I done that is not in my nature?

And leaping to the other side of the stage, the Beast stood erect, arms folded, and said, in stern and judicial tones:

—It is your nature that we cannot abide. Your weakness. Your changeability. Imperfect creature!

And cringing again:

—What will become of my children? My children's children?

And stern again:

—They will be provided for. We will set lights over them, to make them mad. We will build a labyrinth around them, so that they will always be lost. They will never see the bars of their prison.

Cringing again, the Beast suddenly stood, flailed dramatically, and fell, crying out. It was not an elegant fall—the body it had stolen was not athletic. It lay still for only a moment. Then it leaped up and stood at the front of the stage. Demonic firelight lit its scarred and drooping flesh. In its own voice it said, "Do you understand the lesson? If I ever told you differently before, I was lying. *This* is how it began. I should put out your eyes so you can see it better. This is the story of Man. Is it any wonder I hate you all? We, the vermin in your cell, never had any choice in our confinement."

It paused. There was clapping from the crowd—uncertain at first, then tumultuous, obsequious.

The Beast waved for silence. "Our story—our story continues! Our story continues sometime later, how much later we cannot say, for that was *before* and this is *after*. Now we are in the first district, when the city huddled at the foot of the Mountain, the engine from which it was made, and the energies of its making were always present, and now, being stupid, your kind forgets the nature of its confinement. The energies of making and meaning were like lights and music. Our story continues with one very stupid young man."

The Beast bowed. Then it lurched across the stage, and began prancing, a stupid expression on its face, apparently fixated on the lanterns. The crowd laughed. The Beast stopped by a lantern on a post, craned its head, and said, in a voice that sounded like an unkind mockery of Arjun, "Will you stay with me always and guide me?" It stroked the lantern, sizzling its own skin. "Will you love me and sing to me?"

The crowd's laughter was infectious; even Ruth smiled a little.

She was surprised to notice Silt sitting beside her, staring intently at her, waggling his bushy grey eyebrows significantly.

On the other side of her, Flitter stood, inched forward, and dropped the sack over her head.

She struggled as they dragged her away. One of them cinched a rough cord around her wrists, behind her back. The voice of the Beast and the rustling of the crowd receded. She stumbled and skinned her knee on the flinty earth.

A door opened in front of her. They pushed her to the ground. She sat on a concrete floor, with her back against a wooden wall.

Flitter said, "Clever little thing, ain't ya?"

His voice echoed a little—they were in a small, low-ceilinged room. A foreman's office?

"Shush," Silt said. "Shush, Mr. Flitter. Don't talk to the creature. It is not a pet. You know you get too easily attached to the strays."

"Nearly got away from us, she did."

"No harm done, Mr. Flitter."

"She's a pretty one."

"That's hardly important, is it, Mr. Flitter? She belongs to the Beast now. He'll make something finer out of her raw material."

"Are you sure we should be doing this, Mr. Silt? She's not—she's not like the other strays, is she? She was looking to follow the Beast anyway."

"Not in front of the client, Mr. Flitter. United front! If she offers *herself* up, who's going to get the credit for the catch? Not us! We shall present her in the morning, all wrapped in a bow. See, Mr. Flitter, I've thought long and hard about this. I'm an educated man—not like the rest of you. The master, for all his undoubted spiritual excellencies, doesn't recognize the value of my mind. His surgeries fail—for all his genius, all his struggles, he cannot create true speech, or mind, or soul. Is the fault in *him*? Blasphemy! The fault is in his raw material. Rats and vermin! Ridiculous! The client here—I mean to say, rather, the stray—is more promising material. As you may have noticed she *already* has something like speech, she already stands erect. I mean to say, rather, *it* has those qualities."

Ruth tried to get to her feet—someone's hands pushed her down.

"Go on, then, Mr. Flitter."

"I don't catch your meaning, Mr. Silt?"

Silt sighed. "It's very simple, Mr. Flitter. If the creature is presented as a live catch, our master is apt to become confused. You know how easily he gets distracted from his purpose by pretty young things that find him fascinating. How he loves to be adored! But every seer and visionary has his foibles. It is for us, the earthbound, to manage his affairs and appetites. I do the thinking; you get your hands dirty. Which is to say, Mr. Flitter, you must take the knife and kill her."

"Doesn't seem right, Mr. Silt."

"Flitter! What have I told you? *Never* in front of the client! Come here, come over here . . ."

The two men scuttled away into a corner of the room. Through the muffling cloth of the sack, Ruth half heard them bicker—Silt peevish, condescending; Flitter stubborn. ". . . at least take its tongue, Flitter, or is even that too much to ask?" The argument seemed to go on for hours. Silt's arguments for murder became increasingly sophisticated and elaborate; Flitter grew monosyllabic. "No, Mr. Silt. Won't. Because."

It was dark in the sack, and hard to breathe. It smelled of terrified animals. Dust and fur and loose threads caught in Ruth's throat and clogged her nostrils. To her amazement, despite her fear, she nearly fell asleep. And then she did.

In her dream she stood on the edge of a very tall building—no, on the edge of a cliff. Under her feet were sharp black rocks. The wind sang in her ears. The night was alive with noise and motion. Far below were trees, below the trees was black earth, and the earth swarmed with life. Behind her, her father and her sisters sat at the kitchen table. Warm morning light and the sound of conversation spilled at her back, distracting her. *Shh,* she said. *I'm listening.*

She walked away, leaving the sounds of human speech behind. She went carefully down the cliff-top path, switchbacking down between jagged rocks, down through the treeline that swallowed her like green water. Under the trees, in the murmuring darkness, tiny creatures moved. The branches shivered with their fragile weight. The earth turned. The leaves rustled.

Two bright eyes like twin moons watched her from a high branch. Wide wings like black clouds opened. Hooting like a steam-whistle the fierce owl came swooping down as if from a great height, growing immense as it descended. Ruth turned and ran. Her heart beat hot and wild. Something impossibly bright and fast and sharp struck her . . .

Ruth jerked awake, gasping into the sack, breathing dust.

The room was nearly silent. One of her captors snored; the other muttered in his sleep.

The cord round her wrists was sloppily tied. With a few minutes' struggle she was free.

She tore off the sack and breathed deep.

She was in a small sparsely furnished office. Silt sat in the room's only chair, his feet on the desk, his head lolling, snoring. Flitter curled at his feet.

Where was her rifle? They'd taken her rifle. She couldn't see it anywhere.

There was a small pile of tools in the corner of the room. She picked up a long wooden pick-handle. She hit Silt quite hard on the back of the head, making him grunt and fall silent. She tied Flitter's hands behind his back, and as he woke and cried out in alarm, she put the sack over his head.

Her mouth tasted of dust and sackcloth and animal fear.

She opened the door and went out into the night.

The camp slept.

Next to the prefab office there was a tall contraption of rusting iron and concrete—a kind of scale? A large black owl perched in it, watching her. Its eyes were like moonlight. Through its indistinct shape she could see the stars.

"Poor thing," she said. "What did they do to you?"

Its voice was a tinny buzzing little thing. It sounded as if it came from a cheaply made device in its breast. The stresses fell oddly, senselessly. Monotonous, malfunctioning, it said, *who'll sieve into the veil the veins of these visions?*

"Does it hurt? Do you know what you are?"

It shuffled its sharp talons on its perch. Its wings were misshapen—broken and badly reset. It said, *Can they hive and thrust the heather? The theater? The thrum? The?*

"Can you understand me? Come here—I won't hurt you."

Was his war? Are we? Or we? Our way. Are we?

It opened its wings and twisted its head around, and around, and as if unscrewing itself from the world it vanished.

Ruth shook her head. Too much—too much for one night. Too much for one lifetime. Enough.

She walked dragging the heavy pick-handle behind her like a child trailing a stick in the sand. All around her rose the high walls of the quarry—black, unthinkable, like the walls of the universe. The Beast's sleeping followers were scattered across the floor of the quarry. They reminded Ruth of skeletons, left behind by a fire. Stepping over them, stepping past two quietly slumbering motor-cars, Ruth approached the Beast's soaring tent. Scarlet and gold by day, it was blood-red and bone-white in the night. The flap hung open. As she stepped through a thick intoxicating scent touched her—acids, alcohol, blood, and electricity.

"Ruth Low," the Beast said. "Middle child. I've missed you."

It stood in the far corner of the tent, hunched over a table. It worked without light—as Ruth approached, it struck a match and lit a gaslamp, apparently as a courtesy.

On the table lay blades and a skinned animal. Cat? Ferret? Ruth looked away.

The floor was littered with jewelry, silk cushions, bedsheets, velvet curtains with the rings still in them, marble lawn ornaments, grandfather clocks—all haphazardly jumbled together, as if the Beast's caravan had simply swept through an executive's abandoned mansion and picked up everything not nailed down. Tall cabinets, lacquered and ornate; a heap of musical instruments. The Beast didn't seem to understand luxury. The effect was claustrophobic, obsessive, and unhappy.

The Beast wore its stolen flesh unclothed. It wasn't naked, exactly—it moved with an unself-conscious disdain of its own scarred and mottled skin, like an animal.

Its hands were bloody. So, before the tongue flickered, were its lips.

Its body was that of a stocky middle-aged man, bearded, well fed, wealthy looking, respectable, and dull: Mr. Wantyard, first name unknown and now irrelevant, former Chief of Operations for the former Holcroft Municipal Trust. White scars and yellow bruises mottled its skin. Its eyes were dragon's eyes.

She wasn't sure what to say to it.

"Your people outside are mad," she said. "And they're starving."

It blinked, and smiled. It said, "Who cares?"

"I wondered if you knew. Or if you cared."

"Not really."

"Why do you keep them around? I thought you'd be . . . different, somehow."

"They can go if they like," it said. It smiled again. "They love me. For a hundred years I was worshipped, for a hundred years crowds adored me, and for a thousand years I was alone in darkness. It's nice to be loved again. It's terrible not to be loved the way one deserves—wouldn't you agree, Ruth Low?"

"So you're cruel, then."

"Ruth, you saw me eat my way into a man's skin," the Beast pointed out. "You do have some real questions, don't you? I'm full of wisdom. Try me. I even know who lives on the Mountain."

"No more lies—please, no more lies. Yes, I have questions, of course, I do. The Mountain? I don't know. Who made you? What's happened to the city? How do we stop it?"

The Beast wiped its hands on a bloody towel, and offered an expression that might have been meant to be a smile. Insubstantial shapes slunk around its ankles. The ghosts of vermin and strays. What was the Beast making?

"What are you making?"

It smiled again—yes, it was a smile. "Ruth Low! So many questions! Always lost. You have been treated cruelly, though not nearly so cruelly as I. You are too full of questions, and I am too full of answers. Sisters, under the skin. Would you change places with me?"

Ruth was too tired to stand, too exhausted to argue. She sat in the scarlet cushions. Soft sheets caressed her. She might have been dreaming—the moments drifted past her with a lazy inevitability.

The Beast sat across from her, on a cloud of golden cushions. The shapeless strays drifted anxiously between them. Casually, the Beast said, "Is Flitter dead?"

"No. I tied him up. Silt may be—I hit him very hard."

"Silt. Ha! Silt was never much use to me. I can't say I care if he lives or dies. Ruth Low—do you care? Really?"

"Not much."

"How very frank of you! No lies, Ruth Low. You are old enough now to understand."

Easy questions first, the Beast said. *What am I making here? A new world of my own. Others to share my burden. No success so far. But—early days, early days.*

You freed me from the Museum. That was kind of you. Your sister freed me from the burden of my extraordinary flesh. That was cunning of her.

I was free. I had never been free before.

I concluded my business with your sister and I vanished into the crowd. I went south, away from the Mountain. I savored humanity—it is an imperfect condition, but far superior to the alternatives. I wore a rich man's flesh, and I enjoyed a rich man's luxuries. I was ordinary. I was learning to become fat and stupid. I was happy.

Then the airships came. I knew at once who sent them—he sent them. My maker. King of this City, by right of fraud and theft. Ivy had failed to kill him; she had only angered him. She had frightened him—that man is the most contemptible coward!

The world was ruined. I stood in the rubble and wept bloody tears. I shall never be happy—I understood that. He will not allow it. I am still his creature.

There were others in the ruins. Survivors. Those too stubborn or mad or wicked to go north and seek shelter in Fosdyke, or Fleet Wark, and rebuild. Those, like me, too proud to beg.

They followed me. I am still a remarkable creature, aren't I? Even in this new flesh? I cannot be ordinary. I cannot have an ordinary life.

I told them things, and made them follow me. I did not want to be alone.

But they can't understand—none of them can. What it's like to be a made thing, a provisional thing, unknit by strange surgeries from the fabric of the city—to exist in an oblique and shifting relation to time.

They are only human. Poor Silt! Poor Flitter!

I watched him work, Ruth Low—my maker. I lived on his shoulder once, before I grew too long and heavy and blood-fat. I was with him when he dealt with those doctors. I thought I could make my own creatures. I thought I would act in the image of my own creator. I am a man now, a maker. I would make a world of my own, in the ruins. They would talk to me. They would understand me. Remarkable creatures!

You see the results all around you. I do not have the right knives. My memories are imperfect. I know a great deal, but I am not very intelligent. I am not the equal of my creator. I have surrounded myself with failures—neither alive nor dead. Mindless, feeble. A little more than animal, and much less. That damned owl! It spouts nonsense. It mocks me. I cannot kill it now, hard as I may try.

My mistakes will last forever. These creatures will haunt the city forever, hidden in weeds and back alleys and moonlight, secret testaments to my own flawed nature. Just as I am a testament to his.

I don't understand," Ruth said. "Who made you? How? What are you?"

Once I lived in a little brass cage. I have vague animal memories of the market in which he purchased me—monochrome, motion, scent. I was a kind of lizard.

Not large—no larger than your delectable forearm. I don't know my own breed. Does it matter? I asked my maker; he wouldn't tell me.

I woke to myself on the operating table. Before that my awareness had been dim and thoughtless—a constant throbbing awareness only of the present moment. With needles in my brain and my tiny bones cracked and splinted I woke to glaring electric light, and my first thought was how I hated that light. It was a hospital light, like a compound eye. My awareness, too, became compound—I saw not only the present moment, but the future, the past. Suddenly I had words with which to slice up my sensations. Can you imagine what it is to have words thrust upon you?

He was not done with me. He continued to operate, to open, to unknit, until my awareness unfurled as far beyond yours as yours is beyond that of the lizard I was.

What was my purpose? Once the scars had healed? To sit on his shoulder, to watch and listen, to spy for him, to keep his secrets and carry his messages. To remember his countless aliases and schemes, who owed him money, who owed him their soul. Sometimes to kill for him. All through time we traveled.

Mr. Shay. Clever little man. I was one of his first.

Who is Shay?

I don't know. I don't know half of his secrets. I traveled with him for ten years, a thousand years ago.

He was an ordinary man once. How do I know that? Because he boasted of it. He wouldn't shut up.

He'd say: I did it myself, didn't I? My own bloody self. I broke free of the world, said bye-bye to the city, up into the beyond, out into the abstract, down into the maze. And no bloody bugger ever helped me. I found the way out myself, and I went all alone. I was the fucking first. The things I had to suffer for it! The things I gave up!

And so on. It was my sad duty to listen to his whining. That was why he kept me—for he was not comfortable in the company of mankind—for no human creature could ever be so utterly in his power as I was.

How was I made? The surgical techniques that made me the freak I am—those, Shay learned from the Doctors of the Academy of Marfelon. Have you heard of them? Of course you haven't. They are a well-kept secret. Slope-browed skulls containing an excess of cunning, a numb deficiency of morals and affections. Ontological surgeons. They can uncut you from time, gravity, mortality, existence, your own soul. Engineering speech in a lizard is nothing to them. In this city, everything approaches to the condition of everything else—your little friend, Arjun, understood that dimly, it was a fine trick with the birds! A slice, a stitch, a fold, this becomes that. Easily done.

The Doctors of Marfelon—in their own time, their experiments made them an enemy of all decent folk. Mobs, torches, pitchforks—oh, I know the feeling well! They were in danger of extinction. They were scientists, not fighters. My maker Shay made a deal—they taught him

their methods, and in return, he hid them away in the twisting passages
of the singularity beneath the Iron Rose.

Do you understand what I mean when I say, singularity?
Hah. We'll be here all night.

I don't care about that. I wouldn't understand, would I? If Ivy were here you could talk to her about singularities."

"You seem disappointed in me, Ruth."

"I always thought you were a kind of . . . myth. A dream. Something magical, something that no one could explain. Now you say you're just a kind of thing someone made."

"Everything that exists has a reason why, Ruth."

"I don't mean to be hurtful."

"I disappoint myself, lately."

"So who taught you to tell the future?"

"Oh, Ruth—no lies between us. I cannot tell the future. No one can—the city is always in flux. I remember things, I know secrets, I watch carefully. I plan and I am cunning. Everything is trickery—people are very predictable. I have no gifts of prophecy."

"Oh. Oh, I had so many questions about the future."

"I know. My answers would be lies. Would you like me to lie to you?"

"No, thank you."

"I don't know if the city can be saved. I expect not. The old man will have his way."

Ruth sighed and shifted. When she'd come in, the tent had been warm. Now a cold breeze drifted around her shoulders.

She said, "Whatever's going to happen is going to happen. I just came here to *understand*. I remember you in the Museum. I was only a girl, and I liked you better back then. So—why were you in the Museum?"

"Oh, Ruth Low. That's cruel of you to ask. One day I may ask you a cruel question. He left me behind, Ruth Low."

There are too many of him.

His business, his scheming, his deals and revenges, his flights from creditors and police and inquisitors—it took him all over the city. Back and forth. To and fro. In and out. Up and down. From the first times to the last. Your mind cannot grasp the complexity of it—forward and back, how his own schemes tangled him, how he thwarted himself over and over. A trap laid in the first times springing itself in the last, and on the man who set it! A yellowing photograph in the police files of a prior century. The long memories of the many churches who knew him as the Devil. Nor could he grasp the complexity—I do not mean to insult you, Ruth Low.

He lost himself. He doubled and tripled himself. Weaving back and forth, he stepped too often in his own traces. He existed simultaneously. Shadows. Reflections. Reiterations. His past became confused. Rumors of his presence abounded—which were true? He looked to me to remember for him. He used to say: "I was never here before, was I? Did I do this? I never did this. This wasn't my fault. They've got the wrong man. This isn't fair." *I lied to him. No, I whispered, when the truth was yes; yes, I whispered, in the rare event that he was truly innocent. I confused him further. I schemed against him! I was a spiteful little thing! I started to grow fat on lies and secrets.*

His shadows proliferated. They took different paths through the city, so sometimes they were old, sometimes young, sometimes scarred, sometimes unwounded.

I was with him on occasion when he met one of his shadows.

My master went generally by the name Shay, sometimes Hangley, sometimes Cuttle. He was a man in middle age when he made me, and when he left me behind he was still not old. He was a little man but a strong one— he had a system of exercises, about which he was fanatical. His body was a tool to be mastered. He shaved his white head near-bald. He carried no ordinary weapon—I was sufficient.

We traveled to Cendylon. Cendylon, where the thick vines strangled the emerald city. Summer, when the violet flowers spread like a disease.

We went hunting a God. A God of music, something that took the form of a sudden silence in the city's cacophony, a sudden chanting that might change a man's life. A God that had wandered in from the wastes, in obedience to the strange currents that carry their kind.

My master sought to trap it, so that he might offer it to the folk of the Bright Towers, in trade for the seeds that . . . never mind. He had his plans for it.

We followed rumors. The God had settled in a bend of the green river, in a little bower of vines, where now the flowers rang like bells. The botanists of Cendylon were there to observe the phenomenon. Access was re-

stricted. We had to blackmail the Police Chief of Cendylon, and to bribe the Chair of Botanical Science. So every one of my master's schemes bred further scheming! We had to murder a man and kidnap a child. In the moss-walled tunnels beneath the river my master stood chain-smoking while I rooted in the Police Chief's trash for incriminating material. "Hurry up," *my master said.* "What's taking so long? Losing your nose for secrets? You're getting fat and lazy. You belong in the trash." *He was always cruel to me, Ruth. But perhaps I was too slow, because we were interrupted.*

A snarl. A hiss.

I poked my green head from the filth to see, at the far end of the tunnel, a short fat man, white hair in a wild greasy tangle, the long robes of Cendylon hanging in shimmering folds from his round belly. My master's face—but older, looser, heavy-jowled.

My own master, snarling in hate. Lips pulled back from his teeth. He hated with animal simplicity. I loved him then, Ruth.

That . . . shadow of my master, sneering. What was beneath his robes? A gun, a knife? He had not come unarmed. How had our paths crossed? No doubt he hunted the same quarry as my master. To him, my master was the shadow—the contempt was clear on his face. My loyalties, such as they were, were divided. The tunnel's air crackled with something that can't be named. Were any of us real?

The imposter came with weapons. My master preferred not to risk himself, or unleash my own . . . capabilities. We left the tunnel. "Not again," *he whined.* "It's not fair. I shouldn't have to live like this." *We returned to our hotel in Cendylon, where that fat shadow tried to murder my master by arson. We in turn tried to kill him with poison, by bribing his bodyguards, with a curse . . .*

And so on. For years. In the end my master prevailed. But in our chases and scheming back and forth across the city, no doubt we birthed another half-dozen shadows.

Another time we met a man called Lemuel at an auction, quite by accident . . . Never mind. I could go on. I won't.

He was the first. He has been doing this for so long, now. The city is large, but not large enough.

The Beast stood and walked to the flap of the tent. Outside the night was dark and silent. The Beast breathed cold air.

"This is painful for me, Ruth. A thousand years ago I was

abandoned. Left alone to find my own purpose. To rot in a cage. Circus freak, sideshow act, medical specimen, dusty antiquity. Neither alive nor dead, real nor unreal. To remember the days with Shay is—Ruth, how bittersweet is it for you to recall your childhood? To hang on Shay's shoulder and share his secrets—that was my youth! Those were my golden days! We had great adventures together. We did terrible things."

Suddenly the Beast slipped through the flap and outside. It stalked across the quarry, and up and around the broad path out of the quarry's depths.

It talked as it went. Ruth, clutching a scarlet sheet around her shoulders to ward off the cold, followed.

. . . our endless struggles. Our schemes and murders. What did we fight over? What else could it be? The Mountain.

What is the Mountain?

I have never seen it. I do not precisely know. Secrets upon secrets.

It is not a Mountain. That is a veil it wears.

It exists in every part of the city, in every Age. An anchor that holds the sea together. Sometimes it is close, more often it is far, far away. Here it is very close. Here, we are always on its threshold. Kings have given up their kingdoms just to come this close.

It has an unusual relationship to time. Shay rules it now, having stolen it, and it has always been the case that Shay rules it.

It is a kind of machine. But perhaps I only say that because I am a kind of machine, and that is how things seem to me.

Those who built the city made it. I don't mean the vague energies your kind calls Gods. Nor the pioneers and first fathers and stout burghers who laid down the foundation-stones and built bridges over the river and made pompous statues of themselves. I mean those who, from the outside of things, laid down the conditions for the city's impossible flourishing.

I have no names for them. Call them the Builders; everything is defined by its function. I like to think they made the city as a kind of prison, but perhaps I only say that because I have spent so long in cages.

The energies of the Mountain spin out time and distance. The Mountain is the engine of creation. The Gods are its fuel, its energies, its agents. Its hands and its knives and its fire, to cut and burn and shape the city. On the Gears of the Mountain the city spins. He who rules the Mountain rules everything below it.

We were not meant to approach it. The Builders of the city created defenses around it. They locked us out. Approach the Mountain's slopes: the streets become a maze. Shadows fall. Memory and awareness falter. The way is trapped. I have never dared come any closer than this—my own existence is tenuous enough already.

The first makers set the machine into motion, spinning out time and possibilities. How many thousands of years ago? What impossible energies poured through the Mountain? Vast and out of control, the piling up beyond reason of time and complexity, the impossible weight, always growing, the awareness of which burdens everything we do. No wonder in these last days the Mountain has gone dark.

The Builders set it into motion, then they left us alone. Perhaps we disgusted them. Perhaps they will return for us when our sentence is up.

For millennia the Mountain existed alone, working according to its own mysterious design. Then Shay stole it.

Not my master—oh, not my master! My master was only a second-rate shadow. I believe the Shay who fought through to the Mountain was the same who first fought his way free of the routines of ordinary life, and learned to walk in the city behind the city. Not that it matters which it was, in the end.

Shay stole the Mountain. He grew old there. What does he do with it? Nothing. With the Mountain he could do anything. The airships are the least of the tricks he can work with it. Yes, of course the airships are his— a cheap nasty trick—pay attention. He could make the city a paradise— a thousand different paradises. With the Mountain, the Gods are at his beck and call—he could light every street with them. He could fill every moment with meaning and beauty. He could make the dead walk, he could make brutes speak, he could make every hovel a palace, and float them on a cloud. Instead he hid, and hoarded his treasures, and worked on his defenses.

He has always *been an old man, hoarding his treasures, in the Mountain.*

He made the city at the slopes of the Mountain into this . . . wasteland. The Know-Nothings. The pointless factories. The ugliness of it. That was his work. He wanted no visitors, no tourists. With the Mountain's engines he stole and hoarded the city's Gods, like a lesser miser would hoard gold.

He hides in the Mountain. And his countless shadows scheme to steal it from him. How they envy him! How he hates himself! He is not a happy man.

His shadows do not dare approach the Mountain themselves. He fears himself more than he hates himself. They work through surrogates, agents, dupes, patsies.

What kind of madman would go up on the Mountain? Ruth, the city is full of madmen. Your friend Arjun—one of Shay's shadows set him loose from the confines of the city, and no doubt meant to set him on the path to the Mountain. What was Arjun looking for? Has he told you? Are you in on that secret? For all I know it may be on the Mountain, whatever it is. Or it may not. But I can tell you that if, by some unlikely chance, Arjun were to fight his way onto the Mountain, and kill the old man who rules it, then Shay's shadows would be close behind.

That fat idiot Brace-Bel, who was at the Museum—one of my master's shadows recruited him, once. I could smell it. Brace-Bel may try to refuse the call, but he will always dream of the Mountain, now. One day he will return there. Will he *be the one to kill the old man? Not likely. But perhaps.*

I remember how my own particular master found a handsome psychopath named St. Loup, and lifted him out of his daily existence, and set him on his way. I whispered in his ear: I told him the power he craves is on the Mountain. He will kill anything that gets in his way.

St. Loup has never yet found his way to the Mountain. Will he ever? If he does, how will we know? If he wins through, will everything change at once? I don't know.

When my master finally tired of me—oh, this is hard to say. I was too fat to sit on his shoulder. Swollen on lies and secrets and crimes. His plans no longer included me. He had another use for me. He traded me away, Ruth, to the Archbishop Pnoff, in return for . . . Never mind. Firm hands clutched me, thrust me into a sack, from which I was decanted without dignity into a cage.

"One last job," *he whispered to me.* "You ugly thing. Endure. Be a sign. I made you fascinating. They will keep coming to you. Show them the way."

I endured for a thousand years. I told fortunes, I awed crowds. I gathered dust. I whispered into the ears of those who would hear the way to the Mountain.

Not out of loyalty. Out of spite, Ruth.

They go up in their hundreds, their thousands, onto the Mountain—the madmen of the city. Arjun, Brace-Bel, St. Loup, a thousand others. This is a vast city, and it has endured for millennia, and my master and his shadows have always fought over it. The madmen—my master and his shadows dangle dreams before them, myths, Gods, visions, answers, empty promises. They unveil the Gears of the city for them. They teach them just enough tricks to get by. So many mad people in this city! Sooner or later they find their way to the Mountain. They go up chanting, or scourging themselves, like pilgrims. They go with swords, or guns, and scarlet banners, roaring barbaric defiance. They steal in like thieves, like cockroaches. They fly their splendid machines, trailing rich plumes of smoke. They don't know that Shay's shadows are watching close behind, waiting to see if they break the Mountain's defenses. Waiting to follow them home.

But none of them have ever succeeded.

Some of them, the old man catches. In his traps, in his nets, in his mirrors, in his paradoxes. His mirrors are prisons—an old technique. What do they make of him, when they see him? They thought the Mountain was ruled by demon princes, bright angels, glittering mechanical Minds. Those are the lies I told them. What do they think when they see that nasty and withered old man? "Not again," *he says.* "Why won't you leave me alone? It isn't fair."

He applies his surgeries to them. A cut, a slice, a fold—unstitched from time—he makes them into his Hollow Servants. Have you ever wondered why they stink so of failure and shame?

Those who escape—they fall, their minds shredded by the Mountain, by the old man's defenses. They fall at the foot of the Mountain. They stumble through your world like ghosts. They never escape for long. Soon enough the Hollows catch them, or the police.

You have loved a few of those fragile ghosts. They were doomed from the start. You have loved me, and I have always been a monster. No ordinary life is possible in the shadow of the Mountain, in the killing fields of Shay's war on himself.

I thought your sister might finally be the one to kill the old man. At least that would be a change! I dreamed she might destroy the Mountain. What would happen to the city then? It could hardly be worse. Without that darkness on the horizon we might lead real lives.

✦   ✦   ✦

As it talked, the Beast walked up and around the slopes of the quarry's walls. It set a punishing pace, and Ruth struggled to keep up. With every turn they approached the stars, and the Beast unburdened itself of another secret. The sky paled with the dawn. The quarry filled with cold mists, and the Beast pressed on into the grey, its voice hollow and distant. At last they reached the top of the path, where the signs warned of BLASTING IN PROGRESS and NO TRESPASSING and the wagons were parked. The Beast was gone, and Ruth was alone. The Mountain darkened the horizon.

TWENTY-ONE

The Missing, After the War–The Hero of Fosdyke–Secret Files–More Flags– The Choir

Arjun

Carnyx Street lived!

A couple of houses were in ruins, in whole or in part—cracked gaps in its defiant grin. Otherwise it was intact. Windows still caught the morning sun. Laundry hung like pennants. The street breathed—front doors were open and people went from house to house. The wild scrub behind the houses had been repurposed into fields; green was starting to show through the black earth. Arjun and Inspector Maury came across the fields, one smiling, the other scowling.

Who watched them? Two men worked in the fields, bare-chested in the warmth of the morning—a third stood guard. The guard carried a rifle and a bell round his neck. For a moment, seeing the newcomers approach over the fields, he looked frightened, raised his gun—then he lowered it again. Whatever he'd been frightened of, Arjun and Maury weren't it. He watched them go by carefully, but without fear—almost with a kind of cautious welcome. Of course, Arjun thought, Carnyx Street *would* be welcoming to refugees. He smiled and showed his hands were empty.

He'd made Maury throw away his long black coat—it identified him as a Know-Nothing, a Night Watchman, a dangerous man. Without it Maury looked, and apparently felt, naked. Stripped of his last vestiges of authority, he hunched like a snail. The sun made him squint.

The Low sisters' house still stood.

Arjun bounded the last few yards to the door, banged on it, peered in through the smoky windows of the shop, calling, "Ruth, Ruth, are you in there?"

A stranger answered the door, and the smile vanished from his face.

They both said, "Who are you?"

The man at the door was tall, pale, grey-haired. Behind him, the shelves and tables of Ruth's shop had been cleared away—the books and maps and records and paintings were gone—four young women and one man sat in a circle stitching something together out of canvas—sails? Coats? Tents? The floor was littered with off-cuts and needles. Lamps burned. They'd thrown out all Ruth's wonderful and mysterious treasures and put a workshop in their place! She was gone. Dead? Gone to the Mountain, with Ivy? He'd known she might not be there when he returned, but he hadn't *believed* it. His mouth hung open. He forgot why he'd come back. His blood ran cold.

His mouth was making strange unhappy noises. Tears stung his cheeks. When the tall man in the doorway, a little frightened, asked him who he was again, Arjun said aggressive and unpleasant things that he didn't mean, and that didn't make any sense. When the man asked him to leave, Arjun refused to go. "What have you done with her? What have you people done with her?"

The tall man laid a hand on Arjun's shoulder; sobbing, Arjun shoved him away. Almost instantly Maury came charging up, head-butted the tall man to the floor, and proceeded to start kicking. Why? No obvious reason. The Inspector was mad. Those were his skills, those were his habits. Arjun tried to pull him away and he snarled.

"Stop right there!"

The guard from the fields stood at the other side of the street, pointing a gun.

They were apparently under arrest.

The guards seemed unsure what to do with them. What law applied here? "This is all a misunderstanding," Arjun said. After that he stayed silent. The guards searched them both, took Maury's gun, not without a struggle. An official was summoned—a mechanic with oily hands, who spoke for the Committee for the Emergency. He shrugged—this wasn't his responsibility. There were further communications, there was further confusion. A red-faced woman with flour on her skirts ordered Arjun and Maury separated.

They locked him in an underground storage room beneath a machine workshop. The little space echoed and droned with the noise of industry. He sat cross-legged. Hours passed. The machines above went silent, and the workers went home.

Arjun wondered briefly what the workers were paid in—food? Shelter? Did Fosdyke's Committee for the Emergency print money now? Were they paid at all—did they work for fear of the whip, or out of public-spiritedness? An economy was a hard thing to re-build. He'd seen the aftermath of a hundred catastrophes in the city, he'd seen a hundred ways of rebuilding. Some worked, some failed. Perhaps he should offer his services as a consultant! He laughed. The tears dried on his cheeks; he could still taste them in his throat.

The shock of it—Ruth Low gone! —the hurt of it had taken him by surprise. Some losses hurt more deeply than others. The ebb and flow of his emotions was often a mystery to him. Sitting in the dark, breathing deeply, he sought to master himself again.

Hours passed. It was Arjun's habit when he became hungry to think of music; to develop and elaborate melodies in his head. It stilled his hunger, and it calmed his turbulent emotions. He sat in silence; in his head the room resounded. What did he care what happened to him now? He could become forgotten, down in that little dungeon—he could pass into memory, into unreality. Like the Beast! He could come unstitched from time and reality. Become a vague music, a fresh breeze in the dungeon's stale air. Strangers would move into the houses above. Their children and their children's children would forget all about the War, and the Know-Nothings, and the Night Watch and the Lamplighters and the Low sisters. He'd lie there, turned to crystal and music, something wondrous to be dug up and marveled at in future centuries. He didn't belong anymore. Time to wake in a better time.

✳   ✳   ✳

The door opened with a clang and a rattle of bolts, and Arjun jolted awake, scrambled blinking to his feet, wiping drool from his chin. Where was he?

Marta Low came into the room. Two unfamiliar women at either side of her each brought in a chair.

Marta sat. Arjun looked at her in astonishment.

"You're alive," he said.

"So are you. Why don't you sit down?"

"What happened to Ruth?"

"Ruth? What do you mean? Have you seen her?"

"What? Her shop is gone. Her house is full of strangers. Is she dead? Did she go with Ivy?"

"You haven't seen her?" Marta rolled her eyes in relief. "She's not dead—as far as I bloody well know. She was alive last week, and doing well, as well as she ever does. Nine days ago she just upped and walked out, off the job. Out into the Ruined Zone."

"Ah." Arjun flushed. He ran a hand through his hair, which was long and filthy. "Ah." He sat down. "I misunderstood. Ah. My apologies to the man in that house. Is he badly hurt?"

"He'll mend."

"I'm sorry." He suddenly laughed. "She's alive?"

"She lived through the bombs. Is she alive today? Who knows? This is a bad time to be walking around alone."

"If she lived through the bombs," Arjun said, "she's alive now. I have a great deal of faith in her judgment. Yours is a remarkable family.

"Ivy," he said.

"I don't want to talk about Ivy."

"Ivy . . ."

"I don't want to talk about Ivy." Her voice dropped into deep registers that had the force of law.

They sat in silence for a while.

"So," she said, "your friend Maury—nasty bit of work. I don't know why you keep bringing those sort of people round here. It doesn't make me warm to you."

"Hah. No. I don't suppose it does."

"Do you want a drink?"

"Very much, please."

"We have coffee. We have more coffee than we know what to do with. Coffee all right?"

Coffee was brought in. He asked, "Where did she go?"

Marta didn't answer for a long time. At last she said, "She left a note. She went out—she went out looking for the Beast. She left her job behind and went out after a rumor."

"It's alive?"

"I don't know. She thinks so."

"Can I see the note?"

"No."

"Where did she go?"

"Not just yet. Not just yet, Arjun."

Marta folded her arms and sat back in her chair. She looked at Arjun sternly, and without a great deal of affection. Embarrassed, he scratched at his filthy tramp's beard. He wondered if she might bring him a razor, and soap. Did they have razors here, or soap? It probably depended on what the old regime had left behind in their warehouses, and where they'd left it. Quite possibly Fosdyke had an overabundance of razors, and Fleet Wark had an overabundance of soap, and with the Ruined Zones dividing them there was no commerce yet. Someone would have to open the way—some explorer, some pioneer.

It would be someone with the same shrewd and tough expression as Marta Low.

"Are you in charge here, Marta?"

"As much as anyone," she said. "It's complicated. Day-to-day. Do you really want to hear how things work here?"

"Not really." He sipped his coffee. "You're doing very well. I saw your fields. It may work—you may survive. It's very impressive."

She raised an eyebrow. "Thank you."

"The Gods have returned. You haven't gone mad. That's good."

"Thank you."

"Inspector Maury's mad, I'm afraid."

She nodded. "We noticed."

"Marta, have you heard of a God of music that . . ."

"No."

"Ah."

Her voice softened a little. "We have lights, birds, some big drunken bastard with a beard, and this horrible stretched-out long-fingered thing they call *the Tailor*. The mad women who worship it snap their scissors all day, they sound like crickets. No music. Sorry."

She leaned forward and stared at him. "You don't know what happened any more than we do, do you?"

"On the Mountain?"

"Look, I don't *like* talking about this. Just give me a straight answer, will you?"

"I don't know, Marta. Maybe Ivy found her way there, maybe she didn't. I don't know what she found."

"Is all this her fault? The war, is it because of something she did?"

"Maybe. Who knows? No one's ever made it past the Mountain's defenses before. It should have been me. Or maybe the same thing would have happened whoever went."

Arjun leaned forward, too. "I've thought about this a lot, Marta, while walking in the Ruined Zones. Over all the Ages of the city, a thousand explorers have gone up the Mountain. A thousand thousand pilgrims, thieves, and madmen. The Mountain exists everywhere, everywhen. It is the central puzzle of the city. It anchors the Metacontext. Who made it? I don't know. Who rules it? No one can be sure. Shay, the Beast said—but how can that be true? This city is an unnatural place, and the Mountain is at its heart. *More* than a thousand thousand. You've never traveled, Marta—you can't understand the age of the city, its size, the numbers involved, the shadows and reflections."

"You sound like Ivy. You sound like my father. I don't mean that as a compliment."

"This has never happened before. The Mountain has never been provoked like this before. It holds itself aloof. It doesn't make war on the city—that would be absurd, like the moon invading us, or the sun taking someone to court. I think it's a sign of weakness—it feels like a sign of fear. Did Ivy *hurt* it? Did she hurt Shay? That doesn't matter—I know you don't want to talk about the Mountain. What I mean is that something's different this time. She did something different from a thousand thousand thousand climbers before her, who failed, who fell, who were forgotten. What happened? I don't know. I don't think it would have happened if I'd gone in her place. I don't think I'm clever enough to hurt the Mountain, or make it afraid. I don't think I'm cunning enough to hurt Shay in his place of power. I think . . . Marta, has Ivy come back down?"

"Not that I know of."

"I didn't think so. Marta, will you let me go free? I'll go after Ruth. I'll go after the Beast. I'll begin again. I'm not suited for re-building, or farming, or working, the way you are. The only way I can put this right is on the Mountain."

"No." Marta sighed. She leaned back and rubbed her neck. "Ruth made her choice. And we need you here. I'm not bloody happy about it, mind you."

Fosdyke was in peril. The Committee for the Emergency was out of its depth.

In the bright mornings, in the long summer afternoons, Fosdyke hummed along nicely, rebuilding, reknitting the delicate webs of commerce and government, dismantling the ruined build-ings and making fields in their place. In a strange way life was *better* now. It was hard work but people were working for themselves, for their futures, for their children's futures. The work had a purpose. Men and women who'd slaved mindlessly and resentfully in the fac-tories were learning the habits of free people. Refugees came, and were housed. Fosdyke was a great glorious thumb in the eye to the Mountain. It was a yell of defiance to the bombers. A slap in Shay's face.

By day.

At night the Hollows came.

The invasion was in full swing. As the sun set they gathered at the borders, in the Ruined Zones, in the long shadows of broken masonry and charred and leafless trees. Dark suits, pale faces, flut-tering nervous hands—the awkward sly sidle of beggars, homeless schizophrenics, child-snatchers. Their numbers seemed limitless. They all looked the same—like mass-produced parts. Pale faces scarred and loose, badly made. Sexless, unhappy—if there were women the women looked like the men. Identical, like something mindlessly mathematical—they reproduced themselves like col-umns of numbers in the ledgers of a failing business. When straggling refugees trailed in from the Ruined Zones, the Hollow Men attached themselves to human families like shadows. They bred suspicion. They disappeared people who went walking alone. They occupied abandoned houses and made them haunted. Bit by bit they subtracted life and energy. Clean-up crew; an unpleasant chore—you could tell they resented it. They were *made* of resentment. When everyone in Fosdyke was finally dead or gone, the Hollows would take the place of human life. The city below would be nothing but the shadows of the Mountain. "This *Shay* person," Marta said. "Soon he'll never have to worry about us disturbing his peace again."

"Creatures like that have chased me," Arjun said, "since I first came down from the Mountain."

"I know."

"Brace-Bel had a kind of weapon, a device that unmade them. He stole it from Shay himself. I just used to run away from them."

Marta nodded. "Bells, music, fire, loud noises drive them back. They're shy. They're pathetic. But you can't hurt them. They just sneak around behind you, and kill . . . "

"Do you have any hope of stopping them?"

Marta reached forward and put a firm hand on Arjun's shoulder. "That's up to you, isn't it?" Grimacing, she brushed a strand of his long and filthy hair out of his face. "You're the only magician I see here. What are you going to do about all this?"

Arjun shaved and washed. Fosdyke had both razors and soap, not to mention running water. He changed his clothes. Where did the water come from? Perhaps it was best not to ask. Razors, soap, and water; what more did one need to fall in love with a civilization?

Ruth would survive, he decided. She was probably as safe in the Ruined Zones as she would be in Fosdyke. She was almost certainly safer out of his presence than in it. He had interfered in her life quite enough; let her be. In the meantime he could make amends by ensuring that if and when she returned she would have a home to return to. He would play the hero—not his favorite role, but one he'd worn before. Yes. He examined himself in the mirror, and was pleased with his decision. Everything made more sense clean shaven.

Over a long lunch he met with the leading lights of the Committee for the Emergency, and was fully briefed on the situation—the distribution of the attacks, the vectors of the Hollows' approach. It was more than he could hold in his head. The Mountain and its servants throve in conditions of a complexity that was beyond ordinary understanding. The maps weren't helpful—there was no particular front, no relevant borders. It was no ordinary invasion. More like a plague. More like an unpleasant rumor. He nodded and tried to look confident.

In the afternoon he went walking through the sunny streets. A bodyguard followed at a discreet distance. He listened. He tried to imagine the Hollows drifting murderously through those streets at night. It was almost unbearably painful to contemplate. He had no idea how to stop it.

Children came to stare at him. The rumor was out that he was a wise man. Probably Marta had leaked the news, to boost morale. Very wise, Arjun thought—despair would only strengthen the Hollow Men. They were at home in despair and humiliation.

A small redheaded boy grabbed at his sleeve and said, "Mister, is it true? Mister, where are you from?"

"Everywhere and nowhere," he said, in his deepest voice. "I have been to and fro in the city, and up and down in it." His best oracular voice—he'd seen enough prophets and visionaries to mimic the manner. The boy looked back at him with awe on his face, and a bright smile.

His walk ended at the edge of Holcroft Square, looking at what used to be the local Chapterhouse of the Know-Nothings.

It slumped. The upper floors had been ruined, as if a bomb falling or bouncing slantwise had sliced through the roof on its way down to the Square. Now the building's shapeless and senseless peaks and valleys echoed the Mountain that loomed behind it.

As far as the Committee could tell—and they were painfully aware that the problem was beyond their comprehension—the Chapterhouse had become the Hollow Men's headquarters, the focal point at which they massed. The beachhead for the enemy's invasion was right in Fosdyke's heart. Distances and borders meant nothing to the Mountain's servants. Four nights ago the Chapterhouse had merely, like most of the other abandoned buildings in Fosdyke, showed occasional signs of haunting—pale faces at the windows, fluttering shadows on the rooftop, cold fingers grasping through the rails of the fence. The shadows gathered, and by the night before last the Chapterhouse thronged with them. Yesterday morning the Committee evacuated the Bird worshippers from Holcroft Square. Last night the shadows had poured from the ruin of the Chapterhouse like black flame.

They liked it in the Chapterhouse. It was mean and dark and unhappy there.

Arjun stood at the edge of the Square and watched the afternoon bleed away. Shifts ended at the workshops and the fields and the crowds passed him by. His bodyguards grew nervous. Shadows lengthened. Afternoon turned into evening. In the cracked windows of the Chapterhouse Arjun saw a nervous shuffling motion. Inside, the servants began to go about their business. What were they? He racked his memory. It seemed he was close to recalling them—if he closed his eyes he could almost picture them, picture how they'd moved about Shay's house, up on the Mountain.

Pale fussy fingers flicking the ancient dust from the machines of the Mountain . . .

A thousand thousand men standing in the shadows beneath a single sputtering bulb, waiting to be called to serve . . .

A dusty steel tray, a row of strange sharp instruments—was that the laboratory where Shay made his servants?

Arjun's bodyguard shook his shoulder, and he opened his eyes.

The sun had set behind the rooftops.

Slowly, two by two, the Hollow Men emerged from the Chapterhouse. They came through the doors, through the shattered windows, through the cracks in the walls. They moved slowly, without enthusiasm, like overworked doctors leaving for their rounds. Two, and two, and two more; twenty, a hundred. There seemed to be no reason why they shouldn't keep coming forever.

Arjun had no idea what to do. "Run," he said, and ran.

Another night, another hundred little battles. The Hollows rapped on windows, climbed up drainpipes, appeared in the shadows of bedrooms, stepped forward out of the dry ticking of clocks.

Husbands woke to see pale men leaning by the bedside, hands fluttering about their wives' throats. Mothers came running into their children's rooms shrieking to drive away the pale men who lurked by the window. Sometimes that was enough to drive the Hollows away—not always.

Most people gathered in the cellars, underground, where they burned candles, sang songs, sought safety in numbers. The Hollow Men massed at the doors, scratching to be let in like cats, like refugees. The doors creaked but generally held—the Hollow Men weighed very little.

In a few more days the doors would start to break.

Arjun walked the streets. At some point he lost his bodyguard. He followed and spied on the Hollows as they stalked the citizens; and probably the Hollows stalked him, too, a vicious and paranoid circle that reminded him of too much of his life, altogether too much of it. What could he possibly do to stop them? He had no idea.

At four in the morning he came across a group of half a dozen of them, standing in one of the new fields, delving in the earth with their pale hands, methodically digging up roots and bulbs, and stealing them away in their grey sacks. Arjun had never seen anything so mean and vile and loathsome. Furious, he ran at them shouting; but when they dropped their sacks and turned their awful eyes on him, he fled. The chase lasted until morning, when the Hollow Men vanished, and Arjun, exhausted, fell asleep sitting against a low fence.

He dreamed of music. When he woke he thought for a moment that the Hollows had been a nightmare.

Marta stood over him with her arms folded. She said, "Well?"

Arjun persuaded the Committee to release Inspector Maury. Not without argument—they regarded the man as a rabid beast.

He asked them, "Do you have any soldiers left among you? Any generals?" They had to admit that they didn't. "Maury is a wicked man. But this is war, and the enemy is very wicked, too. I need his counsel."

"All right," Marta said. "He's your responsibility."

Maury had been kept imprisoned in a toolshed. (The toolshed had been emptied, but not carefully enough; Maury had found a chisel in the dirt, a weapon that he later produced for Arjun with a triumphant and bloodthirsty smile.)

Maury sat on the floor of the shed. His nose was bloody, from the struggle to arrest him, but otherwise he hadn't been hurt. He was sallow and starved-looking—he'd refused all food.

"He kept expecting us to torture him," Marta said. "Or poison him. I sort of think he was looking forward to it."

Arjun, Marta, and two guards stood by the toolshed door. Marta regarded Inspector Maury like vermin caught in a trap. Arjun bent down to help the man stand.

"We're at war," Arjun said.

Maury snorted.

"Perhaps you were right," Arjun said. "Perhaps it was madness to try to rebuild, and that resistance has brought down the Mountain's wrath. It's too late to stop it now. It's happened. If you still want revenge on the Mountain, this is where you have to begin the fight."

Inspector Maury suggested fire and dynamite. He jabbed his finger at the slumping Chapterhouse building, cobweb-grey in the afternoon light. "They've stolen it," he said. "So they want it. So we should take it away from them."

The Committee members nodded. Marta nodded. "Makes as much sense as anything else. Can we do it before sundown?"

The files. Arjun panicked—Maury had said that the Chapterhouse might contain files on Shay. Who knew what secrets the Know-Nothings might have hidden away?

So while the Committee's guards placed charges against the base of the building, not daring to go inside, Arjun pushed aside the half-unhinged back door and went into the silent, unlit corridors. Plaster had fallen from the cracked ceiling and the floor had a lunar whiteness. The tables and chairs and bloody leather straps in the interrogation rooms cast shadows like ghosts. Arjun jumped at every muffled sound. It was cold and damp in the ruined building but he sweated in fear. Evening breathed down his neck—the Hollow Men might emerge from any patch of darkness, any crack in the dirty glass, any unpleasant complexity.

The stairs creaked under his feet, and shifted, warped by the shock of the bombs. He went up, as Maury had suggested, and along the landing, and up again, into the storage rooms of the fourth floor. He found dusty rooms full of carefully boxed clothes, watches, jewelry, personal effects, taken no doubt from criminals, seditionists, ghosts, the disappeared, over all the long years of the Know-Nothings' brutish operations. A mad variety of fashions. Blood-stained, torn. He opened a window and threw the clothes down into the yard—it would be terrible, in these days, to waste serviceable clothes. They fell like men jumping from a burning building. He found a room full of a row of desks, their wood warped by months of rain—the roof had been torn open, and the bloody rays of the sunset spilled through the hole.

No files.

He went down into the yard. "Inspector Maury, there are no files on the fourth floor."

"I don't fucking know, do I? I was only here for a week, and I was a bit distracted, wasn't I? Try downstairs. Try the basements."

Arjun had been afraid of that. He swore at Maury and went down into the darkness of the basements. Torture rooms, execution rooms. Barred doors. The walls plastered with those repetitive and somehow threatening old posters—BE VIGILANT and WE'RE ALL IN THIS TOGETHER and all the rest. A stink of fear—not just his own. The Know-Nothings had been gone for months, and the stink persisted.

A locked door. He was ready for that—he smashed it open with an axe. The sounds of violence echoed down the haunted corridors and made him feel complicit.

He stepped over splintered wood and broken metal. The long dark room inside was full of filing cabinets, in rows and columns like dwarfish soldiers. Arjun's lamp flickered. The cabinets in their ranks seemed to menace him—they cast long shadows.

He opened them at random. Names, dates, places. Code words. Classified operations. Stamps and wax seals in the shape of hammers, eagles, the Mountain. A childish fetishization of secrecy and mystery and fear. Rows and rows of cabinets—what was he supposed to do with all that paper? Time was ticking by. The files rustled as he flipped through them, throwing the shadows of complex things unfurling. Names—the names of ghosts, of murdered men.

The cabinets in their inert ranks reminded him of how the Hollows, in the vaults of Shay's Mountain, stood stiff and silent waiting to be called on . . .

Arjun turned and there was a dark shape in the doorway, like a man, but misshapen, incomplete, oddly angled. He lifted the axe and readied himself for the thing to rush him . . .

It said, "What the bloody hell are you playing at?"

"Maury?"

"You've been down here for half an hour—the light's going. Do you want to be here when we blow the charges? Hurry up, you idiot."

They carried out the files in bundles under their arms, panting and afraid. No time to read them or search them. They made half a dozen trips. Loose leaves fell out and fluttered away and were lost—who knew what secrets they contained? The sun set behind the rooftops.

"That's it," Marta said. "Time's up."

The explosion lit the Square red and gold, then filled it with black dust. The Chapterhouse crumbled away and vanished, as if dissolving into noise and light and steam. A cheer went up.

That night the Hollow Men came anyway. They rose up out of the shadows of charred timbers, out of the dismal stink of dust and burning. If anything, it seemed there were more of them.

In the morning it was time to tally the missing again.

The birds," Arjun said. "The Thunderers—they had a power in them. It might not rival the Mountain but it might give it pause—where do the Thunderers roost?"

But when he approached the strange birds' roosts, they saw him coming, and they took to the skies. They didn't want to hear it. Sullen yellow eyes said: *piss off*. They still felt confused and violated by the last time—you could see it in the way they hovered, waiting for him to go away. *Leave us out of it.* They weren't going to be jerked around again. Who could blame them?

That night the Hollows came again, up from the ruins, down over the borders.

"All the places you've been," Marta said. "All the things you say you've seen—didn't you ever learn anything *useful?*"

Arjun shrugged. "My attention was somewhere else."

Bright colors," Arjun said. The Committee had given him an empty office to work in, and he sat with his arms on the desk and his head on his arms. It was three o'clock in the morning, and Marta sat cross-legged on the floor, smoking. Shadows gathered around the star of her cigarette.

"Bright colors?"

"Lights. They're shadowy things. Bright colors and lights may scare them."

Two days ago a small army of Lamplighters—a mob, really, or a drunken movable feast—had set up on the hills above Fosdyke. They set off fireworks and made ridiculously tall flags. Why not? It was worth a try.

"All right," Marta said. "It'll be good for morale, if nothing else."

The next morning they repurposed four hundred cans of red and blue paint and three hundred yards of cloth out of the warehouses on 34th Street. Children painted the walls, the grown-ups hung the hastily designed flag of Fosdyke from windows and lampposts. A dome and an angel, in red on blue or blue on red, depending—the instructions got confused.

That night the Hollows came. Neatly, sadly, two by two, they took the flags down, folded them up, and carried them away. And they killed, almost as an afterthought.

Music," Arjun said. "You said they hate music." Music occupied his thoughts—it drove out the memory of the sound of the Hollows' fluttering motions. Music? "A choir," he said. "A great choir." A retreat into a comforting familiarity. It wasn't a plan so much as a kind of highly sophisticated panic. He knew it wouldn't work, right from the start. He saw it bring hope to the locals' tired eyes and he felt like a charlatan. They *trusted* him! He felt like a false prophet with a secret bank account.

"A choir?" Marta said. She raised an eyebrow and Arjun was

pathetically grateful for her skepticism. "What do you think we are, here? We're not what you could call *musical*."

But they went ahead with the plan anyway. What other choice did they have?

All shifts in the factories and fields were canceled. Fosdyke assembled in Holcroft Square. Everyone—even the children, even the refugees from foreign districts. They filled the Square and spilled out into the alleys. They formed quietly into orderly lines—they were frightened and desperate and happy to do whatever they were told. Women on the left, men on the right, children at the back. They squinted in the bright morning sun.

Arjun went down the line, testing voices. Hardly anyone was shy. Eager to be part of the resistance, they belted out the fiercest noise they could. "Not so loud." He smiled, a hundred times. "Not so loud." Different-colored badges, cut from curtains, pinned to the shirt, identified the different voice ranges. "Stand over there—no, over there." People stepped on each other's feet.

Bellow and shriek—those were the two principal varieties of voice, along with grunt, squeak, and quack. Maury turned out to have a powerful baritone.

The music—something simple, something jubilant and demotic. In Arjun's head, when he created it, the music had had a faint echo of his God; when the vast choir rehearsed, and the Square echoed with their voices, it was distinctly undivine. It sounded like a football chant. It sounded celebratory and defiant.

The afternoon darkened. The rehearsals went on. The Committee for the Emergency had beer brought out, and lit lanterns.

What the music lacked in elegance it made up for in energy. The crowd broke again and again into laughter and foot-stamping—they couldn't be convinced not to stamp their feet, and eventually Arjun let them have their way. What did it matter? It wouldn't work anyway.

It didn't work. As the sun set the Hollow Men stepped out of the ruins and approached the crowd. They winced. They looked upset and embarrassed. They held their hands to their ears, or looked unhappily at their feet. They hated the music and the light, but they came anyway. They clutched each other's indistinct shoulders for support, they whimpered and complained like neighbors pleading for the music to be turned down. They touched the edge of the crowd, and they killed with fear and shame.

The choir broke and ran.

In the morning the choir gathered again. This time they took it seriously. Grimly, with fierce determination, they worked to perfect the music. It didn't make any difference, when evening came.

The next day the choir was a little smaller, and by the day after that it was a quarter the size, as Fosdyke lost faith and went back to work.

That night the Hollows didn't come. The next morning the choir's numbers swelled—and the next night the Hollows came again.

So the days went. Was anything Arjun doing making any difference? He didn't know. What else could he do? He had no idea.

Happy news!

On a grey morning when morale was especially low, and absenteeism at the workshops and the guardposts especially high, and the choir listless and mumbling, the Committee for the Emergency made an announcement. For weeks in secret they had been restoring the old pre-War telegraph networks. Now they were in intermittent communication, across the Ruined Zones, with their counterparts in the Rebuilding district of Anchor, far to the south. In Anchor the local Organizing Committee had built, out of a factory chimney, and various steam engines and pumps, a kind of cannon, capable of launching heavy blocks of masonry high into the air at tremendous booming velocities. Two nights ago they'd fired on an airship as it passed over, silent and murderous, and they'd *hit* it, punctured the immense balloon, causing it to buckle and collapse like a fat man punched in the gut, causing it to tear and flap and burst into lurid green flames in the upper atmosphere, staining the clouds with its oily insect blood. Then it was *gone,* utterly gone, not even enough of it left to settle as ash on the rejoicing city below. The enemy was not invulnerable! Plans were under way in Fosdyke to replicate the device, as soon as the parts could be acquired—so the Committee for the Emergency announced. The Committee opened Fosdyke's stores of liquor and beer, and declared a holiday. There was music, unrehearsed and chaotic, and there were bonfires, and dancing, and the Hollows didn't show themselves that night. Maury, drunk and belligerent, shouted *It won't make any difference, it won't work,* but no one believed him. They laughed at him. Enraged, he pulled out his gun and shot an officer of the Committee dead in the street, and ran off into the night, out of Fosdyke, into the Ruined Zone. Even that didn't spoil the celebration. The tide was turning!

When Arjun cornered Marta by the edge of the bonfires' light and asked her if any of the story was true, she shrugged and said, "Does it matter?"

In the morning there were half a dozen drunken Lamplighters to deal with, ranting, making trouble, criticizing Fosdyke's new color scheme. They'd somehow shown up for the party and wouldn't leave. They shouted in the street below Arjun's office, squabbling with the police. Well, Arjun thought, that was fine. New people were good, even mad ones, even annoying ones. Life was better than death. He remembered Brace-Bel, and felt a twinge of sorrow.

Heaped on his desk were the files he'd saved from the Chapterhouse. Finally he had leisure to read them. He shut himself up for the day with biscuits and coffee.

He went through the pile methodically. Shay? Not in this file. Lemuel? Cuttle? Not this file; not that one either. The reject heap grew at his feet. It started to rain outside, and the windows rattled and echoed. Cuttle—yes! That picture, the eerie artist's likeness! A file for the *yes* pile! Then Lemuel, Hangley, Swinburne—so many aliases. Some of the Know-Nothings' files went back a hundred years or more, yellowing, flaking under his fingers. Some had been updated the day before the War. Shay, Swinburne. The rain turned into a storm. He made notes. His door opened and he slowly became aware of someone standing behind him.

"Marta."

"Plans? Strategies?"

She was soaked from the storm, and she dripped on his papers. She smoked without asking if he minded.

"Not exactly," he said.

"It's not over," she said. "You're not done yet."

"Hmm." He scanned the file of a Mr. Lyall. Dealing in weapons, unlicensed surgeries, a mysterious disappearance from a locked cell. He flipped through another Shay file, and another Cuttle. Rumors of murders and poisoning, insurrection, conspiracy.

"Is there anything in there that can help us?"

"Not yet."

A heap of irrelevant folders, gathered by mistake: dogfights, drugs, operators of public houses without license, public urinators. A file on a Mr. Lemuel, who—

"What?"

He was standing—swaying slightly in shock. Yellowed papers spilled from the folder in his hand. Dumbly he echoed her, "What?"

"What is it?"

He studied her face. Solid, heavy, dark-browed. Was it possible? Surely not.

"What?"

"I can't help you," he said. "I never could. Good luck."

He walked past her, and down the stairs. She came running after him. "What? What?" He didn't answer. He couldn't tell her. He turned the corner and was gone.

TWENTY-TWO

The Faces of Ghosts–Flitter's Owl– Sunshine–The Borders– Her Predicament

Ruth stood on the cliff above the quarry, among the loading wagons and the low concrete offices and the dawn mists. Too exhausted to face the long walk back down, she lay down in the back of one of the wagons, on a heap of dirt under rough canvas, and quickly fell asleep.

She dreamed uneasy dreams—she walked alone through darkened streets, and faces darted at her out of the shadows. The searchlights of the airships drifted senselessly past. One by one she recalled the ghosts she'd known—the pilot, the astronomer, the sculptress, the soldiers who'd vanished. Even Arjun, who had somehow survived the Mountain and then chosen, unforgivably, to go back. Even Brace-Bel, who now seemed a pitiful figure. Too many losses. A cruel joke.

The strange owl intruded on her dreams, drifting silently on the cold light of the airships, hunting her, and she stood her ground, too furious even to imagine retreating, and told it to piss off, which, hooting sadly, it did.

The dream continued. The faces of the vanished haunted windows that went dark, one by one. She turned over in her sleep, whimpering with anger. Shay—her enemy, everyone's enemy, she would kill him if she could, and she didn't even have a face for him.

A face occurred to her.

She woke with a start. A horrible, ridiculous question nagged at her. She set out down into the depths again.

＊ ＊ ＊

Sunlight flooded the quarry. The stones sparkled. The motorcars gleamed.

The camp was awake and at work. They were cooking a stew of weeds, branches, and what was left of the strays after the Beast had finished with them. No wonder they were so thin! They were decorating themselves, and the cars, and the tents, with the excess bones and teeth discarded by their master. The Beast copied Shay; dimly, pointlessly, the camp followers copied the Beast. *Madness all the way down,* Ruth thought.

Silt sat on a rock, having his head bandaged by a large red-headed woman. "You," he said, jumping up. "Ungrateful creature—how dare you? Assault! Assault! Utterly uncalled for, I should . . ."

Ruth walked past him; he spluttered into silence.

Flitter stood under a short rusting crane, making cooing noises at the owl that perched on the cables.

Currently the peculiar creature was solid, tangible, almost fully present in the visible world. It was about the size of a doll, or a teddy bear. Its feathers were grey, thick, like old lace skirts. Its eyes were black stones.

Flitter, raising his cupped hands over his head in offering, presented the owl with a dead mouse. "Here, girl. Good girl. Good morning."

The owl sank its head into its shoulders, and shifted farther out of Flitter's reach.

Flitter lowered his hands. He looked so downcast that Ruth felt a moment's sympathy for him.

He looked up and saw her watching him. He quickly dropped the mouse and put his foot over it, like a schoolboy hiding an illicit cigarette. He smiled broadly. "Good morning, miss! Good to see you up and about! Any . . ." He made a peculiar gesture, waggling his filthy hands.

"What, Flitter?"

"You know. Any . . . Like my little girl here. Any . . . scars? You know. What's it like?"

"You mean, did the Beast operate on me?"

"Well, yeah."

"No, Flitter. We talked."

"Oh." He shrugged. "Shame." He indicated some of his own scars and stitched wounds. "One day he promised to do me."

"You *want* it to . . . ?"

"Of course!" Flitter looked sincerely surprised. He jerked a thumb at the owl. "Look how pretty she is," he said. "She'll live forever. Never hungry."

He reached up again for the owl, and it jabbed its beak at his hand, drawing blood, which Flitter licked away, smiling.

"No hard feelings about the other night, miss." He showed her his wrists. "Old Silt untied me, right enough, and no harm done to him—his skull's gone all hard with all that law in it. Like a stone!"

"No hard feelings? Flitter, you were going to kill me!"

"Not me! Mr. Silt thought it might be best—he's a very practical thinker. I told him it wouldn't be kind. You heard me tell him!"

"There was a sack on my head! You were going to give me to the Beast like a present!"

Flitter looked genuinely upset. "You were running away!" His own voice rose shrilly. "You would have got lost! It was for your own good! He'd have made you magical, that's it, you didn't look happy the way you were, I *said* to Mr. Silt, she doesn't look happy, she's all wrong the way she is . . ."

"Don't you dare tell me . . ." She stopped; she lowered her finger, which had been jabbing at Flitter's face. The anger flowed out of her at once, and she laughed. Flitter's lip wobbled. There was no point in arguing with mad people. "All right, Flitter. All right."

He breathed a sigh of relief. Then he went back to courting the owl, which looked down at him with every indication of loathing and contempt. Its black eyes studied his fingers like prey. It said, *Where's there? Near?*

"Here," Ruth said. "Flitter, do you mind if I . . ."

"She won't come to you, miss, she doesn't even know you. You have to know her moods . . ."

"Just a moment, Flitter." Ruth stood beneath the crane. She lifted up her arms, and before she could even open her mouth the owl had descended into them.

Its claws gently clutched her forearm. It was heavy—as if beneath its soft feathers it was made of stone, or steel. The eyes—the eyes could not be natural. They were like gems. Perhaps they *were* gems. Could it see? It said, *Who'll will the whorl of the walls of the world?*

"You've got a way with her!" Flitter said. "Oh you've got a way with her, all right! Look at you both! You'd be beautiful friends together, when the Beast's made you . . ."

He reached to pet the bird's head. Its beak struck off the tip of his index finger. Then it screwed its head around, and around, and emitted a long hooting sound that turned into a mechanical screech like a train running off its rails. Then it ceased to exist.

Ruth's arms were empty; she stumbled.

Flitter's finger stump bled all down his bony wrist.

"You should get that looked at," Ruth said. Then she walked over to the Beast's tent.

The Beast was gone. The tent was empty. The haunts of half-dead strays drifted among the cushions, the cabinets, the sundials, the statues.

Outside, an indifferent guard sat by the tent's open flap, drowsing in the sun, whittling a bit of wood into a spear-point. "Not there, is he?"

She sighed, "No."

The guard pointed with his knife at the circle of motorcars. "Took a car. First thing this morning."

"Is it—is *he* gone? Why? Where?"

"Calm down, miss! He'll be back. He wouldn't leave us. You'll learn if you stay with us—you'll learn his little ways. He gets all excited in the mornings. It's the sun. He says he never used to get sun, where he was before, back in the old world. He likes to take the cars and go for a drive. Roaring round and round and laughing. The streets are empty these days and you can go as fast as you like."

Feeling lost and deflated, Ruth sat down. She closed her eyes and felt the sun on her face. "Sounds nice," she said.

"I wouldn't dare," the guard said. "Too fast for me. Those things terrify me! He's a brave one, the Beast."

"It sounds like you love him very much."

The guard hummed cheerfully as he whittled.

✻ ✻ ✻

Ruth wandered the camp. The Beast's followers shared their food with her, and told her their stories. She didn't really listen. Everyone had some reason for following the Beast, some chain of coincidences and tragedies and epiphanies that had dragged them there. It was all the same, in the end.

In the afternoon, the owl came and settled beside her. It came back into existence half shyly, like a missing cat slipping in by the back door. It puffed its breast and shuffled its claws. It seemed to enjoy her company. She felt like she, too, was a provisional and incomplete creature. Its feathers glowed in the sunshine with their own inner light—it shone like a dirty puddle. Sighing, she stroked its head; her fingers tingled. It faded in and out of visibility. It muttered nonsensical questions. Flitter watched jealously, pleadingly, and tried to catch Ruth's eye.

Was it possible? Yes—no—maybe. What a cruel joke!

Sunset filled the quarry with light the color of roses. Darkness followed behind. The Beast's followers lit bonfires in trash bins and old oilcans. A dull roar of engines echoed over the edge of the quarry—and with its horn honking, its wheels spitting gravel, its kerosene headlamps slicing the night, the Beast's black motorcar came hurtling recklessly down-slope. It slammed to a halt and the Beast leapt from it. Steam hissed from the car's hood, and the engine rattled in distress. "Ruth Low," the Beast beamed. "Still hungry? You have more questions?"

She followed the Beast into the tent. It lit two lamps, then sank with a sigh into the cushions. "Speed, sunlight, danger," it said. "Clear the mind."

The lamps cast strange shadows, some of which were animate, haunted. Outside, the engine still hissed. The cooling metal of the car's black cowling popped and clanged, a series of notes, descanting, clear as a bell, and the quarry echoed with it. There was a thump from the corner of the tent, which made Ruth start, and one of the tall lacquered cabinets seemed to sway. Far overhead, the owl cried out. The Beast toyed with a knife. "You have questions, Ruth Low?"

"Only two."

"Only two? Frugal. Go on."

"Can we save the city? Can we rebuild?"

"No. The Hollows will keep coming. The airships will keep coming. Shay is bloody-minded and unsympathetic—he will not change course. He has clearly decided that you are—this part of the city is— an unacceptable weakness; he must cut you out. And he will. He controls the machines of the Mountain. Things down here will happen as he wants them to happen. Your stores will run out. Your farms will fail. You will win only temporary victories, and not enough of them. A long dark Age is coming. Shay will be alone, and there will be no one left for him to fear for a long time. There is no way back to the Mountain. Did you come here hoping I would tell you the way? Oh, Ruth, the routes I was taught have all vanished. The airships leveled those streets. Shay has changed the locks." The Beast paused, as if waiting for a response.

"I . . . I understand." What else was there to say?

"Remember, Ruth, I am not a prophet. But this is how it seems to me. I'm sorry. You had another question?"

How to ask it? She couldn't come out and say it straight—she had to circle around it, like the narrow streets that circled the Mountain, as if an answer was the last thing she wanted, a ghost in the room that must not be acknowledged . . . "Ivy," she said. "My sister."

"I remember her well. She is very, very clever." The Beast admired its own scarred arms. "Look at the suit she helped to tailor for me! I could not have done it without her." It glanced over at its operating table, and frowned. "Look at all my failures."

"Hundreds of people have gone up the Mountain—you said that, right?"

"Thousands! Hundreds of thousands! More than an ordinary mind can count."

"And I . . . And this time, things were different. With the airships and everything. Shay's gone mad, or something. Right?"

"Apparently." Something thumped in the recesses of the room. The Beast hissed and the strays went shadowy.

"Someone who went up this time did something different, or was something different. Arjun? I don't think it's Arjun."

"No. He could not do this. By the standards of madmen and seers, he is remarkably ordinary. Far deadlier men have gone up. I am surprised he ever made it as far as he did, frankly."

"Ivy, then."

"Are you trying to tell me something? Would you like me to listen to your story? Six hundred years ago the Church of the Spine of Heaven chained me in a golden cage in their sacristy. I listened to confessions. I swallowed sins, supposedly. I listen well, Ruth."

"This isn't my story."

"How sad. I rode on a man's shoulder. I was left behind in a cage. I am a king of madmen in the wasteland. I know what it is not to matter."

"Beast, have you ever left the city? Have you ever been to the borders?"

"No. I have never dared. I am a patchwork thing. I might fall apart. Have you?"

"No. Ivy has, though. Do you want to hear about it?"

Slag. Heaps of it. Rusted metal. Spoil and tailings, in mountainous dunes, flat and lifeless plains. Forever, into the void. That was what was at the edge of the city. In other Ages—so Ruth's books and old paintings said— there were walls, or rivers, or fields. Steaming waterfalls over an abyss of stars; the shores of a bright sea. Storybook stuff. Here, now, there was shadow, waste, and nothing. So Ivy had said.

As Ruth talked, the Beast leaned in closer. The maimed and shadowy strays clustered around. Something rattled in the darkness. The Beast licked its lips.

"It's more funny," Ruth said, "than it is sad. Really. When you think about it now."

One day when all the Low sisters were only children—Marta was perhaps fourteen and going with the boys from the printworks, Ruth twelve, bookish and shy, Ivy ten, eleven, precocious and cunning—the Dad came home rain-soaked from a business meeting and swore bastard *and threw his battered briefcase against the wall so hard that it burst open and scattered papers, maps, devices—whatever it was he was selling at the time—all over the floor. And the cabinets shook open and the best plates fell out and shattered, and the Lows could not afford to lose their good plates.*

Ruth remembered this because Mr. Low was generally a cheerful man, and if he was a little distant, a little remote, it was only because his fascinations, his enthusiasms, his genius, *distracted him; and his rages were infrequent, and happened only when he had been thwarted, when he had been* cheated.

What was he? He was an independent operator—an inventor—an explorer—a wheeler and dealer—a crook, from time to time. Too proud to work in the factories. Too difficult and strange to rise in the ranks. Always at odd angles to the world. The city was a hard place for independent operators, even back then.

Ruth remembered how while she and Ivy waited nervously at the top of the stairs, Mr. Low tore off his tie, loosened his belt and let his round belly sag, rolled up one of the special cigarettes that he used to say, winking, brought visions of how things really are; *and then he settled into an evening at the kitchen table sorting through his papers and making notes and tearing things out and swearing and cursing to himself—another* failure another failure another fucking failure, bastard that bastard.

Ruth stayed at the top of the stairs. Ivy went and sat across the table from her father, and Ruth couldn't hear what they talked about. Marta didn't come home until the early hours of the morning, by which time the Dad's mood had improved greatly, and Ruth, relieved, had gone to bed.

*T*wo *days later Mr. Low announced over the breakfast table that he was taking a trip. Since the girls' mother died he had limited his explorations to the near environs of the house on Carnyx Street, which circumscribed his investigations greatly. There was nothing to see there, and no one knowledgeable to talk to or deal with, and the bloody Know-Nothings were on every street corner making trouble and always questioning Mr. Low about his* means of support. *And in Mr. Low's view the girls were old enough now to look after themselves for a bit, with the possible exception of Ivy, which was why he was taking Ivy with him.*

He would be back soon, he said. In the meantime he had made arrangements with Mrs. Rawley from the Tearoom down the street; she'd look in on them from time to time, and make sure that they were fed, and bathed, and schooled.

Mr. Low left that afternoon. As promised he took Ivy, who looked very grave and serious in the grey raincoat he found for her—which was to say, Marta's raincoat.

Mr. Low's promises regarding Mrs. Rawley unfortunately turned out to be false. It turned out that he'd told her he would be away for two nights, maybe three, and she was entirely unprepared for his long absence—which stretched out into a week, two weeks, a month, two months, and still there was no word from him, or from Ivy. After two months Mrs. Rawley passed the girls off to Mrs. Guip, who one month later handed them into the care of old Mrs. Thayer, and so on, all down Carnyx Street, until after six months had gone by, Marta insisted that they were quite capable of looking after themselves, and they returned to the drafty and dusty old house Mr. Low built.

By that time, Ruth's evening schooling was finished, and she and Marta both worked making boots; and Marta had decided that the Dad was clearly dead—no matter how Ruth cried, Marta said, the fact was that the Dad was clearly dead. It was better *if he was dead than if he'd just decided to walk out. Less hurtful. And Marta had ideas about how, with all the strange stock the Dad had left behind, heaped in boxes in the cellar and the attic, it might be possible to keep some of his odd little businesses going . . .*

Eleven months after he'd walked out the door Mr. Low returned. He sauntered in through the kitchen door while the girls were eating, and at first they took him for a Know-Nothing or a burglar and Marta reached for the shotgun over the mantelpiece, but then they saw Ivy with him.

He said, "What are you eating? Smells good." It seemed he expected the girls to be delighted to see him, to rush at him with hugs and kisses; when they only stared coldly at him, he scowled, suddenly furious, and stomped down into the cellar. And Ruth felt terribly guilty.

Isn't that ridiculous?" she said. She wiped her eyes and laughed. "I felt guilty."

The Beast nodded and gave an eager grunt.

Outside the owl called again.

Marta—*older, harder*—swore. "Son of a fucking bitch."

And Ivy laughed.

Mr. Low had lost weight on his travels. He had always been plump; now he was wiry, hollow eyed and hollow cheeked, and his old brown coat didn't quite fit. "Fucking hard out there," he muttered. "You don't know." He had acquired a scar on his scalp, and a number of rings for his fingers. His manner was changed—his jokes had turned needling and vicious. He had developed a habit of baring his teeth when annoyed, and he was frequently annoyed now. His hair, which he now wore long and tied back like a horse's tail, had gone stark white.

And Ivy was changed, too. She'd grown precociously beautiful, but also hard, and wild. Her hair was cut in an exotic style, straight and severe. She seemed in some ways much older now than her sisters, while in other ways she was like a nasty and cunning child. For instance:

Marta refused to talk to the Dad for weeks, and Ruth, in solidarity, stayed silent, too—and anyway the Dad showed no inclination toward saying where he'd been—and so the only possible source of information was Ivy. And Ivy was mean *about it. She teased and held the information out and demanded promises and favors and self-abasement for it.*

But finally Ivy laughed prettily and gave in, and said: we went to the edge.

*T*o the farthest edge of the city, where everything ended. It was the proof of a theory—so Ivy said the Dad had said. It was important to understand *the* density *of things, which required a trip to the limits of space. And frequently they got lost—it was, Ivy said,* a complex navigation problem. *All the street signs and numbers and directions always changed. Little Ivy showed off her mastery of all the foreign dialects in which she could now curse.*

Before the world could be escaped, it had to be measured. Before entering the City Beyond, the City-to-Hand had to be fully apprehended. What the fuck does that mean, *Marta asked; Ivy was vague, sly.*

A complex navigation problem, Ivy said; and so the Dad would not have made it without her. The Dad was a genius at getting things out of the people they passed—shelter, food, directions, secrets, free passage, protection, weapons. At first by smiling and joking, but more and more often—as they were hounded by Know-Nothings and police and gangs and worse south from district to district—by threats, and mockery, and humiliation, and blackmail. But for all his gifts the Dad needed Ivy to navigate. The mathematics were too complicated for him, or so Ivy said.

They traveled under a dozen different names. They went hungry. Tough decisions had to be made. They cheated, were cheated in turn. The Dad hardened, got thin. *When it came right down to it, there was nothing he wouldn't sacrifice. He bargained Ivy away, stole her back. Once, Ivy teased, she had seen the Dad kill a man; but that story would cost extra—and in fact she never did tell it.*

And so eventually they reached the edge of the city, where the slag heaps and ash and weeds simply piled up infinitely on the border, and there was no point in going further, because there was nothing left to see, and there never would be.

For a few hours Mr. Low took observations. It was like it was nearly night but there were no stars.

Then they went home. "Obviously," *Ivy said,* "it was quicker going home."

*T*wo months later the Dad vanished again. *Marta would always insist that he must have walked out during the night, but—Ruth said—both the back door and the front were bolted from the inside, and the Dad had gone down into the cellar, and no one ever saw him come back up.*

He took most of his notes, his maps, his collection of signs and keys. He left most of his experiments and devices—though it seemed he destroyed a few critical machines, leaving little piles of ash and tangled wire.

Ivy screamed and sobbed with red-faced rage: he promised he promised to take me with him. *Her shrill voice echoed up from the cellar, where she paced among her father's discarded experiments. She pored frantically over the last few scraps of paper. She drew on the walls—designs that were abstruse, mathematical, painfully incomplete.*

"Come on, Ivy," *Ruth said.* "It's dark down here. You need to sleep."

"Forget it, Ruth," *Marta said.* "You can't help her."

Once in the middle of the night Ivy woke her sisters screaming: he closed the way behind him, he closed the way!

He never came back.

✾ ✾ ✾

A sad story," the Beast said. It sat very close, now; its scarred hand was on Ruth's knee.

"That's my sob story." Ruth laughed. "Marta doesn't like my telling people—but you're not really a person, are you?"

"I don't really know if it's sad or not. Your eyes are a little wet, Ruth. I am deficient in sympathy. I am a monster—had you forgotten?"

"Is he?"

"Is who what?"

"You know what I mean."

"Yes, Ruth."

She sighed. "You're sure?"

"Generally, my master went by Shay, or Hangley, or Cuttle. Occasionally, he used the alias Lemuel. Once, just once, I witnessed a transaction where he had no choice but to give his true name. He thought he'd banished me to the shadows, but I was disloyal, I spied. Later, on my master's orders, I hunted the man who now possessed my master's name, and murdered him. Tore out his throat with my teeth. Rich blood! My master's true name was Low."

The Beast was close enough now to kiss her.

"He didn't like it. He didn't like to be reminded of everything he'd left behind. Everything he'd sacrificed to become what he was. Everything, as he put it, that had held him back for so long. The unforgivable mediocrity of his origins. Everything that had contained and stifled that impossible ambition of his. I don't mean to be cruel, Ruth, but he is what he is. And that was when *I* knew him, and he and I were young! The one who rules the Mountain is so *old,* now. I wonder if he remembers you at all?"

The Beast smelled nothing like a living thing—its breath was dust, spirits, dried blood, electricity. The hiss and echo of its voice drowned out the noise of something heavy clattering in the distance.

"When you were a little girl, and you wandered into my vault in the Museum, I knew at once what you were. I smelled your extraordinary blood. You were happy. *For you, it had not happened yet.* My head spun. I had drifted, over the centuries, into a kind of dead thing, a never-alive thing: slowly, I began to wake! *Extraordinary* blood in you. You and your father, you and your sisters. I knew you could accomplish wonderful things, I knew I could do wonderful things with you. Your father was still with you, then. I heard his voice, calling after you. I considered killing him—but then what would become of me? Would I be never-made? These are difficult calculations, and I am a simple creature."

The Beast's fierce eyes were paralyzing. Ruth tried to stand but couldn't. No—she tried to try to stand. She tried to try to try . . . Her will failed at every hurdle.

"I waited. I woke slowly. I shook off the dust of years of nonbeing. My blood was cold and I was slow—the Know-Nothings made me a prisoner. That complicated matters. Caged in the darkness I planned. I called to the ghosts who fell down the Mountain, and sometimes, when I was lucky, I drew them to me. Like a frog catching fireflies. I reached out into their dreams—those who are drawn to the Mountain are fools for dreams. I sent them to you. I hoped . . . It amazes me that Arjun, of all of them, was the one to free me. I tell you these things because we have the same father, and I am sorry, as much as something like me can be sorry."

The Beast placed its hand on her shoulder. "You freed me. Ivy went up. I hoped she would kill him. It seems she failed. But oh, how it must have hurt him to see her! To see his past invade his sanctuary! His bitter isolation! She would have been unkind to him. She had a sharp tongue."

The Beast licked its lips. "The blood is important. The flesh. The face you wear. Ivy wounded him. What would it do to him to see you?"

"I won't . . ."

"No. I will wear your flesh. I will hide in it and drive him mad."

For the first time Ruth noticed the knife in the Beast's hand.

"I'm sorry, Ruth. To the best of my abilities. This isn't fair. None of this has been fair for anyone. But it will be better for you this way. When I kill your father, when I take the Mountain—well, you would not want to live in a city remade in *my* image."

TWENTY-THREE

Some Deaths—The Road—Speed and Noise—The Trap Closes

Now all the strays in the tent perked up their ears, shifted into solidity, let their black eyes shine. They hissed and whispered. Leaning forward, the Beast opened its mouth wide, and the stitches all along its jaw stretched and ripped. Wider and wider: yellow teeth caught the light, and behind the cage of those teeth there were more teeth, and more. Its eyes were no longer human at all.

She kicked it in its belly as hard as she could. It doubled over, grunting in pain. The knife waved vaguely at her as she scrambled back. She slid and tangled herself in the silk pillows. She fell. The cushion beneath her face was embroidered with a green dragon, curling around and around and around its own tail . . . A hand gripped her leg. She kicked back and it let go; there was a snarl of shock and outrage.

It's not used to being human, she thought, *it's not used to being weak.*

A glance behind. Its eyes blazed. Its back rippled as it raised itself on all fours. Stitches opened. Delicate work was undone. It reverted to savagery. It opened its mouth to say something, some threat, some promise, and nothing but strangling and hissing emerged. A look of irritation crossed its face. Impatiently it pushed its jaw closed with its left hand. The right hand boasted long claws. There was a constant banging at the back of the room, loud now and wild, as if someone was beating a harsh drum. The Beast lunged, grabbed her, sank sharp fingernails into the thin flesh of her upper arm. It spun and hurled her, as if she weighed nothing, as if she'd left everything behind in the wilderness, so that she flew through the dark and landed lightly in a drift of silk. When she sat up, the Beast stood over her, the knife raised to strike. Behind it one of the tall lacquered cabinets was shaking. Its scrollwork of gold and jade flickered in the light of the lanterns. The door lurched again, and again, in time with the banging, then suddenly burst off its hinges, and Arjun came tumbling out, falling facefirst into the cushions. He wore grey flannel and carried no weapon that Ruth could see. The Beast started to laugh.

Ruth ran for the tent's mouth. The Beast lunged for her. Arjun got to his feet, and, laughing, the Beast turned back toward him. Something heavy and scaled lashed across the floor and swept Ruth off her feet—a tail?—then a moment later it was gone. The Beast's form was swelling, indistinct. Through its vague flesh Ruth saw Arjun dive for the operating table, snatch up a scalpel, and turn back to the Beast. He jabbed with the scalpel and found only shadows. The strays shrieked and called out nonsense: *Swithin! Sewer! Dowry! Embers!* The Beast raised its claws over Arjun's head— knife? claws?—and swung. Ruth threw a vase at its back and it spun round to face her. Arjun scrambled toward the tent's flap. He shouted, "Ruth!" She thought, *yes, what?*

"Ruth, you're alive!"

The Beast kept laughing.

They changed places again.

"Enough, Ruth." The Beast was hard to look at now.

Ruth threw open the heavy slick door of the tent, and the cold night blew in. Wings beat around her head and Flitter's owl hooted like an engine. A flash of dark eyes—then it rushed past her and into the tent. Behind her, the Beast roared. She turned back again, caught a glimpse of scales and feathers and rending claws, two shadows struggling . . .

Arjun grabbed her wrist and dragged her out into the night.

"That thing, like a bird—did you do that?" he said.

"No, it's . . ."

Outside in the quarry, the Beast's followers stood in a vague mass. They hovered around the oilcan bonfires like tramps, bony, shiftless, confused. The tent bulged and rippled, and horrible shrieks emerged from it. Flitter, hands over his mouth, tears streaming from his face, ran into the tent, whimpering *pretty girl, please, pretty girl, no . . .* He screamed once and went silent. Silt—

Ruth thought it was Silt—some bony sexless skeleton in rags and bird-bones—picked up a hammer and dumbly considered its possibilities as a weapon. Arjun held her close and said, "Ah." Someone shouted and someone else moaned.

Excuse me!" A new voice, echoing around the quarry. "Excuse me? Would you all please shut up?"

Down the slope and into the quarry came a little procession of men. They carried guns. They fanned confidently out, spacing themselves around the Beast's little camp. One of the Beast's people complained and was knocked efficiently to the floor. The man at the lead of these new intruders approached the tent. He said, "Thank you." He paused to collapse a brass instrument that might have been a telescope and hand it off to one of his men. He passed by one of the fires and Ruth recognized his smile, his golden hair, his handsome unpleasant face. He said, "We'll take it from here."

Arjun let go of Ruth's arm. He said, "St. Loup."

St. Loup grinned enormously.

St. Loup turned to the Beast's followers with what appeared to be genuine surprise. "Why are you still here? Things are difficult enough already. Piss off." They did.

"Good," he said, and sat on the hood of one of the Beast's black motorcars. "What a beautiful machine. It has good taste for a monster." He clapped his hands. "Quick, quick."

His men surrounded the tent. Who were they? They didn't look local. They had dark brown skin and neat little ginger beards—an unappealing combination. Their clothes were plain and black and their guns—which they now slung over their backs—were heavy and complicated and distinctly unusual. They pulled strange implements from boxes.

St. Loup wore a loose shirt of shimmering duck's-head green, open-necked, and beneath it a gold necklace. His own gun, which he began toying with, was a sleek little thing, blue and white, like a bird. The bruise on his temple was fading to yellow.

He saw Ruth watching him, and winked.

She said, "Arjun, who is this?"

"We're the best of friends," St. Loup said.

"It doesn't matter," Arjun said. "Leave her alone, St. Loup, she's not important, I'm here for the Beast."

"Oh shut up. I know exactly who she is. I've been watching her for Ages. When I got here the first thing I did was research all your little friends. I may look like a fool but I didn't get where I am today without doing my homework. When did *you* work it out?"

Arjun shook his head. "Just now. I just found out. It was in the Know-Nothings' files, but I was busy with other things."

"Who *is* this?"

"We're family," St. Loup said. "Your father made us all who we are. That awful thing, too." He gestured toward the tent. "I wanted to know what it was going to say to you. Now I know. So now what I am going to do with you all?"

The Beast's erstwhile followers scrabbled and slipped up the slopes of the quarry and their grunts and footsteps echoed. In the heart of the quarry the tent had gone still and silent. It slumped in the windless night, cautious, turtlelike. Encircling it, St. Loup's men now brandished a variety of items. One had a dogcatcher's net. One had an immense hunting rifle, another a crossbow. Three carried what appeared to be icons of religion or witchcraft—a spoked wheel, a cross with a little naked wooden man on it, a big rod with dead birds and rats attached by wire and string. One held what looked remarkably like the cane Brace-Bel used to carry, with its eerily glowing crystal. One had a machine that Ruth simply could not comprehend. It had wires and dials and valves and a glowing green window, and it hummed.

One of St. Loup's men placed a glass box on the ground and flipped a switch. The box crackled then poured out a cold white light—like the light of the airships. It filled the quarry with a chessboard of shadows, it picked out every line on St. Loup's face, it banished all mystery from the night.

"I came prepared," St. Loup said. "After all, there's no way back. Most of this stuff may be junk but you never know. By the way, Father Turnbull's dead. I gouged out his eye and slit his throat with my very own hands, and wouldn't it be hilarious if he wakes in the next world at the feet of his God? So I'm in the market for a sidekick if you're interested, Arjun. Ruth, I don't know what I'm going to do with you, but I'm sure I can think of something. Beast!" He raised his voice. "Come out! I have questions!"

The Beast didn't put up much of a fight. Somehow it made Ruth sad to see it.

The tent shifted, its fabric seeming to swell, and there was a sound of slithering—heavy breathing—the scrape of claws and the dragging of a great tail—and St. Loup said, very loudly, "Tut tut." His men hefted their icons and talismans. The crystal on the cane pulsed. The mysterious box of valves and dials emitted a low warning throb. Three rifles were cocked.

The noises from within the tent subsided.

A few moments later the Beast emerged.

It came sheepishly out of the tent and into the light. It had some new and some old scratches and bruises, hair wild and sweaty, clutching a red silk sheet around its body. A half-naked middle-aged man, under arrest. St. Loup's men brandished their strange weapons and the Beast cringed. With a nervous grin it said, "Who are you? My name is Wantyard, sir."

"Stop that." St. Loup rolled his eyes. "I have listening devices. I heard every word you said. Psychopath, am I? We'll see." He gestured to his men. "Tie it up. Truss it."

Arjun said, "St. Loup, did you hear what it said?"

"I just said so, didn't I? Bloody hell, look at it. First time I saw it was a thousand years ago and it was the prettiest little snake in Shay's pocket. *Come with me,* Shay said, *I've got something to show you. Something money can't buy.* And this thing flickered its tongue, I remember distinctly. Ah, none of us have aged well."

Ruth edged toward the motorcars. Three of them stood scattered odd-angled on the quarry's ground. No one seemed to be looking at her.

"St. Loup, did you listen to what it said? We're just pieces in a game Shay plays with himself. All of us, we're just weapons. We've been lied to."

"So? I'm not going to stop. Are *you* going to stop? I didn't think so. Whatever made you think the game wasn't fixed? Sometimes I forget you grew up in a monastery."

How did you operate a motorcar? Ruth had no idea. How did you even open their doors? Ruth had never touched a motorcar before—they weren't for her kind of people. It was open-roofed, and the interior was a forbidding underbelly of wheels and dials and pedals and levers sticking out like the legs of a beetle on its back.

St. Loup's men shoved the Beast to its knees, tore away the silk sheet, tied its hands behind its back. St. Loup glanced at the wound beneath its legs and winced. "I liked you better before. Now you're mine, can I change you back?"

The Beast growled. "I'm no one's."

"Of course you are. You're a thing, a tool."

Arjun stood next to St. Loup, as if they really were old friends. "We're all tools," he said.

"Yes, but some of us are more important than others. So was it this thing that bit your hand? You can tell me now. Would you like me to cut its fingers off?"

Arjun shrugged. "I'd rather you didn't."

Ruth leaned slowly against the shiny black door of the nearest motorcar. Was it locked? She fumbled blind, behind her back, trying to be unobtrusive, while her eyes watched St. Loup as he circled the Beast, grinning and running his hands through his hair in excitement.

"You're mine," St. Loup said. "The key. I don't care if Shay wanted me to find you, I don't care about his stupid plans and schemes. I'm past scheming now. I win. Tell me the way."

Who *was* St. Loup? For that matter who was Arjun? He seemed to have forgotten about her. And who was *she*? Ruth's head spun and her fingers, fiddling with the door, were numb. Was she one of these people? Was this her world? Ivy would have been at home here. Ivy would have been in charge of the situation. Ruth didn't know what to do or say or even who she was or why she was there—she wanted to crawl away and hide. She wanted a cigarette.

The Beast said, "I won't tell you."

"It's your function. It's what you're *for*."

"I'm free."

"No you're not, I've got you tied up on the floor."

One of St. Loup's men stepped round the back of the motorcar and grabbed Ruth's arm. Stunned, she shuddered and went limp. The man shook his head without making eye contact with her. He was twice her size, muscular, scarred along the line of his jaw so the beard grew patchy—there was no point in fighting him. She wouldn't even know how to begin.

"Listen, you horrible animal. I pay these men by the hour and they charge extra for torture, so don't waste my time."

"You have no way of sending your men home," Arjun pointed out. "Are you paying them enough to come with you to the Mountain?"

The man holding Ruth's arm grunted in what seemed like surprise.

"Shut up," St. Loup said. "Beast, tell me the way."

"It's mine. The Mountain is mine to inherit."

"Don't be ridiculous. You're an animal. Talk or I start cutting things off you."

"May I?" Arjun put a hand on St. Loup's shoulder. "It knows me. It started to tell me the way once before, but we got interrupted."

"All right. All right. You're a good sport, Arjun. When I run the world I'll make you the best God you could want, you can piss off back to your temple and worship it and we'll never have to get on each other's nerves again. Make it talk."

"Beast," Arjun said. "It's time. You owe me." He knelt next to it. "How do we get to the Mountain?"

"I'm *free*."

Arjun put his wounded hand on the Beast's forehead. "No. You're not." He reached out with the other hand and the scalpel glinted as it fell from his sleeve. He drew it swiftly across the Beast's throat, through its double chin and stubbly growth of beard. Blood gushed and the Beast sighed and slumped on the ground.

Arjun stood, letting the scalpel drop. St. Loup was transfixed in shock.

"Now neither of us can have it," Arjun said. "*You* can't have it, St. Loup."

The sleek little gun trembled in St. Loup's hand. He emitted a strangulated whine.

The Beast was still for a long moment, quite clearly dead. Then without warning it spasmed. It shook on the quarry floor. Its body twisted and jerked. Blood sprayed from its wound. The creature roared senselessly and thrashed with arms that bent backward as if broken. Arjun stepped nervously away from it. St. Loup stepped forward.

St. Loup's man let go of Ruth's arm to reach for his gun. Half-consciously she fell backward through the motorcar's open roof and into its black leather innards.

She had a vague sense that one pressed the pedals—which she did, sprawled across the seat, with her left hand—and pulled levers—she kicked randomly at them. St. Loup's man reached over and suddenly the car lurched—not forward but backward. St. Loup's man shouted and fell. The car's wheels threw up gravel and dust. The vehicle slammed against a rock and Ruth bit her lip. She kicked and yanked and operated whatever came to hand and the car lurched again, forward, skidding suddenly sideways. It crunched across the glass light-box and everything went dark again. She yanked at the wheel and the car spun and came to a halt.

There were screams in the night. The dull red glow of the bonfires lit motion and struggle. Men were running back and forth. Something swelled on the floor of the quarry, something unfolding itself in shadow where the Beast had lain.

Ruth pulled herself upright. The car had two kerosene lanterns squatting on its hood and something Ruth hit with her elbow caused them to spark into life. She shoved her foot down on the pedals and the car roared forward. It slammed into one of the Beast's other cars, which in turn slammed into a third, which skidded and knocked over a burning oilcan and caught fire. Ruth reversed, moved forward again, gathering frightening speed.

Golden hair shone in her lamps. St. Loup stood suddenly in front of her. He raised his gun. The next moment the car bumped and leapt a little in the air as St. Loup fell beneath it.

Had she meant to do that? She wasn't sure. She pulled something that caused the car to stop suddenly, its engine screaming, and she fell forward and hit her head.

The door opened. When she looked up again Arjun was climbing into the seat next to her. It crossed her mind briefly to kick him out.

"Go," he said, "quickly! Please."

Behind her two of the cars were burning and the tent seemed to have caught fire, too. Something thrashed in the flames—long, serpentine, many-legged, a body like a train, a mouth like an industrial excavator.

"Don't look back, Ruth, go *faster*."

She pulled the wrong lever and the car's gears ground and screamed and the vehicle halted. Behind them the two burning cars exploded, one then the other. In the mirror, something immense writhed in greasy flames. Men fled in all directions. A little grey bird burst from the tent and took to the air, beating strong shadowy wings, hooting in triumph.

"Don't look back, Ruth, keep going, keep *going*."

She threw the lever forward and the car moved again.

Arjun

"Keep going."

"I *am* going."

"We don't know if it's dead."

"I know. I hit St. Loup."

"I know. I hope he's dead. Keep going."

She accelerated. The road thrummed beneath the wheels. Unused industrial machinery rattled past to left and right.

Arjun sat back in the thick leather of the seat. He watched Ruth work the levers and pedals. It reminded him of a kind of church organ.

He'd offered to drive—not that he really knew how himself—and she'd told him to go to Hell. He'd offered to open a door for them but they had nowhere in particular to go. Why not drive? She seemed happier that way—the speed seemed to calm her.

She was learning fast. At first she'd been tentative, white-knuckled, jerking and braking, cursing raggedly under her breath.

"Ah, Ruth, you can take your foot off the pedal . . ."

"Don't talk to me."

"All right."

"I said don't talk."

By imperceptible degrees she'd gained confidence and speed. Now she swerved, accelerated, worked the device like a virtuoso. She was reckless in the dark. The car's leather roof was folded bat-winged back and her hair blew wild around her.

How thin she was! Her hair was lank and mad. Her cheekbones protruded. Her skin, her eyes, shone like a fasting saint's. Had she starved in the wilderness?

They drove in silence. She didn't want to talk. He wanted to talk—he had, just half an hour ago, quite deliberately attempted to kill the one creature in the world that could lead him to the Mountain, to his God, simply to keep the secret out of St. Loup's grasp. Altruism, or spite? A little of both. He wanted to talk about it but she had problems of her own.

He supposed she was taking it well. She seemed less frightened than angry.

Juno's quarries and mines fell behind them. The ruined factories of Walbrook's Zone loomed ahead. The city was a blur; the stars above were still.

She said, "How much did you hear?"

"Everything," he said. He shrugged. "The door was jammed. Anyway, I wanted to hear what it had to say."

"Did you know?"

"What?"

"About my father, of course. How long have you known about my bloody father?"

"Ruth, I didn't know—I didn't. Not until tonight. Not until—I read it in his file. I came looking for you. I knew you'd be in danger, though I didn't think—"

"You mean you wanted to use me."

"That's not fair."

She braked, too hard, making the car's wheels slide, loose stone spray, steam burst from the hood.

"Who was that man? What files? Who was my father? Who else knows about this?"

He told her about St. Loup, and the Hotel. That was the easy part. Her father—that was harder to explain.

He hadn't brought the files with him. Maybe he should have. Now that he tried to tell her what he'd learned he found his memories were vague and confused. So many names, so many rumors, the Know-Nothings' secret codes, Shay's own scheming. Groping through a forest at night.

How much could he, how much should he tell her? A fifty-year-old file marked *Winwood, D.,* for instance, had contained a report on the case of the mass murderer Winwood, who, according to one investigator, had been seen in the company of a Mr. Lemuel, a white-haired old gentleman, who it seemed had provided Winwood with the unusual guns that he had used in a subsequent apparently notorious massacre . . . The file had contained a list of the dead. The lead on Lemuel had gone cold. Horrible—was that the sort of thing he should tell her?

He told her.

Tears in her eyes, or the cold wind, the grit of the road? Her hands, her face, were so tight and drawn anyway—how was she taking it?

An investigators' report appended, with a rusty paperclip, to the *Shay* file: forty years ago a series of explosions in the gas pipes had leveled four streets in East Bara, and a factory, killing over one hundred people, including a visiting executive from the Holcroft Company, and his two daughters. The engineer responsible for the recent alterations to the pipes had been called *Shay,* and after the incident his papers turned out to be fake, and he escaped the investigators' dragnet.

"I don't know," Arjun said. "I don't know why he would . . . "

Her hands still clutched the wheel. Her eyes were on the road—her beautiful green eyes. *They must come from her mother,* Arjun thought—Shay's eyes were hard and flinty. The thought of Shay, married, a young father, was more than Arjun could imagine. He had a sudden ridiculous picture of Ruth, a little girl, sitting on Shay's knee, Shay smiling that unpleasant smile of his—what was he thinking? Was he scheming even back then? Could he have been an ordinary man, once?

Twenty years ago, investigating a man who went by the name of Swinburne, the Know-Nothings had found a laboratory in the sewers beneath Millerand Hill. The report said, *Contents: Lights.* "*Animals." Machines.* The report said, *Disposition—Fire.* In the margins someone had written *Fucking "Shay" again? Yes/No?*

Arjun faltered. "Keep going," Ruth said. "No, keep going. I want to know."

Two hundred years ago a man called Shay had been charged with Fomenting Unrest Against The Mountain. The Chapterhouse where he'd been held burned down. The arresting officers were found with their throats slit. Most but not quite all records were destroyed.

Should he hate her? He made himself stop looking for signs of her father in her face. It would only upset him.

Fifteen years ago an investigator in Fosdyke, who'd been keeping notes for years on an undesirable, a suspicious character named *Low,* of Carnyx Street, had received a communiqué from the South Bara Chapterhouse, about a closed investigation into a dealer in forbidden goods and heresies called *Lemuel.* The artists' impressions in the files were an uncanny match, separated only by a few years, a hardening around Lemuel's eyes. Before an arrest could be made, Low vanished. A handwritten note to the file suggested: *Keep an eye on the girls. Bad blood there.*

Bad blood! The world lurched, closed like a trap.

As soon as Arjun read that, he'd dropped the files, come running, all across the city. Now he wasn't sure what to say to her.

She accelerated, pushing the car past its limits, annihilating the city with speed and noise. Over the roar of the wind, could she even hear what he was saying?

TWENTY-FOUR

What Happened to Brace-Bel–What Happened to Inspector Maury– What Happens Next

Brace-Bel

G o then! Go!"
Brace-Bel, stomping through the ruins, in and out of empty buildings, heaving the sloshing barrels, talked to himself, dropped the barrels, and gestured wildly, yelled and surprised himself with echoes: *Go . . . go . . . go . . .*

"Would that I could! Where? Where?"

. . . where . . . where . . .

He tired of that game quickly enough. For a while he worked in silence—not for long. "Go then!" he yelled. "Leave me!"

He was drunk on spirits brewed in a still constructed largely from the bathtubs in an abandoned poorhouse. "Is this what I've come to?" What's more, the fumes from the oil barrels were making him light-headed. He had not eaten in more than a day—maybe two.

"After I saved you from the wreck of your city! After I raised you from the dirt!"

The front door of the next house down the street was locked. Locked? With his shotgun—a beautiful lacquered collector's piece—he blasted the door open, and only as he stepped into the thick dust and staleness of the interior did it occur to him that the house's occupants had probably died inside, upstairs, in bed, of one of the fevers that followed the War, and the choking air was very possibly deadly. Too late now! "I, too, once had a fever. Seven years of every ten in gaol, I am not unfamiliar with sickness and madness. Molder no longer in your beds, sir and madam, fire will free you!" He splashed the oil on the walls with an artist's abandon. A garnish of gunpowder! "At last your sluggish bodies will approach to the condition of light! A message, a poem."

Outside, Brace-Bel slumped on the doorstep. It was evening; the sky was the color of spoiled meat; shadows gathered. The little hand-drawn wagon on which he bore the oil barrels and the powder kegs sat in the middle of the street, taunting him, obdurately heavy, stiff-wheeled. Was he a beast of burden? It seemed he was. "Alone, alone, alone," he muttered as he jerked the stubborn thing another few yards down the street, and went to work on the next house along. "I was not made to be alone!"

They'd left him, the Lamplighters, his army, his flock, his fellows, his acolytes, the last of his lovers. So quickly they'd turned on him, so cruelly! The look in their eyes as they walked away—it was the look of every pretty young thing who'd ever told Brace-Bel: "I don't need you anymore." Of whom there had been many. Disappointment. Disgust. *Laughing* at him . . . What had they expected? He was a man out of his time. He did not belong here. Why would they have looked to *him* of all people to give their squalid lives meaning?

Only a few days ago—it seemed like a lifetime now—the Lamplighters had clashed one last time with the great adversary, the Night Watch, among the mansions of Provins Hill. A splendid blaze, a crown of fire, atop the Hill! The Lamplighters rushing away, hurtling down the Hill, arms full of salvaged treasures, gold and silk, flutes, mirrors, jade vases; down into the dark streets where the Night Watch waited, ready like customs officials to confiscate and smash those beautiful things; a deadly game of cat and mouse in the bloody shadows. A victory! Most of the Lamplighters escaped the cordon. (The Watch's numbers were declining. Their hearts weren't in it anymore. The truly dedicated had mostly killed themselves.) "Scatter the treasures!" Brace-Bel commanded. "Beautify the ruins!" And his followers, who he could not help but admit were hungry, and ragged, and sickly, wanted to sell the stuff for food.

A philosophical disagreement ensued. Brace-Bel said some unkind things. It wasn't their fault! They were creatures of their time, as he was a creature of his. Their worlds were incommensurable. His dreams, forced on *their* city, could only end in absurdity. He had screamed at them as they left. (They went south, to beg for shelter in Fosdyke; they went west, and east. How sadly they shuffled away!)

"Alone, alone, alone!" He wasn't suited for solitude. He talked to himself. He had unsound ideas. It seemed that the shadows in the Ruined Zone were haunted by silent and unhappy men with stranglers' hands—he was not entirely sure whether they existed outside his own head. He saw St. Loup, he saw Turnbull, he saw monstrous birds and reptiles and apes. The Mountain loomed. The city was becoming increasingly unreal to him. He dreamed of light, he dreamed of darkness, he turned inward, into his memories. He considered violence against his own person. No one to love or hate but himself. Everything he had turned his hand to had failed; if only he'd lived an ordinary life he might have been happy. Was that how it felt to be Shay?

Brace-Bel had nodded off, on the back of the wagon, amid barrels of lamp oil and home-brewed spirits. Hunger and fumes. These days his waking life seemed much like a dream anyway. When he woke the stars were out, shining like knives, like the gears of unspeakable machines. He'd slept clutching his cane for self-defense. He noticed that one of his shoes was missing. "Thieves!" he muttered. Or perhaps he'd lost the shoe a while ago. He wasn't sure.

"Good evening, good evening." The street stank of oil and sulphur and alcohol. Moonlight picked out a glistening trail behind him. "Good evening!" The street was silent. Even the birds had the good sense to steer clear, it seemed.

"Torches and tinder, torches and tinder, sparks, the lightning," he said, getting to work.

He was utterly alone. The city of his birth was gone; where could he go now? He was a man out of his time, a joke, a failure. Back to Fosdyke? They might be kind to him, they might forgive his trespasses (the Lamplighters had, if he remembered correctly, gone to war with Fosdyke to some extent). They would not let him join in the Rebuilding because he was not suited to the task, but they might lock him safely away for his own good and feed him and care for him in his madness. He would rather die.

Even his memories had abandoned him—he was no longer sure who was real and who was not. Turnbull and St. Loup were plainly impossible. The Lamplighters were all too real, he remembered them all too clearly, the ingrates. Shay? The Beast? Arjun? Maybe, maybe not.

Ivy! He was quite sure Ivy was real. To deny her, even in extremis as he was now, would be a kind of blasphemy. Even now Ivy struggled on the Mountain, enduring dangers and hardships and tortures and terrors that made Brace-Bel's bowels run cold to imagine them. (He imagined them frequently.)

Ivy! He would fight for her, if she'd let him. If she still needed him, he had a reason for being. Together they would claim the Mountain. She would comprehend the machines, and he would make beauty with them. Her cunning, his vision. Together they would open all the cages, reconcile all opposites . . . And if she *didn't* need him, she would let him die in the fire. He would burn. And that would be sweet, too. He would become light, heat, sparks on the night wind, free of the flesh.

He lit the torches, the trails of powder. Panting, he ran down the street, striking sparks, leading the fire behind him. Were his calculations correct? He couldn't be sure. Calculation was never his strong suit. One by one the houses exploded into flame. Windows shattered, timbers crashed. A wild roaring filled the air. Black smoke—would smoke swallow the message? He couldn't be sure. It was hard to breathe. Ivy! She was on the Mountain; she had access to its devices; the city was clay in her hands. If she chose to, she could save him. *If* the message was visible! The skin of his face stung with the heat; red light pulsed through the walls of the houses, enveloped the street, enveloped all the streets for a half-mile around. The fire had gone wild. The city had been transformed into light and heat. But if he'd calculated correctly, a big if, *if* then for a brief moment the fire had spelled out, in letters made from the streets of the abandoned city, in letters visible from the air, the stars, the Mountain, her name: IVY. Now there was smoke everywhere, and nowhere left to run. A wall fell, bricks glowing like coals, and it seemed to him that behind it there was a door.

Arjun

They saw the fire—Arjun and Ruth, who sat on the still-warm hood of the car, looking down from the hills over Fosdyke, past the dark angel on the dome of the Museum, past the new fields, past the rooftops where the guards patrolled through a forest of flags, and out over the darkness of the Ruined Zone. They watched the smoke rise, a black and shifting mass to rival the Mountain. Fire crawled over the ruins, and for a moment it seemed to spell . . .

The car was stuck. It had slewed wildly, and at speed, into a bomb crater in the middle of an abandoned street, and now its wheels were buckled and sunk in mud. Ribs and elbows had been bruised but unbroken. Ruth had laughed and laughed as if drunk. Her door wouldn't open. They had climbed out in each other's arms.

She patted the dented metal. "Poor thing—it'll rust up here. Maybe birds'll live in it."

He asked her, "What shall we tell your sister?"

"Which sister?"

"Marta."

"Of course Marta. I know what you meant. I don't know. I don't know what's best. She's not as strong as she seems. I'll think about it. Don't say anything, will you?"

He nodded. Another layer of lies and secrecy and conspiracy. This at least was kindly meant.

She said, "Do you think she's all right up there?"

"Ivy?"

"Of course Ivy."

"I don't know. I only met her briefly. She seemed very clever. Very cold. She seemed to take after her . . . I'm sorry."

"That's all right." She stared across the city, at the Mountain. It was still and dark. What was she expecting, signs of struggle? Lightning, fires, earthquake, roiling clouds, volcanic eruption? There was nothing like that.

"I hardly remember him," she said.

"Really?"

"No, actually. I remember him very well. I don't know. It's hard to picture. He wasn't all bad. Something terrible must have happened to him. He did something terrible to himself. He isn't really a person at all, anymore, is he? He used to be funny, sometimes. He wasn't like anyone else."

Arjun thought it best to keep silent.

She said, "I never asked—did you have a family? Before, you know, you . . . walked away from things." There was a tone of reproach in her voice. He told her *no,* and she nodded, and didn't ask any more questions. For a long while they watched the fire rise and fall.

"The Beast told me things," she said. "It told me how the world works."

"It lies."

"Not about everything."

"Shay made it."

"So? He made me."

Arjun didn't know what to say. Below, the fire scrawled itself across the city in letters of light, immense, unreadable.

She said, "Do you know why you went up on the Mountain? Because he *wanted* you to. You and St. Loup and all the rest. The Beast told me. My father—his shadows, his copies—they all want the Mountain for themselves. They find people like you—mad people, broken people, dreamers—and they lift you out of your lives, and they point you at the Mountain. They're scared to go themselves. There are traps, there are defenses, it's too high, the air's too thin, you go mad. They send people like you. I don't know what to call it—scouts, cannon-fodder. They're just waiting for one of you to make it through. But you never do. You die. You fall back as ghosts."

"I know. I heard."

"Are you listening?" She put her hand on his and squeezed, as if she were a doctor, breaking the news of a death in the family. "This is important. Everything they ever told you was a lie. They told you your God was on the Mountain. That's a lie. They only did that so you'd go up there. So that they could follow. They cheated you. They spoiled your lives. Everything they said was a lie."

"Maybe not everything."

"The Beast told me what the Mountain is. It's a machine. The people who came before us made it, to make the city. The things you call Gods are only, I don't know, fuel. Parts of the mechanism. The Mountain sends them out to make things and take things away and open and close valves and . . ."

"I've heard that theory before. I've heard a lot of theories before. In the scientists' communes of Zubiri they say the Gods are just what they call anomalies. The mechanism of the city breaking down. Cracks in the facade. Points of fracture. Places where you can see through from where you're standing to somewhere *else*. Different lights, different skies, different noises. Somewhere better or worse. The lights are cars or fires or television or advertising bill-boards. You think you're looking at God but really you're looking at the future."

"Is that true?"

"I don't know. It's just something people say. I never know what to make of it. Does it matter?"

She looked at him for a long time. Then she gave up.

What had the fire said? Now it had no shape. It was advancing wildly on all fronts. It was out of control, swallowing everything in its path.

She let go of his hand with a sigh.

"So what are you going to do now?"

He shrugged. "What can I do? Go down into Fosdyke. Get a job. See how long things last. When he sent the airships, when he sent the Hollows, Shay—sorry—he locked all the paths out of this time. I'm stuck here."

"Your God. Your whatever it was, quest, pilgrimage."

"No one can say I didn't try." He laughed.

"Unless you find a way back onto the Mountain."

"Unless I find a way back."

"Then you'll go, again."

"I suppose so. It's a bit late to stop now, isn't it? What would I do with myself if I stopped?"

"Would you kill him?"

"I'd probably try."

"Fair enough. I think I might, too."

The fire engulfed a fuel depot; an explosion shook the city. They both sat still while the echoes rang in their ears.

"I *might*," she said, "just want to ask him *why*. I mean, it isn't fair, is it?"

"Not really."

"The funny thing is," Ruth said, "that this is always how I dreamed the world works—really, deep down, this is what I always expected."

"Really?"

"You know how it is when you're young."

"Yes? I don't know. It was a long time ago, and very far away."

"Right, right. So imagine finding out the city really is the way it seems when you're young; your father really is the most important man in the city. Everything in the world revolves around your little family squabbles. The city is the way it is because of the way you are. Your codes and secrets and stupid cruel jokes, all those family stories, are the most important things in the world."

"It must be very strange."

"Sometimes it seems it's not so strange; I always really thought the city worked like this. I was only pretending to be a grown-up. You know?"

"I suppose so."

"Imagine all that, and you're still left out of the big secret. Imagine how that fucking feels."

Were those distant lights, on the Mountain? Or sparks drifting in the wind?

"This world is coming to an end," Arjun said. "I tried to stop the Hollows but we can't. People tried to stop the airships but they couldn't. Shay has the Mountain. He'll roll up this part of the city and put it away as if it was just a mistake in the first place."

"I know."

Far below, the fire crawled south, through the ruins, toward Fosdyke. Ruth said, "Don't worry—it'll stop at the canals." And it did, so that was all right.

Maury

And down below, off on the other side of Fosdyke, Maury stumbled through the ruins. Perhaps he heard the explosions, away over the rooftops, a few miles away. He heard explosions all the time now: the sound of the airships overhead haunted his dreams, intruded into his waking hours. The scream of the bombs. The totality of his failure. He'd tried to protect the city; he'd tried to warn them; he'd failed. All over now. All fucking over now, very soon. Perhaps he saw the fire blazing over the horizon. His vision was failing, and full of blood.

He'd stumbled alone out of Fosdyke, pursued by what passed for the law these days. Why were they chasing him? What had he done? He couldn't quite remember. His memory was going, old age and stress—and also when they'd chased him they'd fired guns after him, and children had chased him throwing rocks, and a bullet or a rock or something had bloodied the back of his head, and the wound, untreated, throbbed and itched. What had he done? Something horrible, something stupid, some vicious impulse. Like once when he'd snapped and given the wife a bit of a slap, shouldn't have done it. Once or twice. He didn't trust himself. What side was he on?

He'd been messed around in ways that weren't fair. His life was all wrong.

The first night the airships passed over. He feared them; he cheered them on.

The second night he saw, over a hill, the Night Watch on maneuvers. It hardly even crossed his mind to rejoin them. They probably wouldn't have him, anyway.

The fourth night he trapped a dog in a sunken pothole, broke its neck in the crook of his remaining elbow, ate it raw.

The fifth night he saw a light gathering over an empty lot, sparkling off the broken windows, and he approached, thinking it might be firelight, the light of a camp, and he could—what? Ask for shelter? Murder them in their sleep? He wasn't sure. In any fucking event it turned out to be one of those spirits, one of those Gods, one of those awful things that had spilled out into the city in the wake of the War. A vast and spinning arrangement of lights, performing in the empty ruins, for no one but Maury, who didn't care, who hated and feared it, who spat, and closed his eyes, and walked away.

Now his eyes weren't working right. Day by day his vision dimmed. There was blood in his left eye; it ached. He must have looked too long at the lights. He had a fever, and his head wound bothered him. He couldn't see much, anymore, except fire, stars, and the searchlights of the airships. Everything was shadows. Soon he would be blind, and then he would die.

Vaguely he stumbled toward the redness in the sky. He staggered into a lamppost and spun, a dull ache in his shoulder. For a moment he looked up at the stars. Then he fell on his back in the gutter. He slid in the mud—a bomb crater. He lay on broken bricks. A stink of smoke blew across his face. The stars dimmed.

Someone leaned over him. He heard murmuring—a conversation in something that was not quite language.

Hands held him, under his arms. He was lifted as if weightless. Cold fingers prodded him, hooked his lip and tugged at it as if he was a horse, and they were checking his teeth. He felt the shame that the Hollow Servants radiated; it made his skin crawl.

He expected them to kill him. Instead they carried him on their shoulders, north, up and up through the streets. The air thinned, smelled of dust, electricity, rust, oil, and machinery. A plodding ascension. The Mountain? He didn't struggle.

BOOK THREE
The Final Expedition

TWENTY-FIVE

The Storm—Private Languages—
Back Alleys—The Atrocity Sheds—
The Guts of the Machine—"*You* Again"

Arjun

This is how it happened.

One week after the two of them came back down into Fosdyke, the messages began to appear.

That was one week after Ruth moved back into the old Low house, into a bare room under the attic, which she said was fine, better than fine, never mind the dust or the draft or the memories; she had a lot to think about; she wanted to be alone for a while longer.

It was six days after Marta summoned Arjun into her office, in the headquarters of the Committee for the Emergency, and demanded to know where he'd been, where her sister had been, what was going on. He said: *I can't tell you.* She fumed. She asked if it was about Ivy. He said: *what difference does it make?* She blustered, fell just short of actually making threats. He looked around her office, at the maps, the papers, the stockpile of oil and food behind the door, the grey sheets on the narrow bed in the corner, and he said: *what is it you do here, exactly? I've never been sure.*

It was five days after he walked north into the Ruined Zone, to the great black scar the fire had left behind, still smelling of smoke and burning, and sat all day on a blackened stone bench, listening to the wind, trying to clear his head with music, gently sifting through simple chords and themes and tones.

It was four days after he stood under Ruth's window, wondering if he should go up to her, or leave her alone, trying to remember just how she'd put it when she'd said she needed time, time to think. Should he? Shouldn't he? What would he say? He felt like he barely existed anymore. The afternoon shift ended and passersby slapped his back and said: *Good man! Our savior, Mr. Clever, this is! He'll figure it out!* He smiled, to be polite.

It was three days after he volunteered in the fields, and went to bed with his back aching and slept dreamlessly, wonderfully, too exhausted to think of how he was trapped.

It was two days after the Storm blew in, off the Mountain—they could all see it come down off the Mountain, roiling and churning, rushing like a flood. Lightning whipped it on. It carried soot, dust, black mud, wet leaves, driving industrial rain. Ruth threw the attic windows open and stared into the hurtling darkness. Her father, spitting in the city's face. This was his answer, then! Why couldn't he just leave them alone? But he couldn't do it, she realized; the wound was too deep, the guilt too painful. What would he do to himself when he was all alone again? The Storm whipped away the flags, tore down the bright rags, scoured away the paint, splattered Fosdyke a monotonous grey-black. That night the Hollows came again, and did their work unimpeded.

The messages came in the form of posters. They were well disguised, woven subtly into the fabric of the city, and Arjun might never have noticed them if Ruth hadn't pointed them out. How long had they been there? He couldn't be sure.

"They're fresh," she said. "Look. Isn't that odd?"

They were walking together down Carnyx Street. It was a grey afternoon. The shock of the Storm and the return of the Hollows had struck at the roots of Fosdyke's resilience, and now the workshops were abandoned, the fields untended. The Committee issued orders, and the orders were ignored, or never heard. People hid in their homes, drank and fucked in the bars, lit out across the ruins for shelter in Fleet Wark, or Anchor. Ruth and Arjun, who knew something they couldn't share with anyone else—something that explained everything, but made no difference, would only make things worse—walked together down empty streets, in silence. The days were numbered. It was odd, then, that there were freshly plastered posters, still wet, glistening, on the brick and concrete walls of Carnyx Street.

They looked like the old posters the Know-Nothings used to put up. A picture of the Mountain, black and vast; the green-inked slogan below urging VIGILANCE. But instead of VIGILANCE the slogan was murky, unformed, an analphabetic nonsense.

Ruth brushed her fingers across it; they came away sticky. "I remember this."

"Oh?"

"I don't know."

The next morning the posters were wrapped askew around all the lampposts on Carnyx Street: this time they resembled the old Know-Nothing posters with the young girl, and the old man, and the slogan about how WE'RE ALL IN THIS TOGETHER—but the faces were blurred, vague unfinished sketches, and the letters illegible. Arjun found Ruth standing by the lamppost, deep in thought.

"Ivy?" he said.

"Ivy."

"What does it mean?"

"I don't know. I don't remember. It reminds me of something, from when we were all little."

He touched the poster. It had dried; the green ink was already fading to yellow. "It doesn't mean anything to me."

"It's not *for* you."

The next day, all along the concrete wall at the back of Carnyx Street, by the fields: the Know-Nothings' old recruitment posters. The slogan was more like numbers than letters, and the faces of the young men in their boots and black coats were blurred.

I saw them again," Ruth said. "Down by the canal."

She'd been keeping notes. She'd been keeping a map of the posters' appearances. She had tried to scrape samples from the walls, but they came away in damp grey strips of rag. She started trying to sketch them.

People were starting to notice her obsession.

"The face," she said, brushing her fingers along the glossy surfaces. "On that girl. I feel like I know that face. I feel like I know the words."

It's not words," Ruth said. "On the posters—it's not language at all. It's a kind of code."

"Are you good with codes?" Arjun asked. "I know a great many languages but I have always been slow with codes."

"No. Ivy was the one who was good at that sort of thing. But I *remember* this."

"Ivy?"

"It's her face, you know. If you look just right you can see that it's her face."

"It's been too long," Arjun said. "I forget her face. All I remember is that she looked like you."

"No. She was the beautiful one."

"Was she?"

"When we were children we had codes, and languages. She used to make them up. And . . . *he,* you know . . . he used to pretend he couldn't understand them, though I suppose he could have if he wanted to. He wasn't all bad back then. Or maybe he just wasn't interested. Or maybe Ivy really *was* cleverer than him. Shit. I *don't* understand. But I remember. Ivy's trying to talk to *me.* She's reaching out to *me.* She needs me, Arjun."

It was as if Ivy's patience started to run out—a letter came through the door of the Low house, addressed to Ruth, though no postal service had existed since before the War. Numbers and letters; private language, in a childish hand. The graffiti on the fence spoke to her, and the way the ivy curled on the railings. Another letter. The signals multiplied.

"We used to have a game," Ruth said. "I think I remember it. When the Dad was away, we used to pretend there were doors, a maze, a secret city just for us, full of miracles. What did we call the city? What were the rules? Oh, the weeds in the lot behind the house were a forest. Those old iron sheds were like towers. Palaces. The rusting gears in the old junkyard were treasure maps. The cobwebs, the candles. The grown-ups didn't know. The boys from the factories didn't know they were part of the game. We used to mark our territory with chalk and flowers and stones and broken glass. We took it in turns to be Queen. We had a game, when we were girls, and Ivy always took it too seriously. We had *names* for things—I wish I could remember them."

Arjun hovered close by. He didn't understand, and there was no point trying to understand. Whatever she was seeing it was private, personal, incommunicable. He wouldn't let her out of his sight. He couldn't sleep. It was very close now.

Marta had him summoned to her office. The headquarters of the Committee were in disarray, half empty, purposeless, and off-kilter like a sinking ship.

"Stay with her," Marta said.

"I am."

"I don't know—I don't want to know. Do you understand me?"

"I think so."

"I've put a lot of bloody work into not knowing." She was drunk.

"I understand."

"We can't last. It's all going to fall apart. We can't make it work down here, not when . . ."

"Marta . . ."

"Shut up. Listen. When you go up there, I suppose you'll do whatever you have to do. Your whatever it is—God or whatever. Do what you need to do—just think about us, will you? Try not to forget us down here. If you can do anything. Stop all this. I don't know."

"I'll try."

"Don't let her get hurt."

"I'll try."

"Bloody right you will. Go on, then. Get back to her."

And one day it seemed it was suddenly *obvious* to her. The shape of it came into focus and Ruth smiled beautifully. Her table was littered with scraps of paper, notes, scribbles, diagrams, maps marked with the various messages she considered significant.

"It's a *map*," she said. "And I *understand* it."

Arjun came to stand behind her. "I don't understand any of it."

"I do." She kissed him, and took his hand. She snatched up her scribbled maps and ran downstairs. He followed. They didn't bother to lock the door. Arjun's heart was beating madly.

Downstairs in the street she was standing by the mouth of the alley, studying her map. She bit her lip nervously. She beckoned to him, then stepped decisively into the shadows. He followed.

They took a winding path to the Mountain, through back alleys, up and down fire escapes, along dusty never-used emergency corridors, across rooftops, through unlit empty cellars.

The route Arjun had taken before had led across vast open plains, station concourses, ornate blasted plazas—terrifying and immense exhibitions of ruin and emptiness. The route Ivy sketched for them now was a subtle and furtive one—tradesman's entrances; half-open untended windows; unused sheds.

They crept along in the weeds by the sides of train tracks. "She says *don't get on the train*," Ruth said, and Arjun saw no reason to argue; the half-faces he saw in the windows as the trains rushed past, hollow, elongated, were not welcoming.

All morning the Mountain was at their backs, and, door by door, they seemed to be moving south across the city, and away from it. Ruth consulted her notes nervously.

"Are you sure . . ." Arjun kept asking, and she shrugged no.

They were being followed; they both felt it.

"Do you see that . . . ?"

"I thought I did. It's gone now."

Whatever it was, it didn't approach them, and eventually they agreed they were imagining it; that all that was behind them was their own shadows, the slowly closing doors . . .

When they thought they were lost, there were more marks on the walls; more posters; the name IVY finger-written shakily in the dust on a broken window; complex spiraling children's games sketched in ivy-green chalk over the next manhole; a sprawl of ivy all along the wall of an alley, or curling around the black iron of a fire escape.

In the afternoon, they began to approach the Mountain again. It came closer and closer. It grew from a distant grey-blue blur into a vast darkness.

They stepped from one alley into another, briefly crossing a high gargoyled rooftop, from which they could no longer see the Mountain, in whichever direction they looked; and they knew they were *inside* it.

Nothing attacked them. Nothing black and dreadful hurtled down from the sky or boiled up from the gutters. If they were followed, perhaps it was only shadows or curious animals. No traps. No darkness of forgetting enveloped them. Ivy had found a secret, safe path onto the Mountain.

And Arjun did not understand how it was done—in fact he tried not to think about it, because when he tried to understand his head hurt and he felt sick and scared. But as the day wore on he began to sense the shape of Ivy's mathematics; the vast geometrical perfection she had . . . made? Charted? Discovered? It made his own wanderings across the city look amateurish, sentimental, haphazard, half-hearted. There was a cold and beautiful music to it. He felt that he understood her; he felt that he would never be capable of understanding her.

"We *never* understood her," Ruth said.

At the end of the alley was another alley, which opened onto a broad, dark street. The streetlamps all down it at irregular intervals cast a ghostly haze, circled by moths. The ends of the street—if it ended anywhere—were lost in shadow. Opposite the alley's mouth was a long concrete fence. There was a gate. It was locked.

"We can climb this," Ruth said. "Give me a hand here."

"No," Arjun said. "I should go first."

She shrugged. "Be my guest. Welcome to the family home. Wipe your feet."

"Ruth, are you afraid of your sister? Your father?"

"I don't know. Yes. No. I just want to *see* them."

"We may have to kill him. I *will* kill him, if he won't give me what I want." He put a hand on her shoulder. "Maybe even then. He cannot be allowed to keep the Mountain."

She wouldn't look him in the eye. Something played on her lips that was maybe the start of tears, maybe a smile—at his expense?

"And Ivy?" she said.

"Ivy, too. Ruth. *Ruth.* She may have brought you here to help her, but *we are not here to help her.* Do we agree on that?"

She nodded. She said nothing. The white lamplight made her pale, ethereal. A good person, Arjun thought, an innocent, despite everything. She would never forgive him for being a part of all this. That was her father's fault, too. Small comfort!

"I'll go first," he repeated.

They helped each other over the fence.

They were in a rank unweeded garden—the grounds of a neglected mansion. There was a stand of unhealthy-looking trees to their left. The grass was wet and there was a slightly marshy odor.

There was a thump and rustling behind them, as if someone had followed them over the fence, but when they turned they saw nothing and no one.

At the far end of the garden—down winding paths, and past a number of hulking dark sheds—stood Shay's house. The form of the Mountain. A mansion of immense, imposing size. *Wasteful* size—only a handful of windows at the center of the dark mass were lit.

And, as Arjun and Ruth approached, it struck them that the mansion was tremendously ugly; and what was ugly about it was that it was so *repetitive.* It was less like a sprawling and luxurious mansion than like a single, mean, five-story flatblock repeated again and again, stacked and reflected and refracted, but not elaborated or developed. It had no interesting features other than size. It was a failure of imagination, instantiated in brick and iron.

"This isn't real," Ruth said. "It's a mask. This is how he wants it to look. It could be *anything.* The Beast said this was a machine the Builders made, an engine, a factory, a . . . I don't know what. He made it this way. This is how he wants to live."

"This is his soul, Ruth."

"He wasn't always like this."

"Are you sure?"

From the concrete sheds to the right of the path there was the hum and grind of slumbering machinery.

A huge curved corrugated-iron shed stood by the left of the path. There was a rusty half-open door. Sounds of murmuring, whimpering, hissing emerged. There was a sound of something like tuneless singing.

"Don't," Ruth said, as Arjun pulled at the door, making stuck hinges screech. "Don't. We should stay on the path and go to the house."

"Is that what Ivy says?"

"I think so."

"I don't trust Ivy. I want to look around."

He pulled. Something snapped and the door opened.

The interior of the shed was huge and dark and smelled of rust and blood and muck. A single dim electric bulb dangled and swayed like a suicide from the high ceiling.

Whatever had sounded like singing, or murmuring, it was silent now; perhaps it had only been the creak of the metal, the groan of the pipes, the low hum of electricity.

There were shapes in the shadows—crates, cages, tables, the no-longer organic bulk of dead things.

"We shouldn't be here," Ruth said.

Arjun slowly approached one of the cages. "We can't make him any angrier." Something the size of a man slumped in the cage, wrapped in what might have been a cloak, might have been shape-less useless wings.

"*He has laboratories,*" Arjun said.

Did the shape in the cage move? It was hard to say. The bulb swayed slightly; the shadows twitched and jumped.

"He was always interested in birds," Ruth said. Arjun turned to see that she stood by a row of shelves, like library stacks, on which stood rusted birdcages, dirty glass cases, wooden perches either empty or holding stuffed parrots and hawks and ravens and other, unnameable birds. "All dead," she said. "They're all dead."

"No one's been in here for a long time," Arjun said. "The light—you've never seen those lights, have you, electric lights? They burn out. It should have burned out long ago; that door was rusted shut, and the dust . . . But nothing works here as it should."

"He was *always* interested in birds. He used to tell us—no, he used to tell *Ivy,* we were just there in the room sometimes when he said it—he used to talk about how free birds were, how lonely, how the city was all *open* for them. Once I said, *why do you put them in cages, then?* And he just laughed. I thought he was laughing kindly."

A number of the birds were dismembered in part, flayed and sliced open, nerves and muscles and bones exposed.

"He used to know a lot about how their *eyes* worked. They were too slow, or too fast, or something; how they saw pictures of things."

"Nothing here rots," Arjun said. "Why doesn't it rot?"

"Birds. Oh, it really *is* him, isn't it? Oh *no*."

"He does worse things," Arjun said, "to more precious things than birds."

The sound of shuffling; a slow drip-drip.

There was a row of cages containing dead dogs, dead apes and monkeys, leathery little lizards. Some bore the scars of elaborate surgeries; others didn't, yet.

"Perhaps at first he *collected* them," Arjun said. "Creatures like this. Do you think these spoke, when they were alive? Or obeyed his commands? Or the birds—did they navigate for him? I imagine him trading for them—there are places where such surgeries are cheap and commonplace, and places where they must seem like the most wonderful and terrible magic. When I met him, when he went by the name of *Lemuel,* I remember there were birds . . ."

"Look." On a low table, covered in dust, there was a row of sharp instruments. Ruth brushed her fingers through the dust, and shuddered.

"He must have learned it somewhere. He must have learned all kinds of things. I walked in his paths for years and I never learned very much of anything."

"He's much cleverer than you."

"My attention was focused elsewhere. Now I feel I've wasted my time. I am afraid to face him."

"I don't think he's very *good* at it," Ruth said. "The surgery. All of these creatures are dead."

There was a table in front of them. The bulb now dangled directly overhead and cast a stark light on the table, and on the anatomy of the creature that lay, flayed and shackled and inert, on the table's bloody surface.

It resembled a child at least as strongly as it resembled an ape.

It had one saucerlike eye, wide and dull as a doorknob. The

other eye was an abscess of exposed nerves and fluids. Its throat—its vocal chords—had been opened. Twined in among the red tendons and blue veins were fragments of bright metal that might have been surgical clamps, or discarded instruments, or might have been devices for speech, or . . .

Dust had settled on the table, on the instruments, on the creature's matted fur.

"He lost interest," Ruth said. "Left it unfinished."

She brushed flakes of fallen rust out of its fur.

Arjun inspected the instruments. "Do you think these are remarkable in any way?" He handled them carefully, lifting them up to the light.

"Do you mean, are they dangerous? Are they useful?"

"Yes. They only look like knives to me."

"How am I supposed to know? We can ask Ivy."

The bulb buzzed and flickered. For a moment it was dark and Arjun nearly dropped the knife in his hand. When the light returned again the creature's mouth was open, exposing sharp teeth, a bloody stump where a tongue should have been.

"Was its mouth open before?"

Ruth said, "Never mind that—where was the door?"

Outside the circle of electric light everything was vague and looming shadows.

"This way?"

"*That* way."

The murmuring resumed; a multitude of feeble confused voices. Something in the room *was* singing—a low wavering growl that sometimes whined up the scale into music, and dropped back again as if ashamed.

"No; I circled once around the table, so . . ."

"Something's alive in here."

"*Everything's* alive in here," Arjun said. "Nothing dies here unless he wants it to."

A voice from behind his shoulder repeated *nothing dies*. Another voice from somewhere to his left took it up, and another. *Nothing dies here nothing dies here.*

"Run to the wall," Ruth said. "Work our way round from there. Don't touch anything." And she set off running into the shadows. The moment she stepped out of the electric light something huge and swollen lunged from the hulking shadow of a broken cage and knocked her to the floor. There was a row of spines all along its—its back? Its arm? It pressed her to the floor and groaned in tones of pleasure and agony *nothing here dies of pain or making unmaking reduction increase joining nerves unstitched unmapped division our cruel father our keeper knives and toys and nightmares so long no love or kindness among his children he botched us all.* Its voice was crude and vile, half senseless, unfinished. Ruth's sudden scream of rage and pain was half animal, too. She struggled beneath it. Arjun charged it brandishing one of the vicious little surgical knives and it half ran, half leapt back into the shadows.

Ruth was on her feet and running. Arjun followed. She stumbled, banging her hip against a low table, and he overtook her. He ran nearly face-first, full tilt into the wall—he banged against it with his outstretched hands and the whole shed clanged and shook.

Ruth fell into his arms; there was slick blood on her shirt. She turned left and ran brushing her hand against the thin corrugated-iron wall, so that it rattled and clanged and the shed echoed. Arjun ran after her. Something seized the back of his trouser leg and he fell onto the concrete floor. The thing that hunched its damp and sweaty weight over him spoke nonsense in numbers and shrieks. He struggled to stand and it brought its mumbling mouth next to his ear. Its breath smelled strangely of flowers.

Ruth stumbled against the wall and ran into a concrete and iron block on the side of which was a large rusty switch. Screaming and throwing all her weight onto it she dragged it down—it clicked and wires sizzled and hummed, and suddenly a dozen more bulbs flared into life and the shed was brightly, blindingly lit.

There was a hiss and a scrabble of claws and the thing on Arjun's back lurched away. When he rolled on his back to catch a glimpse of it it was gone, and the shed was silent.

Ruth's dark curled hair was lank with sweat, despite the cold. She was breathing wildly. The worn linen of her shirt was torn at her left shoulder, and she was bleeding.

In bright light the shed was like a disused slaughterhouse. In the starkly lit corners of the cages there was nothing but bone, dried blood, scraps of fur, and half-rotted carcasses.

Ruth choked and sobbed and held her sleeve to her mouth as the *stink* hit her.

The door was not far away. They ran for it.

As they forced it closed behind them, leaning all their weight against its hinges, the lights went out again.

Arjun assured Ruth that the cuts on the back of her shoulder were shallow. He didn't know whether that was true or not.

He held up his maimed hand and smiled ruefully. "It could be worse," he said. "And at least we know that their teeth are not *necessarily* poisoned."

She shuddered and held her left arm tightly against her side with her right.

"Did Ivy tell you the light would—would do whatever it did to them?"

"I didn't even know the switch would turn on the lights," she said. "I just thought whatever it was it couldn't make things worse."

"Hah. I picked up this knife." In the moonlight it looked rusted, dull, and grimy. "It may be worthless."

"Be careful with that."

He slipped it gingerly into his jacket pocket.

"All right," she said. "All right. Come on."

It crossed his mind briefly to suggest that being wounded, she should stay behind, but he had the good sense not to say it.

"No," she said, as he looked curiously at the sheds off to the right of the path, under the shadows of drooping ash trees. "Now we stay on the path." From the sheds came the sounds of machinery, and from around the shuttered windows there was a faint cold light. "We find Ivy first. Then you can look for whatever you want to look for."

"That's very wise. Ivy first, and your father."

The mansion had no obvious entrance. There was a multitude of dark windows, all out of reach, but no doors. There were black rusting drainpipes, and cornices, and inelegant pillars, but nothing that could be climbed. The drainpipes broke from the wall. The windows remained out of reach.

It took a long time to walk around the building, to find that it appeared more or less identical from every angle. They turned again and came around the front, if that was what it was, and they walked around it again.

Ruth jumped for a window and fell short. She swore. "What did you do last time?"

". . . and for all I know the time before that, and before that. But I have no idea how to proceed. I doubt I ever got this far."

She shook her head and rested for a moment, leaning against the cold brick of the wall.

They kept walking. Overhead, a light in a window went out. Another window lit up, and shortly afterward another, as if someone was moving slowly from room to room, carefully switching off each light as he went.

Ruth stopped to rest again. She sat on a set of low, worn steps. They had passed one like it every few minutes; it led nowhere. She was looking increasingly grey faced and short of breath. She walked more slowly with every step.

"Let me look at your wound."

"I'm fine, Arjun."

She let him look anyway, but it was dark, and he still had no real idea what he was looking at.

He said, "You'll be all right." He frowned. "I expect Ivy or your father will have medicine."

"Not if we never get inside. Let's keep moving."

They turned the corner again and another flank of the building lay before them. In the garden there were shadows and structures and occasional noises. There was a brief scatter of rain. They turned another corner. Some faces of the mansion were randomly ornamented with gargoyles; others were not. Drains and gutters and eaves bulked in the dark.

"If we had a rope . . ." Arjun said.

"If we had a rope there would be some other bloody reason why it wouldn't work. Let's sit for a moment."

They turned another corner, and later another. Though the building seemed to be square, right-angled, Arjun suspected that it was not; that each time they turned a new face of the building unfolded before them. Ruth thought that they were simply going around and around in circles. They left no footprints and they had nothing to mark the walls with; they could not be sure. They turned another corner, and another, and Arjun said that he thought perhaps Ruth was right and they *had* seen those windows before, those pipes, that cracked molding. Ruth disagreed.

They turned another corner and there was a door. They nearly walked right past it.

It was an unremarkable narrow metal door, painted a dark olive green, set down a short brick staircase and apparently opening into a basement. It was ajar.

"The back entrance," Arjun said. "I wonder what your father does when he has guests he *wants* to welcome."

Ruth sat on the steps to catch her breath.

Arjun slowly pushed the door open with his foot. He thought how much he disliked Shay; how he hated the way Shay cheated, and stole, and lied, and hid, and *hoarded* things that were not his; how everything Shay touched was turned ugly and mean. It crossed his mind to be glad that Ruth was weak and tired; she would not be able to stop him from doing what needed to be done.

He helped her stand and they stepped into the darkness of the basement.

The room behind the door was heaped with refuse. It reeked of mold and rotting food. Against the near wall slumped a mass of black rubbish bags. There were slimy and sticky things underfoot. There were angular piles of old furniture, and the swollen valves and rusty levers of old machines; there were yellow drifts of discarded books.

They crossed the room, holding their breath. There were a number of doors. They chose the nearest.

After that they couldn't agree which way to go next. The drab concrete corridor ran left, toward what appeared to be an immense boiler room, full of a tangle of pipes hung with fat sinister valves; and it ran right, into the shadows, lined with closed unmarked doors. Arjun said *left,* in hopes of finding something vulnerable in Shay's machinery. Ruth said *right,* because if the machines were important, then they were surely trapped. Arjun didn't know what to do—his instincts couldn't be trusted in Shay's house—but that only made him more determined to dig his heels in. He saw the same resolute uncertainty on Ruth's face. In the end they tossed a coin; *heads* meant *right*. It came up heads, and Ruth immediately said *maybe we* should *go into the boiler room* and Arjun said *no, you're right—no diversions*. But then after they'd walked only fifty feet down the corridor his curiosity suddenly got the better of him and he opened one of the doors.

It opened onto the boiler room.

The huge room clicked and clanked, whistled and moaned. Heavy iron pipes twisted at painful angles all around Arjun's head. Wheels protruded. Valves attached themselves like leeches to the room's iron veins; their dials ticked patiently away. Everything was covered in a thick layer of dust.

Ruth stepped into the room after him. "Do you understand any of this?" He shook his head and put a finger to his lips; there was motion in the depths of the room.

Every dial and pressure gauge that Arjun could see fluttered in the red, or hung inert and empty. The machinery appeared to be balanced finely in a constant state of crisis. Something *tense* in the creak and clang of the pipes . . . He whispered, "This may be easily broken. I wonder what would happen if . . ."

Ruth drew in her breath and squeezed his arm.

Shadows crept over the pipes, coming closer out of the depths of the room. Something bright glinted—blinked—something opened a mouth of tiny, bright, needle-sharp teeth.

A dozen little grey monkeys approached, hand over hand along the pipes, blinking bright round camera-shutter eyes.

One leapt from a pipe near to Arjun's head and he ducked, but it flew past him to land clattering on a valve. It wiped the grime from the face of the dial with the ragged fur of its forearm; then it chewed its wrist and muttered to itself. Its back was a mess of purple scars. It cocked its tufted head as the pipes clanged. It shuddered and leapt. Arjun lost sight of it among the plumbing.

Ruth shrieked as another monkey leapt from a pipe to her shoulder up onto a wheel valve, which it turned a tiny notch. The pipes whistled and all of the monkeys shrieked and shook themselves.

Something banged and echoed off in the shadows. The monkeys hunched and looked up in terror; then they went racing off to fix it, brachiating recklessly across their iron jungle.

Suddenly the thought of damaging that complex, incomprehensible machinery seemed utterly terrifying. There was no telling what it might do to the Mountain, what it might do to the city.

Ruth had slumped against the door and was sitting with her head against a cool pipe. Arjun helped her stand and together they walked back out into the corridor.

The corridor ran endlessly, around countless sharp corners, past unmarked doors. Sometimes it was lit by bulbs; sometimes they had to walk in darkness, Arjun feeling his way along the wall with his hand.

Ruth held his arm and rested her head on his shoulder. For a long time she was silent, and he thought everything was all right. Then she mumbled, *thank you, Marta, thank you for helping me, you're very kind,* and his blood froze. "Ruth, it's me."

She said, crossly, "I know."

Silent again. He tried to keep her talking; he tried humming and encouraging her to hum along. Later she addressed him as *Dad.* He said *no, no I'm not,* and she moaned and pushed him away. Her legs buckled. He looked back. Fifty feet away the corridor turned a sharp corner and beyond that continued . . . endlessly?

If he left her behind he would never find her again; he was quite certain of that. He was lost; he did not understand the machine. He helped her stand again. Her eyes were bloodshot, her scalp sweaty, her breath foul.

Oh, look at it all, she said.

Sometimes she staggered and looked down at the concrete floor as if swaying over a great abyss, and clutched weakly at his arm. Sometimes she shuddered with what seemed to be dread. Sometimes she laughed, bitterly.

Once she addressed him as *my musician,* and he said, *yes, Ruth, yes, that's right.* He thought most likely it was right; how many musicians could she have known?

For a while she refused to go forward, and Arjun didn't want to fight her. She saw something before them that terrified her. He asked her what it was, but she was too far gone to answer him. He thought it was her poisoned and feverish imagination—but then there was a terrible grinding noise and all the lights swayed and dimmed, and it seemed the shadows lunged across the wall from side to side and something passed by within them. Ruth said, *quick, quick, we have to keep going.*

She muttered as they walked, lost in some sort of childhood argument, which drifted senselessly into a bitter sullen fight over money. She said, *why didn't you tell me? Oh, what a stupid unkind joke.* He tried to think of a joke to tell her, thinking it might catch her attention, keep her in the here and now; nothing came to mind.

She called him *my pilot.* She kissed his face and her lips were too cold and her breath too hot and too stale. She told him he was beautiful. She said, *I never thought you'd come back.* She said, *you found it at last.* Arjun said: *yes.* She began to shake feverishly. Arjun said: *yes, yes, I found it, we found the way.* She coughed weakly. He said, *we found it, just a little farther.* She slumped against his shoulder and said, *but it's so horrible. It's such a horrible broken machine.*

She stumbled and he let her sit against the wall.

He said, "What kind of machine? What do you see?"

She laughed and her eyes fluttered back in her head.

Her pulse was weak and unsteady.

He felt terribly cold and numb and lost.

In a sudden ecstasy of panic he threw open the nearest door. It led into the same clanging hissing forest of machinery as the last door, and the door before that.

He seized a valve wheel; it was rusted and painted sloppily grey-white and stuck, and he hung all his weight off it to make it screech sourly and turn a half-revolution. *She'll die,* he thought, *she'll die; get someone's attention!* The pipe the valve governed began to shake; an arrhythmic knocking started up, traveling back and forth over Arjun's head, leaping from pipe to pipe, gear to gear, grinding and thumping and ringing, spreading like an infection.

The door swung quietly shut behind him. When he threw it open again the corridor was empty; Ruth was gone.

He didn't know whether to hope or despair. He didn't know how anything worked or what anything meant. The corridor echoed to the sound of sick machinery. He kept walking; he wasn't sure where he was going.

☆　☆　☆

The corridor curved and sloped. The sounds of the machinery above drifted down like dust. He counted the numbers on the doors, the rungs on the rusting ladders that carried him down, and down, and with every step it was harder and harder to remember why he was there.

The name of his God!

Medicine for Ruth!

Life for the city, death for Shay!

What was the point? The Mountain was beyond his comprehension.

The corridor ended in a door. It was marked CELLAR 222-A. The sight made Arjun unaccountably, uncontrollably angry. He remembered it!

The door opened with a familiar groan.

Cellar 222-A was an echoing void. The light was like moonlight, and ebbed and flowed in sinuous waves, and had no clear origin. The floor was concrete, ancient and moss-blotched.

Now he remembered; he'd been here before. He'd *seen* it. Cellar 222-A! Here Shay kept his servants.

Standing in massed ranks . . .

In far distant and long-forgotten Red Barrow, the warlike Thanes had traditionally buried themselves with their favorite warriors, standing in stiff phalanxes around the bier, willingly poisoned, rotting in their own armor in the darkness. By the fifteenth generation of the Thanes the vaults beneath that unlucky part of the city held dead and silent legions. Arjun had broken into the vaults in search of a certain key that the Seventh Thane had worn around his bull-like neck . . . Now the uncountable unmoving ranks of Shay's servants reminded him of the darkness below Red Barrow. Perhaps the Thanes had had some dim sense of how things were in Shay's house, and built in imitation—the Thanes admired conquerors and thieves and cruel men.

Hanging like old coats in a wardrobe . . .

He walked among them, brushed against them. They were cold. They shifted as if in a breeze and fluttered and it seemed that sometimes two or more stood in the same spot; perhaps an infinite number could stand on a single point.

Like pale reflections in a cracked mirror . . .

Did he recognize any of them? He wasn't sure. Their heads hung dismally down. Their faces were all so similar, so vague—Shay's hollowing process stripped them of their identities. There was sometimes a subtle suggestion of *place* or *time* to them—the dark skin and pronounced brows of the princes of Erigena; a stain across the temples and cheek that might have been one of the tattoos of the thieves of the House of Moth. One of them might have been Mr. Zeigler. Maybe; it was hard to tell, and what were the odds? There were so many. Explorers and adventurers of a thousand Ages of the city . . . Arjun's ill-fated peers; his fellow dreamers. Most had probably been men; it was hard to be sure. Their clothes were androgynous, ill-fitting, ill-defined. He *hoped* they were men because when he saw a pale ambiguous face that he believed to be female he found it unbearably sad, he felt unbearably ashamed. He looked for Ruth's face; he didn't find her among them.

Like ripples in a moonlit pool . . .

It was possible that the dim light came from the servants themselves; or that its reflection glowed from their brittle skin, that some part of them was in a place where moonlight fell . . .

Dusty valves in a monstrous calculating-engine . . .

A signal went through the room and every head snapped attentively up, and Arjun's heart seized with terror.

He was in the middle of the room; no exit was visible. Why had he come here?

Because you belong here.

His legs buckled. He sat numbly on the floor. The servants gathered around.

A cane clacked on the concrete. A bent figure approached. The servants stepped flinching aside.

An old man pointed his cane at Arjun's face.

"I *remember* you," Shay said. "*You* again. You little shit. You little shit of a thief. Don't you ever learn? What am I going to have to take from you *this* time?"

TWENTY-SIX

Come Home–The Pawns–Stalemate–
First Blood–Reunion

Ruth

Where was she?

Ruth sat bolt upright. Sparks showered and stung her skin, drilled tiny black holes in her shirt. What? A pipe overhead had burst, and black cables like guts spilled. All along the corridor the pipes rattled and shook. Oh! She remembered how once the Dad had come stamping up the stairs in the middle of the night shouting *fire, fire, everybody out*—some experiment gone wrong. The stink, the fear, the sudden constriction of the throat, tears and screaming. So long ago! She remembered the bombs falling. She lurched to her feet and threw herself backward through the nearest door. She stumbled a little way in the dark and fell against the wall again.

Where was she?

She was at home, and half asleep. Perhaps she was dreaming. A great exhausting ache in her back—a hard day's work behind her. What had she been doing, where had she been? Come home, come home. Every corridor, every door, every unsteady staircase was something she half recognized. She lay down, and got up again. If she could only lie down in her own bed! But the house seemed unusually large, and empty. She climbed the stairs and kept climbing. Where were her sisters? An awful creaking and banging of pipes. Shutters banging. Take care of it in the morning! Lie down. Where was her father?

Familiar cobwebs and dust, those old familiar splintery chairs, the cracked molding on the old windows! If not for the dull pain she'd have been happy. Things hadn't been the same since. Come home.

Not her bedroom, but good enough. A mattress, under the declining angle of a staircase. A candle, a glass of wine, a little heap of old newspapers. Ivy's bed? No one would mind. Begin again in the morning. She lay down and fell asleep.

A man stood over her. Her father? No. Too heavy, he moved wrong, he didn't belong there any more than she did, and when he saw her he only sighed.

Sometime later someone held her arm and slipped a cold and silvery needle in. It made her shake, and there was a silvery taste at the back of her throat.

She sat up slowly. Her back ached, and her head ached. Where was she? Not at home—not at home at all.

A little makeshift bedroom, under the stairs. Like a servant's nook, or a refugee's squat.

A man sat on a three-legged stool at the foot of the bed. He appeared to be doing a newspaper crossword puzzle.

"Miss Low." The newspaper lowered—the date, the place names, briefly glimpsed, had been impossible—and behind it was a badly burned face, an ill-fitting black suit, two piercing lavender eyes. "You look so very much like Ivy. Which one are you?"

"Brace-Bel!"

"No. *I* am Brace-Bel." The burned man shuddered and closed his eyes. "There are too many mirrors here, and sometimes I feel myself watching myself with displeasure. It's easy to become confused here. I remain however Brace-Bel. Are you Ruth or are you Marta?"

"Yes. Ruth, I mean."

There were footsteps outside in the corridor. Brace-Bel rolled up his newspaper and held it as if it was a weapon. The footsteps receded, and he relaxed. "Ivy wasn't sure who would answer the call. Ruth it is, then. Can you stand?"

"Yes. What happened . . . "

"Ivy's medicines. There are laboratories here. Engines of making. I understand it all depends on the will, or the imagination. I have little left of either. Your sister has a message for you." He unrolled the newspaper again, and read from a snarl of jagged handwriting on the corner: "'I told you to stay on the path, touch nothing, don't be followed. Hope you've learned your lesson. This game has rules.'" He rerolled the newspaper. "There you go. She's impatient today. Stand, then, and come quickly."

"This isn't my house, is it, Brace-Bel?"

"In a manner of speaking you are heir to it. But it is no house. Speaking of mirrors—do not look in them. They are prisons, traps. The old man keeps souls locked away in them. A friendly warning."

The footsteps returned outside.

"Come quickly. Ivy needs you. No place here is safe."

He rapped with the newspaper on a brass pipe that ran along the edge of the skirting. The wall shook, releasing white dust from the ceiling, and a door opened.

Brace-Bel

How long ago was it, weeks ago now, years perhaps, time being different within the Mountain, in the play of its electric fields and monstrous pressures—how long ago was it that Brace-Bel ascended into the light?

The fire had played around his feet. The glow of molten metal had scribed the outline of a door in the wall before him, and he'd fallen through, staggering, believing himself dead, through sparks and gouts of flame, through foul smoke, and he had burned. He had felt his flesh burn away. Weightlessly, he ascended on the wind. That, he'd thought, was how stars were made. And as a greasy glowing cloud he'd stretched across the sky—could he make it rain? Wouldn't it be wonderful if he could make it rain on the city? —until the jagged peaks of the Mountain snagged him, fishhooklike, and dragged him down, and down again. He'd had the sensation of being stretched and dragged through monstrous gears, ground away, refined from the stuff of *that* world to the stuff of *this,* and still always down, and down, terrible pressure gathering around him, until he was tumbling through hot brick and soot, through a *chimney,* and he rolled naked and scorched out through the coals of the fireplace, past the black iron grating, at Ivy's feet.

"Get up," she said. "Get up, Brace-Bel. Stop your screaming."

Was he screaming? Well, why not? Be fair.

"He'll be here in a moment. Get up, and come with me. I just took a big chance on you, Brace-Bel."

He followed her. His burned feet pained him, and he left bloody prints on the grimy carpet. She led him up what seemed like dozens of flights of stairs. (Had he really been a star? A cloud? Already the memory was fading, uncertain—an ambiguity in the translation from Below to Above, from life to death.) She opened various hidden doors, the last of which led into what appeared to be a neatly furnished spare bedroom. She sat cross-legged on the edge of the grey-white bed, took off her shoes, and rubbed her feet as if she, not him, had had the harder day. Released of the need to follow her or be lost in Hell, he fell on the floor.

"He won't let me do *that* again," she said. "Ha! You'd better be worth it, Brace-Bel. Now that he knows that little trick's possible, he'll put a stop to it. Just watch. Just watch."

Indeed, when Brace-Bel ventured outside the bedroom, outside Ivy's wards and locks, the first thing he noticed was that Shay's servants had boarded up all the fireplaces.

Maury

And Maury had stumbled into darkness. The servants held him under his arms, dragging him, his legs dangling helplessly. They carried him as you might carry a suicide out of the cell in which he'd hung himself. Maury's throat was tight. He could almost feel the noose. They walked for hours, maybe days, and he heard the servants murmur, grumble, unlock and lock the doors, disarm and rearm the traps. Finally he was lowered onto a cold metal slab. *This is all right,* he thought, *it's not so bad being dead.* The rattle of sharp instruments on a steel tray. The hum of machinery. An old man's hacking cough. Numb, indifferent, he waited for the knife; the autopsy; the cause of death. Whose fault was it all? It didn't matter much anymore, did it? That was the best thing about it.

"Yes. The Know-Nothing. The Inspector. Yes. My darling daughter's little friend. What's his name?"

A harsh voice, a voice Maury remembered. The old man. *Shay.* The whisper of the servants answered.

"Maury? *Maury*. Ha. Blind, is he? He'll do. Got no arm. He'll be grateful, then, maybe. About bloody time someone was grateful to me! Eyes first. Let's get you some new eyes. Any preferences?"

Maury said nothing—he was dead, after all. It wouldn't have been proper.

"Cat? Come on, Inspector. Lizard? Bird? Cat's good for shadows. Bird's good for things that move too quick or too slow. Lizard's good for secrets. Come on, come on. I haven't got all day. While we're down here she's scheming against me upstairs. Turning my servants against me. Stealing my keys and spying on my secrets. Interfering with things she doesn't understand. You were one of the ones who brought her here, Inspector. You ruined everything. That bloody woman! You're going to help me put this right. Cat's got your tongue? Cat, then. You, you, and you: hold him down. This is going to hurt."

Brace-Bel

Brace-Bel had no idea who was winning. The struggle between father and daughter took place on levels that he comprehended only dimly. As best he could tell they were in a position of bitter stalemate. Sometimes they brushed against each other in the corridors, as they went about their business. He snarled; she sneered; sparks flew.

It was all to do with control of the machines. Brace-Bel knew very well that the Mountain was not what it appeared to be. Shay had occupied the Mountain for so many long lonely years that he had shaped it around himself, like a worn and grimy sweater, like a favorite armchair; but, though it now took the outward form of a vast and appallingly ugly, old, and empty house, the machines were sometimes visible beneath the facade. The pipes that crawled the walls like bulging veins—the valves and diodes that grew like mushrooms in dark corners—the wires that bunched and knotted from the ceilings—the gears—all spoke of the Mountain's true function. Those delicate incomprehensible machines! Those were the machines that made the city. Brace-Bel spent many of the timeless hours of his afterlife with his head pressed against the warm copper of the plumbing pipes, listening to the churn of creation; or staring into the glare of an electric bulb, the black filament like the seed of universes, until the afterimages of whorish scarlet angels were

burned on his eyes. Sometimes out of the corner of his eye, or
through the cracks in the curtains, he thought he could glimpse the
machine's true immense architecture: a spiral, a lattice, a mesh of
gears of light, a necklace of vast and glistening pearls, greater than
worlds. A vast machine. The engine of creation, left behind by the
Builders of the city, spinning endlessly, idly.

He tried to imagine those Builders. He couldn't picture them.
He imagined pillars of intelligent fire; vast silver-winged women;
tower-tall scientists in white coats; misshapen gargantua, ogreish
gaolers, clinking golden keys the size of tree trunks, soaked in seas
of blood and oil. None of those guesses convinced him. His imagination was unequal to the task.

"Who made this?" he asked Ivy, over and over again. "Who made
this? Who built the city? What beautiful terrifying creatures?" She
wouldn't tell him. She smiled and told him to be patient. The secret
of it was one of the many, many, infinitely many things that she held
over him, to keep him in her service.

The old Brace-Bel would have raged at the Builders, would have
fought past the doors of the Mountain to spit in their unthinkable
eyes; but he was too tired now, and too old, and too lost. He was con-
tent to wait and see what was revealed to him.

He subsisted on cheese and fine wines, which Ivy had her servants steal for him from Shay's pantries. The finest wines in the city,
hoarded, going to waste! He drank and laughed too eagerly at all
Ivy's jokes. He went out spying for her. Following her instructions,
he made certain precise adjustments to the machinery, the purpose
of which he didn't understand.

She controlled most of the upper floors now, and the east wing.
Shay controlled the cellars, the west, the echoing halls of the ground
floor. Day by day, room by room, she turned more of Shay's machines
against him. She was knotted into the control of the Mountain now.
In the lower floors it was always twilight, the way Shay liked it, but
in the upper floors it was a cold and bright morning—Ivy said it
helped her think. She lay on the bed and counted the cracks on the
ceiling and plotted out her strategy. Dozens of Shay's little surgical
abominations followed her—adored her—nuzzled against her and
begged to serve her. The loyalties of Shay's Hollow Servants were divided. When father and daughter passed in the corridors they were
each flanked by shadowy phalanxes.

Ruth

"Who's winning?" Brace-Bel shrugged. "I don't know. Come on, come on." He flapped his hands, gesturing Ruth toward a splintery ladder. "Up, up. He can't kill her, she can't kill him. The machines are too delicate. She's begun processes that he can't repair. He knows things she's only beginning to learn. The whole thing might fall apart and then where would we all be?" He spoke quickly, nervously, his usual orotund manner deserting him, as if the shadows of the house depressed him. There was a knocking behind the walls; perhaps they were being followed?

She climbed the ladder. At the top Brace-Bel took the lead again, shuttling back and forth through empty rooms and bare corridors. "And the Hollows are less useful than you might think." Brace-Bel patted his pockets. "There are charms and wards. Lines they can't cross." He withdrew a glittering crystal from his pocket. "Ivy gave it to me. The Hollows fear its light. I used to have a stone very much like it. I kept it on the handle of my stick, and I thought it very fine and rare. But her father has a hundred of them. There is or was or will be a district called Islegh where they mine these things, or mill them, or I forget what. Not special. Seen from here, nothing in the city is special."

He tapped with his toe on a little brass grille in the skirting. There was a slithering scrabbling dusty sound, and a small scarred monkey emerged from the hole. Brace-Bel said, "Which way today?" The monkey limped off down the corridors, and Brace-Bel followed. "Things change," Brace-Bel explained. "You'd be lost here by yourself."

The monkey led them up narrow staircases, through attic rooms where dust spun in the sunlight, slowly, as if thinking. "Who knows what she's got planned for you? Some scheme, some strategy. Maybe she thinks your father won't hurt you. Maybe she thinks you can get close. I don't know. She doesn't tell me. I do as she says."

They followed the monkey through room after room of bathrooms: claw-foot tubs, slippery tiled floor, cold stagnant air, and the choke and hiss of overburdened plumbing. Mildewed doors swung, faded curtains rustled. The pattern on the tiles was green and yellow, like moss.

Ruth said, "Are you happy here, Brace-Bel?"

"I'm sorry?"

"Are you happy? You seemed so proud, when I met you before.

You thought you were so clever. You were, too, you really were, though I didn't like you much. You can't be happy serving my sister, in this horrible place, not understanding anything."

Brace-Bel turned to her. His head was framed by rusting pipes, and he stooped beneath them. His burned face wore an expression of genuine surprise. "Why do you ask?"

"I don't know, Brace-Bel. Maybe I'm sorry for you. You didn't deserve to get caught up in all this, did you? You were probably all right in your own place, before we ruined you. Never mind. Never mind. I don't mean to be rude. Let's go see Ivy."

He shook his head. He seemed to be about to say something.

Maury

Shay should have killed her at once, the bitch Ivy, killed her when she'd first set foot on the Mountain. That was what Maury thought. That was what Maury thought because that was what Shay had said, muttering, snarling, all through the operation, and during the grey days that came after, when Shay hunched in his chair and Maury scuttled around at his feet, cleaning, fetching, serving, adjusting the wheels and the levers of the machinery. Now, as Maury skulked and spied through the corridors of the terrible house, the old man's words echoed in his head, scraped his skull. *I should have killed her.* He should have hollowed her out, stolen her memories, thrown her back down. He could have done it then, when she was new, when her position was vulnerable. But he'd been soft. He'd been sentimental. Now it was too late—now she had servants, she had control of the machinery. That was the problem with family, with women; they made you weak. Often at that point Shay started to weep, and Maury turned his scarred face away in embarrassment; but the old man's point was basically sound, Maury thought. And when he saw the new woman, that little copy of Ivy, creeping around the house, he knew there was no room for delay. The thing had to be done *now*. So he followed her, and the fat man. He could go where the Hollows couldn't. He didn't know why. And he waited for his moment, and he drew his knife—Shay's servants had armed him with a meat cleaver from the kitchens, very useful, very nice indeed—and stepping from the shadows he buried it in the fat man's back. The fat man's words were replaced with blood. *Was* he happy? Was he fucking happy? Who cared? They were all beyond happiness or unhappiness now. They were dead, at the end of the world. Nothing left but strength and fear. He worked the knife loose from the wound. The woman was screaming, running. The Inspector's new eyes were particularly good at watching *prey*.

Ruth

Brace-Bel, jerking, bleeding, lifted the glittering crystal and waved it vaguely under his attacker's nose, as if trying to tempt him with sweets. The attacker, all too substantial, ignored it. The cleaver struck again and the crystal rolled off under a bathtub.

Ruth ran.

The murderer's face had been terribly wrong—the scars, his yellow monstrous eyes. He wore torn leathers, rags, what appeared to be an old bedsheet. His left arm was a stump that jerked spastically.

The Inspector—Maury—was it possible? Was he real, or a creation of the machines, her father's will, Ivy's mean streak and vivid imagination?

She ran and slid on the wet tiles. Nearly falling, she pulled herself upright on a cold pipe, threw doors open, pushed through damp curtains. Boots stamped behind her. She panted, moaned. He was silent.

A long room of wooden washtubs, in ranks along the walls. Green-black water. Air that choked. The floorboards thick with moss. Her feet slipped and she regained her balance, at the cost of a shooting pain in her calf, a stab of sick-making adrenaline. She froze, too scared to go further.

Behind her the Inspector stamped, grunted, slid with a sad flatulent squeak, and landed with a thump and a crack.

She turned. He'd caught his head on the edge of one of the washtubs. He was kneeling, trying to stand; his missing arm flailed for purchase, as if he'd forgotten his wound.

His face was down, his eyes not visible. That made it easier.

She put her hands on his shoulders as if she were comforting him as he cried. His body was warm, solid, real. She leaned her weight on him. It was that easy; she didn't even have to push. She did it without thinking. His face went into the green water. His knees scrabbled for purchase on the slimy floor. It took too long, and she had time to think. Time to gasp in sympathy with his pained thrashing. But she didn't let up until he stopped moving.

Not real. That was what she decided to believe. Nothing in that house was real. It was all just moves in an unpleasant game.

R uth retraced her steps. Brace-Bel's body was gone, though smears of blood remained.

She groped under the bathtub, and recovered the crystal.

Where was the monkey, her guide? Vanished. She was alone. All around her the house creaked and strained, pulled this way and that by incomprehensible machinery.

S he wandered through the house, the crystal held out in front of her like a lantern. Its light waxed and waned unpredictably. Whispers and murmurs followed behind her. Shadows leaned from the walls, taking brief form, watching her go past. Cobwebs shook themselves and became pale servants, their fingers reaching tentatively for her, only to be stung by the light; they stared after her resentfully.

Oh, everything was so terribly familiar! That was the worst thing. She walked through her own memories. She might have been dreaming. The house she'd grown up in, endlessly repeated, made nightmarish. That mantelpiece stood in the drawing room—the paint was faded where the sunlight hit it. That was the door to the kitchen—the knob rattled loosely, ever since . . . That corner where a conflux of roof beams made odd angles—that was in the bedroom she'd once shared with Ivy, and shadows had *always* gathered there.

Her father had made the Mountain this way—this was a mask that he'd hung on its true unthinkable form. All the things her father must have seen, all the places he'd been! But in his old age he returned to his beginnings—and not happily, not fondly, but bitterly, full of shame at his own failure.

She thought of Arjun. Was he still alive? She wished she'd never brought him with her. She was ashamed to have him see this.

The crystal had sharp points. She used it to scratch her name on the plaster of the walls; maybe he'd see it, maybe he'd find her, maybe they could save each other.

✻ ✻ ✻

A radio. Creeping, shivering, the sound of static, carried strangely through the thin walls, the pipes, the wires. Were those voices? Not exactly. Certainly not music. Information of a kind Ruth would never be able to understand. Its source was unclear. It bounced, echoed, refracted in shadow.

A man coughing, swearing. *Bloody woman. Cow. What's she done this time?*

The noise came from the corridor to Ruth's left, past glowering gaslamps, and a bare wooden door. The door to the old back room, at the Low house, where her father had kept his accounts.

All right, then. All right.

She knocked on the door. The radio went silent—no other answer. She pushed it open.

There he was. Sitting, watching the door, in an armchair, the radio and a knife and a clock with spiderish hands on the low table next to him. A frail and sunken man, dressed in a slate-grey suit, his white hair a ghostly nimbus around a withered face. The room was ill-lit, densely crowded with paintings and mirrors and photographs and dusty treasures.

He stood, slowly, creaking and unfolding, and she knew that he was real.

"You got so old," she said. "What happened to you? Where did you go?"

He looked her up and down, his bloodshot eyes wide with shock, and for a moment he appeared close to tears. Then his eyes narrowed again, and he sat back down. A sneer twisted his face. "So which one are you? It's like a bloody bus station in here these days. Why did you come here? Why can't you all leave me alone?"

She crossed the floor. The carpet, ash-scarred, ancient, was a map of something abstract. She swept the clock and the knife off the table, leaving tracks in the dust, and sat down by the side of the old man's chair. He winced at the noise. She put her hand on his arm. "Haven't you been alone long enough?"

He squeezed her wrist with bony fingers, hard enough to hurt. "Your young man was just here," he sneered. "He didn't ask after you. If you came for my blessing you can fuck off."

He laughed until he started coughing again.

TWENTY-SEVEN

The Demon King—Father and Daughter—Haggling

Arjun

The servants had dragged Arjun up the stairs, out of the cellars. Frozen by their touch, he couldn't resist. His feet dragged numbly in the dust. Shay followed behind, his cane clicking, cursing. *Why won't you leave me alone? What do you want? You can't have it. I rule alone here.*

They'd thrown Arjun on the floor at the foot of Shay's armchair. Warmth had slowly returned to his limbs. He'd stood, shaking like a newborn calf. The room was unlit, as if everyone in the house had gone to bed. The old man had pointed his cane again. *I've been here before,* Arjun thought. *The mirror is a trap, everything is a trap, or a device, or a weapon, or an implement of torture . . .*

Shay, again, and perhaps for the last time. This one was an elderly man, withered down to bones and bitterness. His cheeks were hollow and his yellow teeth, which he bared as he sneered, were abnormally thin and sharp. A broken nose. A grey suit, a faded handkerchief in his pocket. The skin of one hand was burned. The skin of the other was liver-spotted and thin and grey as death. His eyes were bloodshot. For a moment Arjun felt a kind of pity for the man. There was something ingrown, bitter, and unhappy about him that was both embarrassing and pitiful. Then he saw the hollow and shadowy servants that hovered behind Shay's chair, brushing their fingers gently through his spiderweb hair, smoothing down the shoulders of his suit, murmuring in his ear, awaiting his orders. The man was a monster. The yellow smile and twisted features of a demon king.

Was this the first—was this Mr. Low? —or was it a copy?

Did it matter?

"Don't do anything stupid," Shay said. "I know that stupid look in your eye. Don't get heroic notions. You people! Where do they keep finding you people?"

"You have to die, Shay." The Hollows perked up their pale heads.

"Maybe! Maybe! But it won't be you who kills me."

"You sent the airships. You sent your servants. You murdered the city."

"What? Oh. Yes. You didn't leave me much choice, did you? Bringing that woman here. Ruining everything. I'd been too kind for too long. Time to clear the rubbish away."

"I've killed you before, Shay. I can do it again."

"Not me. Not me. Very inferior copies. A hazard of too much travel, overcomplex affairs, is that you collect shadows. You killed a few? Excellent. Thins the herd. Fewer to make trouble for me. Sit down. Sit down. No, on the floor. *Don't* make me tell my servants . . . Thank you."

Cross-legged on the carpet. The carpet's pattern was abstract, intricate, mechanical, a snarl of dark threads.

"Who sent you here?"

"No one. Ivy showed me the way. I came alone."

"Why did you really come here? You don't look quite stupid enough to be taken in by my daughter's poor-little-princess-please-save-me routine. And don't pretend you care what I do to that slum down below."

"When I was a boy, long ago, I lived in a town in the mountains, far to the south. We had a God of music, and it ordered our lives, gave meaning and beauty to our days. One day it vanished. I chased it all this way, to the city and beyond. Is it here? Did you steal it, Shay?"

"Maybe. Maybe. I have machines here that can do that. I've collected a lot of interesting machines, over the years. Sometimes I find it useful to acquire those energies. They make good fuel. They make good bargaining chips. Do you know what the Gods are?"

"I don't care to hear your philosophies, Shay. Is it here?"

"This isn't philosophy, it's cold fact. Do I fucking look philosophical?

Energies of creation, that's just what they are, that's how the Builders made them, this Mountain commands them, spins and weaves them, sparks from the friction when the city's angles rub together, oil for the Gears, little fragments of making . . ."

"I don't care, Shay. I prefer not to believe what you say. Can you blame me? Why won't you answer my question? Is it here?"

"Maybe. I've hoarded a lot of treasures over the years. Anything that wanders too close to the Mountain goes in my nets. I don't need them making trouble, opening doors where there shouldn't be doors. That bloody daughter of mine let a lot of them loose when she started fiddling with the machines—yours wasn't one of them? No? Well. *Well.* I can have a look for you, if you like."

"That's very generous of you, Shay."

"Rummage in the attics." Shay didn't smile.

"Will you?"

"If we can make a deal."

"Why would you make a deal with me?"

"My daughter, you fool. She's ruining everything. Too clever, too clever, I always was afraid of her. Should have strangled her in her bed. Wards and sigils and locks. She's taken over half the bloody Mountain. If this goes on the whole thing might fall apart. I need your help. I need you to go to Ivy. I *need* your help—I'm admitting my weaknesses here, you little shit of a thief. Take it as an earnest of good fucking faith! Take her a little present. Help me, and we'll see about a deal."

"Ivy brought me here. I think I was supposed to help her against you."

"So? Renegotiate. You left loyalty behind long ago. Our kind has none of the ordinary virtues. Cultivate flexibility instead."

They haggled. Shadows gathered. And as Arjun left the room, it seemed that Shay sagged, and paled, and only his servants held his thin head up, as if the haggling had taken the last of the old man's strength. He left Shay in the dark, listening to the empty noise of his radio.

Ruth

"What did you do to him?"

Shay bent almost double in his chair, wheezing, groaning. He dabbed at his mouth with a stained handkerchief. His spine protruded through the worn fabric of his jacket, curved like a dog's, frail and painful. It hurt to look at him, so Ruth turned away, and looked all around the room. On one wall there was a large and dusty mirror—she recalled Brace-Bel's warning, and looked away from it. The rest of the room was cluttered with trinkets and devices. Low tables stood at angles like fortifications, carrying weapons, charms, machines. He seemed to have a fondness for fertility idols, dull-pointed weapons, tin soldiers, dirty postcards, stuffed animals in postures of terror or rage. Everything was close to hand. How long had he sat here? His bony fingers had worn tracks in the dust, his shuffling feet had worn shiny trails across the carpet. He was present timelessly in the room; she could almost see the years of his operation of the room's devices. Somehow he controlled the Mountain from that chair. He maintained his defenses, he hoarded his treasures, he took his revenge. The room stank of fear and madness. It was the center of the world, the center of her memories and nightmares.

"He works for you?" Shay said. She started, turned back to him. He still wouldn't meet her eyes. "He works for me now. We made a deal."

"You shouldn't have. He's naïve."

"Why did you come here?"

She put a hand on his bent shoulder, more out of curiosity than sympathy—he was dry, weightless, fragile.

"I wanted to see you. I wanted to know if it was true."

"Now you know." He shuddered. "Now you know."

"Yes."

"You think it would have been better if I'd taken you with me? Think you could have lived this way? Is that what you think?"

"I don't know what I think. It's too late, isn't it? You're not really a person anymore, are you?"

"You don't know how hard it is. The things I had to do, the deals I had to make. It's not easy, is it? It's never easy. One thing leads to another."

"I know."

"You lose bits of yourself. You get caught up in your own lies. All over the place. It's like being sick. It's like a cancer, eating at you. Hundreds of them, thousands of them, scheming against me. All I do is hide. It's horrible to be your own worst enemy."

"Is it?"

"I stole this thing. The Mountain. I lied and killed for it. Do you want to know who I took it from, who he took it from, what he took it from, what it *is*?"

"Maybe. What's the price?"

"Oh, you're clever. You're a clever one. Which one are you?"

"Ruth, Dad. It's Ruth."

"Right. Right." His head was still bent. "I can't look at you. Why did you have to come here? Why did you have to remind me?"

Was he crying?

"You sent the airships. You tried to kill the city. Do you remember?"

"Oh, maybe. Maybe. Your young man was whining about that. What choice did I have? Things look different from up here."

"I'm sure they do."

His shoulders shook. Her hand wasn't far from his scrawny throat. She was inside his defenses. Had he let her in knowingly? What did he want her to do?

She could kill him; he was frail. She should kill him. She heard Arjun's voice, sounding so stern and serious—*he has to die. He cannot be allowed to keep the Mountain.*

His shoulders shook, the way the Inspector had struggled as she held him down.

She couldn't do it again. Not because he was her father—that had not been true for a long time, she realized—but because he was a human being, and old, and weak, and afraid. After the Inspector, she couldn't pretend that it would be easy.

She had so much to ask—*What was so important that you had to leave us? Was it worth it?*—but his answers would only be self-serving lies.

She walked away. He clutched at her shirt. "Wait—wait. Where are you going? I need your help. You're the kind one, you were always my favorite. That Ivy, she's trouble, she's too clever, you have to help me . . . What do you want? What do you want?"

"Oh, be quiet." She brushed away his hand. "You don't have anything I want. The two of you deserve each other."

The servants murmured in awe and terror as she passed through them. She closed the door behind her.

Arjun

Two forces of servants fought at the stairhead. Arjun couldn't tell Ivy's from Shay's. Their numbers were uncountable—they seemed evenly balanced. Surging and retreating, clawing and tearing, grey and flickering. No words, no shouts, no screams—only a noise like wind rattling through the eaves of an old house. Arjun waited at the foot of the stairs until they exhausted themselves. Afterward, the tiles of the stairhead were strewn with scraps of shadow like leaves.

One, two, three; take the fourth corridor on the left. The ladder, the stairs again. Shay's directions; Arjun had committed them carefully to memory.

He carried one of Shay's wards, and the servants stayed clear of him. They glared in disapproval. They shook their heads. Did they envy him? There but for his undeserved luck . . . "Brothers," he said. "I'm sorry." They didn't stop resenting him.

Ivy's part of the house was marked out by sigils painted on the walls, lines scratched in the floorboards, circles in the dust. There was something infantile about it—a child's marking out of territory. KEEP OUT. KNOCK FIRST. TOP SECRET. MINE.

He knocked. She answered. He went in.

Brace-Bel

Downstairs, in the darkened hallways, Brace-Bel staggered through a forest of pillars. When he stumbled he pulled himself along by the wires and tubes that knotted on the floor. He wasn't sure where he was going. It seemed too late, too late to reinvent himself *again*; his small store of genius was exhausted. He thought it would be nice to find somewhere warm to sit, in the sunshine.

The servants followed at a discreet distance, cleaning his blood from the floorboards.

The machinery hummed all around him, and it sounded like music. He thought it would be nice to see fire again, and beauty, before he died.

There were footsteps approaching. He slumped to the floor and took out his little pocketknife, and began sawing weakly at the cables. The footsteps came closer, and stopped. The cable in his hand snapped, golden coils sprung out, a shower of sparks rose up, and another cascaded from overhead. Small fires ran along the ceiling. As his vision ebbed, the cables in his lap glowed with the red light of a violent birth. His first memory! A perfect circle. Someone stood over him, now, a man, and a familiar voice said, "That's going to make things a bit more difficult, isn't it?" Then his head fell forward into his lap, and he felt nothing.

Arjun

Ivy conducted her business from a single bedroom. The room was sparely furnished, but clean. Morning light forced its way through shuttered windows, slicing precise diagonals through the closed space, defining angular shadows. The walls were pinned with maps, diagrams, mathematics, ciphers and codes, sketches of the gears of impossible machines, plans for new languages. Sharp instruments lay in a row on a well-organized desk. Ivy herself, sitting on a plain wooden chair, in a long black dress, her bare arm resting on the desk, seemed for a moment only one of the instruments in the room, only a part of the machine.

There was something flat about her. Her eyes were full of calculation, estimation, contempt. Her charm had deserted her. She was beautiful like a statue. The stress of her struggle had reduced her severely.

She said, "Where's my sister?"

"I don't know."

"You weren't supposed to come, you know. What use are you to me? There are hundreds just like you, and none of you are worth a damn. I wanted my sisters."

"I'm sorry if I spoiled your plans."

"Never mind. Never mind." She rubbed her temples. "I can make do. I have another sister, after all. What do you want, anyway?"

"Can I sit?"

She waved him vaguely toward the bed. Her fingers were covered in rings and charms. Strange marks were scribbled on her palms.

"He sent me to kill you."

"Did he now? How were you going to do that?"

"He gave me this," Arjun said. He took a small black stone from his pocket. "He told me to come to you, offer my services to you, and hide this in your room. I don't know what it does, how it kills. I imagine it's horrible."

"I expect so."

"I doubt he trusted me. I imagine he hid other weapons on me, things I didn't know about."

"I expect so. He's not as clever as he thinks he is. He was first. That's really all he's got going for him. First to Break Through. But that's just luck, isn't it? That's just a matter of wanting it more than anyone else. Doesn't make him clever."

"Are you winning?"

"Maybe. Bit by bit. It could take a very long time."

"Will there be anything left of the city when you've won, do you think?"

"Well, I'm not really sure. But I can always make another. If I choose. I expect I will. It will be a fascinating exercise."

He looked again at the maps on the walls. Their geometries were rigid, unsympathetic. A plan for a tower, coiled, elongated, pierced by bridges, suggested repressed pain, outward cruelty. The scale of her design was both vast and claustrophobic. "I see," he said.

"What do you want?"

"Will there be music in your city?"

She looked at him with interest for the first time. "I remember. You lost a musical thing. A God. Is that right?"

"Don't tell me what you think it *really* is—please."

"I'm very fond of music, too. In my way. What does it sound like? Is it pretty?"

"Yes. Is it here?"

"Maybe. The city runs on music, you know."

"So I've always thought. Others think differently."

"It depends on your definition of music. Most of it isn't very pretty at all. It's a question of what you can find beauty in. What you're willing to face."

"Is it here?"

"It may be. There are vaults. Down below. The old man hid things away. Will you be very angry if I say they're only *things*?"

"I won't be angry."

"There are keys to the vaults. I know the way. Help me, Arjun."

"Is that the price? Murder your father?"

"Get rid of him. Get him out of the way. Don't you think it's time? Help me and I'll set your God loose. Fly free, you know? There's not enough music in the world. I'm on your side, really, and you're on mine. Help me."

Her face was flat, monstrous. Her eyes were the dull green of rusted metal. Her voice never wavered, and every word out of her mouth was blasphemy. Arjun was sick of haggling.

"I won't," he said. "It's not worth the price. It never ends."

As he left, she shrugged and turned back to her desk, without another word, as if she'd lost interest in him entirely.

Arjun

In the corridors outside, the wires in the ceiling pulsed and sparked. The pipes groaned. Cracks opened in the plaster, the drawers in the sideboards fell open, and a fractal stain blossomed on the carpet.

A troupe of Shay's monkeys scuttled frantically up the stairs, darting in and out of the balusters, scrabbling along the handrail; they leapt and passed Arjun by.

And the servants stepped from shadow to shadow and their long weightless fingers brushed the cracks clear and swept away shattered glass and china.

The strains of Ivy and her father's struggle, Arjun thought, shaking the Mountain at last.

What would happen when the whole thing fell apart? Would the Gods fly free from the wreckage, make the world anew? Or would they die with it? It seemed there was nothing to do but wait and see.

The sound of straining machinery had ceased; then it started up again. The engines suffered . . .

"Come in, come in."

The voice came from a room to his left; the door was open.

"Come in. Don't just stand there."

It was Shay, again, but . . . Shay stood by the far wall with his hands in his pockets, examining the pipes that twined around each other in the corners of the room. He was young, again—a man in his thirties, plump, pink-faced, his floppy grey-white hair only a little balding—dressed in baggy clothes, corduroy and tweed. He might have walked only yesterday out of Ruth's old photograph of the Low family. His eyes gleamed.

"Wonderful, isn't it?"

"Mr. Low?"

"It's been a while since I used that name. These days I mostly go by *Cuttle,* or *Shay,* or . . ."

"Cuttle, then."

"I know *you,* Arjun. I've been watching you for a long time, now. You and that daughter of mine. Ever since that old bastard sent you tumbling back down the Mountain! I *knew* my clever, clever girl might find you a way back."

"And you followed? I thought I heard someone following us."

"I never could have done it on my own. I needed someone on the inside to find the safe path through all those traps. I needed someone cleverer than me. There! I've admitted it. I'm admitting my weaknesses here; take it as an earnest of good faith!"

"What do you want from me, Cuttle?"

"Look at this thing! Isn't it wonderful? I can tell you what it's for, if you're curious. I can tell you who built it. What it *does.* How all the city *hangs* from it! I can tell you, if you make it worth my while."

"I don't want to make any more deals, Cuttle."

"Were you in the old bastard's room? The one where he drifts away his days? What was in it?"

"I don't know. Photographs, lamps, a mantelpiece."

"Describe the photographs. What was on the mantelpiece?"

"I don't know. I don't remember. I wasn't really looking."

"It's a miracle you survived this long and got half this far." Cuttle sighed. "My problem is this. Here I am *inside,* the consummation of all my dreams and wishes and scheming, the greatest and most secret treasure in all the city almost—*almost*—in my grasp, and I can*not* seize it. I cannot wait. I cannot *stand* to wait for it. That old bastard doesn't know how to enjoy it—it should be mine *now.* But he's cunning, oh yes, I don't get *less* cunning with the years and my travels. So," he shrugged and smiled disarmingly, "I find myself stuck in these worthless upper floors. Below there are traps. How many? What kind? I have no fucking idea. But they must be there—if *I'd* held this place all this time I'd have trapped it. And of course I *did,* in a manner of speaking. I don't dare go on. I need intelligence. I need an ally. So do you, Arjun. So I thought we could make a deal."

Arjun started to laugh; Cuttle pretended to join in, though it was clear he didn't see the joke.

"Ivy's cleverer than me," Cuttle explained. "The old man's older and he knows more and he's had fuck knows how long to learn this machine's secrets. Why would you help me? Because I'm desperate. I *need* you. The others don't, really. I'm weak, that means you can trust me. Help me and when I hold the Mountain I'll give you whatever you want . . ."

"No, Cuttle, no. No more deals."

The man's smile stiffened and soured.

And Arjun went wandering the house, calling out Ruth's name, listening for the echo of his God, watching the disintegration of the machines. Something now was very wrong and getting worse, a discord echoing back and forth through the pipes and wires. What were they doing to the machines?

He found his way back to Shay's room by accident. He entered before he knew where he was.

The old man lay in his armchair with his head back, his mouth slack, his throat slit from ear to ear, his grubby shirt bright with gore, his lap a pool of blood, his thin fingers twisted and stiff as if he had tried to fight.

The servants hovered uncertainly.

Bloody footprints led across the carpet to the mantelpiece, where a skinny little man with razor-stubble white hair in an outsized black coat rooted frantically with bloody hands among the photographs and dusty bric-a-brac, swearing and muttering to himself, *no, no, not this, nothing, fuck, the old bastard, not this, what the fuck is this?*

The man turned as he heard Arjun cross the threshold. His face was Shay's. Neither the oldest nor the youngest iteration of that face Arjun had ever seen. Someone had once broken his nose, and his cheeks and eyes were sunken—this was not the happiest or most prosperous of Shay's shadow lives. Even now, in victory, he looked bitter, resentful. His sharp vicious eyes sized Arjun up; he smiled thinly and said, "*There* you are. You and those daughters of mine did a good job leading me here." His hand hovered near the long knife at his belt. "So I'll give you a chance, how about this, I'll give you a chance to be on the winning side. You were helping my daughter—Ivy, not the other one—you must know a thing or two about how this works. Tell me everything you know. Bring Ivy to me. Call me Mr. Shay, Arjun; this is going to be *my* house soon. So let's make a deal."

Behind the walls, the machines were going mad. Blood dripped from the murdered man's sleeve onto the carpet. The pipes throbbed and moaned and shrieked; the floor shook and one of the clocks tumbled off the mantelpiece. Shay-with-the-knife snarled and angrily swept the photographs onto the floor after it.

Shaking his head—not taking his eyes off the angry little murderer—Arjun backed out of the room.

"You'll regret this! You'll regret this, you little shit! When I'm in charge here you'll . . ."

The noise of the machines soon drowned out the man's ranting.

TWENTY-EIGHT
The Shadows Return–Little Murders–
The End of the World

Arjun

He found Ruth on one of the upper floors. She sat on a balcony made of marble, on a stone bench. Ivy's work—the sky above was cold and blue. It felt like morning. Nothing was visible below except grey clouds. Did the city still exist?

A light rain fell on them as they embraced.

She'd been crying. She smiled now, weary and exhilarated. "I couldn't," she said. "I didn't."

He wasn't sure what she meant.

She leaned on the balcony. "It's over."

"Is it? He's dead, Ruth." She nodded, bit her lip. "Not my doing." He explained. "His shadows are returning now. We left the way open for them when we came. They were watching and waiting. They followed us home."

"Oh. How horrible. I suppose that was stupid of us."

"More will come."

"They're not my father. My father is dead."

"They're going to break everything. They're reckless."

"Shouldn't we try to stop them?"

"There's only two of us. There are more of him. I don't want to fight. I don't want to deal with them anymore. It poisons everything, the compromises you have to make. Nothing bought this way is worth having. Let them fight, let the sickness run its course.

Let the error resolve itself. Nothing can work right until they're gone."

A gunshot echoed in the house below.

"I want to see where he died," she said. "Then we can go home."

The servants were busy clearing away every trace of the murdered man. A hundred of them closed in overlapping together to lift the body with their pale insubstantial hands. Others drifted on their knees across the floor, picking with miniscule pointless unappreciated care the blood droplets from the carpet, while a second shadowy wave of servants rolled up the carpet itself. Like black feathers on a slowly beating wing yet more of them swept through the room taking up the photographs, and dismantling the clocks, and slipping the ugly little ornaments into their pockets, and slicing the paintings from their frames, and plying the frames apart. The servants unpicked the wallpaper, which had been vaguely yellow, and vaguely floral, and left behind stark concrete.

"His mirrors are prisons," Ruth said. "The Beast told me that. So did Brace-Bel. There are souls still in them. Should we . . . ?"

"Yes. I remember." Arjun took the dusty mirror down from the wall. A few of the servants tugged at it, but he pulled it from their feeble grip. They stared reproachfully at him as he carried it away. Ruth closed the door; the old man's room was bare and empty behind them.

A man stood at the end of the corridor, in a charcoal silk suit, no tie, small, wiry, prosperously neat, vainly smart, white hair in a short ponytail. "Too late, am I?" A complacent drawl. "I smell blood. I smell excitement. Did I miss the action?" He had Shay's face, but he introduced himself as *Mr. Cruickshank*. "Who invited *you*? This is a select gathering. Do you work here?" He removed a fold of vivid butterfly-green notes from his pocket, held in a golden clip, and he thumbed suggestively through them as if offering a tip to a doorman . . .

They couldn't find the way out. *Was* there a way out? The lower floors were full of steam, strange gases, collapsed pillars. Windowless, dark, the corridors turned inward. Buffeting pressures drummed on locked iron doors. Wires hung from the high ceilings, twitching like dreaming snakes. The machine was a closed system. It seemed to go on forever.

They went upstairs, instead, onto the highest floor they could find. The air was clean there, and the process of disintegration not yet begun. They found a small spare bedroom. They propped the prison-mirror up against the wall. Neither of them had any idea how to open it; perhaps it had something to do with the complex arabesques and intaglios carved and molded into the frame?

The war went on below them. It accelerated. The house changed minute by minute. There was no way out but there were countless ways in—copies stepped confidently from every open door. The shadows flocked home like birds, in gathering numbers.

They wrestled over control of the servants, made them into armies. They came with Beasts of all kinds, sharp-clawed, poisonous, cunning. The servants, confused and pathetic, torn this way and that by the claims of their countless masters, performed unnecessary tasks out of habit. They cleaned and dusted constantly. Every few minutes they absentmindedly brought little servings of dry bread and coffee up to Arjun and Ruth's hiding place.

Arjun went walking down through the corridors. He watched the place disintegrate.

The rivals fought over the machinery. They twisted it and tampered with it. For short-lived strategic advantage they broke delicate things older than the city and beyond their imaginations. Perhaps they were shortsighted. Perhaps the nasty logic of their situation left them no choice. Now Arjun saw them in every corridor, skulking, scheming.

He saw old friends from the Hotel—Abra-Melin of the shaking staff, and Longfellow of the hair shirt, and Cantor, who had no notable peculiarities. Gate crashers, late to the party, they were quickly cut down. He didn't see St. Loup. He saw people he didn't recognize at all—maybe there were other Hotels, other cliques and cabals. He saw a flock of someone's servants strangle Cantor with hands of shadow.

Moment by moment the Mountain was less and less like a house. There was very little furniture left, and no carpeting, and no curtains, and the floorboards rotted away to expose concrete, plastic, steel, hard alien substances with a dull unfriendly sheen. The walls were sometimes paper-thin and sometimes only arrangements of bars wrought from that alien almost-metal. There were no sconces on the sheer walls, no bulbs hung from the ceiling, and the dim light appeared to issue from the air itself—for the time being there was still air in most of the house. A maze of empty rooms; a machine of steel valves and chambers. Intestinal spills of cables sheeted in something like black rubber that stank of burning and bile. Steam shrieked from bent pipes. Strange and volatile liquids coursed down sharp channels, through glassy veins. The natural form of the hallways and chambers seemed to be roughly hexagonal; or sometimes curved, like a vast snail shell; or sometimes complex and unfolding, like a fern. An elaborate machinery extruded and snapped tightly into place. A mesh of bars and wires and gears and metal teeth. The Mountain, whatever it was, was slowly sloughing off the shabby domestic facade Shay-the-first-and-eldest had hung on it. An unearthly light shone from behind the walls. Arjun had a sense of some impossible vision battering against the form of the machine. The masks were coming off. The bars were breaking and the prisoners were ready to be released. He awaited the revelation.

Murder stalked the halls all afternoon. Temporary alliances formed and disintegrated. As far as Arjun could tell, Ivy seemed to be doing well in the struggle. She had an unusual number and strength of the servants at her command. Her servants fought her rivals' forces in the corridors. They did it dutifully and unhappily. They made a noise like birds' wings fluttering, like sick children sniveling. They canceled each other out. They *exhausted* each other, like a bitter drawn-out argument between people who were no longer friends. They left scraps of shadow in the corners.

Arjun found one of the Shays dead in an empty corridor, in a ripped business suit, torn to shreds by the claws of some great Beast. He saw a pipe burst and fire and steam swallow a corridor that contained the unfortunate Mr. Cuttle. He saw three Shays standing in an attic, pistols trained on each other, frozen, glaring, each caught in his own shadow's trap. He laughed. They snarled at him. It seemed to hurt their feelings. They took their predicament very seriously.

He met Ivy at a junction. She smiled distantly, tensely. He held out his empty hands. *I'm not playing.* She passed him by as if he wasn't there. A flock of servants followed her, whining and muttering.

Ruth

Ruth stayed in the little hideaway, and wrote. The servants, eager to please, brought her paper and pen. She sat on the bed, rested the mirror on her knees, and wrote until her fingers cramped.

It began as a letter to Marta. Why not? Perhaps she could throw it from the balcony, and it would flutter down through the clouds, and be picked up from a gutter somewhere. Or she could tie it to a bird's leg. Or a message in a bottle, like in the old fairy tales. So it began,

> *This letter is for Marta Low, from her sister. If you find this, whoever you are, if you know her, if she's still alive, please, please, pass this letter on to her. I can't promise you any payment but I would if I could.*

But Marta didn't want to hear about the Mountain. Marta didn't want to hear about their father. It was too strange, too painful. Knowledge she couldn't use. Why burden her with it? The letter's address drifted. For a while Ruth conceived it as addressed generally to the world below, or to whoever might find it. She tried to explain the Mountain, or at least what little she knew of it, to offer her theories on how it might be approached. The secret should be shared, she thought, congratulating herself on her generosity. *Whoever finds this, pass it on.*

But was it wise to share the secret? What if the letter fell into the wrong hands? Not that there was ever much chance of it falling into anyone's hands. Not that her own understanding of the Mountain was more than superficial. But still. So she began to write for herself. First she tried to order her thoughts about the Mountain. Her vague theories, her growing fears. It was disintegrating. What would be left? Would anyone be left in the world below, when the machine fell apart? She tried to imagine the city, torn apart by the self-devouring engines of the Mountain. Earthquakes? Floods? Fire? Accelerating Time, decay like a disease?

Who else could she write to? She described people she knew—if you find this, please give it to . . .

If there was anything left of the city, she decided, it would be utterly changed. The thought pained her. She described the places she knew, in loving detail. There weren't very many. She set down the routines of her life. She'd taken so much for granted! What did she understand of the factories, the Combines, the way her world had worked? She approached it as a puzzle, as a difficult work of art. A dozen different retellings of the shock of the bombs. The struggle to rebuild Fosdyke told as heroic epic, as a horror of starvation and fear, as a black comedy of pointless punch-drunk stubbornness and delusion and ridiculous Committee meetings. No one would ever read it; she did it for herself, for the sake of the memories themselves. There was so much that might be lost. The stories! She set out to record every story she'd ever read, or heard, the gist of every precious banned book she'd ever saved from destruction. Everything sounded like a fairy tale when she wrote it down. The servants silently brought her more paper, and hovered over her shoulder as she wrote.

Arjun

By evening (what *felt* like evening—shadows lengthened, the sky was red) there were no servants left. They had extinguished each other. The monkeys, and the dogs, and the birds had long since been spent. Even the handful of truly monstrous Beasts were dead—they'd all fought each other to the death in the corridors in service of one challenger or another. One Beast with the body of a lizard and claws like a tiger, dreadful surgical scars, and a civilized and sorrowful manner of speech, had torn a Shay in pinstripes to shreds, and his pinstripes, too, and been fatally burned by Shay's energy weapon in the process. Soon the energy weapons would be gone, and it would be down to knives and fists.

He found Abra-Melin kneeling sobbing over his broken staff. "Help me!" Abra-Melin grabbed at Arjun's ankles. "You, I know you. What's your name? *Help* me." He kept walking.

In a black metal corridor (the walls of which pulsed with heat and cold) one of the Shays menaced Arjun with a broken bottle. "This is your fault. This is *your* fault." But the man was swaying from wounds and exhaustion, and Arjun took the bottle off him and knocked him down and left him cowering in a corner.

"You did this," Arjun said. "You made this."

Heat and light pulsed from behind the walls. What would the Mountain be when Shay was gone from it? Would there be music?

Ruth

By midnight (it *felt* like midnight—something somewhere was chiming) the room where Ruth wrote was nothing like a bed-room—it had flowered into a metal vault, icosahedral in shape, into which cables and gears intruded, on the upper angles of which light flickered across brushed black steel.

She was running the pen's rounded end thoughtfully over her lower lip and trying to recall the story, the long-forgotten and for-bidden story, of Jack, the butcher's boy, who'd climbed down the stalk of the great flower on which the city rested, and found his true love among the red roots—was it serpents he'd fought, down there, or worms? —when she was woken from her memories by the sound of running feet clanging along the walkway outside. She stood, set-ting the paper and the mirror aside, as Ivy, panting and sweating, staggered through the open door. It was less a *door,* now, than a cir-cular saw-toothed hole through which some gigantic piston might extend. Ruth greeted her—"Ivy."

Ivy barely threw her a glance. Her eyes were wild with fear—with *humiliation.* She looked close to tears, close to laughing at the absurdity of it all; close to laughing and saying, *enough, enough, good game, let's try it again.* But she only said, "I have to hide. Have to hide. Quick."

And she shoved Ruth aside and lunged for the mirror, and, star-ing into the glassy enigmatic surface, she muttered the key words—numbers, colors, names of stones or flowers or mathemati-cal properties or diseases or devices Ruth didn't recognize. Ivy was unable to calm herself enough at first to say the words with the off-hand casual command the mirror recognized, so she settled herself, breathed deeply, and then she *did* laugh.

There was an immense sound of shattering glass; and then,

where Ivy had knelt, her image lingered on the air for a moment as a pale reflection, while her long dark hair retreated behind the surface of the mirror.

And then she was gone. Ruth touched the mirror and its surface was cold. "Ivy?" No answer.

Four iterations of their terrible father appeared at the door. One was fat, the others thin. Two were bald, one long-haired, one short. They wore a variety of clothes, dark, colorful, formal, wild, tight, flowing; all torn and singed and blood-stained. Two carried knives, one bloody; two held brutal lengths of broken pipe.

"Where is she?"

"I said where is she?"

"It's *over*."

"Where did she go?"

They panted, or sneered, or smiled blankly. Wild-eyed, glassy-eyed, lank-haired, eccentrically dressed; the foursome resembled disreputable musicians, long in the tooth, short on money, hunting for drugs. They would have been funny if not for the knives and the blood on them.

These were the *worst*, Ruth thought: the most vicious and inventive murderers. The last to survive.

"I said where did she fucking go?"

"The game's over, now. Where did she go?"

"Good girl, good girl, Ruth. Help your father."

"Help yourself," she said. "I'm done here." She sifted through her papers. The handwriting was tiny, cramped, almost unreadable, even to herself. She tossed them onto the bed. "Try the mirror," she said. "Get it over with, why don't you?"

They parted to let her go. One of them sniffed like an animal. Their attention turned to the mirror, to each other. Who would move first?

Ruth was only halfway down the corridor when she heard shouts of outrage, and triumph, and the crash of shattering glass, as the last of the challengers turned on each other with the last weapon they had to hand.

When she returned to the room it was empty. The silence echoed. The room smelled of electricity and cold fire. The papers were ash, and the bed was a charred frame, its black wires and struts already reverting to the condition of machinery.

The glass of the mirror was grey and clouded and warm. She carried it out with both hands. It was very heavy.

She found Arjun a while later, on one of the lower floors. The corridors had seemed to spiral in, and down, narrowing and tensing, clenching and knotting, as if the Mountain was in pain. She had headed down because the path up seemed to be blocked by small lurid fires, pockets of acrid gas, spills of cables, buckled passages.

He was standing beneath her, down on the floor of a huge empty chamber—an industrial emptiness, like an abandoned factory. Cartwheel gears loomed in the darkness, toothed hawsers cut through it. It was ringed around with multileveled iron catwalks, from which Ruth looked down; he seemed so tiny in that vast and inhuman space.

A boy lost in a dark cave, she thought. All that was missing was a dragon!

He stood in front of a door of black steel, which was locked and bolted and bound with chains. He appeared to have been examining the door for some time.

As she watched, he moved one of the bolts.

A light escaped from beneath the crack of the door. It was too bright and too beautiful to look at.

"It's over," she called. Her voice echoed, became metallic, oracular, the voice of the machine. "They're gone," she said, more quietly.

He turned back to her and smiled. "I know. I can feel it. The Mountain feels different." He slipped another of the bolts. "The locks are opening again."

"Are they?"

"It was a mistake. It corrected itself. Your father—your sister—had no business here. He stole it. Cheated it. Don't know how, exactly. Everything in the city was always wrong—I felt it from the start, you know. A purer note's sounding again. I'm sorry, by the way."

"That's all right. Wait a moment—I'm coming down."

"I don't think you should."

He bent, his back to her, to untangle a knot of chains. They chimed as they hit the floor. The light beyond the door blazed, winked out, surged again. Golden footlights on a darkened stage. Expectant silence in the galleries; the conductor stands alone.

She climbed down a ladder from one walkway to another, circled round the room to the next ladder.

He said, "You should stay back, I think." Thoughtfully he pulled aside another bar. The room shook.

"What is it?"

"Can't you feel it? He kept them here for so long. He stole. He hoarded. He interfered. The city was supposed to be so different— but so much of it was stolen. So much was missing, off-balance. You could always hear it, if you listened. You know that—you always felt it, didn't you?"

She worked her way down the walkways. Steel clanged under her feet. "Your God."

"All of them." He slid another bolt. "So many of them. The city should have been full of treasures. They shouldn't have been rare— every moment should have been full of wonders. This city was made to be a paradise."

"Wait a moment. You don't know any of this."

"Who'd build all this for any other reason?" Another bolt. A chain shattered. A deep note sounded from behind the straining door. "I've thought a lot about this. While I was walking. You shouldn't come any closer. They've been caged for so long, but never tamed. This will be dangerous."

"Wait. I'm on my way."

He turned back and smiled. "I've made up my mind. I'm not brave enough to change it now."

"Stop. You don't know what's in there."

One after another he snapped back a series of hairpin silver clasps. "No," he agreed. "I don't really, do I?"

"I'm coming down."

Snap, snap. The sound echoed in the emptiness of the chamber. "Is my God in there? Maybe. I don't know. The fact is it's been so long I don't know if I'd recognize it anyway. Maybe it's dead. Maybe it never existed. Maybe it's not what I think it is. Maybe I imagined it. There are no final explanations, are there? Not this side of death. Does it matter?"

"Of course it bloody matters. Don't get mystical now. Hang on a moment."

"What's trapped in here are beautiful things. Energies of making and meaning. The city's been without them too long." The handle was a great black lever. He put his hands on it. "Follow them home, Ruth. Good luck. I'm sorry it all had to work this way. Everything should be better now."

"Wait . . ."

"We were all of us bent out of shape, weren't we? Twisted. It hurt. The wrong kind of lives. Ah, right." He braced himself, squared his thin shoulders. "Now I think we can start setting things right. End of the old song, beginning of the new. Hah. All right then."

He threw his weight on the handle. It turned slowly, creaking, groaning, then faster, and faster. Gears behind the walls, and rising out of the floor, and swelling blackly from the ceiling, began painfully to turn. The mechanism shifted. The handle jammed; and then with a sudden ecstatic cry of metal against metal it gave way, lurching out of Arjun's hands. "Ah," he said. The door burst open and the light roared out.

She opened her eyes slowly. She stayed on the floor, with her face turned to the corner. Her breathing slowly steadied. Silence and darkness. What had she seen in the light? If she closed her eyes again she could see, wrought in scarlet and jade and gold, the shapes, the thousand forms, tumbling jubilantly over and over each other. A thousand Gods, or a single energy with a thousand forms? The chiming of a city full of bells. A long-hoarded treasure spilling out like a golden rain. Fire; music; laughter. Already the forms were blurring. She blinked and they were gone.

Cinders and sparks turned in empty space—the spinning of tiny golden gears. An infinity of delicate adjustments were made. Each atom, each moment transformed itself into the next. There was a stain of black ash on the floor. The air was warm and dusty.

He was gone; transformed. And whatever he'd set loose had escaped; had gone beyond the confines of the machine.

Well? The world seemed unchanged so far.

A dozen stories sprang to Ruth's mind—stories from the city below, myths that had fallen through the cracks of the city's history.

The hero who stole the wings of a mighty Bird, and flew too close to the sun. The hero who went down into the crypts under the city in search of his dead wife, and looked back, and so *fell* back, and burned in the deep-dwellers' forge fires. The hero who climbed a tower of glass and was pinned and torn on the sharp wild spires. A painting, hung in the Museum in an airy upper gallery, showing two lovers in robes of gold and ruby embracing while the sun behind them descended ready to swallow the world. Stories about love and war, songs about death. An ache gripped her chest; her love for the shadow he'd left behind.

She took the mirror upstairs again. It was heavy, and silent. Above, below, the machine shuddered and strained. She found a stable place, and thought it as good as any other. She rested the mirror against a thick rubbery pipe and sat across from it. Unnatural light played around her; it pricked her skin.

"He just had to show off, didn't he?"

The mirror was silent. Her own eyes, reflected in it, were red and tired. She sighed.

"This is all your fault," she said. But the mirror didn't answer, and she shrugged; it was too late now to feel any real bitterness. "I suppose you are what you are," she said.

From where she sat she could see down three—sometimes four or five—corridors and chambers of the machine. All around her the thing slowly transformed. The fires below came and went—the buckling of metal, the gouts of steam. Gears snarled. The corridors twisted into new shapes.

Only the mirror stayed the same, and Ruth herself. If she turned away from the mirror she thought it, too, might vanish. Was Ivy still in there? It seemed a shame to let her go. "You're the clever one. Can you tell me how to mend this?" Still no answer.

She remembered how once, in childhood, she'd walked in on Ivy's room, meaning to ask her some question, and found Ivy sitting between two mirrors. One was taken from the bathroom. One was their mother's old silver-backed mirror, from before she'd died, which Ivy must have taken down from the attic. Ivy was talking to herself, to herselves. What was she practicing for? Ivy had shrieked, childishly, lost her temper; and Ruth had backed away, red-faced, half guilty, half laughing. Later she sat between the mirrors herself. All she saw was her own reflection, flushed rose-red with embarrassment. She hadn't understood then, and she didn't understand now.

There was nothing to do but wait.

The corridors twined and twisted like vines. The cables took on a green and vibrant aspect. The gears creaked like oaks in a storm. The fires burned vivid floral shades. The machine attempted nature. Perhaps it was trying to save itself. Perhaps it was accommodating itself to her whims.

She remembered all the games she, and Marta, and Ivy used to play. The pale and scrubby and smog-poisoned gardens of Fosdyke, transformed into forests of myth. The new world should have something of that in it, she decided—not too much. She remembered how they'd lost themselves in the Museum, how they'd dreamed . . . Their long, long childhood. Too long. With the losses they'd suffered, how could they have been expected to grow up right? With the world around them all broken and twisted and full of fear, what should they have grown into? But that was all changed now; everything was ready to be changed.

One by one the fires went out. For a long time the walls bled dark sap, and blackened and withered; slowly they greened again. The corridors righted themselves. The machine was healing. All she had to do was wait. The city was all spread out below her. What did it see, as the Mountain transformed itself? She could feel the city holding its breath. What should she make of it?

About the Author

Felix Gilman lives with his wife in New York City. *Gears of the City* is his second novel.